THE
CHINGLES
AND THE
VAMPIRE
KING

PATRICIA MURPHY

POOLBEG

Published 2007
by Poolbeg Press Ltd.
123 Grange Hill, Baldoyle
Dublin 13, Ireland
Email: poolbeg@poolbeg.com

© Patricia Murphy 2007

Copyright for typesetting, layout, design
© Poolbeg Press Ltd

ISBN 978-1-84223-230-9

Typeset by Patricia Hope in Goudy 11.5/16.3
Printed by Litografia Rosés, Spain

www.poolbeg.com

ABOUT THE AUTHOR

Patricia Murphy grew up in Ballygall, Dublin, the eldest of six children, and turned to storytelling to amuse her brothers and sisters and sixty cousins. After reading English and History at Trinity College Dublin, she has worked in television as a reporter and documentary maker. She has produced and directed a number of acclaimed documentaries for the BBC and Channel 4, including several on children's lives. She is married and lives in Oxford.

The Chingles and the Vampire King is the third book in the Chingles trilogy. Her first children's novel, *The Chingles from the East*, was the winner of the Poolbeg "Write a Bestseller" Competition 2004.

The Chingles Trilogy is dedicated to
my husband, Marc

This book is dedicated with love to triplets
Aaron, Kealan and Ronan,
and both sets of twins
Saoirse and Aoife and Lucy and Grace
And Finn, James, David, Colm, Leo,
Oscar and Éabha

INISH ÁLAINN

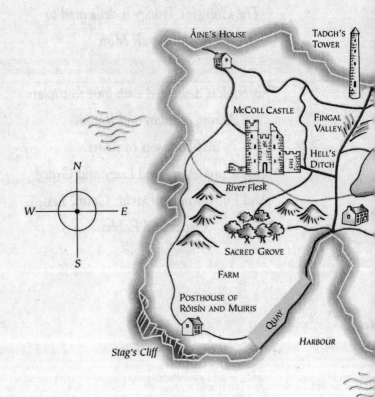

ÁINE'S HOUSE

TADGH'S TOWER

McCOLL CASTLE

FINGAL VALLEY

HELL'S DITCH

River Flesk

SACRED GROVE

FARM

POSTHOUSE OF RÓISÍN AND MUIRIS

QUAY

HARBOUR

Stag's Cliff

N

W — E

S

INISH ÁLAINN – 3km LONG – 6km WIDE

〜〜 Boreen

—— Main Road

FAIRY FORT
& FIELD

FAIRY FORT
HOUSE

POOLBEG ROCKS
& COVE

 sh

BO MEN'S BOG

's

FLOWER
MEADOW

MERING LAKE

LY'S

River Flesk

Boogan Beach

TEASHOP

JARLATH'S WORKSHOP

FERRY

TO MAINLAND
ONE HOUR →

PROLOGUE

*I*n a shady forest a shaft of light cut through the dense canopy like a spear. Into the pool of light stepped a pale slight man with colourless eyes. With trembling hands he unfurled a parchment made of human skin. A spell (for which he had just sold his soul) was written on it in his own blood. It read:

> *The sacrifice of a baby not of human mother born,*
> *At a fault line where a giant sleeps,*
> *By an island with a tower of power.*
> *From above, a space stone of the soul splitter,*
> *From below, the gems of all elements.*
> *When the earth's shadow darkens the blood moon,*
> *All power will be yours, Vampire King of All Worlds.*

CHAPTER 1

O n the surface, Cassie, Thomas and Nancy McColl seemed quite ordinary children. They lived in East Croydon near London, went to school, ate healthily but preferred sweets and liked each other most of the time. Cassie was twelve and a half, tall for her age and loved reading and chocolate cake. Eleven-year-old Thomas was the best runner in his class, was good at puzzles and hated it when Cassie pulled rank on him just because she was older. Nancy who was four had a mop of brown curly hair and liked organising vast tea parties for her dolls and teddies. But when they visited the magical island of Inish Álainn off the west coast of Ireland for their summer holidays they were transformed into superheroes with special powers, known as the Chingles.

Nancy was perhaps the most remarkable of all. Before she was three she swallowed a magical stone, the Star Splinter, and helped her brother and sister annihilate an evil giant called Balor when he tried to destroy Inish

3

Álainn. When she wasn't yet four she helped rescue the lost goddess Finnen and defeat Balor's wife, the evil sorceress Caitlín of the Crooked Teeth. Like her brother and sister Nancy could shape-shift, travel in dreams and journey to the Otherworld. She could also shoot accurately from a sling and best of all she could talk to animals.

So when Nancy said to her sister that a spirit had just waved to her from outside the airplane, Cassie took her very seriously indeed.

They were flying from Shannon Airport on the mainland to Inish Álainn, on the way to spend the summer with their Uncle Jarlath, his wife Áine and their new baby.

Cassie peered outside the window to where Nancy was pointing urgently.

"All I can see are clouds," she said, screwing up her eyes in an attempt to see shapes within the misty billows. But then everything went wobbly as the plane was suddenly buffeted by a rolling wind like a wave.

"Fasten your seatbelts," said the pilot. "We seem to have hit an unexpected bit of turbulence."

The small plane bumped up and down as if on some invisible roller-coaster ride that made their stomachs flip inside out. Thomas fussed over his one-year-old twin brother and sister, Mattie and Matilda, in the two seats beside him. In fact, there was no need – they were fast asleep and gurgling through their dreams despite the constant lurches. But Thomas was enjoying feeling grown up.

The addition of the twins to the group was due to a most unusual situation. When the Chingles were at Gatwick

Airport checking in to their flight to Shannon, their mother had fallen and broken her leg. One minute she was chatting to the flight attendant at the check-in desk. The next she tripped over a piece of baggage that mysteriously appeared out of nowhere and she landed awkwardly on her left leg. Their father was in deepest Africa on business and their grandparents were in Australia. So it was hastily decided that the safest place for all the children was Inish Álainn with their Uncle Jarlath.

While Thomas worried terribly about his mother and her poor leg, he was secretly delighted to have the twins travel with them to Inish Álainn. He was entirely devoted to them and had been dreading the separation from them over the summer. He hoped their mother might be able to join them before long.

"I wonder if someone is trying to get in contact with us?" said Cassie, peering at the streaming clouds as the plane steadied itself. She blinked, thinking she was beginning to see a pattern emerge in the cloud shapes. "I wonder if it's the Tuatha Dé Danann reminding us that we have to decide if we want to go to Tír na nÓg?"

The Tuatha were the gods and goddesses of Ireland who, in recognition of the Chingles, having twice saved Inish Álainn from destruction, had offered them the gift of immortality in Tír na nÓg, the Land of the Ever-Young. The children were supposed to give their answer at the end of the summer.

Thomas frowned. The subject had been a bone of contention between them all year. Cassie was determined to accept while Nancy, despite being only little, was adamant that there was no way she was going. Thomas felt undecided and dreaded having to make up his mind.

"Let's not spend all our time going on about that," he groaned.

"It's not them Toothy Danny Irish gods," said Nancy decidedly. "It's some other spirits from somewhere else." She half-closed her eyes and squinted, trying to work out the cloud formation on the other side of the glass.

Outside, a billowy form arose in a stream from the gold-lined cloud cover that obscured the earth. It took on the shape of a woman cradling something in her arms.

"It looks like a mother with her baby," said Nancy.

Cassie could see it now too. "Or a child with a doll," she speculated.

Then the cloud shape did something unexpected. Sinister grey wisps formed on its outer edges and began to flutter in the breeze. Then it threw the baby shape into the sky where it became a shower of hailstones beating down onto the airplane. The mother shape turned first into a ghoulish ghost that appeared to scream, then into a skeleton that also became a shower of hail dashing against the window of the plane as if trying to force its way in.

Cassie and Nancy both shuddered. It was a deeply unsettling vision.

Cassie glanced around the plane to see if any other passengers had noticed the strange cloud formations. But everyone was absorbed in their own activities, napping, chatting or fussing with their sea-belts.

Almost everyone on the small airplane was from the island. There was Donnacha the bodhrán-maker playing on his latest instrument, Mrs Moriarty, the world's most enthusiastic knitter, crocheting a blanket and sour old Mrs Prendergast from the teashop scowling at a magazine. The only stranger was a man in sunglasses slumped in his seat a couple of rows away. He was pretending to be asleep but actually was looking furtively around. He caught Cassie's eye, then immediately let out a false yawn and pretended to fall asleep again. Cassie thought she knew him from somewhere but she couldn't remember exactly where. There was something about him that made her uneasy. But she had no time to dwell on it. They were coming in to land. After the bumpy ride they were rather looking forward to solid ground.

The airplane was a new venture started by Patch, the brother of Podge the ferry-captain, and this was its maiden flight. So the rest of the island, almost everyone who wasn't on the plane, greeted their arrival. There was Muiris the postmaster and his wife Róisín, Mr Mulally the publican and his twin sons Macdara and Cónán and quite a few other friendly smiling faces.

Towards the back of the crowd, they saw Jarlath's curly head. He waved at them frantically and plunged through to greet them. Cradled in his arms was a large child with a mane of long golden curls.

"Can that be Lorcan?" wondered Cassie to Thomas. "He's only a few months old and that child is at least twice the size of the twins who are over a year!"

7

"Well, his mother *is* a goddess," said Thomas as he gently placed Mattie in the double buggy beside his sister, their dark curly heads touching.

"An *ex*-goddess," corrected Cassie. "Remember Áine's taken human form – or what was all that about last summer? *Duh!* You know, the bit where we had to find her sister Finnen before Áine could get permission from the Tuatha Dé Danann to marry Jarlath?" Cassie could never resist putting Thomas in his place.

"Of course I know," said Thomas tetchily. "Wonder how Finnen's getting on looking after the sun as well as the moon?"

Áine used to be the Sun Goddess and the Swan Maiden Finnen, Goddess of the Moon, had taken over Áine's job when her sister had taken human shape to marry Jarlath.

"Apart from that weird hail shower on the way over, she seems to be doing quite well," said Cassie, gazing up at the sky where a few clouds lazily scudded by a blazing sun.

As they were gathering up their bags and making sure their bikes were safely off the plane, they were astonished to see the huge baby leap out of Jarlath's arms and land on his feet beside Nancy, before falling on his bottom. He burst into peals of laughter as a worried Jarlath ran to check if he was all right. But the baby was strangling Nancy in a big hug. The child beamed at them all and laughed as loudly as a man.

"Children!" Jarlath exclaimed with delight. "So these are the twins! They're the spit of their aunties, Holly and

Ivy, when they were little." He bent down to the buggy and kissed the twins, then encircled the other three children in a big hug.

"Lorcan is a ginormous – I mean, a beautiful baby," said Cassie, catching hold of the child as he tried to crawl into the buggy. She picked him up, staggering under his weight. He threw his arms around her, half-squeezing her to death, and planted a big sloppy kiss on her cheek.

"He's a big one," said Thomas.

"I don't know what Áine's feeding him," agreed Jarlath. "Apart from Connle's porridge. He spends half the day making it as the little fella eats so much!"

Lorcan suddenly launched himself from Cassie's arms and dived-bombed towards the ground, landing on his bottom once more. Then he wrenched Nancy's suitcase from her and crawled with it, carrying it in his mouth. Cassie steadied herself, winded from the force of his propulsion from her arms.

"He's crawling early," said Jarlath proudly. "He doesn't take after me. I was a year before I could crawl. He'll be walking in no time at all!"

"He's the biggest baby in Ireland surely, with the strength of ten men," said Róisín the postmistress, running to greet them. "Legend has it we haven't seen such a big baby since a god married a local girl!" She kissed them all lightly on the forehead and oohed and aahed over the twins, who still slept soundly, oblivious to the antics of their giant cousin. Having dropped the suitcase, Lorcan was giving Nancy a ride on his back.

"We're so glad to have you back," said Róisín. "There's been some very odd goings-on in the last while."

"Like what?" asked Cassie, hoping she wasn't talking about bouncing baby Lorcan. Even though his mother, Áine, had taken mortal form to marry Jarlath, clearly some divinity had passed through to the child.

"I can't explain," Róisín continued. "Like the place is crawling with ghosts and spirits. I can barely walk anywhere on the island from Boogan Beach to the castle grounds without breaking out in goosebumps."

"Don't listen to your one," said Muiris her husband. "She's away with the fairies herself."

"Whist, quiet, you!" said Róisín. "We all know this is a magical island where the veils between the worlds are thin. But now the whole island is so full of clattering and commotion at night, people are afraid to leave their beds."

Muiris winked at the children. Their being Celtic superheroes with magical powers was supposed to be a secret but the children often felt the islanders knew more than they let on.

Outside the airport terminal, which was really just an old-fashioned Irish cottage with a thatched roof, their dear old friend Connle was waiting for them with Derry the faithful donkey.

They threw their arms around Connle and hugged Derry too.

Cassie was now taller than Connle, but otherwise he remained unchanged, his red hair combed into an elaborate quiff and his patchwork waistcoat looking more patched than ever. He was delighted to see the twins.

"They're the image of their twin aunts!" he exclaimed.

Right on cue the twins woke up and smiled and gurgled.

As Connle fussed over the babies, Nancy suddenly felt a cold breeze whip her face, even though it was a warm day. She tugged Cassie's arm and pointed up to the sky. Once more they saw strange wispy cloud formations. But in the blink of an eye, the shapes were gone.

When Cassie looked around, she thought she saw the furtive little man in sunglasses from the plane watching them from behind a rock. She was about to go and investigate when Jarlath called them all to set off towards Fairy Fort House, which was in the north-east of the island.

As they cycled their bikes along the island's main road, the Chingles felt an eerie nervousness in the air. The place did feel different, even though the hedge-lined boreens blooming with red fuchsia bushes, drifts of orange spiky montbretia and clouds of honeysuckle looked the same. They tried to keep pace with Connle, who kept beaming at them and dancing a little jig of delight as he pushed the twins in their stroller. But it was difficult to cycle that slowly, so they took off after Jarlath who was up ahead with Lorcan and Derry the donkey. Jarlath had his hands full, as Lorcan could hurl himself into the air with ease from Derry's back and land on his bottom.

Nancy kept getting strange tingles in her stomach that nearly made her fall off her bike. Since she'd swallowed the magical stone, the Star Splinter, two summers ago, she was hyper-alert to supernatural forces. Reaching the top of one of the many hills of the island, they turned and cycled back to Connle.

"It feels like there are fairies and gods everywhere," Cassie said. "A strange feeling."

"That's what Róisín said in the airport," said Thomas.

"Now that you mention it, we've had a few strange occurrences all right," said Connle. "Not usually during the day – but at night it's terrible! The fairies are up in arms about it."

Cassie told him about the strange wispy shapes in the sky outside the airplane.

"That's odd," agreed Connle. "I've had a few such visitations myself. I don't know what but there's something up."

"You don't think it's anything to do with the Tuatha Dé Danann wanting us to make up our minds about immortality at the end of the summer?" asked Cassie.

Connle shook his head. "That's not their way."

"It's a hard decision to make," said Thomas. "Connle, just checking – if I decide not to go, I won't be able to keep my magical powers when I grow up, right?"

"You will lose your powers when you're grown up, most likely," said Connle.

"So we won't be able to have magical adventures in the Otherworld?" asked Cassie.

"I expect you'll have other things on your mind," said Connle.

12

"It's a good reason to go to Tír na nÓg," said Cassie.

Thomas said nothing, preoccupied with the problem.

"And when exactly are you grown up?" asked Cassie.

"You'll know at the time," said Connle, smiling at her.

"Cassie thinks she's already grown up," said Thomas with a withering look at his sister.

"Let's get you home," said Connle. "You have all summer to worry about all that and a good few years yet before you're grown up!"

Jarlath, pursuing Derry and Lorcan, was already nearly at the house.

"Yes, let's hurry! I'm dying to see Granny Clíona," said Cassie as they passed the Fairy Fort Field.

Granny Clíona was a former witch and their ghost ancestor who lived in a silver bottle. She'd been Connle's foster mother and had originally come to the island from Scotland in the sixteenth century. After she died she'd hung around the island as a ghost but in the eighteenth century she had the misfortune to be captured in a silver bottle. She'd stayed locked in it for over two centuries until the Chingles found her two summers before and opened the stopper.

Connle gave Cassie a worried look. "I'm afraid Granny Clíona has got mislaid, what with all the upheavals in the house. Wee Lorcan is going through a phase of hiding things."

"I hope she's not too lonely," said Nancy.

Granny Clíona wasn't able to come out of her bottle unless someone opened the stopper.

"Now don't worry, children," Connle reassured them. "She'll be somewhere about. Just keep your eyes open for her."

Jarlath and Lorcan were already inside the house. But just before the Chingles reached the bottom of the garden the Pooka, rising out of a ditch from a stray patch of fog, intercepted them.

"Well, if it isn't the oh-so-great Chingles, I don't think!" said the talking horse, whose form was ghostly and transparent in the early evening. "And what's in there?" he brayed, sticking his head into the babies' buggy. "Some more little chinglets?"

Thomas shooed him away bad-temperedly. He was never sure about the Pooka, who was a troublemaker.

"What has you out in the day?" asked Connle. The Pooka normally only appeared at night.

"I'll have you know this is costing me a lot of effort – but you lot are in deep trouble with the fairies," said the Pooka, shaking his white, shaggy, almost transparent mane in a disapproving manner. "They want you to attend the Midnight Court."

"The children are tired," said Connle, annoyed.

"Look, don't shoot the messenger," said the Pooka. "Their reputation as some kind of underworld action heroes is what's causing all the problems. Be there or run the risk of annoying the little people." He raised his front leg and shook it at them. "And you, Connle, should know what side your bread is buttered on – they're your only relatives, after all."

Connle, besides being the caretaker of the house, was a gruagach – half-fairy and half-human – and over five hundred years old.

"And what if we don't come?" said Cassie defiantly.

"You have some new arrivals there," said the Pooka, gesturing towards the twins. "The fairies have been known to take a shine to little babies and replace them with some crabby article of their own."

"They'd have to answer to me if they tried any nonsense substituting changelings," warned Connle.

"If they so much as harm one hair on the head of Mattie or Matilda, I'll do to them what I did to Balor and Caitlín," bristled Thomas.

"Well, you might have left some loose ends," said the Pooka, looking with scorn at Thomas. "Your old friends the Merrows – those cheeky hussies with the fishes' tails who hate Áine's guts and yours too – they're very busy over at the place where Balor croaked his last. And they've been boasting they've got something you'd very much like to get hold of!"

With that he turned on his hooves and cantered off.

While Connle and Thomas exchanged dark mutterings about the cheek of the little people, Cassie's memory was pricked. She was alarmed by the Pooka's message about the Merrows. Last year during the battle to destroy Balor's wife, Caitlín of the Crooked Teeth, she had lost an amulet made of a meteorite that had fallen to earth. The Chingles were meant to have destroyed it because it still contained some of Caitlín's dark powers. It was worrying to think it was still lost. It was more disturbing to think it might have fallen into the hands of those thoughtless, spiteful Irish mermaids. They'd never forgiven Áine for marrying Jarlath. They claimed they'd once saved him from drowning and so he belonged to them.

"I suppose we'd better not risk displeasing the fairies," sighed Connle.

"The fairies wouldn't really harm Mattie or Matilda, would they?" asked an alarmed Cassie.

"They are so full of it these days, you'd never know what they might do," said Connle darkly. "And as for those Merrows, they're capable of anything!"

CHAPTER 2

All thoughts of having to face the fairies and the Merrows were banished by the vision of Áine greeting them at the door of Fairy Fort House. Despite having the biggest baby in Ireland, Áine looked radiant as usual and was overjoyed to see them. She was ecstatic to meet the twins even though they woke up and signalled their arrival with great sobs and roars. Lorcan, who had been smiling and gurgling a minute before, joined in out of sympathy and cried such huge tears that a puddle formed under his baby chair.

Nothing was going to happen until the babies had all been settled and put to bed. This was easily accomplished with a song from Áine, whose voice had such sweetness and purity it lulled them into a sleep. The Chingles then realised why it was no bother to Áine to deal with a strapping great child like Lorcan. Thomas was delighted that the twins' wooden cots that used to belong to Holly and Ivy were placed in his room in the attic while his sisters as always shared the adjoining bedroom. He had a quick look under the beds to see if he could find the silver bottle containing Granny Clíona. But all he saw were cobwebby shadows.

As soon as all the babies were asleep, Áine made the children hot chocolate.

Jarlath was pacing up and down and tugging his hair.

"Perhaps you should visit your workshop and do some more work on your equation," suggested Áine gently.

Jarlath, who was a mathematician and an inventor, beamed at her. "If you don't mind," he said, as he ran out the door.

Áine laughed. "Your uncle is a very responsible father but I know his mind is often elsewhere. Now, while he's gone, let's talk about all the mysterious goings-on on the island."

"Since you visited the Norse gods and the Celtic gods in Europe," explained Connle, "and met Inuits and Native Americans on the other side of the world, your fame has spread far and wide." The children looked puzzled. "So all these mysterious magical creatures have turned up out of nowhere. They are currently just hovering around and won't talk to anybody, they say, except the Chingles – though, mind you, not one of them knows how to pronounce your nickname properly. We told them you're not here and sent them away but they keep coming back."

"Perhaps they think you'll be able to help them in some way," speculated Áine.

18

"But their presence is causing havoc," said Connle. "The stupid fairies want to put up a force field – a magical barrier – to stop any more arriving."

"But it's best you go and see for yourselves," said Áine. "I'll stay here and mind the babies."

"What about the Merrows?" asked Cassie. "The Pooka just told us they're boasting that they have something we would want to get hold of. Could it be the lost amulet?"

"I tried to find out but I was told not to interfere by my father," sighed Áine. Her father was Manannán Mac Lir, the King of the Sea and notoriously bad-tempered. "He's still very mad at me for taking human form." She sighed loudly again. "But at least he did me one great favour – he got so sick of the Merrows' jealousy and spite against me that he put them under a binding promise not to talk about me to anyone. Or they'll be turned into cod."

"So he still cares about you," said Cassie. "He still protects you despite his anger."

"Yes, that's true. But, after all, Lorcan *is* his grandchild . . . even if he's a human one . . ."

He's a lot bigger than any human baby I ever saw, thought Cassie but didn't like to say so. Then she noticed Áine's eyes were full of tears.

"Oh, Áine, don't be upset!"

"I'm just a bit tired," said Áine. "To be honest, I have my hands full with Lorcan." For the first time they realised she was a bit strained, like most mothers of young babies.

"Now you don't be fretting, Áine," said Connle gently.

"Now that the Chingles are here, we'll sort it all out. But first we need to find out who or what's causing all these other disturbances on the island. We should do a quick tour. And check in on those pesky fairies at their Midnight Court."

It was after eleven when Connle and the Chingles trooped outside.

"I think you'd better go equipped," said Connle, leading them to the shed where their weapons from warrior training with Scáthach, their legendary teacher from the Sean Gaels, still remained.

Nancy took up her sling and Thomas a fearsome lance and a shield of beaten copper bearing Celtic symbols around its edge with a centrepiece of a silver stag's head. Cassie decided to leave aside the Gae Bolga, a lance in the shape of forked lightning with a bulging tip like a harpoon, as perhaps too threatening. Instead she took up a rope, ingeniously woven with elaborate Celtic knot symbols. Cassie marvelled to see it. It had belonged to Scáthach. She held it in her hands, feeling a connection with their teacher who had gone missing in action presumed killed during their fearsome battle with Caitlín of the Crooked Teeth. Cassie felt a surge of power that gave her strength. She hoped the rope was imbued with some of Scáthach's magic. She also took up a silver sword wrought with intricate gold emblems of a leaping salmon and an erect wolfhound.

Thomas also made sure to pack their torches. As a last thought, Cassie went back for Ogma's ring, which allowed her to communicate with deities in their own tongue, just in case they encountered any foreign strangers. Standing outside the shed, she held up the ring, admiring its multicoloured facets and swirling diamond light – just as Thomas started playing Frisbee with his shield. The shield came whizzing in Cassie's direction, the edge of it colliding with the ring, which flew out of Cassie's hand.

"You moron!" shouted Cassie at her brother as she picked it up.

"It was an accident," Thomas said sheepishly, retrieving his shield from a ditch.

Cassie was dismayed to see that the ring now had a hairline crack through the multicoloured jewel. "It's your fault if it won't work any more," she seethed.

"Shush, you two!" warned Connle in a whisper. "I thought you had grown out of all that sparring. Do you want to walk backwards?"

Cassie and Thomas mumbled an apology. The last thing they wanted was Connle's special punishment that made their legs feel like they were clapped in leg-irons as they walked backwards – especially in the dark.

The moon brightened the night as they quietly advanced towards Fairy Fort Field.

The fairy fort was a raised circular ditch in the middle of the field. It was surrounded by a thick clump of hawthorn trees. Normally, when the Midnight Court was sitting, the

21

fort was illuminated with lighted torches and tapers and teeming with little people flying about on rainbow-coloured wings. But now the place seemed desolate and there was no Otherworldly music filling the air.

"That's odd," said Connle.

"Maybe we're too early," said Cassie.

"But they should be here already making their preparations," said Connle.

"Yeah, you know how fussy they are about having everything just so for their precious court," said Thomas.

They crept through the trees and peered over the raised circle of earth of the fairy fort. It was deserted.

But to their surprise, a shaft of moonlight illuminated a pile of old clothes at the bottom of a tree inside the earthen ring.

"It looks innocent enough," murmured Thomas as they tiptoed to the entrance and into the fairy ring.

Thomas approached the bundle of old clothes and nudged it with his foot and the most spine-tingling, bloodcurdling roar split their ears!

"*AIEEEE! AIEEE!*" wailed the bundle and immediately sparked into the terrifying shape of a giant insect like a tarantula with large front prongs and a hairy back.

The Chingles jumped back aghast. A quick-thinking Cassie spun the rope into the air and deftly lassoed the insect, which fell back dejected and immediately turned back into a miserable old beggar in tattered clothes.

His face was deeply lined under his sooty black hair. His

eyes were red-rimmed as if he had been crying for days. He had a vaguely South American appearance, like the panpipe players in the Chingles' local shopping centre who came from Peru. On closer inspection he was indeed wearing a poncho and a sombrero, but they were ragged and filthy.

"Who are you?" Cassie demanded as she moved closer to undo her lasso. He seemed harmless enough and there was no need to tie him.

At first he seemed to talk gobbledygook and slurred his words. Then Cassie blew on Ogma's ring.

"Me talka only *Les Chingalez*! How you say, the Persons of the Roof-Tiles?" He did have a South American accent.

"We are them," said Cassie. She turned on Thomas. "See what you've done! The ring used to translate everyone into perfect English, clear as a bell!"

"But you are leetle children. I speak only them, *Chingalez*, the roofers," muttered the stranger.

"Well, you see, myself and my sisters, Cassie and Nancy – I'm Thomas by the way – are called the Chingles," explained Thomas slowly. "We are known by that nickname because there was a prophecy on the island that it would be saved from Balor of the Evil Eye by the 'Chingles from the East' and –"

"When we arrived Nancy told everyone that we were 'chingles from the east'," Cassie butted in, "because she couldn't say 'children from East Croydon' properly."

"So, you see, people who knew the prophecy thought we were sent to save the island –"

"I can say 'children' now," said Nancy. "And 'Tyrannosaurus Rex' and 'anemone'."

"But there was a mix-up," continued Thomas, "because the island was really meant to be saved by this other band of warriors, the 'Sean Gaels' – which sounds rather like 'Chingles' and had got changed a bit over the centuries. The Sean Gaels were legendary: Lugh the God of Light, Scáthach the Warrior Woman and Sennan the Druid."

"Luckily it turned out we did have some special powers, because the Sean Gaels were late so we had to save the island ourselves," said Cassie. "So we are known as the Chingles now."

"Ah, the Sean Gallays," said the beggar, who had listened intently to them. "Them I speak."

"But you can't," said Cassie sadly. "While we were fighting Caitlín of the Crooked Teeth, Scáthach went missing in action and Sennan disappeared. And Lugh, we don't know where he is. He's an awfully busy god."

The beggar hissed and spit out a viscous liquid like a web, driving them back several metres to the bank of the fairy ring.

"Gosh, he's a bit upset!" said Thomas.

"Why don't we just ignore him and leave him to stew here?" said Cassie.

"No!" said Nancy. "He's making my tummy tingle. He must be a god."

"We'd better find out a bit more about him," said Thomas. "He just doesn't realise who we are. He's not exactly unfriendly."

"He's not exactly friendly either!" said Cassie.

"The fairies will be up in arms about this. They are very precious altogether about their Fairy Field," whispered Connle. "We better go easy and not cause too many ructions."

"At least tell us your name!" cried Cassie.

"*VIRACOCHA!*" screeched the beggar.

A moonbeam hit his brow and for a moment he stood tall and imposing.

They had to shield their eyes from the bright light pulsating from his head. When they squinted at him, they saw he wore a crown made of points of light that radiated like sunbeams. He held out his hands and thunderbolts rent the air but then he closed them together and the sudden storm stopped. They saw that tears descended from his eyes like rain. Then the moon disappeared behind the clouds again and Viracocha once more became a beggar, except he continued to cry and curled up into a ball. The children stood, awestruck by his sudden transformations.

"He's definitely some sort of god," muttered Cassie. "The God of Misery!"

"Oh, merciful hour, this will be the last straw for the fairies!" said Connle.

"Don't cry," said Nancy. She approached the stranger and gently touched his brow.

Viracocha smiled up at her through his tears. He snuffled and dried his eyes.

"It is how I make rain for my own people," he said. "But here is the land of *mucho* rain." He wrapped his poncho round him and turned his back on them, sighing loudly. "I came here travelling over the water as if it were land, without sinking. Now I very tired and very sad." He sighed again and waved them away with his hand.

"I think he must mean he walked across the ocean," said Thomas.

"Gosh, he's depressing," said Cassie. "I wonder why he's so sad?"

"Let's ask Tadgh who he might be in the morning," said Thomas.

Tadgh was their friend the local librarian who lived in a round tower and seemed to know everything.

They backed away as the Pooka cantered up, now in his full horse form for spooking the unwary at night – large and glossy white. His magnificent snow-white mane shook with urgency.

"You lot should shift yourselves over to Bo Men's Bog! It's an emergency!"

"You three better get there now," said Connle. "I'll follow you over on Derry."

"Can we still salmon-leap?" asked Thomas. "I can't remember how to do it."

"You jump up, turn yourself into a salmon, then mid-air change back into yourself and land on your own legs," said Cassie. She felt a bit rusty herself. "Concentrate all your energy into a point," she remembered. "Jump and think of the graceful arc of the salmon as you leap. Then, as the earth rushes up to meet you, shape-shift back into yourself."

"Okay – ready – steady – go!" shouted Thomas as he

vaulted forward athletically and leaped upwards. He felt silver scales and fins grow as the air coursed over his smooth silver belly.

Cassie and Nancy followed. They felt themselves change into salmon midair and soared gracefully through the night.

In one deft move, the children salmon-leaped all the way to the edge of the haunted Bo Men's bog where the nasty creatures tickled people to death. Just before landing, they thought themselves back into children. But they were still out of practice. Cassie landed in a crash on a prickly blackthorn bush. Thomas narrowly missed colliding with a boulder. Only Nancy landed elegantly on her feet.

"Wow!" said Cassie, fighting free of the thorny bush but laughing with the joy of changing form.

"I'd forgotten how much fun that was," Thomas said with glee, dusting himself down. "I wish I could do that all the time."

Their magical powers only worked on the island or when they travelled on a special mission for the gods. And even though they'd been instructed in magical skills by Sennan and Scáthach of the Sean Gaels, they could never take their powers for granted.

In the deathly gloom of the fog at midnight they could see nothing. But then they heard a thrashing, squelching sound like a giant whale beached on a shore.

They heard the distant rumbling of the Bo Men and then peals of ghostly laughter rent the dense night air. Their hair stood on end and their skin crawled and prickled. Bizarrely, they heard a clicking sound.

"That sounds like a kangaroo," said a bewildered Cassie.

Thomas flashed his torch and thought he saw a thrashing tail. "No, it's a crocodile," he said. "A giant one!"

Nancy peered into the bog and thought she saw something slithering in a flash of moonbeam. "It's a snake," she insisted. "Its body is all scaly."

"Well, whatever it is, we're not going to capture it in the dark."

"It seems to have figured out how to defeat the Bo Men anyway," said Cassie.

The Bo Men would tickle you to death unless you made them laugh.

"But I didn't hear it tell any jokes," said Nancy.

"Maybe it tickled them with its crocodile tail," said Thomas.

"It's a kangaroo!" said Cassie.

"It's a snake!" Nancy stamped her foot. She was usually very good-tempered but she could get very cross when contradicted. Having to stand up to an older brother and sister had taught her to hold her own. But their argument was interrupted by a huge slopping sound and a foghorn coming from several miles away. Even this far away on the island, seawater splashed their faces.

"It's getting worse! Some weird creature is landing over on Boogan Beach!" exclaimed a breathless Pooka, cantering up. "You are for it with the fairies, I warn you now."

"Please, can you tell Connle to follow us?" asked Cassie.

The Pooka harrumphed but nodded his head in agreement.

With no time to waste, the children salmon-leapt in the air and landed sure-footed on the soft sand of Boogan Beach to the south-east of the island. The Boogan, a kindly seaweed creature that lived in a cave, ran out to meet them, the bladder wrack around his head quivering.

"It's a monster!" he exclaimed. "I fear Balor is rising from the deep!"

The sky was bright with moonlight like frosted breath.

Thomas saw a great glistening snout emerge from a huge backwash of water.

"It's huge!" exclaimed Nancy. "What can it be?"

"It's a whale!" shouted Cassie.

"A shark!" Nancy cried.

They stood, frozen to the spot. But then the huge creature jumped nose-up out of the water and landed with a slap on the surface. Its skin was glistening black and looked like iron, and it had a tower on its back. It advanced towards the beach.

"It's a submarine!" Thomas exclaimed. "It looks a bit like a Darkon!"

"What's a Darkon?" asked Cassie.

"A Russian prototype nuclear submarine and the quietest one ever designed. It was supposed to be fully automated so a small crew could run it. But nobody knew for sure if it ever got off the drawing board. Wow! I hope

Inish Álainn isn't being invaded." Thomas stood transfixed. He was going through a submarine phase. "It's got a double hull," he said excitedly. "The inner one is made of titanium."

"Trust you to be a submarine-spotter!" joked Cassie, although she was feeling rather nervous. A few spears and a rope wouldn't be much use against nuclear weapons.

The submarine beached onto the shore in shallow water and a trapdoor sprang open. The children stood poised, weapons at the ready.

But then a woman emerged, clutching a bundle. She was tall and thin with masses of long raven-black hair and around her neck she wore a necklace of many-coloured gemstones. She waded in towards the shore.

"Hold fire!" commanded Cassie.

The bundle in the woman's arms stirred and began to cry.

"She's holding a baby," said Thomas.

A man emerged from the interior of the submarine, blinking in the bright moonlight and carrying a baby's buggy and some bags. He held a hand up.

"We need water!" he called. He sounded foreign.

The children looked at each other, mystified.

The woman's face was deathly white and she was on the verge of collapse. The children ran to help her as she reached the shore and, while Cassie and Nancy escorted her up the beach, Thomas returned to help the man with his baggage.

Then another young woman emerged from the

submarine. She looked sulky and even more miserable than the South American god.

At that moment, three heads popped up out of the waves a little way off. It was the Merrows, wearing thunderous expressions. Cassie spotted them out of the corner of her eye and ran down to the edge of the sea to confront them.

"What's all this malarkey?" called out Mara, her long blonde hair licked by a sea breeze. "I hope you're not trying to rob any more drowning people from us!" They had never got over having to relinquish Jarlath.

Cassie looked nervously about but only the sulky-looking woman had noticed the Merrows. She was standing knee-deep in the waves, staring transfixed at Mara. On the beach Nancy and the other woman were absorbed in tending to the baby and Thomas was helping the man who was struggling with his baggage.

Cassie turned back to the Merrows just as Mara rose slightly in the water and the moonlight illuminated something red-gold around her neck. It was the lost amulet! She was sure of it!

"Hey, I want to talk to you about that amulet!" Cassie shouted.

"Why?" screeched Sionna, her little red cap of feathers as usual perched on her brown curly hair.

"It's not yours! It was used against Caitlín the Soul Splitter!"

"So what? She's dead!" called Fand mockingly, her dark hair spread around her like tendrils of seaweed.

"It still has some of her essence in it!" Cassie yelled. "It's

31

made of a meteorite from outer space and dangerous in the wrong hands!"

But the Merrows merely stuck out their tongues and disappeared beneath the waves.

Cassie suddenly realised she'd probably said the wrong thing to them. They'd be only too happy to know it was a dangerous object. Worse still, she'd been shooting her mouth off in front of strangers.

The sulky young woman waded in towards dry land.

"Did you see something in the water over there?" Cassie asked her as she reached the beach, trying to sound casual.

The young woman looked at her blankly. "I see water in the water," she said moodily in a heavy accent that sounded Eastern European. "I hate water."

"Oh, it was just some stupid night swimmers," said Cassie casually.

But she was rattled. Mara had definitely looked like she was wearing the amulet around her neck. But now wasn't the time to follow it up.

"Do you have any nuclear weapons?" Thomas was asking the man.

"No, no," he answered, horrified. "This protein type, no war."

"I knew it was a prototype," said Thomas, self-satisfied. "But what are you doing in it?"

At that moment Connle arrived with Derry the donkey so the man didn't have to answer.

"Best get you all back to our house," Connle said,

gesturing to the woman with the baby to climb onboard the donkey. "We'll take care of you."

Cassie held the baby, who was no more than a few months old, while Derry bent down and Thomas helped the woman onto the donkey's back. Cassie put the baby into her arms and they set off. They would have to wait until they were back at Fairy Fort House to follow up their enquiries.

The man, laden down with luggage and the buggy, seemed incredibly nervous and looked around anxiously as if he was being stalked. He was sweating madly and could barely talk. He stumbled so much that Cassie and Thomas had to help him with his baggage. The other young woman kept muttering in disgust to herself but she refused all offers of help and lagged behind.

"This lot are very weird," Cassie whispered to Thomas when the man went to see how the woman on the donkey was doing.

"I bet they're fugitives," agreed Thomas.

"I wonder does their arrival have anything to do with those weird cloud formations," Cassie pondered.

"I think it might," said Nancy. "The women make my tummy tingle. The one with the baby in a nice way but the other one is more like a pain." But the others weren't listening to her.

"Did you see those cheeky Merrows butting in?" said Cassie.

"No!" said Thomas in surprise. "Were they there?"

"Yes, they were! I think that younger woman saw them

but she denied it. I said it was just some night swimmers. But, listen to this, I'd swear Mara was wearing the lost amulet!"

"That's definitely worrying," said Thomas gravely. "But I wouldn't fret too much about what that sulky woman saw. She'd have no reason to believe they were anything other than swimmers – well, unless the Merrows showed their tails. Did they?"

"No. Their tails remained underwater," said Cassie.

"Well, no sweat then," said Thomas.

"Well, except," said Cassie shamefacedly, "I might have gone on about the amulet being dangerous and the stone of a soul splitter."

"You and your big mouth! But, so what, that's unlikely to mean anything to her. Anyway, I think these new arrivals are the ones who owe us an explanation!"

Back in the kitchen at Fairy Fort House, Áine welcomed the strangers warmly. They seemed subdued and weak and almost cried with gratitude to be on dry land. Thomas was buzzing with questions about the submarine but Áine gestured to him to be quiet.

"So what brings you to our shores?" she asked the unexpected visitors.

The man, a good-looking thickset man, slightly balding but with soulful eyes, gazed at the woman. "Please, I am Sasha and this is my wife, Willa, and baby Tatiana."

Áine looked keenly at Willa, taking in her tall, willowy form, her long, wavy jet-black hair and sharp, slanted features. She was very beautiful in a slightly spooky way.

"And Natalya is our, how you say, our nanny goat." Sasha's English was somewhat erratic.

The children tittered.

"I am childminder," Natalya said grumpily. "Only baby. No mind any other child persons." She looked daggers at Sasha, who hung his head, even more crestfallen.

"And where are you from?" asked Cassie.

The man looked at his wife, his eyes darting around nervously. "Far away," he said vaguely.

"Where's 'far away'?" persisted Cassie. She stared into his face. There was something vaguely familiar about him. "I know your face," she insisted. "Have you ever been in one of those TV talent shows? You look like a singer. Are you?"

The man shrugged, embarrassed.

"Have you been in an advert? Or do you live in East Croydon like us?" interrogated Cassie.

"Maybe you're a criminal on the run," said Thomas gleefully. "How else would you get hold of a submarine? They belong to the military."

The man shifted around in his seat and looked even more uncomfortable. Beads of sweat broke out on his forehead again.

"Or you could be a spy," continued Thomas with relish. "It's a good disguise bringing a baby."

Again the strangers said nothing. Willa seemed to be in another world and clung to her baby. Sasha shook as if he was having a panic attack. Áine threw the children a warning look and kindly gave Sasha a glass of water.

"Can I just ask, what kind of controls does the sub have?" said Thomas.

"It has, you know, the funny stick and like a computer window." The man gesticulated as if playing a video game. He seemed relieved to talk about something concrete. "Very easy. Go very fast."

"Wow!" exclaimed Thomas, excited. "A digital joystick and an animated graphic touch-screen! That's a real innovation. It means a really small crew can run it. And what about the hull? Has it got pump jet propulsion?"

"Now, children, let our guests relax," Áine intervened. "They are tired."

Natalya the nanny was already snoring, her head slumped on the table.

Áine picked up a sound-asleep Lorcan as if he was as light as a packet of crisps. Even though he was huge, she never seemed to have any trouble carrying him.

"You can sleep in my room," she said to Sasha and Willa. "Jarlath will be away all night in the workshop. I can double up with Cassie and Nancy."

"Yerra, you can have my room, Áine," insisted Connle. "I can go to your old cottage, to give you room. Natalya can have the couch. I'll be back first thing in the morning."

Áine nodded in agreement. Her cottage was in the far north-west corner of the island.

Natalya sleepwalked her way to the couch, then Sasha and Willa with Tatiana followed Áine up the stairs to the bedroom on the first floor. Áine lent them Lorcan's old

Moses basket and with Connle's help moved Lorcan's rather large cradle to the other room.

When the visitors were settled, the children followed Áine into Connle's bedroom to talk.

"Those strangers are weird," said Cassie as soon as the door of the bedroom was firmly shut. "I don't trust them."

"I don't like that nanny woman. She makes my tummy feel funny," said Nancy.

"And I don't like the fact that the Merrows stuck their noses in," said Cassie. "We really need to chase them about that amulet. The nanny said she didn't see them but I bet she did. Though I don't think they showed their tails." She was reluctant to tell Áine how she had shot her mouth off in the presence of Natalya and the others.

"It is no matter if she did," said Áine. "You will have plenty of time to take the Merrows to task. And as for the visitors, we must show them hospitality and let them rest."

"But, Áine, these fugitives are beyond suspicious," said Thomas. "That kind of submarine technology is only in the control of navies. They'd have to be mega-mega-rich to get their hands on that class of sub. I hope I get a chance to see inside."

"They have some need," said Áine. "But we will find out what soon enough. Now off to bed with you!"

They kissed her goodnight and climbed the stairs to their attic bedrooms.

"We still haven't faced the fairies at the Midnight Court, wherever it is hanging out these days now that Viracocha is squatting in their field," whispered Thomas to Cassie as they reached their rooms.

"We'll just have to hope there isn't hell to pay," sighed Cassie as she bid him goodnight.

Thomas checked on the twins. He smiled when he saw they were both sleeping soundly in their cots. He quickly got into bed but his head was buzzing with questions and he found it hard to go to sleep. Never mind the creature in Bo Men's Bog and the Beggar God in the Fairy Fort Field, they probably had international criminals under their very own roof!

CHAPTER 3

*T*hat night Cassie's sleep was once more troubled by strange cloud formations that drifted through her dreams. She thought she saw a cradle of billowy cloud burst into flames. She awoke feverish and sweaty. Now that she was back on the island her "long sight" was returning but she was unable to interpret the visions. When she was on Inish Álainn, she was often visited with prophetic dreams but it wasn't always easy to know what they meant. She longed to be able to consult her old teachers Scáthach and Sennan. But sadly they were gone.

Downstairs, the living-room resembled a crèche. Áine and Willa were engaged in a production line of nappy changing while the sulky nanny looked on, playing with her hair.

When Áine asked Natalya to pass a jar of cream for Lorcan's nappy rash, she shrugged and said, "But I look after only Tatiana. She have no rash on bum."

Cassie brushed past her and handed Áine the cream.

"I hungry now," said Natalya.

"Cassie, could you get our guest some breakfast?" said Áine.

Cassie wanted to say no, but one look from Áine made her reconsider.

"Follow me," she said gruffly to the lazy, grumpy nanny.

Connle was in the kitchen stirring a huge pot of porridge. He ladled a large serving into a bowl for the visitor. But Natalya turned her nose up at it even though it was Connle's famous porridge that tasted of whatever you wanted it to taste.

"It look like, how you say, the baby sick," she said, wrinkling her nose.

Cassie noticed that two of her front teeth at the side of her mouth were very pointy. She was also deathly pale.

"This isn't a hotel," said Cassie in exasperation. "And just exactly why are you here and where are you from?"

The nanny shut her mouth and then launched into a flurry of complaints in a language that sounded like Russian.

"Are you Russian?" asked Thomas. "Lithuanian? Latvian? Czech? Slavonic? Estonian? You must be. That's a Russian submarine you've stolen, sorry, are travelling in."

Natalya just kept up her volley of moans and complaints. Then she arose out of her seat in a huff and stormed out of the room.

"What's wrong with her?" said Cassie. "Silly cow!"

"She might be a deadly assassin," said Thomas. "I'd be careful about insulting her to her face. She might have those shoes with retractable knives or umbrellas with poisoned tips or lethal radioactive substances in her pocket."

Sasha appeared in the kitchen, looking hollow-eyed and miserable.

"I sorry. Our ninny not very well in head." He gestured to his head. "She not likes the soupmarine."

"Submarine," corrected Cassie automatically.

"What brings you here?" Thomas asked kindly, trying a different tack. "Are you having some kind of problems?"

But Sasha just looked miserable and jumpy and gazed beseechingly at them. "All of us sick. Please, just a few days," he pleaded in such anguished tones that Nancy took his hand and held it in a reassuring way.

Connle placed a big bowl of porridge in front of Sasha and big salty tears splashed into the bowl. But with Connle's reassurance he began to eat.

"This tastes like home! Like blinis and cinnamon and poppy seed!" he exclaimed, a brief smile crossing his lips. But then he started to cry even more.

Connle waved the children out of the room as he tried to soothe the big man between his big racking sobs.

"Let's go and consult Tadgh about the mysterious beggar and the creature in the bog," suggested Thomas.

The children jumped on their bikes and headed off to Tadgh, who lived in a round tower near the north coast of the island. The wind blew hard as if trying to push them off their bicycles but then it stopped abruptly. It started to rain.

"The island feels very unsettled," remarked Cassie to Thomas as they freewheeled down the hill. "That fog came out of nowhere."

Thomas glanced over at his sister and to his astonishment she was enveloped in a big puffy cloud. "Cassie, it's just you – you're under a cloud for some reason!"

Cassie peered through the mist and thought she saw the shape of a baby before it dissipated. She felt a sudden coldness. It felt like the fog had shifted to her bones and brain. "It's weird. I keep having these cloud visions of something to do with babies!" She had a gnawing fear in her stomach that something awful was going to happen to a baby. But she decided to say nothing about that to her brother and sister.

At the crossroads, they took the fork in the road that led to Tadgh's tower. As they rounded the corner, they were met with an extraordinary sight.

Previously the area around the tower had been a terrain of rock, marsh grass and low thorn bushes. Now, it looked like a giant's vegetable patch. Cabbages the size of bushes grew in profusion alongside cauliflowers as big as horses' heads. Amongst them stood Tadgh.

Tadgh ran the local library but he used to be a professor who travelled the world in search of lost civilisations and myths. He was a tall, thin man, constantly on the go. His creased face beamed with joy to see them.

"Welcome!" he exclaimed. "Now what question do you

have for me today?" Tadgh was used to their obscure enquiries about various mythological issues.

"Well, first off, how have you managed to grow these vegetables?" asked Thomas, throwing his bike against a tree that on closer inspection turned out to be a giant Brussels-sprout stalk. The sprouts were the size of footballs.

"It's very intriguing," said Tadgh, laying down his trowel and ushering them towards the ladder of his round tower. "I don't know exactly how or why this garden has blossomed. But I read that the sites of the round towers of Ireland correspond to the position of stars in the northern sky during the winter solstice, the shortest day of the year. Jarlath said there is some scientist who has a theory that round towers were actually a sort of magnet drawing wave-lengths of magnetic energy from the earth and sky. It might explain why I've suddenly become such a great gardener. Something has triggered the sudden growth. All I know is that since last year everything I've planted has grown to enormous proportions."

"Finnen," mouthed Cassie silently to Thomas.

Since Áine's sister, the Swan Maiden, had returned to the island, flowers and vegetables grew in profusion, tropical and native side by side.

"When the winter solstice comes you can always check out the stars with your telescope and see if their position matches up with the round towers," said Thomas as they climbed the ladder up to the door, which was a few metres up from the ground. Tadgh had a very powerful telescope right at the top of his tower.

43

"I'll be looking forward to the coming lunar eclipse first," said Tadgh. "You know, when the moon darkens because the earth lines up exactly between it and the sun. It's a magical sight. The moon turns a dark red colour and it's associated with blood and black magic. But come on in – no doubt you have more questions about gods and goddesses."

Tadgh led them up through the twisty-turny spiral staircase inside the tower. All along the walls grew ivy and wild roses of the most delicate hues – a pink blush, an orange tinge, a deep yellow bloom. There was even a blue rose, the colour of the early morning sky, and a rose with a silvery sheen. It looked like the bower of a fairytale princess.

But the manuscript room was just as they remembered it, crammed full of dusty volumes and leather-covered books lining the bookcases right up to the ceiling.

As soon as they reached it, the children began to bombard Tadgh with questions.

"Do you know of a kind of god called V-something – from South America somewhere?" demanded Cassie. "It sounds a bit like 'verruca'."

"And could there be a beast with the head of a kangaroo, the body of a snake and the tail of a crocodile?" asked Thomas.

"There was a little old man who turned into a big ugly spider in the Fairy Field last night," said Nancy.

Tadgh smiled indulgently at her.

44

Once Cassie and Thomas would have rushed to shut her up, fearful that she would reveal too much. But they knew Tadgh so well now, they were sure he wouldn't bat an eyelid. He was always tactful and seemed to accept that Nancy had a vivid imagination.

"Well, let's take the V-man first, what do you think?" he said, reaching for a large book covered in battered red leather. "This is the *Dictionary of Mythological Beings*." He thumbed through the volume. "Ah, Viracocha! The creator god of the Inca tribe of Peru!"

The children crowded round.

"According to the legends of the Incas, he created the world. He is represented as having the sun for a crown, thunderbolts in his hands and tears descending from his eyes as rain."

"That's right," said Nancy. "He likes crying."

Thomas and Cassie exchanged excited glances. They were on the right track.

"At first he moved among the people he created as a beggar, teaching them civilisation and performing miracles. But he was so disappointed in his creations that he fled in disguise. And has been wandering lost ever since."

"That must be him," said Thomas to Cassie as Tadgh searched out another volume in the upstairs room. "I was wondering what was up with the beggar disguise. And if he was disappointed by his creations, it explains why he's so miserable."

"That's all we need, a depressed god on our doorstep,"

sighed Cassie. "As well as mysterious Eastern European fugitives in our house."

"And a funny crocodile, snaky thing in the bog," added Nancy.

Tadgh hauled a large book bound with green leather into the manuscript room. It was inscribed: *An Illustrated Bestiary of the World*.

"This book contains all the beasts and animals that crop up in legends from around the world," explained Tadgh as he thumbed through beautiful, detailed illustrations of a chimera, a dragon and a monkey god.

"The head of a kangaroo, the body of a crocodile and the tail of a snake, you say," he said, leafing through a section headed "Mixed Species Beasts".

"No, the body of a snake and a tail like a crocodile," corrected Thomas.

On the very last page was a graphic pen-and-ink drawing of the beast they thought they'd seen thrashing round Bo Men's Bog.

"*Almudj is an Aboriginal deity from Australia sometimes known as the Rainbow Snake*," read Cassie.

"The Aborigines in Australia believe that the world was created during 'Dreamtime', the time before time," said Tadgh. "It's a beautiful notion. The ancestor spirits like Almudj roamed the land and brought everything into existence."

"So what's he doing on Inish Álainn?" whispered Thomas.

"Perhaps he got lost in his own dreamtime or was having a nightmare," speculated Cassie with a shrug.

"Maybe we should talk to Finnen," whispered Thomas, glancing at Tadgh who had his head in the *Illustrated Bestiary* and was obviously oblivious to what the children were saying to each other. "She has experience of moving between other countries and mythologies. You know, the way some gods and goddesses pop up in different cultures and traditions and even change their names."

Last year, they had to seek Finnen through Celtic and Norse mythology where she had hidden for thousands of years from the wrath of Balor after a battle.

"I'd really like to see Finnen anyway," said Cassie. "I'm very worried about that amulet – I'd like to ask her about that."

"Okay. Let's go to Glimmering Lake right now and try to contact Finnen," said Thomas. "Though by all accounts she's very busy."

They thanked Tadgh for his help and set off for Glimmering Lake.

The island really was looking astonishingly beautiful these days. The boreen that led down to the lake was lined with a beautiful hedgerow with a profusion of wild flowers – honeysuckle, Michaelmas-daisies and red fuchsias like fairy bells. There were also clumps of trumpet lilies and magnolia bushes dense with pollen-dusted pink blossoms. The grass was a fluorescent green and the rocks and pebbles were covered with silvery lichen and soft moss.

As they approached the lake, Nancy doubled up. "My tummy's tingling," she said.

The hairs on Thomas's arms prickled and Cassie felt goosebumps down her spine.

"Ssh!" said Cassie, darting behind a bush. "There's something stirring by the lake."

They watched as a dense cloud descended and settled by the shore. When it lifted, an odd assortment of travellers lay on the ground. They looked to be Chinese, wearing elaborate outdated warrior clothes and kimonos and carrying an unusual assortment of weapons. There were eight of them. Immediately three of them broke into a high-pitched argument in what did indeed sound like Chinese. One was a middle-aged woman in a kimono carrying a lotus blossom; another was a dirty old man with a scraggy beard cradling a bottle made out of a hard-shelled fruit, known as a gourd, and leaning on an iron crutch. Another was tall and distinguished looking and carried a flute.

Cassie blew on Ogma's ring, which was looking worryingly cracked. Since it had been damaged by the shield, it had been coming out with some very odd translations and she hoped it hadn't got worse.

"Now, Mr Smarty Bum! What do we do now?" said the middle-aged woman, shaking her lotus blossom at the dirty-faced old man.

"We have to find these Simpletons of Ease," he replied.

"But we know nothing about them apart from the fact they are not very clever or industrious. Are they fat, thin, young, old?" badgered the woman.

"They will be simple persons of a lazy disposition. I say

48

fat," said the dishevelled man with the crutch and gourd.

"So that is going to be very helpful to get us back to Penglai Shan. Some work-shy idiots. You silly man, this was your idea!" scolded the woman who was dressed in an elaborate kimono decorated with cherry trees and white butterflies. "Maybe you should join them – you have all the right qualifications!"

"Have you any better ideas than being trapped in a cloud over the Poison Palace?" retorted the dirty man with the crutch.

"Please, friends, let us not quarrel," said the man with the flute.

The children looked at each other, mystified, as all the Chinese visitors burst into a flurry of argument, like a flock of noisy starlings.

Cassie coughed loudly and they froze. The children emerged from behind the bush.

"Excuse please, can you help us, little child?" began the kindly looking man with the flute. "I am the Philosopher Han and these are – the Immortal Woman –" He gestured to the woman with the lotus blossom and was about to introduce his six other companions when the old man interrupted, waving his crutch in the air.

"Is this Inshau Arring?"

"If you mean Inish Álainn, then yes," said Cassie. "And who's asking?"

"Iron Crutch Li, that's who," said the old man, jabbing his crutch in the air in a bad-tempered way. "And do you know of some stupid people who like to take their leisure?"

"The Simpletons of Ease," added the Immortal Woman.

The children grinned at each other. Thomas winked at Cassie and whispered, "I think our nickname has got lost in translation again!"

"The island is full of people like that," said Cassie mischievously. "Can you be more specific?"

"They defeated this Bal of the Crooked Eye and found the bird woman Hu Fang, even though they are not very bright and inclined to like an easy life."

Thomas and Cassie shook their heads, laughing.

"But they are famous, these stupid persons who enjoy free time and gentle activities – you must know of them," puzzled the flute-playing philosopher.

The children just continued to laugh.

The old man with the crutch frowned at them. "Silly younger persons, do not trifle with the Eight Immortals!"

To the children's astonishment the eight strangers leapt in the air like Kung Fu masters. Some of them carried odd but lethal-looking weapons. A distinguished man with a long black beard held a weapon that looked like a flywhisk but had deadly barbs. Another in formal warrior clothing brandished a lance and performed martial-arts high kicks. The old man, Iron Crutch Li, launched his crutch into the air at them but Nancy shot it down with her sling. As the bearded one with the flywhisk charged Cassie, she leaped over his head and when the warrior aimed his lance, Thomas deftly stood on its point.

"Put down your weapons," admonished the philosopher flute player, Han. "If their children are so strong and clever, these Simpletons of Ease must be truly marvellous – even if inclined towards wasting time and not having many brains."

"We are us!" exclaimed Cassie. "We are the Chingles from the East!"

"Yes, but we must find the idiots who are work-shy, the fools who take life easy," insisted the Immortal Woman, shaking her lotus for effect. "It is velly important."

"But we are the ones you seek," said Thomas.

"Indeed," said Han courteously. "Please, noble children, take us to your elders."

Thomas and Cassie lapsed into vexed thought.

"How can we convince them we are who they want?" said Thomas. "They've got it into their heads we must be adults. And lazy simpletons at that!"

"Oh well, let's try!" Cassie sighed. She turned to Philosopher Han. "*We* are what you're looking for. But you've got our name wrong. You see, the name has gone from 'Sean Gaels from the East' to 'Chingles from the East' and now 'Simpletons of Ease'." Then she explained about the confusion that had arisen because Nancy couldn't pronounce the word "children" properly and called it "chingles" instead. And how the real "chingles", the Sean Gaels, had turned up too late! And how it had all worked out well in the end but they were stuck with a nickname that no one seemed to be able to pronounce properly.

"Ah, English whispers! 'Sean Gaels from the East' becomes 'Chingles from the East' and ends up as the 'Simpletons of Ease!" marvelled Han the Philosopher.

"Funny, we call them Chinese whispers," said Cassie.

Thomas went on to recount to their surprised visitors how they saved the island from Balor and then last year from his vengeful wife Caitlín of the Crooked Teeth.

"Ah, it is good that you are brave. But let us explain to you our mission," said Immortal Woman graciously with a low bow. "Like you, we are a band of legendary warriors. We are known as the Eight Immortals because we each attained immortality through a bizarre chance or fate. We each have a power that can give life and destroy evil."

"Not being proper pedigree gods, we can't live in their immortal heaven," sniffed Iron Crutch Li. "So we set up home in Penglai Shan, an elusive island that can only be reached by air."

"It is so beautiful!" cut in Immortal Woman. "The most beautiful scented flowers grow among coral trees and all the birds and animals are white. Even the insects!"

"Your island too looks very beautiful," said Philosopher Han diplomatically. "And beautiful white swans here on the lake. It is a good omen."

"But we have quarrelled with the so-called king and have been exiled to a cloud over Poison Palace on Penglai Shan," said Immortal Woman. "We heard from passing spirits that you have helped other gods so we have come to seek your help. Except Iron Crutch Li has too much wax in the ears to hear clearly and no brains in the head." She glared at her companion.

"Passing spirits speak very softly unlike Immortal Woman who screeches like a crowing hen," he retorted.

"We'll gladly help, but only if you promise never to call us 'simpletons of ease' again," smiled Cassie.

"We can call you Clever Children of Busy Disposition. How's that?" offered Iron Crutch Li.

"Chingles will be fine," laughed Thomas.

The Eight Chinese Immortals also laughed heartily. It started as a titter but soon they were crying with laughter, doubling over in hysterics. Clearly they were somewhat excitable.

When they finally caught their breath Han the Philosopher asked anxiously, "But you will help us?"

"I'm afraid there is something of a queue," said Thomas, explaining about the Beggar God in Fairy Fort Field and the mysterious Aboriginal creature in Bo Men's Bog.

Just then, a shaft of sunlight hit the water and Finnen arose in a blaze of light from the lake, her swan's wings outstretched.

"Children!" she exclaimed. "Your fame has travelled far and wide!"

She looked even more beautiful than they remembered her. Tall and stately, her snow-white hair billowed like a cloud behind her and was tinged with gold. Her skin glowed and her eyes sparkled. Her swan's wings made her look like an angel. She wore a beautiful gown embroidered with the sun and moon in their different phases. The threads of her dress seemed spun out of sun and moonbeams. Around her head was a diadem of rays wrought in gold and silver. It shimmered with alternating sun and moonlight. The Chinese Immortals fell to their knees in awe and bowed low. She opened her arms wide to greet the children and they ran to hug her.

"My dear friends," she laughed with joy. "Oh, how happy I am to be home again! I am so busy these days looking after both the sun and the moon!"

"It seems to be agreeing with you," beamed Cassie.

The Chingles were so overjoyed to see Finnen, they nearly forgot about the Eight Chinese Immortals until Iron Crutch Li coughed loudly.

"We have quite a lot on our plate too," said Thomas. "The island is full of visitors from other realms, all needing help. These are the Eight Chinese Immortals. Immortals, this is the Swan Maiden Finnen, Moon Goddess and current caretaker of the sun. She is a very special friend of ours."

The previously talkative visitors became tongue-tied and were struck dumb at the sight of this glorious goddess so Thomas told Finnen about their plight.

She listened intently to Thomas's account. Having spent so long in exile, she was sensitive to the difficulties of other gods who sought refuge in other mythologies. She nodded at them sympathetically. "I know what it is like to be exiled from your home," she said kindly.

Still on their knees, the Eight Immortals bent their

heads low in adoration, glued to the spot. Iron Crutch Li sighed, swooned and fell over.

"Velly beautiful goddesses you have here," he muttered. "Too beautiful to look at. Make Immortal Woman look like old toad face."

Immortal Woman grunted in annoyance. "Too beautiful for Mr Ugly Crutch Li with his crooked leg!"

"What should we do, Finnen?" asked Thomas. "Can we really help all these deities from different countries?"

"You helped me," said Finnen.

"But will we have enough time?" worried Thomas. "We only have until the end of the summer before we go home."

"If we accept the gift of immortality from the gods, we can travel in the Otherworld forever," said Cassie.

"Ah, yes," said Finnen, "I remember – you must give the gods an answer at the end of this season."

Thomas nodded gravely. "We don't like to talk about it as we only end up arguing. I don't know what to do. What do you think?"

Finnen smiled. "I know only what it is like to be a goddess. Only your own heart will tell you."

"I'm not going," said Nancy stubbornly,

"And I definitely am," said Cassie.

"I don't really want to leave the twins," said Thomas. "Could I bring them with me?"

Finnen looked at them kindly. "Perhaps these other visitations are tests to help you make up your mind."

"There's one thing bothering me," said Cassie, abruptly

changing the subject. "That amulet that flew from my hand when I fought Caitlín. Did you ever find it?"

A worried-looking Finnen shook her head. "No, and I hear reports that the Merrows are constantly at the site of Balor's demise."

"The Pooka was hinting that the Merrows have the amulet," Cassie said, "and I saw one around Mara's neck."

"The Merrows will not talk to me," said Finnen. "They hate me almost as much as they hate Áine."

"Is it possible that Balor or Caitlín could come back?" asked Thomas.

"It is possible but unlikely," said Finnen. "It would require a huge surge of power and someone evil enough to want to summon them. The Merrows cannot do it on their own and I doubt they want to. They are silly and thoughtless but I cannot believe they would do anything really bad. But we must be ever vigilant. It is impossible to completely destroy evil. Sometimes it just takes different forms."

"We'll try to smoke the Merrows out," said Thomas. "But for now, we'd better get back home. We promised Áine we'd mind Lorcan and the twins this afternoon – we're going to take them for a walk. Can the Chinese Immortals stay here with you in the meantime?"

"Yes, they are most welcome to stay here in Glimmering Lake under my protection," said Finnen.

The Eight Immortals prostrated themselves on the ground in gratitude. They gazed up at Finnen with stupefied expressions of worship on their faces.

"But, please, my friends, do not bow down before me," she said kindly, helping Iron Crutch Li to his feet. "I was made welcome in other lands and I extend you the same hospitality."

The Chinese Immortals stood up but continued to bow repeatedly.

"I'm glad you welcome the newcomers," said Thomas. "The fairies don't seem quite so pleased."

"We keep getting orders to come and see them," said Cassie. "And I don't really want to."

"You cannot avoid it forever," said Finnen. "You must remember the fairies are small-minded and haven't seen much of other worlds. Now I must away to tend to sun and moon. I am always weaving light for day and night!" And in a spark of light, she was gone.

CHAPTER 4

As the children approached the house they heard the most beautiful eerie singing, like the sigh of the sea mingled with the rustle of the wind through forest branches. Enchanted, they peeked through the windows. It was Sasha and Willa, singing together. Sasha sang mournfully and melodiously in a deep baritone while Willa's voice soared through his notes with the tones of a nightingale. When they caught a glimpse of the children watching them through the window, they stopped, embarrassed. Something stirred in Cassie's memory. She was sure Sasha was a singer. But why all the mystery?

As they entered the house, grumpy Natalya flounced by Cassie in the hallway. Cassie made a face behind her back in the mirror but then, with a shock, realised the nanny wasn't reflected there. But she passed right in front of it, thought Cassie. Her blood froze and there was a deep cold feeling in the pit of her stomach. Humans always had reflections. Could Natalya be something else? Then there were those strange pointy teeth and the deathly pallor. Could Natalya be some sort of vampire? They also came from Eastern Europe. The thought was too awful to contemplate. Nancy didn't like her much either. Cassie felt panicky and wanted to talk to Áine or Connle about what she had seen, or rather *not* seen, but the house was too busy and she couldn't get them alone.

Then she began to wonder if she was mistaken. Maybe it was a trick of the light? She should check it out and be sure of her facts before she terrified everyone needlessly – and made a fool of herself into the bargain. She didn't like Natalya after all and maybe she was just being mean-spirited. She decided to keep an eye on her and discuss it with her sister and brother.

She was soon caught up in the detailed manoeuvre of getting Lorcan and the twins ready for their walk. She and Nancy had a real job coaxing Lorcan out of his sandpit where he was busy scratching in the sand with a stick.

Nancy scrutinised the symbols of vertical lines slashed with horizontal lines. "They look like the Ogham alphabet," she marvelled, speaking of the magical tree alphabet invented by the druids that they'd learned last summer with Sennan.

But Cassie was losing patience and didn't pay any attention. Despite Lorcan's protests she confiscated his stick and yanked him, bawling loudly, from the sandpit.

After his brief moment of song, Sasha was slumped dejectedly in the kitchen and Willa was lying down in

Connle's bedroom with a headache. Cassie kindly suggested to Sasha that they take Tatiana on the walk with the other babies. Sasha hesitated but then, with a weary sigh, agreed.

"Small walk, yes," he mumbled. "Not far. Tatiana very young baby. She need her mother."

"You go and lie down, Sasha," said Áine. "You're exhausted. Natalya will go on the walk too and she can bring Tatiana back if she's fretful."

"We'll only take them as far as the Flower Meadow, Áine," said Cassie. Cassie eyed Natalya warily as they set out, wanting to see if she had a shadow. Vampires had no reflections and weren't supposed to have any shadows either. But the sun was at its noonday height and cast no shade. And weren't they also supposed to shun daylight? thought Cassie.

Natalya was behaving oddly. She was restless and agitated. She twitched and seemed to be smelling the air like an animal looking for scents.

As they reached the top of a small hill there was a glorious view of the north of the island. They could see all the way across to the north-west coast, where the rolling contours of the land were lapped by the rugged sea – and there, in the middle distance, was Tadgh's tower surrounded by luxuriant vegetation.

Natalya seemed startled by something that snagged her interest.

"What is that thing?" she demanded urgently, pointing at Tadgh's tower.

"It's a round tower," said Thomas. "Our friend Tadgh the

librarian lives there. There are lots of them in Ireland. The monks used them in the old days to shelter from the Viking raids. But Tadgh told us they might be able to channel magnetic resonance. Imagine that!"

Natalya muttered something under her breath.

"What are you saying? Why are you so interested?" said Cassie suspiciously.

But Natalya became distracted again and sniffed loudly like an animal in a disconcerting way.

As the path went downhill Tatiana's buggy hit a pebble.

"That's it," Natalya moaned, flouncing off. "I go back. You walk filthy road."

"Natalya! Come back!" shouted Cassie. "You're supposed to take Tatiana back to her mother if she starts to cry!"

"Let her go," said Thomas. "We'll be better without her. I'll take Tatiana back to the house if necessary. She seems quite happy at the moment anyway."

So Nancy pushed Tatiana's buggy, while Thomas managed the twins and Cassie nearly gave herself a sprain pushing Lorcan.

Cassie decided to tell her brother and sister about Natalya lacking a reflection in the mirror and her suspicions.

"Are you sure?" asked Thomas anxiously.

"Well, I suppose I could have imagined it. I need to check it out again. But, besides, she gives me a cold clammy feeling like something in a graveyard. And she's behaving oddly. She doesn't seem to like being out in the day. And she's so pale!"

"And has pointy teeth," said Nancy.

"These are all marks of a vampire," said Thomas with a shudder.

"I told you she wasn't nice," said Nancy. "She makes me shiver with a cold feeling in my tummy."

"That's a bad sign," agreed Cassie. "She behaves so weirdly. Why did she develop this sudden interest in Tadgh's tower? She's been acting bored with everything else . . . except the Merrows."

"Well, at least the babies are here safe with us," said Thomas. "We'll smoke her out when we get home."

When they got to the Flower Meadow, the Chingles were delighted to see that a picnic was laid out on the grass. The white tablecloth, loaded with food, looked inviting among the violets, ragged robins, yellow cowslips, ox-eye daisies and the small purple flower called self-heal. They supposed the picnic must be Connle's doing. He was always springing delightful surprises on them. He must have taken a shortcut and reached the field before them.

"Connle! Connle! Come out!" they called, thinking he was laying in wait for them in the meadow.

But there was no answer so they figured he had slipped away and would later jokingly deny that he had anything to do with the surprise picnic.

Best of all, when they took Lorcan from his buggy, he was clutching the silver bottle containing Granny Clíona, their ghost ancestor who was a witch!

As the babies played around in the grass, Thomas popped open the stopper.

"There you are!" exclaimed Thomas in delight. "Connle was so worried! Lorcan must have had you hidden away all the time!"

"Ach, ye wee dearies!" exclaimed Granny Clíona, passing through them, which was her version of a ghostly hug. It gave them a warm, tingling feeling. "Isn't it great to see all the wee bairns around the place?" she enthused in her Scottish Irish accent.

"They're not the only recent additions to Inish Álainn," said Thomas.

Cassie gave Granny Clíona a troubled look. "There's a beggar in the Fairy Field who seems to be a god and we might even have a vampire."

"And eight Chinese people with Finnen and they thought we were stupid but we're not!" interrupted Nancy excitedly. "A dreamy crocodile thing from Australia in Bo Men's Bog!"

"And the fairies want to erect a force field!" said Thomas.

Granny Clíona threw up her hand, bewildered. "Och, I've missed such a lot surely! Now explain it to me from the beginning."

So Cassie told Granny Clíona of her worrying forebodings because of the cloud visions, the arrival of the strange gods, the suspicious visitors in the submarine and the nanny with no reflection.

Granny Clíona looked puzzled and perturbed. "I tell you to be vigilant," she said. "But there is one thing I can do now for the bairns. I ask ye to place all four of them together so

I can give them my blessing, a wee spell for times of need."

The children did as she asked and put the four babies on the ground in a small circle.

Granny Clíona solemnly walked around them and ruffled their heads with a ghostly hand.

"May ye bairns always have strength when ye need it most to protect yourselves from harm! May ye be surrounded by a protective shield of love!"

As she finished speaking, a strange thing happened. A halo of light with all the colours of the rainbow circled over the children's heads.

"It's blessed you are surely," said Granny Clíona.

Just then they heard Stephen Guilfoyle, the local farmer, clattering by on the road in his tractor. Granny Clíona immediately went back inside her silver bottle and Thomas put the stopper back on and hastily hid the bottle under the edge of the tablecloth.

The tractor came to a halt.

"Hello, children!" the farmer called over. "Great to have you back! You haven't seen a stray lamb on your travels by the way? One of the flock that grazes over near your house has gone missing!"

The children said they'd keep an eye out for it.

As the tractor disappeared over the hill, the children were suddenly overcome with hunger. They placed the drowsy babies back into their buggies so they could concentrate on their feast.

"How thoughtful of Connle to lay out a picnic for us!" said Cassie.

"And what a practical joker he is!" said Thomas. "I wonder how he got time to make all this stuff?"

They approached the tablecloth laid out with goodies, suddenly ravenous. There were gingerbread men, chocolate brownies and lots of little sugared fruits.

"But how do we actually know it's Connle who left this for us?" said Thomas, suddenly wary.

"Who else would it be?" tutted Cassie, already tucking into sugared almonds and cream pastries.

She became slightly crazed with greed. Her face lit up with such divine happiness that Thomas soon overcame his scruples and joined her. Nancy's mouth was already full to bursting.

As soon as they'd stuffed themselves stupid, the children felt heavy and sleepy and lay down in the Flower Meadow. Then their eyes closed and they fell asleep.

As they slept, Cassie, Thomas and Nancy found themselves in the same dream. A woman appeared in a torn dress, her face haggard, her eyes bloodshot and puffy from crying.

"My little ones!" she wailed.

She then suddenly held four babies, whose faces they couldn't see. Then the babies became insubstantial like clouds, faded and got thinner and thinner. The dream woman began to wail. The children tossed in their dream. The woman turned into an old hag dressed in rags and held four sticks in her hand that burst into flames.

"Be warned!" she wailed.

Then in their dream they saw a dark cloud descend over Poolbeg Rock and the flick of a Merrow's tail in the water.

The three Chingles awoke sweaty and panicking.

"We've all had the same dream about the flaming sticks, haven't we?" Thomas said.

His sisters nodded in confirmation.

"And what about the cloud over Poolbeg Rock? What can it mean?" wondered Cassie with a shiver down her spine.

"Look!" said Thomas in alarm.

To their amazement the babies' buggies were surrounded by a thick, clammy fog. The Chingles panicked and ran to the buggies, fearing the worst. But under the fog the babies were all present and correct, sleeping the sleep of the innocent.

"There's something up," shuddered Cassie. "That dream, it seems to suggest that something will happen to the babies! I have to confess I've been having vague dreams and presentiments." She gazed anxiously at the babies.

"It was strange," agreed Thomas. "But as far as I can tell, nothing has happened. The babies look normal. But why don't we ask Granny Clíona?"

"Let's wait until we're back at the house. I don't want to hang around here," urged Cassie. "And look, now there's a large bank of fog rolling in from the sea!"

Quickly they packed up everything and set out.

"Where is Granny Clíona's bottle anyway?" asked Cassie as they left the field.

"It's in my pocket," Thomas replied.

Losing no time, they hurried home in the fog, feeling cold and miserable and worried about having the babies out in such weather.

They found Áine and Willa fretting anxiously at the door. Jarlath, who liked Sasha, had decided to cheer him up by taking him on a marathon fishing trip and tour of the island by boat that was likely to go on all night. And there was no sign of Connle.

"Oh, we should never have let you take the babies out!" said Willa.

"But the fog appeared out of nowhere," said Áine. "I know our weather is changeable but that came out of a clear blue sky!"

"Everything's all right," Cassie reassured them. But she knew her voice betrayed her uneasiness.

"But where is Natalya?" asked Willa.

"You mean she didn't come back?" asked Cassie.

"No," said Willa. "Why would she come back? She was responsible for Tatiana."

"Oh, she got into a sulk," said Thomas, "and took off."

All of the babies were still in a deep, profound sleep, so Áine and Willa put them to bed.

Cassie and Thomas were anxious to investigate Natalya further but there was no sign of the sulky nanny. They lurked about in the neighbourhood of the landing during the evening in the hope that she might arrive back and they could check her out in the hallway mirror. But bedtime came with no sign of Natalya.

❧

Later, when the entire house was asleep, Cassie awoke to hear the babies crying and Willa and Áine moving around the house speaking in hushed voices. Jarlath and Sasha were obviously still out fishing. She peeked in at the twins and discovered Thomas was soothing them, quietly singing a lullaby.

He looked up at her with a worried expression on his face. "I think they've caught a cold," he whispered, concerned. He was very protective of the twins.

Cassie peeked at them in their cots. Their dear little faces did indeed look very pale and their breathing sounded harsh. She laid a hand on each little forehead in turn but they felt quite cool.

"No, they don't have a temperature," said Thomas. "I already checked."

"Well, that's good," said Cassie, "but they certainly seem unwell. And the other babies are awake and crying. I'll go and talk to Áine."

Cassie tiptoed down the stairs and came upon Willa and Áine standing on the landing trying to comfort their crying babies.

"Are the babies okay?" asked Cassie.

"We don't know what's the matter with them," said Willa. "They're crying but won't eat anything."

Cassie squinted at Tatiana. She didn't look too good – rather pasty and weak. Even the normally bouncing Lorcan looked weak and pale.

"The twins don't look too good either," she told them.

They all went upstairs where Áine and Willa gazed anxiously at the twins who never stirred despite the fact that Tatiana and Lorcan were wailing loudly.

"Perhaps they caught, how you say, a coldness in the field today?" said Willa.

Cassie looked stricken. "That fog was terrible but it was a beautiful day when we set out."

"Nobody's blaming you, my dear," said Áine. "Babies often come down with strange illnesses that pass quickly. Let's see how they are in the morning. If they're still poorly, we can consult Róisín, who knows many things about babies. Come, Willa."

Cassie wondered if she should tell Áine about their strange dream but thought it might terrify the anxious mother needlessly – perhaps the babies might be better by morning. And she really needed to talk to her about Natalya but now was not the time – Áine was too distressed. Biting her lip, Cassie went back to her room feeling very uneasy indeed

All night the babies slept fitfully, their crying fracturing the household.

In the dead of night, Cassie was abruptly awakened from her own tossing and turning by a shout from Thomas. She and Nancy ran into his bedroom.

"Mattie and Matilda!" cried an anguished Thomas. "Something weird is happening!"

Cassie looked into the cots and to her horror the babies appeared to be fading, literally, as if they were holograms that were weakening. Thomas and Cassie immediately reached into their cots to grab a baby each but a force field repelled them. The babies were locked in a bubble of enchantment.

"Nancy, go and call Áine!" said Cassie urgently.

Nancy ran out of the room and down the stairs. She stopped as she heard an anguished cry from Áine and Jarlath's bedroom where Willa and Sasha were staying.

Willa was in tears, bending over Tatiana in the Moses basket. "My baby!" she wailed, too distressed to notice Nancy come into the bedroom. Willa reached her hands into the cradle but she was knocked back, just like Cassie and Thomas had been when they tried to lift the twins from their cots. Nancy ran from the room to alert Áine.

Áine was in Connle's room, rocking Lorcan in his enormous cradle, the size of a small boat. He too looked thinner and smaller than usual, as if he was disappearing in the pale moonlight.

"There's something wrong with the twins!" cried Nancy. "Cassie and Thomas can't lift them! And Willa can't lift Tatiana either!"

With a panicked look at Lorcan in his cradle, Áine tried to lift him but to her shock she too was repelled by some invisible force.

"The babies must be under some enchantment!" she cried.

With a stricken look at Lorcan, Áine hurried upstairs behind Nancy. As she passed Willa's room, she briefly stuck her head around the doorway.

"I'll come back in a minute," she said. "I need to check on the twins." Willa nodded anxiously.

In the children's bedroom Áine watched in dismay as

Thomas tried again to reach into one of the cots but was repelled.

"I fear some bewitchment," she whispered to Thomas and Cassie. "I cannot take Lorcan from his cradle either."

"Oh, Áine, I'm so sorry!" said Cassie. "There's something I should have told you but I didn't want to frighten you . . . We had a disturbing dream earlier this afternoon that foretold of babies being lost." And she told Áine of their dream vision when they fell asleep in the Flower Meadow.

Áine looked aghast. "This dream was a bad omen," she said, horror rising in her voice.

"It gets worse," said Cassie guiltily. "I really should have told you – I'm worried Natalya is some kind of vampire. She has no reflection – at least I couldn't see one in the mirror in the hall – and she has weird pointy teeth."

"You may well be right," said Áine soberly. "Somebody has put a spell on the babies."

"I've been such an idiot!" cried Cassie. "I should have realised something was wrong."

"Hush, don't fret now," said Áine gently.

"Is Natalya downstairs now?" asked Thomas. "Did she come back last night?"

Áine shook her head. "No, she's not here. But we will worry about her later. First we must do something about the babies. I cannot use my magical powers on pain of death, as I have foresworn them in order to take human shape. We must appeal to my sister Finnen and my father Manannán Mac Lir."

71

"Maybe Granny Clíona can help!" said Cassie. They were inclined to forget about her when she was tucked away in her little silver bottle. "We found her, Áine! Lorcan had her! And she gave the babies her blessing. Surely nothing bad can happen to them? Oh! It wouldn't be her spell gone wrong, would it?"

"No. A blessing could never turn bad in this way," reassured Áine. "This is some other enchantment."

"I'll go upstairs and get her," said Thomas. "The bottle's in my jeans pocket since yesterday." He made for the stairs.

"She was with us at the Flower Meadow, Áine," Cassie explained, "but unfortunately she had to jump back into her bottle when Stephen Guilfoyle came along looking for a lost lamb. Then Thomas put the stopper back on so she wouldn't have heard or seen anything after that. She probably slept through whatever happened to the babies!"

"Still, maybe she can help now," said Áine.

But a few minutes later Thomas came tearing down the stairs, his face a picture of dismay. "It's gone! The bottle's gone! I was sure I'd left it in my pocket! I've searched everywhere upstairs in case it fell on the floor and rolled off somewhere."

"Maybe Lorcan took her again," said Áine. "Though I don't know when – he was in a deep sleep when you came back yesterday."

"I looked in his cot, though I couldn't really search it of course," said Thomas. "She could be under his covers – but it really didn't look like it."

"Let's look around here," said Cassie.

They searched the whole place and even upended the buggies. But there was no sign of Granny Clíona anywhere.

"I hope we didn't leave her in the Flower Meadow," said Thomas in great alarm.

"But you said you put her in your pocket!" said Cassie.

"I thought I did," said Thomas lamely.

"Children, I am sure Granny Clíona will turn up," said Áine. "You must search the Flower Meadow as soon as you can, but for the sake of the babies, let us now contact Finnen without delay."

"But what will we say to Willa?" Cassie said. "You cannot risk revealing your secret to her."

"We will tell her it is herbal medicine," said Áine. "Send Nancy to alert Finnen and ask her to bring some of the water from Glimmering Lake. Now that she is once more its guardian, it may have regained its magical healing properties. I must go to Willa now."

But as Áine reached the bedroom door, the house was rent with a terrible wailing. Áine rushed to Willa's room to find her standing, the baby's blankets in her hand, weeping over Tatiana's basket. There was no baby inside – all that was left was a pile of wooden sticks!

Then Willa fainted into Áine's arms.

Just then, Connle, who had been sleeping over at Áine's cottage, rushed into the house alarmed by the outcry. He charged up the stairs and helped Áine and the Chingles to lay Willa on the bed. She was in some sort of numb shock.

Then Áine ran out onto the landing and into the other bedroom and the air was rent with fearful shrieks as she too discovered a pile of sticks when she pulled back Lorcan's covers.

Back upstairs, Cassie and Thomas approached the twin's cradles with mounting horror, their hearts thudding in their chests, dreading what they might find. Cassie put her hand on the coverlet of Matilda's cot and knew instantly. She was gone! Thomas pulled back the covers of the other cot but he too was confronted with a pile of wood where Mattie should have been.

Immediately he exploded into a towering rage. "Whoever has taken the babies, I'll hunt them down!" he vowed.

"Natalya!" Cassie cried. "It's something to do with her!"

They rushed back down the stairs to the others.

"The twins are gone too!" cried Cassie.

"Was it the fairies?" said Thomas. "Didn't the Pooka say they liked to steal babies?"

"The fairies have other things on their little minds," said Connle. "I visited them last night. They've set up their court in the Sacred Grove and are spoiling for a fight. But all they can think or talk about at the moment is this magical barrier they want to set up to keep foreign spirits out! They're obsessed by the notion!"

"Besides, our fairies leave a baby of their own, not a bundle of sticks," said Áine.

"Then it must be the work of some dark forces from somewhere else," said Connle.

"Does that mean some evil spirit entered the house just now and substituted sticks for our babies?" asked Thomas, bewildered.

"No, no, Thomas," said Connle. "Don't you see? Those were changelings – not the real babies! That's why they were fading away."

"Somehow the substitution was made earlier," said Áine gently, "when you were on your walk."

The Chingles looked at each other, remembering the picnic when they had fallen asleep leaving the babies unattended and the horrible fog that had surrounded the buggies.

"You didn't leave a picnic in the meadow for us this afternoon, did you, Connle?" asked Cassie, already knowing the answer.

Connle shook his head gravely.

"Someone left a huge picnic laid out on a tablecloth," said Cassie. "We thought it was you, Connle, surprising us. That food must have been drugged. That's how they managed to trick us and steal the babies. Oh, we've been so stupid!"

"Don't blame yourselves," consoled Áine. "If they were intent on kidnap, they would have found a way."

"It has to be Natalya!" said Cassie.

"But she couldn't have been working alone," said Thomas.

"It was clever to substitute changelings that turned into sticks," said Connle. "It gave the kidnappers time to get away."

"But why didn't Granny Clíona's spell protect them?"

75

asked an anguished Cassie. "She asked for them to have strength when they needed it most so they could be protected from harm. And for them to be surrounded by a protective shield of love."

"Maybe it's not the time they need protection most," said Connle thoughtfully. "Blessings and spells don't always work instantly or in the way you think."

"It's some comfort," said Áine.

"Oh, I hope they haven't snatched Granny as well!" moaned Cassie.

"We don't know that yet," said Áine.

"But what has happened to Natalya? She has to be our number one suspect," said Thomas. "Connle, we think she might be a vampire!"

"That would account for a lot of things," said Connle.

"I haven't seen her since she left for that walk with you," said Áine.

Their anxiety rising, they left Áine to care for Willa while they searched the surroundings of the house for Natalya but there was absolutely no sign of her.

Just then, Sasha and Jarlath arrived back from their fishing expedition, oblivious to the tragedy that had befallen the household. But as soon as they walked in the door, they sensed the turmoil that churned around the house.

"What has happened?" said Sasha fearfully.

"The babies have been kidnapped!" shouted Thomas. "And I'll kill whoever did it!"

Sasha, his face white, ran to the bedroom where his wife lay in a stupor. Áine embraced her husband in floods of tears.

Connle moved around the house, administering a healing drink to help them all with the shock. "Now, everybody, try to calm down," he said gently. "We must try to work out what has happened."

Sasha and Willa came downstairs. Willa looked like she had been struck by lightning and had to be helped onto the couch. Connle gave her some healing draught and offered some to Sasha.

But Sasha burst into sobs and literally tore his hair out. "It is all my doing!" he cried. "I so stupid! But I have a confession to make. Please sit down."

Everybody sat around the kitchen table.

CHAPTER 5

"Cassie, once you asked me if I was a singer," Sasha began. "It is true. Once I was the best-selling singer in all of the Eastern Europe. Until I go against that evil man, V-Vladimir . . ." he seemed unable to continue speaking.

"I knew I recognised you!" exclaimed Cassie. "But who is this Vladimir?"

"Vladimir is the most powerful man in all of the East now," continued Willa in a husky voice. "He want everybody think he is now a respectable businessman and politician but he is a bad, bad man. A criminal of the underworld who robs ordinary people and steals and lies and cheats!"

"This a most horrible, evil man," said Sasha. "He want me to make a song saying him the best, the greatest, so he can become president of all the countries. But I not like him, not one little, little bit, so I say no. We hear that he plan to steal our baby to force us to do what he want. But before baby born we hide. Then nobody see the baby. Nobody know what she look like, if she boy or girl, when she born, how old she is. Then the police say they want to arrest me for crimes against music. It is stupid charge they make up. But now, I am wanted man. So we escape on the submarine with the help of our friends. My friend, he inventor of submarine and he give me. 'Don't worry about navy,' he say. 'They forget I make this.'"

"You must be talking about Boris Borloskony," said Jarlath, impressed despite the circumstances. "He's one of the most famous inventors in the world!"

Sasha nodded briefly.

"So that's how you got your hands on the Darkon!" exclaimed Thomas.

"And we find you, with luck, just as we run out of water," continued Sasha. "But somehow Vladimir or his bad people follow us here and steal the babies."

"He must have been unsure which baby was yours so he took them all," said Jarlath, whose face had turned snow white. "Sasha and I must go to the mainland as soon as we can and alert the police."

"Please, please, no police! It will be no good!" wailed Sasha. "Vladimir, he powerful and rich. He too clever. I thrown in jail or worse. I had to escape because he want me killed."

"But we must do something!" said Jarlath pacing up and down, agitated. His eyes narrowed and he threw Sasha a suspicious look mixed with sudden anger. "How can we believe your story? How do we know *you* didn't take the babies?"

Sasha looked at him with big, sorrowful eyes. "But, my brother, I was with you in the fishing boat all night. I die before I hurt babies."

Jarlath looked remorseful and hugged his friend. "I'm sorry. I just feel so useless."

"What about Natalya?" Cassie asked suddenly. "How did she come to be working for you if you were so careful about keeping your baby's identity a secret? It doesn't add up that you'd have a nanny."

"She was already on submarine when we leave," said Sasha. "She claim our friends tell her to go with us to help us. We only discover her when we already underwater. Then it is too late to make her leave."

"I sorry I trust her," said Willa. "Now it is too late."

"I want to believe she friend but she betray us somehow," said Sasha.

"Let us go find her now," said Thomas resolutely.

They decided to split into three search parties, the children forming one. Jarlath suggested Sasha accompany Áine and he Willa but Áine was insistent that she and Willa stay together.

"We would only hold you back," she said to the men. "Willa is still very weak. Without us you can cover more ground."

Jarlath and Sasha looked uncertain but obviously thought Áine had a point.

"If you spot Natalya, don't you dare approach her! She might be dangerous," said Jarlath.

"Come and tell us," said Sasha.

"Yes, we will," said Willa.

Then as the men prepared to leave, Áine drew Cassie aside. "I want to try to talk to Willa," she whispered. "There is something of the Otherworld about her and she is more likely to confide in me. I do not think the babies are still on the island. They may have been taken to the Otherworld. But I may be able to pick up traces of supernatural visitors. You see if you can find Natalya. Be careful if you do. From what you say, she is some kind of demon."

"I bet she's a vampire," said Cassie, an edge of fear in her voice.

So Willa and Áine set off to the west side of the island while Jarlath and Sasha headed to the east. Thomas, Cassie and Nancy were to scour the rest of the island. It was decided Connle should stay at the house in case Natalya arrived back there.

When the others had left, the children took up their weapons. "This is a calamity," Cassie confided to Thomas. "I can't believe we were so slow to tackle Natalya despite our suspicions. I've been so stupid not to heed the warning in the visions."

"But nothing has been very clear," said Thomas. "We'll have to make up for it now."

Suddenly Nancy doubled up in pain.

"I feel something is wrong near the farm," she gasped,

clutching her stomach. "I can hear horrible noises. A cry like a wolf. I can hear a hen cry for help and a calf!"

"Something is attacking the animals on the farm!" cried Cassie.

"We'd better get there immediately!" exclaimed Thomas.

In one quick motion, all three of them jumped into the sky and landed at the farm as animals – Thomas as a stag, Nancy as an eagle and Cassie as an Irish wolfhound.

Immediately their keen animal senses smelled blood. Fresh blood that had been newly shed. Around the chicken coop lay several dead hens, their feathers in disarray as if a fox had invaded and feasted on the easy prey. But then they heard a sharp, terrified cry from the direction of the barn as if someone's throat was being cut.

A newly killed calf lay on the ground and, biting into its throat, her face distorted with a savage greed, was Natalya! She looked up from her grizzly meal, blood drizzling from her mouth, and they saw she had two terrible prominent fangs in a wolf-like hairy face. Her face contorted into a slavering grin and her pointed teeth flashed.

"She's some sort of vampire or werewolf!" cried Cassie, as the Chingles assumed their own shapes.

Quickly Thomas aimed his lance in Natalya's direction.

"No!" cried Cassie. "We must get information from her."

She threw the rope into the air and lassoed the jittering, juddering shape of Natalya before she could attack. The creature tore at the rope with her teeth, thrashing like a wild animal. But the magic imbued by Scáthach into the rope held her firm and subdued the beast temporarily.

The creature snarled at them, thrusting out her claws.

"Who are you and what brings you here?" demanded Cassie.

The creature released a blood-curdling roar. "Ah, better ask Willa that! She is herself a fiend!"

"You monster!" shouted Thomas. "What have you done with the babies?"

"You will never find them," snarled the creature. "My Lord's spirits have taken them."

"What spirits?" cried Cassie. "Were they the ones who enveloped us in the fog at the picnic?"

Natalya flashed her teeth. "Stupid greedy children eat the food. So spirits come take babies."

Thomas moved closer and held the lance to the creature's heart. "And who is your Lord?" he demanded.

Natalya let out a blood-chilling, spine-tingling laugh. "Vladimir!"

"Do you mean the Vladimir that Sasha just told us about, the underworld boss?" asked Cassie, her eyes wide with wonder.

"He will soon be Lord of All," crowed Natalya.

"What do you mean? Is he some sort of vampire too?" asked Thomas.

But Natalya just cackled.

"And who are these spirits that left the enchanted picnic for us? Are they vampires?" demanded Cassie.

The creature gloated, exultant. "No. These special spirits I summon. Baby-stealers. Tell them come and take Willa's baby! They take the babies and leave you changelings that change into sticks."

A thought struck Thomas. "Did they take a silver bottle too?" he asked urgently.

But Natalya just looked blankly at them. "They only steal babies. Why they want silver bottle?"

"But why did they take all the babies? You knew which one was Willa's," said Thomas, feeling more and more enraged at this hellish creature.

Natalya cowered. "I hungry. I no energy after summon spirits. I must eat blood so I hunt instead of meet spirits. The spirits come but I not there. They not know which baby is Willa's. Only I know. So they take them all."

"That doesn't make sense," said Thomas. "Why didn't they just go and find you? It's only a small island and they are spirits after all!"

"I not know. But they not come find me or summon me. They very stupid spirits." She grinned, baring her terrible teeth. "But maybe they want to keep other babies for themselves!"

"But they don't know which baby is Willa's!" said Cassie. "They will have to give all of them to Vladimir!"

"Ah, but they will find out which one! When I summon them I tell them about women in the water! They will ask! Nothing can stop my Lord and Master!" crowed Natalya.

Cassie's blood ran cold. In their dreamscape in the

meadow they'd seen a cloud descend over Poolbeg Rock – the favourite hangout of the Merrows.

But did the Merrows even know about Tatiana and the twins? They certainly had never laid eyes on the twins and Tatiana was bundled up in a blanket while she was being taken off the submarine – they probably hadn't even noticed her, they were so taken up with their taunting and mockery. Besides, they were forbidden by Manannán Mac Lir from even mentioning Áine so they wouldn't be able to tell the baby-stealers anything about Lorcan.

"So that lamb that went missing from Stephen Guilfoyle's flock – you attacked it?" Thomas was saying. "You were meant to be at the picnic to identify Willa's baby but instead you went away and savaged a lamb?"

Natalya greedily licked her lips. "Very tasty. But human better. And I want to kill all of you next but then you catch me." She flailed against the rope but she was bound tight. "But I make good discovery for my Lord! He will be very interested in this island!"

"What do you mean?" asked Thomas. "Why would this Vladimir be interested in this island?"

Natalya grinned. "Because here is tower of power and stone of splitter of souls! This is what he search for!"

"That's right!" said Cassie. "You were very interested in Tadgh's tower. And you saw Mara wearing that amulet, didn't you? And you heard me mention Caitlín was a soul splitter!"

"Ah, yes!" laughed Natalya, baring her teeth. "Good discoveries!"

85

"But you haven't had a chance to tell your 'Lord' about anything yet," said Thomas, "and we won't let you go!"

"But I tell baby-stealing spirits already!" Natalya smiled devilishly, opened her lungs and bayed to the moon. The noise was deafening and unsettling and made their nerves taut as piano wires.

Just then, Willa and Áine, drawn by Natalya's roars, came running into the farmyard behind the Chingles.

It all happened in a flash.

As the startled children swung round momentarily towards the women, the creature broke loose from the rope with unnatural power and lunged towards Thomas.

"Watch out!" screamed Willa.

And as Thomas spun back towards the vampire, it lurched onto the point of his lance. The creature fell to the ground and at once crumbled into dust.

For a few moments they all stared in shock.

"What is going on?" Cassie then demanded of Willa, more roughly than she meant.

"We've just been speaking to Natalya!" said Thomas. "And it's all your fault!" Thomas leapt forward and held her at the point of his spear. "Are you some kind of fiend too? Time we had some straight answers from you!"

Willa burst into tears.

"Children," intervened Áine, signalling Thomas to put down his lance, "let us not fight among ourselves. We face darker powers than we supposed. First let Willa speak, then you can tell us what you learned from Natalya."

"The child is right," sobbed Willa. "It is all my fault."

"Tell the children what you told me," urged Áine. "The real truth – that you are no ordinary mortal woman."

The Chingles put down their arms to listen to her story.

"I am a vila," said Willa, calming down, "a wood nymph from the magical forest deep in what humans call the Carpathian Mountains. One day I hear Sasha sing in the forest. He is a shepherd. I fall in love with him."

"That is the weakness of gods and goddesses," said Áine sympathetically.

"I could not rest, you see," said Willa. "I must enchant him. So I decide to take mortal shape. I go to magical place, the Cascade of the Golden Water. But I did not see another human follow me. He spy on me. He see me change form."

"Vladimir," guessed Cassie.

"It was him," confirmed Willa. "You see, I change shape without the permission of the gods. He know this is a bad thing. So he – how do you say – blacked me?"

"He blackmailed you," corrected Áine.

"Yes, blackmail, and he say he tell the gods and Sasha my secret. This is bad for Sasha and me, very bad," continued Willa, her eyes downcast.

"I can see that the gods, wherever they come from, don't like any changes without their permission," said Thomas, ruefully glancing at Áine.

"To my shame," Willa continued, "I beg Vladimir to let me go and I promise him anything." Here she broke down in sobs again. She took a deep breath and continued. "He

87

Patricia Murphy

demand and I promise him – oh, I can hardly say it – my first baby. I think I trick him later or make him change his mind when the time come."

"Why did he want your baby?" asked Cassie. "It's a strange thing to ask."

"There is a prophecy in my land of a spell. To know the secrets of the Otherworld, you must have a child not of human mother – other things too but I do not know them," said Willa.

Áine gasped but said nothing. Cassie and Thomas realised why. Lorcan was another such child and he was now in the clutches of this evil Vladimir.

"Natalya said he is also searching for a tower of power and the stone of a splitter of souls," said Cassie. "They must be part of the spell and Vladimir can find them here."

"Natalya saw an amulet around the neck of Mara, an Irish mermaid, when you were disembarking from the submarine," Thomas said and explained to Willa that it was made of a meteorite from outer space and was used against Caitlín, a soul splitter. "We defeated her in battle but the amulet was lost. Later the Merrows found it."

"And when Natalya first saw Tadgh's Tower here on the island she was transfixed," said Cassie.

Willa gasped. "Yes, you see, Vladimir not just a human crime lord. He must get the secrets of the Otherworld. He is, how you say, obsess . . . ?"

"Obsessed," suggested Cassie.

"Yes, he obsessed," continued Willa. "When he was a

child he apprentice to sorcerer. But he abuse the secrets of the supernatural. He is a very bad man and his gifts – kaput! They took them away. Now he busy, busy, busy until he capture all the magical secrets. He wants them so he can be king, of this world and of the Otherworld. Of spirits, humans, the living and the dead. He must rule everything. He hate that he is just ordinary man but with black, black heart."

"Oh, this is terrible," said Áine. "He has come for your child to fulfil the bargain and he needs her for some fiendish spell. And Natalya, who is she? Is she one of his people?"

Willa looked at the pile of dust. "Natalya was not a person. She a vampire ghoul that take over a dead body."

"But I thought vampires just had fangs," puzzled Thomas. "Natalya turned into something like a wolf."

They looked at the pile of dust but it yielded no clues. An owl screeched in the dark night and the Chingles felt a sickening fear tighten their stomachs. They realised they would have to face unknown horrors to find the babies.

"There are also creatures who are half-werewolf, half-vampire," explained Willa. "Many types of vampires in our land."

"So she wasn't a person?" asked Cassie.

"Perhaps once but she now a spirit. She take a body that dead a long time. That is why crumble away to dust. You see, vampires exist in many forms. There are also spirits that capture live bodies, some who go for the dead, some who take on animal shapes. Many types. I hear rumours Vladimir once more get power in black magic. And this Natalya show he get vampire spirit to work for him."

Thomas glanced at Cassie. Willa looked exhausted and drained but they felt they had to gather as much information as possible.

"What other kind of vampires are there?" asked Cassie.

"There are those called Eretsuns," said Willa. "On point of death a sorcerer take their soul and their body become the Undead under his control. The body can only exist now by sucking blood – animal but better if human. These ones are good for evil sorcerers because they are entirely in his power. Spirit vampires like Natalya more difficult to control. Let us hope he does not yet know the secret to make Eretsun."

"So why didn't you realise Natalya was a creature of Vladimir's? I mean, she was a terrible nanny – you must have been suspicious!" asked Áine. Willa looked a bit embarrassed. "Like Sasha say, she already on submarine. She say our friends provide her. We not like her but no time to throw off. Besides, we very, very tired. She did help a little."

Cassie felt a sudden pang of sympathy for the wood nymph and Sasha trying to cope with a bewildering ordeal and a young baby. There was something innocent and childlike about them. How desperate their situation was! She vowed to herself to do all she could to help them.

"You were lucky she didn't eat the baby and Sasha too," said Thomas.

"Vampires last for days without a kill but then they get

desperate," said Willa. She faltered, going pale. "I am so, so stupid. This Natalya, I should know she bad. I put you all in danger."

Cassie and Thomas related to Áine and Willa how Natalya failed to turn up at the picnic to identify the babies because she had to satisfy her hunger by killing a lamb. So Vladimir's spirits took all the babies because they weren't sure which one was Willa's child.

"Natalya told them about the Merrows," said Cassie. "She thought they would identify Tatiana."

"But the Merrows cannot," said Áine. She frowned. "But why did the spirits not simply find Natalya and ask her?"

"She said they were special baby-stealing spirits and that maybe they wanted to keep some of the babies for themselves," said Thomas.

"There are spirits in my land who steal babies," said Willa faintly. "I have heard of them but do not know them."

"Well, Vladimir has kidnapped the babies rather than kill them because he wants them alive," said Áine. "That is at least one good thing."

"Yes, he needs a live baby for the spell so he can take over the Otherworld," said Willa. She seemed very weak and dazed. "But maybe later he sacrifice!"

"But you don't know that for sure," soothed Áine. "We won't let it happen. You are lucky to have found the very people who can help you." She glanced at the children.

"It was not luck," said Willa. "It was no accident we

came here. I hear of your wonders. The, how you say, Tingles."

"Chingles," corrected Nancy.

"I think you older, fully grown persons," said Willa. "I think maybe you can help me in some way with your special powers. Maybe stop Vladimir."

"A lot of people need our help," sighed Cassie.

"But now we will rescue the babies as a priority," said Thomas.

Willa smiled wanly. "You give me hope," she said, her voice wavering.

"It would help if you knew something else about this spell that will enable Vladimir to take over the Otherworld," said Thomas. "Then we might be able to figure out where the babies fit in."

"A child not of human mother born is all I know," said Willa. "I am wood nymph. I not know black magic." She suddenly faltered and looked like she might faint again.

"Well, we know the tower of power and the stone of the soul splitter have some significance," said Cassie. "We'd better talk to the Merrows."

Áine looked at Cassie with concern and took Willa, who was barely able to stand, gently by the arm. "Children, I will take Willa home. She is exhausted." Time was moving on and Áine was anxious.

"Please take this," said Willa, taking off her multicoloured necklace and thrusting it into Cassie's hands. The gems glinted and shone with a radiant glow. "These are special stones of power. The gemstones will help you if you face spirits from my world. They give you strength."

Cassie examined the necklace. It had stones of emerald, sapphire, diamond, red rubies and amber. A blood-red stone streaked with white and silver was the centrepiece.

"That is a bloodstone – jasper," said Willa. "It has the strongest magic – save that for your hardest fight."

"Do you think we may have to go to your part of the world?" asked Cassie.

"Perhaps that is where Vladimir take the babies, deep in the mountains in the east," said Willa.

Cassie pressed her for more details but Willa's understanding of geography was vague.

"This is dreadful," said Thomas to Áine in a whisper. "If he realises that Lorcan is also related to the gods and goddesses this horrible Vlad might try to blackmail you to reveal the secrets of the Tuatha Dé Danann."

"He must not find out," said Áine fiercely.

"I hope we're right in thinking that the Merrows haven't told Vladimir's spirits," worried Cassie.

"They cannot," said Áine. "As I told you, my father has bound them not to speak of me to anyone on pain of being turned into cod. They fear him – rightly. But, in any case, we must move fast. I think you should travel in dreams to discover what you can about where the babies might be."

"What about Sasha and Jarlath?" Thomas asked. "Jarlath wants to go to the police."

"I will find a way of stalling him," said Áine. "My father

owes me one blessing for our son Lorcan. He cannot refuse me this, despite our quarrel. Now make haste – the events are recent and there may be traces of spirits still near."

Áine went and, putting an arm around Willa, led her away.

The night felt thick and threatening and the smell of blood curdled the air. The children felt sick to their stomachs.

They decided to go to the Sacred Grove to travel in dreams.

"Let's travel as birds," said Thomas. "We may be able to see something from the air."

So they took to the sky on strong wings as falcons, scanning the ground with their keen sight for any unusual activity. It was a moonlit night, the sky the dark blue of summer rather than pitch black. As they flew all they saw were the familiar little fields and maze of boreens. Nancy thought the small mice, rats and voles seemed more nervous and agitated than usual. Maybe that was because a vampire had so recently been in their midst.

The Sacred Grove was to the west of the island and was part of the castle grounds. It was in a narrow valley where the trees grew along the hillside in a clump around a well. It was a special place, long venerated by the islanders, the home of truly mysterious trees. The trees were once the loyal band of warriors of the King of the Isles. When they died they were buried together and grew back as a magical birch, a hawthorn, a willow, an apple-tree, an oak, an alder and a hazel.

But some of the essence of the warriors was embedded in the trees. Those they blessed were permitted to see their human essence. So in the blink of an eye they transformed from tree to person and back again. Sometimes they appeared as a mixture of both.

Last year the trees that were half-human and half-spirit had grown back as mischievous tree children, having been destroyed in a fire by Balor of the Evil Eye in his human incarnation of Sir Dignum Drax. This year they were mature young adult trees, standing aloof and silent in their grove. But when the trees sensed the Chingles in their midst, they graciously flickered into humans for a moment and gently touched the children with their boughs.

The air felt charged with magic and the bloodstone on the necklace given by Willa glowed in Cassie's hand as she held it. Thomas and Nancy touched the gemstone necklace in her palm and felt charged with electricity.

"Spirit of the Trees, be ours, guide us to the answer of the babies' disappearance!" the children chanted over and over again as they sat amongst the trees.

Soon they found themselves drifting into a trance, lulled by the mantra of their words, and their spirits were able to temporarily leave their bodies to travel in the Otherworld.

In their dreamscape, they emerged through a crystal cave into a forest alive with enchantment. The trees glowed an unnatural emerald green; the bark shone with a jewelled hardness. Birds, with plumage of fire and rainbow-coloured wings, flitted from bough to bough. Then a ladder of flame appeared in the sky. At the top a ghostly woman shimmered before them, surrounded by fluffy clouds.

"Can we trust her?" asked Cassie.

Nancy patted her stomach to see if she could pick up messages about this supernatural being from the traces of the Star Splinter. She felt a tingling and fizzing, a good feeling. She nodded her head.

They ascended the ladder of fire up to dizzying heights in the sky. But the flames did not burn them or the ladder.

The woman was almost transparent, as if a breeze might blow her away. As they drew closer, they saw she was made of clouds herself. Cassie recognised her as the spirit who had first tracked them in the airplane.

The woman began to speak. Cassie blew on Ogma's ring.

"I am Dodola," the spirit woman said in a wispy voice. "The Goddess of Clouds. I tried to warn you but my powers were weak in the Other Place. Unlike you, I am not a good traveller."

"Do you know where the babies are?" asked Cassie urgently. "Have they been kidnapped by the crime lord Vladimir?"

"I know not of whom you speak. Evil is about. Many evil things stir in the forest. I know something bad will come to pass. So I try to warn you. It was Poula and Doma, the foolish old spirits, who stole your babies and replaced them with changelings."

"So this Poula and Doma, where can we find them?" asked Thomas.

"I search for them high and low," said Dodola in her breathy voice. "But they have vanished. These spirits steal babies and then think they are their own. They are stupid and misguided but not unkind. I will try to find them and send you word. My messenger will say the wind sent him."

And with that, she vanished.

The children felt their own spirits weakening and felt compelled to return to their real bodies. But as soon as their spirit bodies slipped back into their physical bodies they were confronted with a thousand pairs of hostile eyes glinting in their direction and brandishing lighted tapers in their dazed faces.

CHAPTER 6

"Seize them – it's all their fault!" said a snotty voice.

"They've been nothing but trouble since they darkened our shore," said another querulous tone.

The children blinked in the harsh light of the tapers. Thomas reached for his lance but found himself bound in the soft cords of a spidery web, gossamer light but stronger than steel.

"The fairies of the Midnight Court!" he exclaimed. "Of course, Connle said you'd come here now that Viracocha the Beggar God is in your field."

"Contaminating our special place!" said a scornful voice. "We've had to move here for the time being."

"It's all your fault. You've lured all these foreign spirits here, causing trouble!" piped up another.

"Quiet, all din be ceased!" said a commanding voice.

It was King Finbhearra, the King of the Fairies. His torch illuminated his face. Like all the fairies, he had delicate pointy features and slanting eyes and on his bald head was a garland of whitethorn blossoms. He wore a waistcoat of flowers woven together as if embroidered. His trousers were of plaited grass, his cloak of glistening rowan leaves and his shoes were made of gnarled tree bark.

"And release these Chingles," said the soft lilting tones of his wife Úna. "We will have no binding here." She smiled anxiously at the children, her long hair as black as ravens' wings and threaded with precious stones shimmering in the moonlight. Her dress was woven out of flowers like a summer meadow and in her hand she carried a hazel staff with a bunch of hazelnuts at the crook.

The children were released from their bonds. Cassie recognised among the main agitators the crabby little purple face of Dris, the Fairy of the Blackberries, well known for being a cross-patch. She was glad to see the Pooka behind him nudge the bad-tempered little fairy – accidentally on purpose knocking him off his feet.

"What's all this about?" demanded Thomas, brushing cobwebs from his arms. "Don't you know four babies have been kidnapped? I hope you have nothing to do with it."

"It wasn't us!" Cam, the yellow-haired Fairy of the Buttercups, immediately piped up. "I bet it was all those troublemakers, those blow-in gods who've just arrived."

"Silence!" shouted King Finbhearra. "It is well that you have come to our Midnight Court. For we must pass judgement on what we can do."

Just then Connle burst in. Cassie noticed that some of the fairies looked at him with disdain.

"He is part human," said Dris, "and should have no say in our fairy realms."

"But Connle is our relative," said Queen Úna. "Let us begin this discussion."

Dris stood up and cleared his throat.

"It all began with these Chingles," he said with a dirty look in their direction. "Since their fame has spread far and wide we have been invaded by strange spirits and evil folk."

"It was bad enough when they were just hovering about but since these human children have arrived, we've been invaded!" thundered Cam.

"There is that beggar in the field," Dris complained, "and those eight monsters around Glimmering Lake. The creature in Bo Men's Bog – an abomination. They upset the natural balance of things!"

"But they have come to seek our help," said Cassie.

"Besides, we have a crisis on our hands. We don't have time for this," said Thomas.

"Be quiet, you earth-dwellers!" said Rua O'Rogan, the Fear Dearg, the two-faced red-faced leprechaun dressed all in red who was always appearing and disappearing. "You have no say in our court."

"But we cannot turn the foreign spirits away just because we don't understand them!" said Connle.

"We must erect a special barrier by fairy magic against any more spirits entering!" cried Dris.

"And what about the ones who are already here?" asked the Pooka. "They'll have to be sent packing."

"But we need to keep the channels open, what with the babies being kidnapped!" said Connle.

"They wouldn't have been kidnapped in the first place if we'd had a fairy barrier to keep the foreigners out," said the Fear Dearg, the Red Man, disappearing and then reappearing in that disconcerting way of his.

"They are not proper fairies," said Dris with indignation.

"And what is a proper fairy?" asked Connle. "I myself am a gruagach, half-human and half-fairy. Perhaps you should banish me?"

"Perhaps we should," said Slieveen, the sly clurachaun, dressed all in green.

Cassie glared in his direction. She'd never liked the thin-faced rascal.

"But you cannot take such a step without the favour of the Tuatha Dé Danann," Connle argued.

"Can't we?" wheedled Slieveen. "They themselves are incomers. They arrived in a cloud from who knows where. I don't think we should care a tinker's curse what they want!"

"Please, it could be disastrous for our search!" pleaded Cassie. "We may be sent messages by other deities and they may not be able to penetrate your fairy barrier."

"We should tell all the outsiders to leave and put a spell on those who don't," pronounced Dris.

"You are so mean!" protested Nancy. "Don't you care about the babies?"

"That was the work of outsiders," said Dris. "Nasty criminals and thieves the lot of them."

"The next thing you know these unwanted aliens will be demanding to come to our Midnight Court!" fumed Cam. "And trying to change our traditional ways."

Queen Úna raised a tiny bell and rang it, its tinkles cutting though the simmering arguments. "We must now cast our votes. My husband and I will abstain. On my left for the magical barrier, on my right against."

"So they're abstaining," murmured Thomas to Cassie. "Crafty move. They mustn't like the idea themselves but they don't want to risk alienating their court."

The fairies burst into action and the Sacred Grove became a blur of fairy wings. Each dropped a feather at Queen Úna's side. It was soon apparent that every one of them had voted for the erection of a magical barrier. Only Connle and, surprisingly, the Pooka had voted against it.

Cassie looked with dismay at the toppling pile of feathers to Queen Úna's left.

"The Midnight Court has spoken," said the queen.

Cassie saw Úna and Finbhearra nervously glance at each other and got the impression they weren't happy at this result. Thomas had been right – they didn't favour the force field themselves but had guessed their court would vote overwhelmingly in favour. As Thomas said, abstaining was a crafty political move.

"This is a disaster!" warned Connle.

"What say we ban this traitor from the Midnight Court?" shouted Dris.

"No need," shouted Connle back angrily. "I'm leaving of my own accord. Come on, children!"

"We should punish these Chingles for causing all this trouble," demanded Dris, his purple face half-crazed with vengeance.

The Chingles bristled.

"You might be forgetting the little matter of them saving the island from Balor in the first place!" Connle shouted back in indignation.

A group of fairies made ugly by hatred surrounded the children and Connle.

"Peace!" commanded King Finbhearra. "Let them go in peace. It is wrong to have enmity between kith and kin."

Finbhearra looked almost embarrassed at the fairies' behaviour. Connle threw him a reproachful glance and led the children from the Sacred Grove.

"Of all the petty, small-minded behaviour!" fumed Connle as they neared Fairy Fort House. "They'll make a mess, they will."

The Chingles were surprised to see the Pooka trotting after them.

"You stunned us by voting against the magical barrier," said Thomas. "Surely you're not becoming a good guy in your old age?"

"Oh, you know me," said the Pooka nonchalantly. "I like it when things are a bit mixed up. Makes life more interesting."

"I never knew you were so tolerant and fair-minded," said Cassie.

"Shut up, I'm not!" said an outraged Pooka. "It's just those little jumped-up fairies get up my nose. Squawky little things, full of their own importance, like that Dris, Lord of All the Blackberries. The blackberries, I ask you! Hardly a great kingdom, that one. I've a good mind to go and trample all his brambles!"

The night was beginning to fold into the day as the whisper of the early light of dawn slowly suffused the eastern sky. The Pooka began to seem a little less substantial.

"Well, whatever your reasons, I'm glad you're on our side," said Connle.

"I'm not on your side as such," quibbled the Pooka. "I just can't be doing with all this nonsense. Where do that shower of chancers think they come from in the first place? Some of them have quite murky origins, I don't doubt."

And with a toss of his now almost transparent snow-white mane, he cantered off into the brightening dawn.

"He's such a contrary fellow, that Pooka," said Cassie.

"But that's not the first time he's sided with us," said Thomas thoughtfully. "I think he likes us more than he lets on."

Suddenly, there was an odd crackle of electricity in the air. The Chingles and Connle looked around. There was no visible change but they sensed some shift in the atmosphere. Abruptly, they were all lifted off their feet as a great whoosh arose from above. They looked up to see tiny pinpricks of light spanning the island in an arch across the sky.

"They're doing it already," exclaimed Connle.

"We must stop them!" shouted Cassie.

But it was too late. For a moment all the lights fused and licked together and a gleaming web of luminosity encircled the whole of the island as far as the eye could see, like a bright net hovering over the earth.

Then the lights rose beyond the clouds and to the children's horror Connle was sucked into the sky! Then the children saw Áine and Willa run out of the house but they too were sucked far into the magical barrier. The children immediately turned into eagles and rose on a current of air, high into the clouds. Higher and higher they soared until they felt they almost touched the roof of the sky. There, tangled in a cobweb's mesh of light, they found Connle, Áine and Willa.

"The spell has gone wrong," gasped Connle. "All of us captured are of mixed human and fairy origin. I'm half and half and both Willa and Áine are goddesses who have taken human form."

"Go see if any of our visitors have been sucked into this force field – or Granny Clíona if she's turned up!" said Áine.

"What about Finnen?" asked Nancy.

But their friends didn't respond. They were now frozen in the fairies' net of lights, unable to move or speak.

Finnen should be all right, Cassie thought. She was probably off attending to her business elsewhere. Besides, she was a powerful goddess of the Tuatha Dé Danann and surely too strong to be caught up in a stupid fairy spell. And the sun was beginning to rise as usual.

But the fairies' spell seemed very faulty.

The children searched the skies but found no others caught up in the fairies' cobweb of light. Then they swooped down and surveyed the island. In the undergrowth of Bo Men's Bog, the crocodile's tail of Almudj the Aboriginal creature was still visible. But as they dived down closer, they saw him shrink and turn into the size of an ordinary lizard. He fled and hid under a rock.

On Glimmering Lake, the Eight Chinese Immortals slept on a cloud above the water's surface, oblivious to all the commotion on the island.

The children swooped down and changed back into children.

Han the Philosopher blinked at them through his kind eyes.

"I dream of angry buzzing lights," he said in a sleepy voice.

"That was the fairies erecting a magical force field designed to expel you all and keep others out," explained Thomas.

"But we are still here!" said Immortal Woman. "But I feel weak and sleepy like lizard on rock in sunshine," she added, yawning.

"But otherwise you are unharmed?" enquired Cassie.

The Eight Immortals shrugged. Han reached for his flute

but when he tried to blow on it, no sound came out. The others had also been robbed of their special powers.

"They want us to go but now we cannot leave," sighed Iron Crutch Li in a heavy voice. "We are stuck here now."

"These fairies have poor spelling," sighed Han.

"Is Finnen all right?" asked Cassie.

"I opened my eyes just now before you came and saw her, looking beauteous as ever," murmured Iron Crutch Li. "And that was after my dream of the buzzing lights."

"That's a relief," said Thomas. "It would be hard to do without the sun and moon."

The children told them about the kidnapping of the infants.

"This is velly bad," said Han. "If we had our powers we would help you. Now we are invalids – crippled Immortals."

"You must find the children on your own," said Immortal Woman sadly.

"If I ever see that Dris again, I'll wring his little neck," said Cassie vehemently.

"I will wring his neck and arms and legs for good measure," agreed Han.

The children took their leave and discussed what to do next.

"I wonder where Granny Clíona is," worried Thomas. "She's not in the fairy force field anyway."

"We must search for her in the Flower Meadow," said Cassie. "Let's hope she's somewhere safe and her silver bottle protected her from the ill will of the fairies."

"We better check on old misery-guts Viracocha first," said Thomas.

They changed back into eagles and took to the air.

They flew over the fairy fort in the Fairy Field near their house and saw the Beggar God was still in residence. He snarled at them but remained still a beggar.

"I cannot change now," Viracocha sighed. "But nothing good ever happens to me!"

Just then the children, circling high into the sky, noticed a commotion out at Poolbeg Rock and heard an angry chattering. They caught an air current and headed over towards the rock in the north-east of the island.

They saw that the fairy barrier had stopped short of the rock. Below in the water, the Merrows were cackling in an angry flurry.

"Sod off, you little monster!" they heard a Merrow yell.

Swooping down, the Chingles landed on a bluff on Poolbeg Rock and changed back into themselves.

"That fairy spell is very faulty. It hasn't stopped us despite our witch's blood and magic powers," said Cassie, dusting herself down. "But maybe we don't have enough of Granny Clíona's blood in us?"

"We should be thankful they're rotten spellers," said Thomas.

"Oh, look who's here!" jeered Mara, shaking her blonde tendrils that snaked like eels from her head. "We might have known you'd be all up to your necks in this."

"There's some horrible little creature hiding behind that

rock. A friend of yours, no doubt," mocked Shauna, sporting her jaunty little red cap. She spattered the children with sea foam.

"I want to talk to you," said Cassie thunderously. "First of all, I think you have my property!"

"Do we now?" said Fand, popping her head above water and sticking out her tongue. Her dark hair had the silvery sheen of mussels and she moved with lightning quickness.

"And have you been speaking to someone recently out at Poolbeg Rock?" demanded Cassie, undeterred by their bad manners.

"So what if we have? Where's your proof?" said Sionna.

"You have then! We saw it in a vision. What did you talk about? Caitlín? Balor? Tell me – it's very important," pressed Cassie. "Something awful has happened . . ." She trailed off, not wanting to give the Merrows any information about the kidnap of the babies. The less they knew the better.

She tried to see if Mara was wearing the amulet but she kept bobbing beneath the waves.

The three Merrows rose on their tails in the water and made mocking gestures at Cassie. And there, plain to see, was the red-gold amulet around Mara's neck.

"That's my amulet! Give it to me!" Cassie yelled.

"You'll have to catch us first!" squealed Mara.

Furious, Cassie, fishing her rope from her pocket, trashed the air in the direction of the Merrows who ducked under the water.

They popped up again, jeering, then disappeared once

more beneath the waves. Cassie was about to leap off the rock and turn into a salmon to pursue them when a small voice called out. It sounded like a high reedy note made by blowing on a blade of grass.

"Quick, blow on Ogma's ring, Cassie!" said Thomas. "It might be a messenger from Dodola, the Cloud Goddess!"

She hesitated, desperate to rescue the amulet from the Merrows. But then a vision of her twin brother and sister came into her mind. She blew on the ring.

"I seek the Chin Girls," said the high voice from behind the rock.

"Chingles," Nancy corrected automatically. "That would be us."

"No, no, the girls with chins. Or maybe it's the Chicken Poxes, how you say, Shingles, the bad rash on skin," the creature said.

"That's us too. Please come out," coaxed Thomas.

There was a rustle from behind the rock and a very curious creature stood before them. He was tiny, smaller than Nancy, with a hunched back. He had rather battered-looking grass for hair and his clothes were made of hay. They looked intently into his face and saw he had different-coloured eyes, one blue and one brown.

"I am Jarek," he said. "I am a polewik, a spirit of the fields. I tried to go to your island but the band of light stopped me."

"How do we know you are not a fiend sent by Vladimir?" demanded Thomas.

At the mention of this name, Jarek shrunk into himself and his green hair turned into bleached hay.

"The wind sent me," he said.

It was the code Dodola had given them.

"Dodola and the sky-seekers have discovered where the babies are kept," said the little creature.

Thomas gasped and clutched his sisters. For a brief moment, they felt the faint stirring of hope.

"The babies are held deep in the mountains," Jarek said. "We think in the secret stronghold of the Baba Yaga."

"The Baba Yaga?" repeated Cassie. "What's that? We thought they were kidnapped by Vladimir the crime lord with the help of spirits?"

"Dodola thinks Vladimir is in league with the Baba Yaga that we also call Grandmother Bony Shanks," shuddered Jarek, his voice turning even reedier and thinner. "She is a terrible hag who flies through the air in a pestle and mortar."

"What's that?" interrupted Nancy.

"It's a pot with a sort of club thing that Mum uses to pound herbs and garlic," answered Cassie.

"She must be very tiny then. I'm not afraid of her," said Nancy stoutly.

"It's a giant one," said Jarek. "She travels through the air in it and sweeps away her tracks with a broom. She lives in a revolving house that stands on chicken legs surrounded by a fence made of things I am too delicate to mention."

"You won't scare us," said Thomas. "We've been in the

Norse kingdom of Hel and she has furniture made of human bones."

"How did you guess? Her fence is made of bones and skulls!" said Jarek. "They say she aids those who are strong and pure of heart and eats those who are not. But she is unpredictable. She likes to eat children when she can."

Cassie gave an involuntary shudder. To think of those four beautiful babies in the grip of such a monster.

"We need to go there," said Thomas. "Just tell us where it is."

"Deep in the magical mountains," said the polewik.

"Could you be more specific?" said Thomas. He was used to dealing with Otherworldly creatures but sometimes they could be annoyingly mysterious.

"I came from the east. I do not know what you call it in your human tongue."

"It must be Eastern Europe," reasoned Cassie. "Can't you give us a few more clues?"

"Some messenger you are!" scoffed Thomas.

Two fat tears rolled from Jarek's different-coloured eyes.

Gently, Nancy held his hand and helped dry his tears. "Leave him alone!" she scolded her brother. She smiled at the miserable little creature. "Tell us everything you can about your home."

"Our magic mountains were once a paradise," said Jarek. "Then the people came and we had to hide."

"So people live in your mountains?" said Cassie.

"Nearby. Some they come in our forest, but many are

afraid. Before we lived in harmony but now this bad one, Vladimir, he raises an army of the Undead and our land is parched and scorched where they touch. But there are many kingdoms in the magical mountains and forest and streams and rivers."

"So to rescue the children from the Baba Yaga, we have to get through these Undead ones first?" said Cassie, screwing up her eyes and realising the situation was worse than she thought. If Vladimir was raising an army of the Undead he must have worked out how to make Eretsuns.

"Did you have to travel over the sea to reach us from your home?" asked Thomas.

The creature nodded. "Over many salty seas that lick the land."

"And are there cities in your magical mountains?" asked Cassie.

"No cities. But some say Vladimir make a city underground," said the creature. He became cross-eyed. "You are asking me so many questions!"

"Just one more. How are you going to get back?" asked Nancy.

"I am very tired," said Jarek, curling up on a rock. "Perhaps I rest here first."

"Just be careful the Merrows don't scare you away," said Thomas.

"We really should pursue them," said Cassie.

"It's not as urgent as rescuing the babies. We've got to figure out how to track down this Baba Yaga," said

113

Thomas. "Besides, it's probably pointless. The Merrows will just run to Manannán and hide behind him. And we won't be able to do a blind thing about it."

"You're right but I'm still uneasy," said Cassie.

"Look on the bright side," said Thomas. "The Merrows aren't great but I'd rather the amulet in their clutches than Vladimir's. And they certainly didn't hand it over to his spirits."

"You're right again," said Cassie. "Let's get back to the house."

"We must look for Granny Clíona," said Nancy.

"Thanks for reminding us, Nancy!" said Thomas. "We mustn't forget her in all this commotion. Time we ruled out the Flower Meadow."

So they took to the air as sea eagles and wheeled many a time over their picnic area – but their eagle eyes caught no glint of a little silver bottle. They alighted and poked about a bit. But there was no sign of Granny Clíona.

I've really done it this time, thought Thomas, who was still sure he had put the bottle in his pocket. Maybe I've lost her for good.

Back home, there was no sign of Sasha or Jarlath but the Chingles were dismayed to see a very unwelcome visitor snooping around their house. They landed behind a nearby bush and regained their human shape.

Their visitor was a small man. He was very tanned and had elaborately gelled hair and a very large moustache. He had a camera around his neck with a large telephoto lens.

"It's Finbar Flash!" exclaimed Thomas with annoyance. "Of all the blasted bad luck. Let's get rid of him quickly and do nothing to arouse his suspicions!"

"So that was *him* slumped in the back of the airplane pretending to be asleep the whole flight," said Cassie. "I thought I knew his face."

Finbar Flash was a journalist who used to work for Drax Universal Media, the television company set up by Balor in his human incarnation of Sir Dignum Drax. No one, apart from the Chingles' magical allies, knew about Drax's true identity as Balor. All the world knew was that the loathsome tycoon Drax and his yacht had eventually exploded. But after his demise, his foul deeds in human form were exposed, including his destruction of the Sacred Grove trees. And Flash was discredited as a bent journalist. The last time Finbar Flash was on the island, he'd ended up being thrown into the sea.

Flash was looking in their windows. Tentatively, he tried the top half of the back door. It was open. Looking furtively from side to side, he gently pushed the door in.

The children sauntered up the path.

"Look what the cat sicked up!" said Cassie loudly.

Finbar Flash jumped out of his standing with fright.

"Oh my gosh!" he breathed. Then, when he saw who it was, his lip curled in disdain. "Oh, if it isn't the three environmental campaigners known as – let me remember – was it 'the Chancers'?"

"Chingles," said Nancy.

Finbar Flash knew nothing about their supernatural powers. But the children, despite attempts to suppress the story, had been featured on television about their failed protest to save the trees of the Sacred Grove when Drax Universal Media had destroyed them.

"So what are you doing snooping around our property?" asked Thomas boldly.

"Thought I'd pay my favourite children a visit," he mocked, fingering his camera. Cheekily he raised his lens and snapped them, all with thunderous expressions on their faces.

"You have no business being here," said Cassie. "Go on, shoo!"

"Well, that's for me to decide." He took a card from his pocket and tossed it at Thomas.

It read: *Finbar Flash, the Pap with Dash! All Your Celebrity Sneak Shots. Supplier to* Daily Scumbag, Celebrity Shame, News of the Worst.

"You're a pap now?" said Cassie. "Short for paparazzo," she explained to Nancy. "It's an Italian word meaning annoying little mosquito and it's used to describe the horrible photographers who stalk the rich and famous. He sneaks around and tries to get photographs of famous people when they don't want to be seen."

"Just the perfect job for a malicious little sleazeball like you," said Thomas scornfully.

"Oh, come on now! Bet you liked it when your picture got beamed around the world. Child heroes, my foot! More

116

like meddlesome little show-offs. Thought you'd ruined my career when Drax Media went down the pan," he continued bitterly. "But I've come back and I know you have a dirty little secret somewhere. I'm on to you!"

"Not around here, you aren't," said Cassie menacingly. She was nearly the same height as him and she faced him eye to eye.

Finbar Flash blenched, taken aback by her fierceness. Then, at a safe distance, he said slyly, "Know anything about a missing Russian pop star?"

"He's our friend," said Nancy.

"Oh, is that so?" said Flash.

"She means she's a fan of his songs," said Cassie quickly.

Not for the first time, Nancy realised there were some adults you had to be careful what you said to.

"And do you know that this 'friend' of yours is wanted by Interpol, the international police, for stealing a submarine and for crimes against music?" said Flash.

"Our daddy doesn't buy those rags you work for," said Thomas. "He says they are rubbish." But he was rattled. Finbar Flash was dangerous and he knew too much.

"This is big news," said Flash, "and I intend to have a scoop. I've had a tip-off that the submarine was last tracked coming in this direction. As we speak, the Irish, Russian, English and American navy are getting ready to come and intercept the missing vessel. Sasha is toast!"

Cassie threw Thomas a worried look.

"So when are they coming?" Thomas gulped.

"My sources have told me today or tomorrow," boasted Flash. "It's a major international operation. And I intend to get the exclusive photographs. '*Pop Star Sunk*' – that kind of thing. He's got his wife and baby with him. We think. Nobody has ever seen the baby. Don't even know if it's a boy or girl. So that would be a scoop in itself – some nice shots of a sobbing mother – that will go down well."

"They're not here!" blurted Cassie, instantly regretting it.

"So where are they then?" sneered Flash. "Has he killed them or something juicy like that?"

"You really are a scumbag," said Thomas, signalling surreptitiously to his sisters as he backed towards the shed. Cassie got the message and kept Finbar Flash talking.

"So this Sasha? What's the story or are you really a news reporter at all?"

"Well, Vladimir Chornovsky – you know, the big industrialist and politician – owns football teams, airlines, entire countries, a music business. Sasha was under contract to him. Vladimir demanded that he write a song saying he was Mr Wonderful, best thing since sliced bread, blah blah blah! Now the thing is, Vladimir is very powerful. You don't mess with him. This dumb singer refused to make the record. So Vladimir wanted him executed for crimes against music and Sasha went on the run. Some enemies of Vlad, some old crackpot inventors in the Russian navy, 'lent' Sasha a submarine. And now he's going to be captured. My guess is Boogan Beach. I'm on my way there now."

"No, you're not," said Thomas, tossing his sisters two spears with large shiny points.

The Chingles formed a circle and surrounded Flash, holding the quivering points to his neck.

Flash's look of contempt froze on his face. "Now let's not be hasty," he said, raising his hands.

Cassie took her rope from her pocket and with one hand formed it into a lasso and, whipping it round him as if he was a spinning top, trussed Flash up to his neck. His face froze in a rictus of fear.

"Please, children, I can do a deal with you," quaked Flash. "Lead me to Sasha and I'll say you found him. You'll become heroes all over again. I'll give you half the cash."

"We don't know what you're talking about," Cassie retorted.

"Come on, you're obviously up to your necks in this," he weaselled. "Why else would you stop me?"

"Oh, do shut up!" said Cassie as she checked her rope work. He was nicely coiled in the rope. It wasn't too tight. She didn't really want to hurt him, just stop him causing trouble.

"I'll get you for this," he shouted as they bundled him into the shed.

"We'd better get to Sasha and warn him," said Cassie. "The last thing we need is him being arrested. The house looks empty but we better make sure."

They checked the house but there was no sign of Jarlath or Sasha. Then they found a note from Jarlath on the kitchen table saying they were in his workshop near Boogan Beach.

With one leap Thomas, Cassie and Nancy took to the air and headed for the east of the island.

Sasha was with Jarlath in the work barn, poring over maritime maps. It looked like they planned to go out on the boat.

"An international navy force is coming to arrest you, Sasha," Thomas told him breathlessly. "Finbar Flash – a reporter – told us. You'd better leave now!"

Sasha put his head in his hands. "Oh, what am I to do? I am just a simple singer!"

"Maybe you should just explain everything to the police," said Jarlath. "You *are* innocent."

Sasha laughed bitterly. "If only it was so simple. This Vladimir wants me dead. I go to jail, have little accident and never return. This man is very powerful and will stop at nothing to get what he wants."

"You can't stay here," Thomas said with urgency.

But Sasha just slumped to the floor. "Jarlath is right," he said dejectedly. "I can do nothing. Let them take me. I go to my wife now and tell her."

Sasha got up off the floor with an air of resignation.

"No, you can't do that. Willa and Áine . . . they're . . ." Jarlath and Sasha looked at Thomas intently, "they're following a line of enquiry using their underworld connections," Thomas improvised desperately. He glanced at Nancy and she winked at him.

"But Willa has no connections to underworld," said a puzzled Sasha.

"Nor does Áine. She's a herbalist," said Jarlath.

"Trust us, please," pleaded Cassie.

"Well, you know, Willa's a singer," said Thomas. "Maybe she worked in a nightclub frequented by shady characters before she met you?" He was worried he was digging himself into a hole with his inventions.

Sasha hesitated. "My wife is very mystery woman. She always say she not speak about the past, she born anew when she meet me. I think she have past in shade."

"Do you mean shady past?" asked Thomas

Sasha nodded. "But I don't care – I love her like heavenly creature." He sighed.

"I too worship Áine like a goddess," agreed Jarlath passionately. "We have so much in common, my friend." He gave Sasha a big hug. "And I can't believe you are a good friend of Boris Borloskony, the inventor of the Darkon. He's one of my heroes!"

Cassie threw Thomas a look, not sure if they were convinced.

"But I don't understand," said Sasha. "How they contact those underworld people from here on this island?"

"Yes," said Jarlath. "How? When? Where? I mean phones don't work well on the island. We can't get mobile coverage. It's the same for most electronic equipment."

"Um . . ." Thomas looked at his shoes, hoping to find inspiration. Then it came to him. The safest place for Jarlath and Sasha was the submarine! It had equipment that could evade surveillance. "They think the babies are being held in Eastern Europe. They said you were both to go at once and keep the sub hidden off the coast of Poland while a rescue in the mountains is launched. Willa knows the territory. She has contacts in the police as well. Maybe the police went to the same nightclub . . ."

Cassie threw Thomas a look, warning him to stop inventing Willa's colourful past. She was also alarmed at his hastily devised plan.

Sasha and Jarlath looked at each other.

"Please," said Sasha, "this is all very strange. We need to talk to our wives about all this before we leave. Where are they now?"

"They had to leave the island suddenly and didn't give us many details," Cassie blurted out. "They said they were sorry."

"They've left the island without telling us?" said an alarmed Jarlath. "But how?"

"They said we were to give you instructions," said Cassie, ignoring the question of how Willa and Áine were supposed to have left Inish Álainn – or have contacted the "underworld connections". She had a sinking feeling neither Jarlath nor Sasha was buying their stories. But at least the stories were more plausible than the truth that they were captured in the fairies' dodgy magical barrier, thankfully now invisible.

"Are you sure that is what Willa and Áine want?" asked Jarlath uncertainly.

"Absolutely!" said Thomas, with greater conviction than he felt.

Cassie showed Sasha the necklace that Willa had thrust upon her, somehow feeling he would recognise its significance. "Look, Willa gave me this to show you," she said.

Sasha fingered it. "She told me she would only part with this if our daughter was in danger. Maybe you speak the truth," he said sadly.

"There's another complication," added Thomas. "This reporter, Finbar Flash, is a sleazebag and he's about to turn you in. You really must leave now."

"Maybe Sasha should go and I should stay. I need to find Áine," said Jarlath.

"Out of the question," said Thomas frantically. "We don't know where she's gone. And Sasha needs your help to navigate. Trust me. This is the best plan."

Jarlath hesitated. "How are Áine and Willa travelling to Eastern Europe? I mean, your explanation is full of holes – you must have got some of it wrong. And even if this Flash does turn us in, we're innocent."

"Please just trust us, there really isn't time," said Cassie imploringly.

"Jarlath, Flash is going to tell them you've been harbouring a criminal," said Thomas. "You'll get arrested too."

Sasha looked beseechingly at Jarlath. "Please, my brother, I need your help. For the sake of our children! The submarine is good plan. I escape in it once already."

A seagull that was hovering overhead let out a squawk. It was a message for Nancy, who could talk to animals.

"Warships and submarines! Gathering off the coast! Will be here within a few hours' time!" Nancy told Cassie and Thomas to their horror.

But Jarlath in particular didn't seem convinced. Then Cassie had an inspiration. She remembered Áine saying that her father, Manannán Mac Lir, owed her child a blessing. Now was the time to call it in. She winked surreptitiously at Thomas and Nancy and mouthed "Manannán" at them.

"Okay. Thomas, you go and see if Áine and Willa are still here. They may not have left yet. If they haven't, get them to come here and talk in person. Maybe they'll change their minds and go with you in the sub. We'll all meet on Boogan Beach."

Thomas got the message and ran off, hiding behind a rock when he was out of sight.

This seemed to satisfy Jarlath and Sasha. Quickly they all ran down onto Boogan Beach.

As Jarlath and Sasha looked out to sea at the submarine, deep in conversation, Cassie indicated to Nancy to follow her. They walked a few paces to where they could conceal themselves behind a large rock.

They faced out to sea.

"Please, Manannán Mac Lir! If you can hear us, compel Jarlath and Sasha to do as we say and help them escape for the sake of your grandson!" shouted Cassie out to the waves. They watched the steady rhythm of the lapping waves for a long time. The sea was calm, indifferent to them.

They shouted again and again but nothing happened.

"Let's go," said Cassie, disappointed.

But as they turned to go a large wave rose from the sea, crested with foam that turned into a mane of white hair. Beneath it, they saw the craggy features of Manannán. He said nothing but nodded his head and sank back into the sea again.

They ran back around the rock to where Jarlath and Sasha stood on the shore facing the submarine.

"You must go now," urged Cassie.

This time neither Jarlath nor Sasha put up any opposition. Their eyes were glazed, their movements hesitant. Cassie knew they were under a spell.

"We will do what you say," said Jarlath in a daze.

Without further ado, they waded out to the submarine and boarded it.

"Please tell my wife I love her and I will die for her," said Sasha before closing the hatch.

"That won't be necessary," Cassie reassured him. But as the hatch was secured down, she suddenly felt frightened of the forces ranged against them. The world was closing in.

"I think Manannán will help them," said Nancy. "I'm sure of it."

"I hope we've done the right thing," said Cassie. She felt a gut-wrenching fear in the pit of her stomach. Events were moving very quickly and she felt out of her depth. She was conscious that every second's delay put the defenceless babies in further danger. Worse still, the Chingles were

Patricia Murphy

going to have to face the forces of darkness without any of their normal supernatural help, thanks to the fairies' meddlesome ways. Even though it was a long time since Áine had been able to use her magical powers, she had always been on hand to dispense useful advice. Connle was ever their faithful ally but he too was trapped in the fairies' magical barrier. Finnen had her hands full tending the sun and moon. The other gods of the Tuatha Dé Danann were too remote or self-absorbed to intervene. Manannán Mac Lir hadn't exactly bowled them over with friendliness. How they wished they could summon the Sean Gaels but Scáthach was presumed dead, Sennan was in the Kingdom of the Dead and Lugh was lost in the Otherworld. And they couldn't find Granny Clíona.

It's just the three of us, thought Cassie, biting her lip as they headed home. Let's hope we're as good as everyone seems to think.

126

CHAPTER 7

B ack at the house, they discussed their options.

"We have to get to these mountains in the east and we have to do it before the international navy arrives," said a panicky Thomas.

"We could try shape-shifting – fly as birds or swim as fish across the waters," said Cassie. "But away from the island our powers are weaker. I'm not sure we'd make it."

"The same goes for travelling in dreams. We can only do it in short bursts without magical help. And we may need a lot of time to track down the babies," said Thomas.

"Besides, Vladimir is human and operates in the real world as well as the Otherworld. We will have to do the same. If we travel in dreams we are confined to the Otherworld and a strange one we don't know," said Cassie.

"But it's hardly like we can row there!" said Thomas. "We don't even know where we're going!"

"Some misty magical mountains in Eastern Europe

where there's a deep, dark forest. That's like a big place," said Cassie bleakly.

"At least we know we can get through the force field, as we were able to reach Poolbeg Cove," said Thomas. "Despite our witch's blood."

"It would help if we knew something about these Eastern gods and goddesses – and vampires as well," said Cassie.

"Let's go to Tadgh," said Nancy. "He has maps."

Cassie and Thomas smiled at their little sister. They could always depend on her for good ideas!

"We don't have much time," said Thomas. "The navy is closing in and we won't be able to escape by boat. But I can't think what else to do."

Mindful not to sap their magical strength, the children set off down the boreen on their bicycles.

They arrived at Tadgh's breathless and anxious.

Tadgh was in his garden tending his giant vegetables. He pulled out a carrot that was the size of a child's arm.

"So what can I help you with today?" he asked with enthusiasm.

Good old Tadgh, thought Cassie, he's always so dependable.

In his manuscript room, they pored over maps of Eastern Europe.

"Know any magical mountains with mystical forests in Eastern Europe near the Carpathian Mountains?" asked Thomas hopefully. "Eh, we're doing a school project about the mythology of Eastern Europe."

"I'm very impressed by the way your school encourages an interest in mythology," Tadgh beamed as he leafed through a dusty old volume. "Any more information?"

"Some old hag called the Baba Yaga lives there and maybe these old vampires called Eretsuns and some Slavic gods and goddesses – one is called Dodola."

Tadgh looked at them with interest. "Well, let's deal with the vampires first. Interesting, as I've just been writing all about them."

The children smiled. Tadgh was an invaluable source of information on the Otherworld.

"Did you know nearly every culture has some kind of blood-sucking monster?" he said, showing them illustrations of terrifying ghouls with fanged teeth and dead eyes.

A shiver ran down Cassie's spine. She had been feeling quite confident about facing Vladimir and the Eretsuns. After all, they'd defeated both Balor and Caitlín. But she was suddenly filled with a sense of pure evil like a punch in the stomach. She realised Balor and Caitlín were mere child's play compared to these monsters. Vladimir was a human dabbling in the black arts. This made him more dangerous because he himself didn't understand the forces he might be unleashing.

Tadgh turned the page onto another illustration. It was a female demon with demented eyes and fanged teeth.

"This is Labartu, the Babylonian vampire. She was a hellish creature who feasted on the blood of humans and animals alive but preferred to drain the life force of young children. She would ask mothers to entrust their babies to her and would then drink their blood."

At the mention of babies Thomas felt his stomach flip inside out.

"In fact, many of the vampires prey especially on babies and young children. For example, the Aswang in the Philippines, a beautiful female by day but a flying demon at night, also the Obayifo in Ghana, which is the spirit of a witch that leaves its body as a glowing ball of light and devours babies."

"How disgusting!" said Cassie, inwardly shuddering.

"The Bramaparush in India is also pretty vile," said Tadgh. "It drinks its victims' blood through their skulls and eats their brains."

"I think I'm going to throw up," said Thomas, turning green.

"What about the ones in Eastern Europe?" asked Cassie. She was conscious that time was short before all hell broke loose with the arrival of the navies.

"Well, of course, the myth of the vampire is most commonly associated with Dracula and Vlad the Impaler, a real figure from the Middle Ages who liked to drink blood," said Tadgh.

"Vlad?" said Thomas. "That's a coincidence!"

"Yes?" said Tadgh encouragingly.

"Oh, it's just that I heard the name recently."

Cassie and Thomas looked at each other, the same question in their eyes. Could Vladimir the Criminal be a reincarnation of Vlad the Impaler? They had met that sort of thing in their previous struggles against evil. But then Thomas shook his head and Cassie nodded. Willa was clear on the matter: Vladimir was an ordinary man with an evil heart.

Tadgh was looking at them inquiringly.

"Have you ever heard of the Eretsuns?" Cassie pressed on.

Tadgh's face lit up. "Yes, indeed, but they are more obscure than vampires. The common belief is that you become a vampire when bitten by another one and you can only operate at night. But the Eretsun is a living vampire created when a sorcerer possesses the soul and revives the body of one on the brink of death. The Eretsuns are supposed to be a cross between a werewolf and a vampire, with fangs and wolfish hair and features."

"And how do you kill them?" asked Cassie.

"Well, with ordinary vampires, the usual way is supposed to be a stake through the heart and garlic helps to ward them off – but I'm not sure about Eretsuns, never having met any," he said with a laugh that died when he saw their open-mouthed horror and realised how seriously they were taking all of this. "It's only a myth," he went on. "It's not real. The famous novel *Dracula* was written by an Irishman, Bram Stoker, in the nineteeth century and he never even went to Transylvania. There was also another nineteenth century account of a vampire city near Belgrade in what is now Serbia, formerly Yugoslavia. You know you are there when a distant bell tolls twenty-three times. The ground is dull and dark as if a rain of ashes has fallen on it. The sky turns grey and clouds cover the sun. The traveller feels weak in the knees. The darkness fades and the city of Selene appears."

"Sounds quite detailed," said Thomas thoughtfully.

"It's a work of imagination. The same writer suggests extracting the vampire's heart and then burning it into ash, which can then be used to sprinkle on the vampire to kill its body, which keeps going even with the heart torn out, or on other vampires, making them explode in a bluish flash."

"What about the land of forests and magical mountains?" asked Cassie.

"The Slav folk also have beliefs similar to the Norse World Tree," said Tadgh. "They have deities like most of the gods in other cultures. They regulate the elements."

"And the Baba Yaga?" queried Thomas.

"Yes, the Baba Yaga. Old Grandmother Bony Shanks!" said Tadgh. "She's an interesting one."

"How do you find her?" asked Nancy.

Tadgh laughed. "Well, I don't know that you can. It seems she finds you. All the tales about her are about children lost in the forest."

"So to find her, we'd have to get lost first," said Thomas. "And what forest would that be in?"

Tadgh took down a large colourful map of Europe and indicated a vast swathe of forest across a mountain range.

"Well, all the Slavic tales are set in the area of the Carpathian Mountains. Here there are many ancient forests, meadows and mountain pastures. The area contains

Austria, the Czech Republic, Slovakia, Poland, Ukraine, Romania, Serbia and Northern Hungary. It also includes Transylvania. It's between the Baltic Sea and the Black Sea and surrounded by large grassy plains known as steppes."

Thomas was relieved to see that he'd made a lucky guess where to send Jarlath and Sasha in the submarine – Poland was on the Baltic Sea. But he was daunted by the size of the Carpathian Mountains. The babies could be anywhere.

"So it's a vast area," pondered Cassie. "Are there any specific areas associated with magical forests?"

Tadgh waved his hand over the map. "Not that I know of. Take your pick."

"And what about Eretsuns or vampires?" asked Thomas. "Where are they?"

"They are a common myth all over Eastern Europe," said Tadgh, climbing the ladder to fetch a volume from a high shelf.

Cassie frowned in puzzlement. It was all worryingly vague.

Nancy moved closer to her sister to peer at the map. As she did so, she brushed against the necklace around Cassie's neck. She felt a sudden jolt in her stomach.

Nancy tugged on Cassie's jumper. "Give me Willa's necklace," she whispered.

Cassie shrugged and handed her the necklace. When she was sure Tadgh wasn't looking, Nancy passed the necklace over the map. The bloodstone began to throb at certain places. Cassie looked at her little sister with interest.

133

"I think the Star Splinter and the necklace together do that," whispered Nancy. "I think it will help us find the place."

"Like some kind of magical satellite-navigation system!" said Cassie excitedly.

She watched as her sister passed the necklace back and forth over the map to see if she could identify certain places where the necklace lit up. It was difficult to tell because the map wasn't very large or detailed but it seemed to throb most right in the heart of the mountain range.

Cassie took the necklace back as Tadgh came down the ladder empty handed. Trust Nancy to come up with a solution. Cassie winked at Thomas and signalled they should leave.

"We have to sort out Finbar Flash before we go," she whispered.

"Well, thanks, Tadgh," said Thomas, conscious that they needed to concentrate on the huge problem of getting to the Carpathian Mountains in the first place. "We must get back."

They left rather hastily, thanking Tadgh again for his help.

"We really need to go to Eastern Europe," said Cassie as they got back on their bikes at the foot of the round tower, having waved goodbye to Tadgh. "If only we could figure out how."

"What about Dick Headley?" asked Nancy suddenly. "The nice man said we could take his plane."

Cassie and Thomas looked up with interest.

"Of course," said Thomas.

Dick Headley was a plane-loving Hollywood movie star they'd rescued from Caitlín last year. He had helped them return to Inish Álainn after they had travelled to Hollywood in search of Finnen.

"Only problem is we don't know how to reach him. The phones are all rubbish here," said Thomas. "It will take ages to get a message out through Patch or Podge."

They had reached their house.

"We'd better decide what to do with Finbar Flash," said Cassie. "Much as I'd like to, we can't leave him rotting in the shed."

But as they approached the shed they heard a scrabbling noise and several muttered curses. They flung the door open.

To their surprise, Finbar had managed to wiggle his shoulders out of his ropes and was attempting to dial a mobile phone with his nose. Cassie plucked it out of his reach and raised it above her head, intent on dashing it to pieces on the concrete floor.

"Don't, Cassie!" Thomas shouted. "We can use it to phone Dick Headley."

Cassie lowered the phone.

"You can't take that!" Finbar pleaded. "It's a super-sophisticated satellite phone, the only type that can work on this godforsaken island! And why would you be phoning Dick Headley? Dick Headley the movie star?"

"None of your business," Cassie retorted.

"I'll do you a deal. Release me and I'll give you the security pin code that allows you to use it," Flash wheedled. "You can't use the phone without that."

"Perhaps we could just leave you here instead," said Cassie, heading for the door.

Thomas hurried after her. "I think we should consider the deal," he said. "After all, we can't use magic to summon Dick Headley and we haven't much time."

Reluctantly Cassie turned back into the shed and looked Finbar Flash straight in the eye. "Don't try any tricks," she said. "Tell us the number and I'll untie you."

"I'm not telling you the number unless you untie me first," said Finbar.

"This is stupid," said Thomas. "Look, tell us a digit and we'll untie you a bit each time. How many digits?"

"Three."

"Okay," said Thomas. "First one?"

"Six," said Finbar.

So Thomas undid the rope as far as Finbar's waist. Flash rubbed his wrists with relief.

"Six," Flash said again.

Thomas untied the rope to his knees.

"And six again," said a relieved Finbar as Thomas untied his feet. He shook out his legs and jumped up and down.

Cassie felt a bit guilty for tying the rope so tight. She went outside the shed to conduct the call. As luck would have it, Dick Headley was already flying over the Atlantic on his way to Africa. Since his incarceration by Caitlín last year, he'd become a reformed character and devoted much of his time to charity work. His flight path passed directly over the island.

"Dick! It's Cassie!"

"Cassie, my friend!" he exclaimed. "I'm cruising thirty thousand feet above sea level. How great to hear from you!"

Cassie briefly explained their plight.

"No questions asked," said Headley in his deep, reassuring voice. "Estimated arrival time Boogan Beach fifteen minutes from now!"

Cassie nearly cried with relief.

She rushed back into the shed and tossed Flash his phone back, triumphant.

"No time to lose," she told her brother and sister.

She hustled Flash out of the shed and hoisted him onto the back of Derry the donkey. Hitting the donkey's rump she said to Flash, "You try and print anything nasty about any of us and you'll have me to answer to!"

"And I love you too," said Flash facetiously. "We'll see."

Derry suddenly burst into a canter and they were gone.

But when Finbar was out of view of the children, he got off the donkey and shooed it away. He hunkered behind a bush, took out his mobile phone and pressed the redial button. Dick Headley's number flashed up. He pressed another button. His phone was fitted with a feature whereby all the calls were recorded. He pressed play and listened with glee to Cassie's entire conversation.

He laughed and shook his little fists in triumph as he pressed another button.

"Hi, *Daily Scumbag*? Get me the editor! Pronto!" He waited, sniggering to himself, until the editor came on the line. "Finbar Flash here. I need to charter a plane to the Carpathian Mountains. Sasha may have killed the babies. He's on the run. That lunatic inventor Jarlath McColl is his accomplice. I suspect both their wives have disappeared. And get this – Dick Headley, Hollywood's all round do-gooder and highest-paid leading man, is aiding and abetting his escape. Trust me, this is the big one!"

It was only when they were settled in the vast aircraft fastening their seatbelts that Thomas realised they'd forgotten something very important.

"We don't have any magical weapons," he said suddenly. "In all that business with Finbar Flash we forgot to arm ourselves properly."

"I have my rope," said Cassie, feeling it in her pocket.

"And I have my sling," said Nancy.

"Well, it's too late now," said Thomas, watching the earth recede below the clouds as the plane gained altitude. Below he saw powerful military ships en route to the island. "I'll just have to depend on my own secret weapon."

"And what's that?" said Nancy.

"My mind," said Thomas jauntily, hoping to get a rise out of Cassie.

She gave him a big grin. "Then we really are sunk."

CHAPTER 8

It was towards dusk when Cassie, Thomas and Nancy were lowered from the flying craft deep in the Carpathian Forest in the mountains. The children still weren't sure of the location of the Baba Yaga but Cassie and Thomas had watched closely as Nancy held the necklace when they flew over the region. The bloodstone throbbed right in the heart of the mountains above a dense forest. Cassie and Thomas felt weak with relief. The combination of Nancy and the necklace had created a magical compass to guide them.

This was the place to start.

As they landed in the forest, they assessed their surroundings. The forest was dense with trees and dappled sunlight barely penetrated the lush canopy. Here, high in the mountains, there were mainly evergreen trees, fir and pine mixed in with some beech trees. There were pine needles and cones underfoot on the dark forest floor. They walked on, descending through the carpet of needles into a less dense part of the forest where the evergreen gave way to deciduous trees. Cassie recognised beech trees, silver birch and mountain oak mixed in with some stands of pine and fir trees. Willow trees, honeysuckle and raspberry bushes flourished in the undergrowth.

Beautiful wild flowers carpeted the forest floor. Here, where the tree cover wasn't so thick, shafts of light fingered the ground through the overhead canopy, revealing a path through the trees. They walked stealthily along, uncertain how to find the home of the Baba Yaga.

"I suppose we could follow the path," said Cassie, pointing right.

"Why not go left?" said Thomas. "Since we don't know where we're going anyway."

"Because I said it first," huffed Cassie. Typical Thomas! Always wanted to do the opposite of her.

Nancy started to pick flowers. She tended to ignore her older brother and sister when they began arguing pointlessly.

"Both of you follow me," insisted Cassie. "I'm the eldest and anyway we're supposed to get lost. We'd better get a move on."

"If you say so," Thomas conceded truculently.

Impetuously, Cassie rushed ahead of them onto the path. She didn't realise it took only moments before her brother and sister lost sight of her in the thicket of trees. She plunged on, unaware that the trees were becoming denser, the undergrowth more bushy and the path not very clear.

Thomas and Nancy tried to catch up but Cassie was going faster than she realised. They turned a corner and there was no sight or sound of her.

"Wait for us, Cassie!" Thomas called. His voice sounded eerie and echoing in the vast forest. A bird cried out and the plaintive sound made him jump out of his standing. But there was no reply from his older sister.

Cassie didn't notice the change in the rough path under her feet. Instead of bare earth worn by animals or human tracks, she now walked on a carpet of ferns.

She was peeved about her brother and sister lagging behind. Why couldn't Thomas ever accept she was older than him? Why did he always have to shove his oar in? She ploughed on, paying scant attention to her trail. She was unaware of the slight scurrying sounds behind her.

She stopped suddenly, for the first time aware that there was no path under her feet.

She had stridden into a deeper part of the forest where the overhead branches grew so dense she could no longer see the sky. It was inky black and quiet, all sound muffled and deadened in the dense growth.

She shivered. She thought she heard a branch snap as if someone was following her. Maybe it's an animal, she tried to reassure herself. Not a bear or a lynx or a wolf, she hoped. This was the kind of forest that would contain frightening predators like that. Silly her, it must be Thomas and Nancy.

"Thomas! Nancy!" she called in a voice half-hopeful. "Sorry I rushed ahead of you!"

There was the shushing sound of someone's clothing brushing leaves.

"Thomas!" she called nervously. "Stop messing about! Nancy?" But her brother and sister didn't reply. Whatever about Thomas, she knew Nancy wouldn't play games like this.

She hesitated and decided to turn back. But which way? The dense thatch of trees looked identical whichever way she turned. Everywhere she looked, she saw gnarled branches with twisted ivy clutching onto bark and lianas of vine hanging from the boughs. Barely any sunlight penetrated the thick canopy of tree cover. Above was a ceiling of dark green leaves. Her head began to spin.

She really felt afraid now. Out of the corner of her eye, she thought she saw creatures loping towards her with long front arms grazing the forest floor. Maybe they were Eretsuns! She felt a sickening stab of fear and broke out in a cold sweat. She was about to turn round but panicked as a high-pitched growl rushed around her ears. She ran for it, her heart beating in her chest like a captured bird. Then she felt silly. Maybe it was only her imagination. It must have been tendrils of liana that had stirred in the breeze and the wind that growled. She made herself slow down and breathed deeply. She looked behind her. Silly girl, she chided herself, there's no one there. But she was so intent on looking behind her, she tripped and felt a sickening lurch in her stomach as she plunged deep into the dark earth.

She screamed, terrified by the loss of control in falling. Then suddenly the ground came up to meet her and she landed badly on her left ankle. She was trapped in a hole and couldn't see much beyond a blur above. She felt around and realised the hole was lined with fern leaves.

She touched her ankle. "Ow!" she cried, on the verge of tears. It felt tender and stiff but she didn't think she'd broken any bones.

She felt very frightened. The Chingles had survived all kinds of terrors but they had usually faced them together. There was something about these deep, dark woods that terrified her to the bone, an instinctive fear of wild predators that might attack the unwary and defenceless.

She whimpered softly and lapsed into a daze, unaware of three pairs of beady eyes that gazed down at her.

Thomas and Nancy hesitated when they came to the part of the forest where the trees became more impenetrable and the path became unclear. They decided to wait to see if Cassie would turn back.

"I wish we'd kept up with her," said Thomas ruefully. "But Cassie always has to be in a hurry."

"Cassie! Cassie!" they called anxiously, fearful of calling too loudly in case they alerted any enemies to their presence.

Nancy peered anxiously into the darkest part of the forest. "We have to try and find her," she said. "But will our powers work here?" She rubbed her stomach but felt no twinges and Cassie had the necklace. "Let's try to shape-shift," she suggested.

But when she screwed up her eyes and tried to become a deer, she just remained Nancy.

Thomas concentrated and tried to shape-shift into a fox. He broke into a sweat and his heart thudded. But nothing happened.

They tried holding hands and intoning the magic formula: "*With all the powers that are strange, change Chingles change!*" But after a minute it was clear it wasn't working.

They said nothing and, holding hands, plunged deeper into the forest in the direction they thought they'd seen Cassie disappear.

Cassie stirred beneath the forest floor and came to. She felt a twinge in her ankle but could see nothing in the inky blackness. But she was definitely hearing the murmur of voices. She desperately hoped it was Thomas and Nancy. She was about to call out but suddenly felt cautious. The sound was muffled, as if she had cotton wool stuffed in her ears. She tried to focus but couldn't make out the words. The voices sounded high-pitched, not gruff or unfriendly. Perhaps they were hunters and she had fallen into a trap for animals. They seemed in no hurry to pull her out. She tried to ignore her ankle. She had one thing in her favour, the element of surprise. She fingered her rope in her pocket. She thought it through. Her ankle was sore but she might just be able to manage a salmon leap and have her rope to hand. Her other option was to turn into an animal, a mouse perhaps, and scurry out of the hole. But changes went badly when she was injured. A sore ankle could transfer as a broken leg. And anyway they didn't work so well away from Inish Álainn. But just as she was about to make the leap, the roof of leaves above her head was pulled back. She realised that it was a crude animal trap of branches interwoven with foliage covering the hole. She shielded her eyes from the sudden rush of light.

Three anxious pairs of eyes peered into hers. They looked no older than she was. Instantly she felt a bit more confident. They had long wild hair and very dirty faces that she could hardly see from the tangle of hair.

"What do you think you're playing at?" Cassie demanded. She had been the victim of some stupid children's game and she felt very foolish. "Let me out at once!"

A boy spoke in a harsh, guttural language to his companions.

Cassie thought to blow on Ogma's ring.

"Who are you?" a thin boy with sharp pointy features and straw-blond hair asked her.

She felt weak and wobbly and was glad she hadn't attempted a salmon leap in the circumstances. They threw down a crude ladder of interlocking branches. Breathing hard, she struggled to climb it. Her ankle was raging now and a piercing pain shot through her left leg when she put her weight on it. She winced, but mustering all her strength she pulled herself up the rungs. She faltered a bit near the top and the boy with straw-coloured hair extended his hand to pull her out. She was glad of his help. Back on solid ground, she breathed deeply and tried to conceal her injury.

"Who are you?" she managed to say.

Three boys surrounded her and regarded her with a mixture of interest and wariness.

The boy with the straw-coloured hair was about to speak but was interrupted by a taller boy with heavyset features and matted black hair that had formed into sorts of dreadlocks around his head.

"Don't talk to her, Kicker," he said. "She might be one of them. Or a witch or something."

"I'm nothing of the kind!" retorted Cassie.

"You're right, Basher. But she could also be one of us," said the other. "Let's take her to Ivo. I know he just sits around and mopes all day but he's seen things we haven't. Agreed, Conchy?" He turned to the third boy, who was small and slight with red hair that hung in bedraggled curls past his shoulders.

The boy nodded. He had a delicate face and shining green eyes that looked full of mischief and tricks. She was rather surprised when he gave her a dazzling smile.

"Perhaps this will jerk him out of his fug," said Conchy

in a sweet, melodious voice, like someone in a church choir.

Cassie calculated. It was three against one. And yet, wasn't she lost and injured? They didn't seem particularly hostile. Perhaps they would lead her to the Baba Yaga. She could possibly take them out but her ankle was screaming. She was split up from Thomas and Nancy. She had to find some way to let her brother and sister know where she was. She thought about letting out a shout of battle but she was winded and her breath rasped in her chest. She raked her hand through her hair in despair, her arm glancing off Willa's necklace around her neck. That was it! She could drop some of the beads at intervals. Maybe they would connect with Nancy's traces of Star Splinter in her stomach. While the boys were consulting each other in muffled whispers she slid the necklace from her neck and broke the string, gathering some of the beads into her hand. Then she retied the string to secure the remaining jewels, including the jasper bloodstone.

The strange boys plunged through the forest with Cassie, their prisoner, stumbling between them. Cassie's attempts to engage the boys in conversation met with a resolute silence. She was limping badly now and seriously slowing them down, so they forced her to sit across two sticks. But when they weren't looking she dropped the beads from the necklace at intervals. For one heart-stopping moment the red-haired Conchy stared at her fingering the beads. But she sighed loudly and made it seem as if she was fretful and nervous.

Finally, after what seemed like hours, the boys called out. "We're back at camp," explained Conchy.

But all Cassie could see ahead was a small clearing by a flowing stream. No settlement was obvious from a distance but, as they drew nearer, Cassie saw that a crude stone fortress had been cunningly erected between the trees. Ivy and ferns disguised it. As they approached a tiny opening, a sentry – a boy, or it could have been a girl, with matted hair and a skinny waif-like appearance – waved them through.

Inside, tree houses constructed from willow branches swirled organically around the trees. Some were egg-shaped, others square. But all looked part of the forest. Cassie realised she was in a village. Groups of boys and girls, all equally waif-like, filthy and bedraggled, moved purposefully carrying wood and water in wooden pails. There was no sign of any adults. One group of children around a fire peeled and cut vegetables and put them into a huge black pot. Some just lolled in their tree houses, polishing knives. Another troop looked to be transporting a cache of weapons. It looked like a medieval settlement or the camp of Robin Hood and his Merry Men. Goats and chickens ran about and she saw a pigsty at one end. Everyone stared at her, curious, but nobody said a word.

They brought Cassie to a hut formed of wooden staves carved into a point, with interlaced branches overhead, and pushed her inside. She slumped down exhausted and in pain. She felt disoriented but tried to settle herself by trying to recall the details of all she'd observed and concentrating on the here and now. I am in some weird back-to-nature village populated entirely by children in the middle of a forest, she told herself. My ankle hurts. I am hungry and tired. Yet I've faced worse dangers.

But she felt light-headed and missed Thomas and Nancy.

At one point somebody shoved some black bread and water through the door. She wondered if it might be a trick but hunger overcame her reservations and she greedily tore into the bread. It tasted delicious, like the black rye bread her school friend Renata's mother, who was Polish, baked.

As the light began to fade, the door to the pound opened tentatively. The dark boy called Basher and Kicker the straw-blond boy beckoned her out. After the darkness of the hut, she blinked in the salmon-pink glow of evening light and was taken aback when she saw what seemed like hundreds of dirty faces peering at her. Most of them looked as dishevelled and unkempt as the first boys she'd met. They regarded her with keen scrutiny as she was ushered to the centre of the clearing where a tall muscular-looking boy was sitting on some rush matting. He seemed somewhat cleaner than the others, perhaps a little older and had a strong, intelligent face dominated by large green eyes. They reminded her of the eyes of the red-haired boy, Conchy – perhaps they were related. His long blond hair extended in a ponytail down his back. She guessed he was some sort of leader. But he seemed self-absorbed and depressed.

Cassie blew on Ogma's ring.

"Look, can we stop all this nonsense and can you just

tell me who you are and I'll tell you who I am?" said Cassie in a loud, clear voice.

The gathered children gasped, as if surprised that she could speak.

"On an island in the sea," said the tall boy, jumping up and pacing about, "sits an old bird who has seen it all. She has seen the tsar in Moscow, the king in Lithuania, the infant in her cradle, the old hermit in their cell. Of whom do I speak?"

Cassie sighed. "How the hell do I know?" That's all she needed, some mysterious joker.

"Death," said the boy solemnly. "I speak of Death." He bid her sit on a tree stump. He went back to his matting and pulled out a cloak of sky blue, embroidered with stars, from a basket beside the matting. He wrapped it around him. It was beautiful and all the more so in comparison to the rags that everyone else seemed to wear. As he stood up, Cassie was struck by how compelling the boy looked despite his strange appearance. She sat and waited, more curious than afraid.

He went to where a hen sat on a nest and pulled out the newly laid egg. He approached Cassie carefully, holding the outstretched egg as if it was a hand grenade and he was walking over landmines. Cautiously, he stopped just at arm's length and held the newly laid egg in his palm under her nose. The assembled children held their breath. The boy looked into her face defiantly but Cassie saw a flicker of fear in his luminous green eyes.

Oh dear, thought Cassie, they are setting me bizarre

tests. Maybe it's because they think I'm some sort of witch. The boys who found me were worried about that. Her heart beat wildly. She debated what to do. If they knew she had special powers, this might confirm their suspicions. A show of strength might make them respect her more. But she wasn't sure her powers worked here. The pain in her ankle had become a dull, throbbing ache and her head felt woozy. She couldn't think straight. She wished Thomas was with her. He was always quick-thinking in these situations. She decided to be friendly. She looked into his face, an enquiring smile playing on her lips.

"What do you want me to do with that?" she asked. "Am I supposed to eat it?"

The boy laughed awkwardly and turned to his followers. "You see, she didn't run away. Witches are supposed to flee at the sight of the freshly laid egg of a young hen."

Cassie breathed a sigh of relief. She'd passed the first test.

The boy threw the egg into the sky with a wild cry. The wild children took up his cry. But it changed to a gasp of amazement when Cassie, with a reflex action honed over many lessons with Scáthach, put her hand out and caught it without crushing the shell. Without thinking she spun it on her fingertip with a flourish. She stopped, realising too late her showing off had just unwittingly reawakened their suspicions. An uneasy murmur spread through the camp like a crackling fire.

The boy called Ivo gasped in alarm.

"She's a witch!" someone shouted in a high-pitched voice. "Kill her, Ivo!"

"No, there will be no killing," said the boy firmly.

"I'm really not a witch," said Cassie, alarmed. "I could be your friend. Maybe we can help each other."

"Please, we cannot talk to you unless we do our tests," said the boy. "We have to be sure. Bring me the candle and aspen wood."

Conchy, the redheaded boy, went into one of the tree houses and emerged holding a candle and stick. He lit them from the fire.

Cassie watched them intently and tried to stand straight. She began to feel a little bit afraid. She didn't like the look of this candle – what if they tried to burn her! She wasn't sure if her powers would work but, as Conchy came closer and she became mesmerised by the flicker of the candle, instinctively she found herself taking in large gulpfuls of air. Before she thought it through, she was preparing for the Breath Feat. She fingered the bloodstone around her neck and breathed in a massive lungful of air. Puffing out her cheeks, she expelled the air like a bellows. As Conchy tried to hand the candle and burning aspen branch to Ivo, the flames went out.

He lit them again and this time managed to hand the lit candle and branch to Ivo. But Ivo only got about five paces closer to Cassie when the candle and the branch were extinguished. He looked at Cassie intently.

"I don't know why the flames keep going out. But she is

still standing up straight. If she was a witch, she would have turned upside down," he pronounced.

"You have to go closer," said Kicker.

Ivo relit the candle and the branch and strode resolutely towards her, confident that they were still burning. This time she held her breath.

As he got closer and Cassie didn't blink, the expression on his face softened.

"Don't you want the ashes?" he asked.

She laughed nervously, not wanting to betray her fear. "Will these ashes defeat vampires?"

Ivo let out a sigh. "That is not a joking matter."

Cassie cursed herself. Why did she have to make a stupid joke? She decided to risk the truth. Maybe if they knew Thomas and Nancy were looking for her, they'd be more careful.

"Look, I'm not a witch. My name is Cassie. I'm here on a mission to rescue four kidnapped babies. As we speak my brother and sister are looking for me. They have special powers and so do I."

Ivo and the children gasped in astonishment.

Cassie tested her ankle on the ground. It still ached but she felt she could risk it. She fingered the bloodstone, as it seemed to give her strength. She stood on her good right leg and in one sudden fluid movement jumped high in the sky and landed again on her good leg.

"She's a witch!" screamed several children.

Ivo turned on them roughly. "That was an acrobatic

feat. She didn't turn upside down and stay that way and she doesn't want the ashes."

"But these are stupid tests," said Basher. "Ivo, just because you survived the Baba Yaga – or said you did – doesn't mean you know everything."

"You know the Baba Yaga?" Cassie asked urgently. "That's who I want to meet!"

Ivo looked at her for a second as if she was mad. The children were becoming restless and unsettled. They began to clamour but he stopped their cries with a raised hand.

"Let's try the wheel test," he insisted.

Conchy went to a shed and fetched a crude little cart. The wheels were roughly hewn from bark. A group of children grabbed the cart and in a kind of frenzy wheeled it around Cassie.

"It hasn't shattered," said Ivo. "I told you she just performed an acrobatic trick. I doubt she has special powers."

Cassie suddenly felt annoyed that he had dismissed her claims. I'll show the arrogant so and so, she said to herself, and before she realised it, she had once more performed the Breath Feat, blowing the cart high into the sky. It rose on the current of air and bobbed above them. Cassie manoeuvred it towards the fire. She inhaled and allowed the cart to drop lower towards the flames. The crowd of children watched her, spellbound in mounting fear. Ivo looked at her with a dismay that was turning to anger. She exhaled, pushing the cart away from the flames, and manipulating her breath, lowered it safely to the ground.

Ivo took a pace towards her. Feeling suddenly afraid, she let out a tremendous Shout of Battle, stunning the assembled children who ran this way and that, grabbing rough weapons of sticks and cudgels.

A ragged group with lighted tapers rushed towards her. Fear rising in her throat, Cassie jumped into the branches of a solid oak tree.

"Burn the witch!" they cried.

"Be careful!" shouted Ivo.

A couple of children began to shimmy up the tree. They were going to attack her. Then instinctively she looked up and saw two eagles hovering in the air above the clearing. Instantly she knew they were Thomas and Nancy. They swooped towards her in the boughs of the tree and grabbed her arms in their beaks, raising her into the sky. They flew left and rose upwards through an opening in the high trees but were surprised to get caught in an artfully concealed net of ropes that the children had woven between the branches as some sort of defence. Beating their wings, they tried to push their way through but were forced back. They had no choice but to land as themselves as the net was pulled to the ground. Thomas hit the ground first and managed to break Cassie's fall. The wild children watched in astonishment as Thomas and Nancy changed from eagles into humans.

"Kill them!" shouted Basher. "They are sorcerers!"

But Ivo thrust himself in front. "You'll have to kill me first," he said. "I want no more killing. Look, one of them is hardly more than a baby!"

The wild children backed off.

"I'm not a baby," said Nancy indignantly, pulling the net off her. "I'm a Chingle."

"Who are you?" asked Ivo. "Your sister has failed my test for sorcery but not in the way I would have expected. I was wrong to doubt her. You have magical powers."

"We are the Chingles from the East," explained Thomas. Noticing her sore ankle, he helped Cassie to her feet. "We are not from here. We have come to rescue four babies who have been kidnapped by the Baba Yaga." The wild children froze, dumbfounded.

"Thanks for coming to my rescue," said a grateful Cassie to Thomas and Nancy.

Thomas handed her back the glinting beads from Willa's necklace. "Luckily you were able to lay a trail," he said. "Nancy sensed where they were."

Cassie threaded them back on the necklace. "I think the necklace is helping me in the use of my special powers," she said.

"That would explain why we were able to change after we found the beads," said Thomas. "When you first disappeared after we got off the plane, neither Nancy nor I was able to shape-shift."

Ivo regarded them intently. "Please, children, tell us your story. I am sorry, Cassie, that we had to put you through those tests but we don't know who to trust."

"There's no point in testing my brother and sister, Thomas and Nancy," Cassie said. "They have the same powers as I have."

Ivo nodded in agreement. "I will trust you."

Ivo led them to a fireside and bid the other children bring food for Thomas and Nancy. Unobtrusively the other children, now meek and respectful, sat around them, focused intently on the newcomers. Some of the younger ones smiled shyly at Nancy, who nodded back in a friendly manner.

So Thomas and Cassie explained to Ivo and the wild children what had happened to them. How Willa and Sasha had fled to Inish Álainn to escape from Vladimir who was trying to raise an army of vampires and wanted Willa's baby for some spell so he could take over the Underworld. As the Chingles recounted their story, gasps of recognition escaped the children. A look of fear flickered over Ivo's face, as if some unpleasant memory clouded his brain. Then they told how the babies had been exchanged for changelings who turned into bundles of sticks. How they had been spirited away and the Chingles had followed them here.

As the story unfolded the mood in the camp changed. The wild children listened open-mouthed. Thomas noticed that Ivo and Conchy nodded at certain points. Ivo questioned them closely about their special powers and their experiences in the Otherworld. He seemed impressed and a little troubled but gave very little away.

"So now you have to tell us who you are," said Cassie.

"We have something in common," said Ivo. "Vladimir is our enemy too. He has captured the souls of our parents and turned them into Eretsuns."

"Eretsuns?" gasped Thomas. "The Undead who are half-werewolf and half-vampire?"

"So you have heard of them," said Ivo in a low voice. And as he spoke, a terrified hush came over the children. "Vladimir learned how to steal our parents' souls and turn their bodies into the Undead. Normally a sorcerer can only inhabit one body at a time but he has found a way to possess multiple souls. He is truly evil. I think my father was one of the first to experience the dark side of Vladimir's power."

He explained how his father and he had lived in an isolated cottage on the other side of the Carpathian Mountains.

"My mother died when I was little. So I was raised by my father. He was a woodcutter who wanted to send me to a very special school where I'd won a scholarship but he needed money for clothes and books. So he borrowed from Vladimir who was the local moneylender." Ivo's voice cracked with the memory.

"Go on," urged Conchy. "My cousin blames himself for what happened to his father," he said in an aside to the Chingles.

"One day I came home and I heard strange voices in the house. They were raised in argument. I had a strange feeling so I didn't go in. I thought maybe they were thieves breaking into the house. Quietly I crouched down outside the window to check if I was right. I couldn't see much. There was a man with a high-pitched voice and another taller man. Later I discovered they were Vladimir and his wizard sidekick Raznik. When my father said he couldn't repay him, they tortured him." His hands flew up to his face but his eyes remained dry. "I can still hear the screams today." Ivo halted and fought for breath.

Gently Conchy took his hand. "They turned my uncle into an Eretsun before Ivo's eyes. He has never been able to cry since that day."

"I tried to run for help but I was frozen to the spot," Ivo said, his voice croaky. "Something compelled me to look in the window. I saw my father tied to a chair and Vladimir looming over him with a sharp knife in one hand. Raznik held a large box with something glinting in it like a jewel. They were so intent on what they were doing they didn't notice me. Then in that split second my father caught my eye and signalled me to stay quiet. His eyes pleaded with me not to give myself away. He fingered the wooden cross he always wore around his neck – maybe as a sign that he had faith and would be strong and was not afraid of suffering. I saw his hand was bleeding. Then I turned and ran into the woods." Ivo faltered and closed his eyes but then continued. "There was no way I could have overcome Vladimir and Raznik. And my father's wish was that I should escape. But I still blame myself for leaving him."

The Chingles looked with sympathy at Ivo. Cassie then glanced around at the gathered children. Some cried softly; others just stared blankly ahead.

"And the rest of you?" she asked quietly. "Your parents have met a similar fate?"

They all nodded their heads.

Ivo picked up his story. "My only thought was to fetch help for my father but in my panic I lost my way. I plunged deep into the forest, then a cornfield and that's when she, you know who, caught me."

"The Baba Yaga," Thomas mouthed to Conchy who nodded in affirmation.

"But I escaped," continued Ivo. "Then by some miracle Conchy found me when his parents were also harmed."

"We began to find other children and realised children from all over Eastern Europe were seeking refuge here," Conchy said.

"As you can see, we've set up a camp," said Ivo. "They look up to me because I survived the Baba Yaga and that means I have a pure soul, or so they say. But I don't know what to do."

"You will have to fight Vladimir," said Cassie decisively.

"How can we?" said Ivo sadly. "It will mean fighting the Eretsuns. And they are our parents. We cannot kill our mothers and fathers while their bodies and souls are separated and in Vladimir's possession."

"But is there any way of bringing them back to their former selves?" asked Cassie. "Or is it too late?"

"They are in the grip of a terrible power," said Ivo. "But there is still some hope. I have to believe this."

He paused and Cassie could see that he was holding himself together.

"It's difficult for you to talk about it," she said kindly.

He smiled at her and continued in a low, tremulous

voice. "Vladimir brought my father near to death and somehow trapped his soul. I couldn't see it all happening. But he seemed to have some device in that box that enabled him to store spirits, while taking control of bodies."

"It sounds a bit like Caitlín the Soul Splitter," said Cassie. "We've dealt with this before. She did it to us."

She explained how they had been soul-separated by the evil sorceress Caitlín of the Crooked Teeth, the wife of Balor of the Evil Eye, who wanted revenge for his death. How she made replicas of their bodies and stole their life forces to bring the replicas under her control. And how sometimes she did it the other way round, storing souls in replicas and using people's bodies.

Ivo nodded thoughtfully. "You give me hope. How did you reunite body and soul?"

"We faced Caitlín in a battle," said Thomas. "And we overcame our shadow selves by using ingenuity and magic. Then we were able to reunite."

"I do not think it will be so easy for us," said Ivo.

"We have been told that you can kill a vampire by grabbing its heart, burning it and sprinkling the ash on the body," said Cassie. "And any leftover ash can be used to kill other vampires. Is that true?"

"And what about all the stuff about stakes through the heart and garlic?" said Thomas.

"Hollywood nonsense," Basher scoffed. "That's just in books and films."

"Anyway the Eretsuns are the Undead," said Ivo. "Our

parents, uncles and aunts. And I will not allow them to be killed. They are victims too and we have to rescue them."

Cassie looked at the boy thoughtfully. She could see why the other children looked up to him. He had fierceness but a basic decency that even at her age she realised was very rare.

"Tell us about the Baba Yaga," said Thomas.

At the sound of her name Ivo shuddered and seemed reluctant to talk.

Thomas changed course. "What else do you know about Vladimir? Do you know of a spell?" he coaxed.

"That night at my father's house, Vladimir was cocky and boastful," Ivo continued. "He revealed that his ambitions do not stop in Europe – he plans to raise an army of vampires everywhere in the world. He is also searching for other ways to augment his powers."

Cassie felt a cold tingling in her spine. It was bad timing. So many gods of Otherworlds who could have helped were trapped in the fairies' force field in Inish Álainn. "What did he say exactly?" she asked.

"He said he had the recipe for raising a vampire army that would control the world," he mumbled, not wanting the other wild children to hear. He beckoned the Chingles to follow him to his tent.

Inside, he signalled to them to stand close and barely breathed the words.

"This was the recipe. A child not of human mother born–"

Thomas and Cassie gasped, recognizing the spell.

"A space stone of the soul splitter, a tower of power . . . and something about a supernatural death at a fault line in the earth. Then he mentioned something about stones of the elements and when the earth darkens the moon. I couldn't hear all of it . . ." Ivo stared down at his feet as if trying to recall something else.

Cassie and Thomas were horrified. Natalya had revealed that Vladimir would be interested in the information about a tower of power and the stone of the soul splitter connected to Inish Álainn. Their dream revealed that the spirits who kidnapped the babies might have spoken to the Merrows about Caitlín and Balor. Too many elements were worryingly slotting into place and pointing to the island.

And now there were more . . .

Thomas took a deep breath. "When we fought Balor of the Evil Eye, we annihilated him at sea," he told Ivo. "Balor's death might have opened up a fault line in the earth at the very spot. We had information that enemies of ours, Irish mermaids called the Merrows, were spending a lot of time there. And the earth darkening the moon sounds like the description of a lunar eclipse. Our friend Tadgh said there is one due shortly."

"The amulet I used to protect myself from Caitlín in the battle was made of meteorite stone that had fallen to earth," Cassie added. "As we told you, Caitlín knew how to divide souls. And in saving me it captured some of her dark power."

"Do you still have this amulet?" asked Ivo.

"No. I lost it and the Merrows, found it," said Cassie. "At least Vladimir doesn't have it yet. But he does have another important element. Willa's child is born not of human mother because Willa is a vila. Unknown to Vladimir so is our cousin Lorcan because his mother used to be a goddess."

"As for the tower of power," said Thomas, "there is a round tower on Inish Álainn and our friend Tadgh told us that there was some theory that round towers could draw magnetic resonance from the sky and earth."

"But 'the stones of the elements' – what could that mean?" pondered Cassie.

"Vladimir will be busy finding out," said Ivo. "I thought there was a jewel in that box held by Raznik when they tortured my father. Perhaps it has something to do with precious metals or stones."

"I hope it doesn't mean this necklace Willa gave me!" said Cassie. "It has magical powers!"

"You had better guard it closely," said Ivo gravely.

Cassie felt sick. It sounded more and more like Inish Álainn figured somehow in Vladimir's plans. Had their victories over the dark forces somehow made the island more exposed to future troubles? It was a terrible thought.

"Vladimir is close to getting all the ingredients he needs for his spell to help him unlock all the secrets of the black arts," Ivo whispered. "Then he will be fully able to recruit the dead of all nations and take over the world. The

Baba Yaga is somehow in his power or is working alongside him. I cannot tell."

"So where can we find her?" urged Thomas.

Ivo led them back to the campfire. "In the Broken Fields. The Crooked Mountain leads to the Destroyed Plain, then beyond the Magic Mountain and the Enchanted Forest there are her broken fields." He stopped as if recollecting something, then continued as if thinking aloud: "The rain can help the wind."

"What's he talking about now?" shrugged Cassie at Conchy who sat tending the fire.

"Ivo likes to talk in riddles. He thinks it outwits the evil powers," explained the red-haired boy.

"I will help you only on the condition that you help us," said Ivo.

Cassie looked at Thomas. "We don't necessarily need you," she said to Ivo.

"Don't you?" Ivo said evenly. "Even if you were able to rescue the children on your own, don't you think you have a responsibility to take on Vladimir? You'll only have to do it sooner rather than later. Strike now before he gets too powerful."

"But our prority is to rescue the babies," said Cassie. "We can't make promises."

"He's an evil, clever, ruthless man who will stop at nothing," said Ivo with passion. "He is in league with the dark side and intends to unleash a spell. The sorcerer Raznik, who is reputed to be a specially powerful vampire, is in his pocket. Vladimir doesn't understand the forces that he is unleashing and is all the more dangerous for that!"

This last point chimed in with the Chingles' own fear. They asked for some privacy while they discussed his offer. He gestured to them to return to his tent.

Inside, they sat and went into a huddle.

"I like Ivo and all the little children," said Nancy. "I think we should help them."

"We could go it alone," said Cassie. "After all, these kids don't have special powers. You got into the camp easily enough and they seem sort of underfed and hysterical."

"But Ivo is a different matter. He's a thinker," said Thomas. "He's right that Vladimir is everyone's enemy. It's not enough to get the babies back." The image of the defenceless infants in the grip of such a monster burnt the back of his eyes. "We mustn't delay. We are in unfamiliar territory here and need all the help we can get."

Cassie hesitated. "I'm not sure. Ivo seems honourable but kind of mad too. All those weird habits and riddles and stuff."

"He's just different," shrugged Thomas. "We know what that's like."

Cassie thought about how she was teased in school because she was clever. She knew what it was like to be prejudiced against. "Okay," she said. "Let's give it a go."

They returned to tell Ivo their decision. He responded with a whoop of joy. He insisted on them all sealing their agreement by conducting a ceremony. He instructed all the children to gather around them in a circle. Then he bent down to the earth and with his left hand scooped up a handful of dirt. He took up a piece in his right hand and, rubbing it onto his brow, proclaimed: "I now solemnly vow to help these children find the Baba Yaga in return for their aid in freeing the Eretsuns!"

To the Chingles' surprise, he then placed a piece of dirt in his mouth and swallowed it. Cassie glanced at Thomas in horror, already questioning their decision to co-operate with the tribe of wild children. Ivo approached Thomas and asked him to swear likewise. Thomas hid any reservations and complied, swallowing the piece of dirt with a gulp. Cassie eyed Ivo's approach with the clod of earth with distaste but reluctantly she took the lump in her mouth, determined not to gag. It tasted salty and peaty and wasn't as bad as she'd supposed. Nancy accepted her clod with interest, as she was still young enough to experiment with flavours.

Then one of the children gave Ivo a small glass filled with oil. Cassie watched in alarm, hoping he wasn't going to ask her to drink it too. But he turned towards the east and poured a few drops into the ground.

"Oh Moist Mother Earth, hold evil spirits in check!" Next he faced west and pouring a few drops of oil said, "Oh Mother Earth, send your fierce fires to consume the forces of evil!" Turning to the south he again poured oil and asked Mother Earth to soothe the southerly winds and prevent bad weather. Then looking north, he poured out the remainder of the oil and intoned, "Deliver us from the cold northerly, bringer of heavy snowstorms, clouds and icy blasts!" He finished by smashing the empty oil jar to the ground. All the children cheered.

Cassie felt the ceremony was slightly silly but she tried to conceal her amusement.

"We will accompany you to the edge of the territory of the Baba Yaga," said Ivo. "It is very dangerous. Eretsuns lurk in the plains. There are also powerful and capricious spirits in the Enchanted Forest and I have forbidden our children to venture there. The Broken Fields belong to the Baba Yaga and I dare not presume to survive a second encounter with her. Once there, you are on your own. However, I will give you this."

A large wooden box painted with images of the firebird and a stag, in bright gaudy colours, was fetched from the tree house. With great ceremony, Ivo reached inside and took out a small wooden object. He offered it to Cassie.

She looked at it and examined it closely. It was a small little doll like the Russian dolls known as "Matreshka" where little doll figures are encased within each other, each smaller than the next and all exactly the same. She gave it a twist to open it but this one seemed to be just one doll. It looked gaudy and cheap.

It had a painted smiling face of a woman wearing a red headscarf with painted black spiral-shaped curls peeping out. She wore a painted yellow cloak and carried a painted orange flower.

"What do we do with it?" she asked. Compared to an amulet of meteorite or a jewelled talisman necklace it looked rather ineffectual.

Without realising it, Cassie hadn't given it the amount of reverence that Ivo felt appropriate. He looked hurt.

"It is not so fine as a gemstone necklace," he said, glancing at the sparkling jewels around Cassie's neck.

Nancy grabbed the doll from her sister with both hands and lovingly cradled it.

"Well, what's its purpose?" asked Cassie in puzzlement.

"My mother left it to me. I didn't tell you earlier but it was this doll in my pocket that stopped me entering the house when Vladimir came. You will see when the time comes if it helps you or not." He turned away to hide his anger. "Of course, I have no control over whether or not you are pure of heart," he added with a tinge of hardness in his voice.

"Surely such a pure one as you wouldn't lower yourself to sarcasm?" said Cassie.

Ivo bristled. The other wild children became unsettled.

"Pure is not the same as perfection," he said. "I've never denied I have a temper. A very bad one. Particularly when people don't trust me."

Cassie was finding Ivo very perplexing. They kept rubbing each other up the wrong way. "I'm disappointed in you," said Cassie teasingly. "I thought you were a paragon of virtue. Some kind of saint."

"It is easy for you to make jokes. You have not lost your parents," Ivo said seriously.

169

"Well, having your baby brother and sister and your little cousin kidnapped is hardly a picnic," said Cassie.

Ivo looked away. "Then I don't understand why you make these jokes."

"I'm not taking it lightly but being miserable doesn't help anybody," Cassie said in exasperation. "I don't believe in going around with a long face with the weight of the world on my shoulders."

Ivo looked stung.

Thomas glanced at his sister. Her cheeks looked hot and her eyes narrowed and glittered and he saw she was losing patience. He knew all about her quick temper and impetuous nature. Now that she was nearly a teenager she was getting even more moody. Ivo also seemed quite temperamental. Thomas was used to Cassie blowing hot and cold in an instant and was intrigued to see how this strange boy would take it. Maybe she had met her match.

"I have to think of many children," said Ivo with dignity.

"Except you don't seem to do anything for these children," Cassie said with scorn. "How come they are so dirty and thin? You're older, you should make sure they have baths."

"I did not choose to be their leader. They chose to follow me," said Ivo.

"We don't like baths," said a small voice. She was a very dirty little girl with straggly hair almost to her waist.

"Well, you could at least feed them properly," continued

Cassie on her high horse. "Instead of moping about all day, feeling sorry for yourself and talking nonsense."

"I am a bit hungry," admitted Conchy.

"It's a disgrace," continued Cassie, who was like a dog with a bone when she got her teeth into her own brand of outrage. "I bet these woods are teeming with game you could catch and roast."

"I don't eat meat," said Ivo. "I cannot bear to kill any creatures."

"Well, that's all right for you," said Cassie a bit more uncertainly. Her best friend was a vegetarian and she had been brought up to respect people's views. "Anyway, even if you eat vegetables, you should make sure it's a balanced diet."

"Perhaps you would like to stay with us and take care of the little ones and lead by example," said Ivo in a quiet, threatening voice.

Several children cheered at this and nodded their heads in agreement.

"She can do magic," said one admiringly.

"She knows her own mind," said another.

"See, you've already swayed my followers," Ivo said. "After all, they are so desperate for a leader they chose me."

"You know very well I have to find the babies," Cassie said angrily.

Ivo said nothing.

The children began to murmur and quarrel among themselves, some saying they'd like Cassie to lead them,

171

others that it should be Ivo. The mood threatened to turn ugly.

"I have no intention of staying here," said Cassie emphatically, to put an end to the matter. Her ankle began to throb again and she felt like she might pass out. But she turned her back on Ivo so he wouldn't notice.

"You should make your preparations," Ivo said finally. "Do you want the doll or not?"

Nancy, holding the doll, ran to him and sweetly kissed him on the cheek. "I will mind the doll," she said, hugging it tight. "I like dolls."

"We'll give it a whirl," said Thomas soothingly.

Ivo smiled at Nancy and relented. "We'll get going at sunrise and I will come and tell you about the doll later."

"We ought to do something about Cassie's ankle," Thomas said to Ivo.

"I'm just about to," he said.

The Chingles were led to a tree house shaped like a giant beehive, nestled within the boughs of a great oak tree. Inside, it was lined with carpets and rugs and there were colourful blankets. It was simple but surprisingly cosy.

"You and your big mouth! Why did you keep clashing with Ivo? You'll never learn, Cassie, will you?" said Thomas. "You have to be gentle with someone like him."

"But that Ivo is so full of himself," she fumed. "And he wants us to take on some bloodsucking warlord while he hangs back from doing it himself. Plus he has no sense of humour."

"I think he's intelligent and kind of interesting," said Thomas. "He's been through a lot."

Cassie felt a bit confused herself about why she and Ivo seemed to have got off on the wrong foot. "I suppose he's been through a trauma," she conceded. "But he could be a charlatan. He could be just trying to control the others with stories of bravery of how he survived the great Baba Yaga."

A rustle of leaves indicated someone was climbing up the stepladder. Ivo's head peeked into their tree house and he came in and sat down.

Cassie saw instantly from his grim expression that he had overheard her. She coloured from embarrassment but said nothing.

"The Baba Yaga will set you certain tests," he said. "When she does, ask the doll what to do." He looked significantly at Cassie. "It worked for me even if you don't believe me," he added quietly. He was holding a small phial of ointment and some ferns. He gestured towards her leg. "I know about healing plants from my grandmother."

Reluctantly, Cassie allowed him to pack the ointment around her foot and bind it in the fern leaves. He touched her tenderly and, despite herself, Cassie felt a surge of electricity between them. He caught her eye and looked away and she realised he felt it too – some sort of connection. Both of them were too shocked to look at each other again.

Immediately she felt the throbbing subside and muttered a grudging "Thank you" to him while avoiding his eye.

"I wish you success," Ivo said quietly.

"We will soon find out," said Cassie to his departing figure, trying to keep the scepticism from her voice and her own confusion in finding that, despite their disagreements, she rather wished they could spend more time together.

CHAPTER 9

The next morning, the Chingles got ready to enter the domain of the Baba Yaga. Cassie was amazed to discover that her foot had got much better overnight. She tested it gingerly on the floor, then flexed it and was able to stand as normal without wincing. Ivo might be a weirdo but he certainly knew something about healing. Feeling hungry, she poked her head out of the tree house and was surprised to discover that the camp was a hive of activity. She immediately noticed Ivo's blond head as he strode around the camp. She caught herself thinking again he was quite good-looking if you ignored the ragged clothes. She saw the children were lined up in an orderly queue for some sort of unappetising grey gruel ladled out from a pot and some even appeared to have washed their faces. Obviously her words had hit home with some children, she thought with pride.

"Nice to know my advice had some effect," she called

over in a friendly way to Ivo, pointing over at the wild children's scrubbed faces as she descended the ladder.

But Ivo scowled at her and walked away.

"Be like that," she said airily. But she felt a bit hurt at being rebuffed for tendering him an olive branch. She walked over to the pot and sniffed the gruel. It looked very unappealing but then so did Connle's porridge. She joined the queue for a bowl.

Ivo walked over to the children that stood in line and told them to reapply the dirt to their faces after breakfast. The children bowed their heads and meekly agreed.

"That's just pig-headed," Cassie turned on him. "Just because they want to take pride in their appearance!"

Ivo walked calmly over to her and looked her hard in the eye. "You arrived in an airplane and were winched down. You foolishly rushed ahead of your brother and sister and got lost and then you walked into our trap."

Cassie was taken aback. The wild children had tracked their every move since they'd arrived and they'd never been aware of it. Cassie felt annoyed at herself for not realising that they'd been followed the whole time.

"How do you think we escape the attentions of the Eretsuns and the forest dwellers? Our ragged clothes and dirty faces disguise our appearance and our scent," Ivo said. "How did the great superior children with magical skills not notice our beady eyes following them through the forest?" He spoke evenly but with a hint of condescension.

A sleepy Thomas and yawning Nancy descended from the ladder and, seeing Cassie in the queue, joined it.

"Hide!" Ivo suddenly commanded. Silently and quickly the wild children scurried behind trees or climbed into boughs. Some just curled up in the earth. They blended with the fallen leaves, the bushes, with the trees and the branches, their tones of grey, green and brown melding with the earth and foliage. Their matted hair covered their faces.

Cassie stood alone in the encampment with her brother and sister. She could barely hear anyone breathing beyond the rustle of the trees. The wild children's ragged clothes and wild hair and dirty faces were perfect camouflage for their surroundings. How stupid of her not to notice!

"You have made your point," she said coldly, scanning the area to find out where Ivo had concealed himself. Surely his yellow hair would give him away. But he had blended like the others into his surroundings.

He dropped down from a high branch, nimbly landing on his feet, his hair flying in the wind.

Cassie regarded their own ordinary clothes. They were dressed sensibly in fairly neutral colours but compared to the wild children, they stood out like traffic lights.

"Perhaps you could help us disguise ourselves," said Thomas.

Ivo flashed him an appreciative smile.

The gruel was rather tasteless but at least it was hot and there were also apples and rye bread. Cassie wanted to suggest adding the apples to sweeten the gruel but she didn't fancy being rebuffed by Ivo again.

After breakfast, the Chingles were kitted out in the wild children's forest attire. To their surprise the leggings and tunic that looked ragged and tattered were made of the most delicate, comfortable cloth in the colours of the forest – earth, green and russet browns. They seemed to blend and change depending on the background. Ivo also gave them each a cloak of a fine material as soft as butterflies' wings, in tones of green and brown. They enjoyed daubing their faces with mud. Some of the little girls threaded Nancy's dark curls with branches and twigs but Cassie refused to let them touch her own hair on the grounds that its lustrous nut-brown colour was camouflage in itself. Ivo also gave them each a brown kerchief, which he told them to use as a facemask. Conchy and Basher brought them crude cudgels as weapons.

"You will encounter Eretsuns on the way," Conchy said. "So do not go about at night. They reek of death. You will need to learn to live with the smell."

"How will we deal with them?" asked Thomas.

"All I ask is that you don't annihilate them," Ivo said quickly. "In any case, they are difficult to kill. They fear fire and bright lights and do not like to cross running water."

"That's a whole lot of help," muttered Cassie but Thomas glanced at her to be quiet. He had quite enjoyed her sparring with Ivo at first but it was beginning to get on his nerves.

They left the camp, accompanied by Ivo, Basher the heavy-set dark boy, Conchy the redhead and Kicker the straw-haired boy. They plunged into the gloomy centre of the forest. At one stage they walked alongside a river and eventually came to a part of the forest with rocky outcrops and terrifying spiky rocks. The sky hung overhead, leaden and dark. They were glad of the company on the gloomy journey, although nobody spoke much. Ivo seemed to be sulking again and responded to Thomas's questions with only a gruff yes or no.

Thomas watched how stealthily the children moved without even disturbing a twig. He realised they were used to being unobtrusive, moving through the forest like deer or mice. They had learned to incorporate these qualities into themselves. The Chingles would need to develop such skills. They wouldn't always be able to just change into an animal. This got Thomas thinking about whether it would be better to be a human or immortal. He finally got Ivo's attention when he asked him his opinion on the subject.

"Sometimes I think it would be better to be immortal, so I could fight Vladimir," said Ivo. "But if I was immortal I probably wouldn't care. I would live forever and silly human matters wouldn't concern me."

"I enjoy having magical skills. From what I've found out, we won't have our powers when we become adults. It's hard to think that when I'm a grown-up I'll lose them," said Thomas. "I think they will come in handy in rescuing the children and fighting Vladimir."

"That may be so," said Ivo thoughtfully. "But Vladimir is a human and we can only outwit him if we think like humans. Of course, he wishes to be supernatural and I am suspicious of anyone who craves special powers. I want to be the best human being I can be, not some arrogant godlike person who lives forever."

"We have the choice to be immortal at the end of this summer," said Thomas. "Last year, the gods of the Tuatha Dé Danann offered us the chance to live in Tír na nÓg, the Land of the Ever Young. We could stay the same age forever and never grow old. Tír na nÓg is a kind of heaven. Cassie has already made up her mind to accept but I'm not sure."

"Your sister already behaves like she is one of the gods," said Ivo contemptuously. "She thinks her magical powers make her better than mere mortals."

Cassie overheard him and her face turned red. She rounded on him with equal contempt. "You can talk! I got the distinct impression that you yourself have been trying to master sorcery, what with your stupid tests and silly rituals!"

"Ivo's just trying to protect us," interrupted Conchy, his face growing hot. Instinctively the three wild children drew closer to Ivo and put their hands on their cudgels.

Cassie bristled and Thomas was taken aback.

But Ivo held up his hands to calm his companions.

"I do not approve of the black arts and I too once thought all these rituals silly and superstitious," Ivo said reasonably. "But in our fight against Vladimir, I am willing to give many things a try. Including an alliance with strange children who can perform magic tricks."

"Oh, how kind of you to let us risk our lives on your behalf!" mocked Cassie.

Conchy and Thomas caught each other's eyes and both

looked up to heaven. Good, thought Thomas, he's as irritated by Ivo and Cassie's touchiness as I am.

"Hey, shut up, you two!" said Thomas with a grin. "We're all on the same side."

"Yeah," agreed Conchy. "We have enough enemies without fighting among ourselves."

Basher and Kicker nodded in agreement. Together with Nancy and Thomas they strode on ahead, leaving Ivo and Cassie to follow in sulky silence.

"Those two are more alike than they realise," Thomas confided in Conchy.

"They both like to be in charge, even if Ivo denies it," agreed Conchy. "I kind of admire the way your sister takes him on. Sometimes he does need a good shake."

"She's very brave," said Thomas proudly. "Even if she has a big mouth."

They climbed up the steep mountain and passed through a sub-alpine meadow of grasses and wildflowers. Higher up, the terrain became rockier and vegetation was sparse. Here and there stunted sycamore and alders clung on against the onslaught of a constant battering wind. Near the top, it was tough-going, treacherous scree until finally they reached a gap where the wind whistled through, rushing into their ears. From the summit they saw a desolate plain, then a dark forest covering another mountain range capped by snowy peaks. It was so noisy they had to shout to talk.

"Beyond the Magic Mountain and the Enchanted Forest

lie the Broken Fields," pointed Basher, "where there are cornfields and the domain of the Baba Yaga. To get there, you have to cross the plain and follow a path over mountain ridges to a deserted village in a long valley at the edge of the forest."

"This is the edge of our safe area!" Ivo was shouting to overcome the sound of the wind. "It was out there beyond the Magic Mountain by the cornfield in the Broken Fields that I got lost and fell into Grandmother Bony Shanks' hands! You must wander round until dusk. If you reach the cornfield, sleep in it. They say the sway of corn means the passing of the Baba Yaga. Try not to talk to her, and do whatever she tells you even if it seems absurd." He gave Cassie a look. "And as silly as it seems, ask the doll for help. Her name is Vasalisa. I will post sentries here to wait for your return."

As they turned to go, Ivo touched Thomas on the arm.

"I saw that you can shape-change," he said. "I would be careful about doing it in the Enchanted Forest, lest you attract other attention. I do not know for certain but I have always sensed it is haunted by unfriendly spirits."

"What do you mean?" asked Thomas.

Ivo shrugged and turned away. "I can't always explain my hunches but I do not like it there." Then he added enigmatically, "The quarry will draw the hunter. Even a liar can tell the truth."

"You're talking in riddles again," sniffed Cassie.

Just as he was about to leave, Ivo turned to Thomas and

said, "If you see an Eretsun wearing a wooden cross, please get word to me. It may be my father."

Thomas nodded. They briefly shook hands and with that Ivo and his companions left.

Cassie barely said goodbye and then felt bad for being ungracious. He had after all cured her ankle. She turned around at the same moment that Ivo turned back to look at them. They caught each other's glance and turned away as if scalded.

The Chingles were on their own and set off down the mountain. The air was thick with a noxious scent and they were glad of the kerchiefs loaned to them by Ivo.

Cassie fingered Willa's necklace. Luckily Nancy and Thomas had found all the stones and she'd threaded them back on. Did Ivo think her shallow because she had an expensive necklace? All she did was ask him questions about his precious doll. He made her feel awkward. Oh, what do I care what Ivo thinks, she told herself. I'll show him!

The path down the mountain was rough and they had to concentrate on their every step. As they reached the beginning of the desolate plain that led to the Magic Mountain and the Enchanted Forest, they realised it would be many miles to the open cornfields that lay beyond.

"It doesn't make sense," said Cassie as they surveyed the bleak landscape. "All the other information is that the Baba Yaga lives in a forest and yet now Ivo is telling us to sleep in a cornfield."

"Look, you just don't trust him, do you?" said Thomas.

"Understandably. He's very contradictory," said Cassie. "How is he ever going to defeat Vladimir if he doesn't want to harm anything?"

"But he has a point. The Eretsuns are their parents. It's different with demons and monsters and gods. They are spirits and pure evil. A person is different. Even an evil one is still a human being," reasoned Thomas. "That's why Sennan went to the kingdom of Donn of the Dead to try to retrieve the souls of Caitlín's fighters." He spoke of their former teacher, the druid Sennan, who had travelled to the Irish underworld in the hope of reuniting the bodies and life forces of those soul split by Caitlín.

"You are falling under the sway of that waster Ivo," said Cassie. "He's such a know-all!"

"And you're not!" quipped Thomas.

Cassie said nothing but as they walked towards the plain, she resumed the conversation.

"But Ivo, he's so touchy, did you see the way he –"

"For someone who doesn't like him you seem to want to talk about him all the time," said Thomas slyly.

Cassie blushed with embarrassment and shut up.

"We should stay quiet," said Nancy sternly. Her words seemed to echo in the still air. Thomas and Cassie realised she was right.

All day they tracked their way through the barren plain. It seemed to be vast and much wider than they'd thought. The wind beat them like a weapon. The sky was leaden and low as if it wanted to press down on the earth. Here and there, they saw burnt-out buildings, abandoned sheds and rusting farm machinery. Everything seemed blackened and desolate. They felt nauseous and light-headed with the stench of death. They also felt exposed and vulnerable with few hiding places.

They tried to stick to the open plain as much as possible but as they journeyed on the terrain changed. It became rocky and steep, falling away to narrow ravines. They were in the foothills of the Magic Mountain. Luckily there was an old worn path that took them over rocky outfalls and cliffs. A fast-flowing river cut through the landscape and on the opposite bank they saw waterfalls cascading down the high bank and crashing into the river below. The path narrowed and took them over a ravine that fell away steeply down to the river. Then the path dropped into a long, narrow valley with a lake and a wide stream flowing through it. The deep valley was pockmarked with burnt-out and deserted dwellings and buildings. At the end of the valley, cut by the stream, they saw the mountain became thickly forested, dressed in greens of every hue.

"I don't like this place," shuddered Cassie. "It gives me an eerie feeling."

"But we have to go through it and cross the stream," said Thomas.

The valley looked as though it had been bombed. There were piles of rubble everywhere. Where buildings stood, their roofs had been burnt off or blackened and glass windows had been blown out. Here and there were odd reminders that it had once been inhabited by people – a torn teddy bear with a missing ear, a blackened shoe, a squashed soft-drink can.

They walked warily and silently, picking their way through the rubble and debris.

Nancy's stomach began to throb. Instinctively they quickened their pace. But it was slow going. Unchecked by humans, wild nature had asserted itself in the valley. The path was almost completely obliterated and obstructed by brush, herbs and thick grasses. Riotous thorny bushes stood in their way. On the right-hand side a wide meander from the stream had become cut off and formed an oxbow lake shaped like a horseshoe. Clouds of mosquitoes hovered over its stagnant depths.

They walked on, their nerves on edge. Ahead they saw the bridge covering the stream had decayed but there were fording stones and it looked easy to cross. Before the stream crossing was a group of high derelict barns. Beyond the stream they saw the silhouette of tall trees in the distance etched by the late evening sun.

They held hands, Nancy in the middle with Cassie to her left and Thomas to her right. As they passed by the open mouth of a disused barn with rusting machinery blocking the entry, Nancy practically leaped off the ground. They heard a low, animal howl. All three of them spun round. To their horror about twelve paces behind them two Eretsuns stumbled from the barn, closing in for the kill. The creatures winced in the daylight but their ravenous hunger propelled them forward.

They were hideous and terrifying, a mix of half-vampire and half-wolf. They stood upright with long front arms that ended in bristling claws. There was little trace of humanity in their faces that had become snouts with huge snarling jaws. Large vampire fangs extended from their upper jaws and gleamed as they roared with blood lust.

"Salmon leap!" shouted Cassie.

The children concentrated their energy into a point but nothing happened. Frantically, they ran and hid behind a crumbling wall. Cassie took out her rope and Nancy her sling. Thomas jumped out from behind the wall and hurled rocks at the Eretsuns. Nancy managed to hit one on the head with a stone but he just stumbled and pushed forward. Howling filled the air.

Thomas crouched against the wall and looked up. A pack of maybe ten Eretsuns emerged from a corrugated shed ahead of them further up the valley.

The Eretsuns were closing in.

"The necklace!" said Nancy. "It helped us before!"

Cassie took off Willa's necklace. The jewels slithered in her hands, which were sweating with fear. The gems pulsated with a strange power.

"Right. Let's try a salmon leap again," she said.

Thomas and Nancy touched the necklace, feeling power emanating from its jewels.

This time it worked. They rose in the air in a great

spiralling arc, changed into salmon and then back to themselves, landing on the opposite side of the stream, at the forest's edge. They watched as the Eretsuns gathered on the stream, howling with frustration and hunger.

"Ivo said they won't cross running water," Thomas said.

The children plunged into the Enchanted Forest that grew up to the rocky snow-covered peak of the Magic Mountain.

Cassie peered into its dense interior. The trees seemed huge. Everything about it was more intense than a normal forest. The gnarled trunks of broad-leaved deciduous trees were topped with glossy emerald leaves that glowed. The polished brown barks of oak, beech and walnut trees were intermixed with tall, thin rustling willows and the silver bark of birch. Apple-tree boughs were heavy with golden fruit. Thick clusters of catkins grew on hazelnut trees. Wild flowers of an intense blue and violet carpeted the grassy forest floor, and stones were furry with moss. As they walked further up, the deep green of pines sheltered them overhead and huge silver firs that towered into the sky put in an appearance, lichen bearding their branches.

Through the trees they glimpsed the rosy sky of the dying day as the sun began to settle in the west. It would be twilight soon.

"We're not going to make it through here before nightfall," Cassie said. "I think we ought to shape-shift."

"Our power is weaker here than any other place," said

Thomas. "Maybe we ought to conserve it and not waste it in shape-shifting when we can travel the distance on foot."

"Our powers are intermittent here," admitted Cassie. "But Willa's necklace seems to help and I feel I'm getting stronger. Doing the salmon leap has given me more confidence. You've both shape-shifted but I haven't yet."

"Maybe a bad thing will find us in the forest," piped up Nancy.

"Nancy's right," said Thomas. "And it might be a disadvantage if we're animals. We should remain as children."

"Didn't Ivo say we had to seek the Baba Yaga in a cornfield? Wouldn't it be tempting to just fly across the forest?" coaxed Cassie.

Thomas was torn. He'd have loved nothing more than to transform into an eagle and cover the distance in a soaring flight.

"Ivo said shape-shifting's a bad idea," he said. "But maybe you're right. I don't want to encounter any more Eretsuns tonight."

"They are scary," said Nancy.

"Let's turn into deer," urged Cassie. "They can run fast and it doesn't require as much effort as an eagle."

Seeing the others were giving in, Cassie closed her eyes and concentrated all her attention into a point. She felt her stomach contract, her head buzz and her bones creak as they stretched and elongated. In moments, her skeleton was rearranged. There was a hammering inside her skull as it expanded and her face was pulled into a snout. She breathed in through her glistening black nose and felt her long tongue flick out of her mouth. She squealed in delight and did a dance on her four fleshy footpads and looked around at her glossy fur back. She saw the world pin-sharp through her black and white vision, the veins on leaves, the bracken underfoot. Her nose was filled with the scent of the forest, newly opened buds, green grass, the trails of mice and the acrid scent of bears. And the mossy smell of Thomas and Nancy in their forest clothes. She saw Thomas and Nancy smile and with a waggle of her tail trotted off through the trees as a sprightly doe.

Thomas told Nancy they'd better do the same. So they too became deer, Thomas a stag and Nancy a young fawn.

After the tension of escaping the Eretsuns, Thomas enjoyed the sensation of running gracefully through the forest. Their black and white vision was exact and they flew over branches and logs, their brown coats blending in with the dappled foliage. It was great to feel an animal's naked freedom. The magic of shape-shifting absorbed their clothes and weapons and they always knew their worldly goods would appear when they re-assumed their human shape. It was one of the wonders of shape-shifting. But how good it was once more to be an animal and not to have to worry about material things! They began to gambol and play, relishing the freedom of their unencumbered bodies. About halfway through, they came to a small brook in the forest. Thomas and Nancy were a little way ahead.

Thirsty, Cassie stopped for a drink. The cool water felt so good on her panting tongue. She was so absorbed in slaking her thirst that it took a moment for her to realise she was being watched. She heard a twig break and, startled, looked up. Across the brook she saw the flash of a poised arrow in a bow. A hunter!

She had a split second to act. If she ran, she could be shot down as quarry. She changed back into herself.

"Don't shoot!" she cried. "I'm a girl!"

A tall, imposing woman marched out of the trees, still aiming her arrow at Cassie. Cassie felt for her rope but before she could use it she froze, unable to move her limbs.

A split second later Thomas and Nancy changed back to themselves and ran to join Cassie. She tried to call out but her tongue was numb in her mouth. Then they too were frozen in some invisible bonds.

The woman was very tall, dressed in animal skins and had a handsome, weather-beaten face. She regarded them with a savage expression. It's a supernatural being, thought Cassie. Ivo was right. It really was an Enchanted Forest. I probably shouldn't have had anything to drink. It's not wise to eat or drink anything from the Otherworld. But she seemed to be all right and only hoped she'd got away with it.

The woman began to speak. "I am Devana the Goddess of Hunting. Who are you creatures who dare to trespass on my domain?" She raised her bow once more.

Cassie felt the woman's power and realised that the

force emanating from her was sapping her own. The woman nodded towards them and suddenly Cassie was able to speak.

"Please, we seek only to pass through here. We wish to find the Baba Yaga who has kidnapped four babies, including our cousin and our twin brother and sister. Also the child of a wood nymph called Willa."

"Willa!" The woman laid down her bow and arrow. "But Willa has left us," she said sadly. "Disappeared."

"No, she has just taken human form to marry Sasha, a human," explained Thomas.

A flash of anger clouded the woman's strong face and she tossed her coal-black hair that hung down her back in plaits. "Our nymphs have this weakness. I warn them not to get mixed up with humans. I choose not to. This is my domain. I allow no one to trespass here. All who do can be hunted."

"But we have special powers," Thomas said, realising Devana was one of those deities who disliked humans and had to be placated.

"You deny you are humans?" she demanded. "Not that it matters. I also punish any gods who disobey my decrees."

"We are humans," Cassie conceded. "But we will be immortals by the end of the summer."

"Then you will be more sport to catch," said Devana. "You have broken the laws of my forest and must be punished. I command you to change back to deer and I will hunt you. If I do not catch you before dark, you are free to go through my domain if you agree to one favour. If you refuse to be hunted I can kill you now – you are entirely in my power."

"And what is that favour?" asked Thomas. He glanced anxiously at the glowing sky. The sun was sinking below the horizon.

"I want you to bring a gift to Leshii, the fat peasant who thinks he is Lord of the Forest. Tell him I command him to leave."

Thomas looked at his sisters. He appraised Devana. She exuded a dark, brooding power and was sharp and quick. He reckoned as deer they didn't stand a chance.

"It will be too easy for you if we are deer," he said. "It's far more of a challenge if we can change shape."

"What do you propose?" Devana demanded.

"Say if we soared as eagles, slithered as snakes, hopped as hares? That would make us all the more unpredictable and show just how good a hunter you are," said Thomas persuasively.

Cassie looked at him with interest. Only a minute ago he had been scolding her for wasting their energy shape-shifting. Now he was proposing a full-scale menu. He must have some plan. Thomas seemed to have a lot native cunning when it came to dealing with capricious magical beings.

"Agreed," said Devana and placed her arrow back in her quiver. She threw back her head and laughed in a savage manner.

Then she waved at them with a swirling gesture in the air and the spell freezing their limbs was lifted. She ushered them to the other side of a giant, gnarled oak tree where stood her chariot. It was a beautiful vehicle of gold and silver pulled by two sleek, powerful horses, one black and one white. She revealed her cache of weapons: finely wrought swords, slender spears and cudgels.

"I enjoy the chase as much as the capture." She walked up beside them and in one deft move sniffed each of them in turn, acquainting herself with their scent. Then arrogantly she dismissed them and turned her back on them.

"I will allow you ten minutes' advantage," she said imperiously. "Now go. Do not try to escape – you will not pass through the magical barrier that protects my domain when the hunt is on." Then she let out a high-pitched cry that chilled their blood and marrow.

"Eagles," whispered Thomas. "Follow me."

They soared into the air on golden wings, following Thomas's lead. Scanning the forest below them, Thomas saw that even with a powerful eagle's flight they wouldn't reach the edge of the domain within an hour. Devana was heartless and there was no guarantee that she would give up within the agreed time span. Their only hope was to catch the huntress.

They settled on an outcrop in the craggy forest and, following Thomas's lead, transformed back to themselves.

"We're going to have to fight her," he said.

"We have no magical weapons. All we have are my rope, Nancy's sling and the cudgels given to us by the wild children," said Cassie. Now she bitterly regretted the fact that, in the rush to get away from Inish Álainn, they'd neglected to fetch their magical weapons.

"We can throw stones," suggested Nancy.

"You've got to be kidding," said Cassie dismissively. "She's a goddess. We're good but not that good. It would be like trying to beat Scáthach or Lugh. And she's on her territory."

"We'll have to steal her weapons," said Thomas.

"But she's able to sap our powers," said Cassie, beginning to feel a bit frightened. "We're no match for her and she will track us down even if we become the tiniest insect scuttling across the forest floor."

"That's it. Let's be insects. We'll scuttle into her chariot," said Thomas. "That's the last thing she'd expect."

So Cassie took out Willa's necklace and they made the change to wasps. There were so many bees and wasps abounding in the forest they hoped she wouldn't be able to distinguish the buzzing of their wings from the others'. But they were able to communicate through pheromone chemical signals, movement and vibration.

Within minutes Devana tracked them down in her gold and silver chariot. Cassie felt panicky as she watched her through her little wasp eyes but following Thomas's lead continued to suck nectar from a wild rose bush. Devana homed in on the spot where the scent led her, parked her chariot and jumped out but was dismayed not to see any sign of them. She was only inches away from them. Each of the children in their wasp shape crawled deep inside a bloom. Devana sniffed the air loudly. But despite picking up their scent she was frustrated that she couldn't see them. Angrily she kicked the rose bush, causing a flurry of petals and a cloud of bees to scatter from it.

She jumped back into her chariot, then rose above the forest canopy to survey from on high. At a signal from Thomas, the three Chingles flew up on their wasp wings, and as Devana hovered they attacked her. Nancy stung her on the nose, Thomas on the wrist and Cassie on the back of her neck.

Taken by surprise, Devana dropped her sword and tried to swoosh the angry wasps away with her bare hands. Quick-thinking Thomas transformed into a spider and instantly spun a web across her eyes.

"Demons!" shouted Devana, losing control of her chariot.

Deftly, Cassie transformed back into herself and grabbing the reins avoided a collision with the earth. They landed with a bump in a clearing. Devana tore at the web with her hands but Thomas had become himself and held her own sword to her neck. Nancy also turned back into herself and held a spear to Devana's chest.

"Surrender!" said Thomas. "You may be able to take our power but you cannot put your own weapons under a spell."

Devana looked thunderous but then a look of genuine

admiration came across her face. "Clever children," she said. "You have outwitted me!"

"Oh, we know you only let us win because we are children and you are too good a sport," said Thomas humbly.

Cassie looked at him quizzically but Thomas ignored her.

Devana smiled indulgently at him. "You are right, human child, and for realising it I'll give you a piece of advice: if like me you ever have the misfortune to encounter a three-headed beast, the three of you must make it choke on your bloodstone." She glanced at the bloodstone on the necklace that hung around Cassie's neck.

The Chingles were puzzled by the strange advice but thought it better not to question this prickly goddess.

"Thank you for your generosity," said Thomas.

Devana looked pleased at this further flattery. "I will deliver you to what Leshii thinks is his domain. If you encounter him, tell him I wish to heal our quarrel."

Thomas looked at her, puzzled. Earlier she said she wanted Leshii to leave. He was about to correct her when he thought better of it. She was truly capricious and contrary.

"Whatever you say," he said.

"But I warn you: he will try to cheat you. You may think you are cleverer than him but he is a trickster. Whatever you do, don't ask him for a favour. For the price is your soul."

Devana flicked her whip and the chariot of gold and silver rose in the sky, pulled by the white and black spirit horses. The clouds parted and they flew through the air in an instant, covering vast tracts of forest in the blink of an eye. It was a thrilling ride for the Chingles, who'd wearily trudged so far on foot, but all too short. Almost immediately, they were at the forest's edge, where a river and a meadow broke up the dense growth.

As they got out of the chariot Devana handed them a silver and gold bottle with an emerald stopper.

"Give this as a gift to Leshii. He is partial to the liquid from my sacred well."

They thanked her.

"I advise you to turn your clothes inside out and wear your shoes on the wrong feet as a precaution. Leshii is very unreliable. Goodbye."

With that, she swung her chariot around and was gone.

Puzzled by her instructions, they did as she told them, not that it made much difference with their earth-coloured, forest-hued clothes from the tribe of wild children.

Cassie sat down on the grass, exhausted and relieved from her encounter with Devana.

"Perhaps we ought to have a little rest before we journey any more," she yawned. "I'm worn out."

"Well, at least you know why Ivo thought it was a bad idea for us to shape-shift in that forest," said Thomas. "His suspicions about unfriendly deities were bang on."

"I seem to be making a habit of getting captured," Cassie said guiltily.

"It's okay, sis," Thomas laughed. "It's good practice for getting caught by the Baba Yaga."

"Devana was silly," said Nancy.

"You're right," said Thomas. "She's one of the stupid, vain ones that puts me off being immortal."

"Good," said Nancy.

Cassie said nothing, not wanting to start an argument about immortality again.

"I wonder what she meant about a three-headed beast?" Thomas said, puzzled. "These divine beings do like to talk in riddles."

Cassie was about to say something but she felt herself drift asleep, lulled by the sweet air and a warm breeze. She dreamed the grass was tickling her feet and she laughed in her sleep. Then she woke up suddenly. Somebody *was* tickling her feet. She jerked up abruptly.

"Thomas, don't do that!" she reprimanded him. She heard him laugh in reply.

"You stop doing that to me!" he giggled.

Then Nancy joined in, chuckling happily. "You stop too!"

The other two rose to their feet and they all stared at each other in surprise.

"Maybe it was just the grass," laughed Cassie, still feeling ticklish.

They heard a voice and all three of them jumped out of their standing. Cassie blew on Ogma's ring. Mysteriously, it seemed to be working a lot better in the Carpathian Mountains than on Inish Álainn and the hairline crack was barely perceptible. Perhaps Willa's jewelled necklace was helping it repair itself.

"What did you say?" asked Cassie.

"Maybe it wasn't the grass," said a sonorous deep voice that seemed to be coming from a tree.

Just then an old fat man dressed like a peasant from the Middle Ages appeared. He wore a baggy grey tunic and green leggings and they noticed his shoes were on the wrong feet. His somewhat piggy eyes gleamed with curiosity.

"Greetings, travellers," he said in a friendly voice. "I see you have taken the precautions to avoid meeting Leshii. Likes to tickle his quarry to death."

"Just like the Bo Men back home. Do you know this Leshii?" Cassie asked warily.

"Know him?" laughed the man. "We are old sparring partners!" Then he said in a confidential whisper, "He's a thoroughly bad lot. You know, he gave a spell to a mortal who has to sacrifice a baby for absolute power. Written on human skin it was, with human blood."

The children felt muddle-headed and laughed heartily and somewhat uncontrollably. Somewhere at the back of her mind, Cassie dimly realised he was speaking of Vladimir but she couldn't join up the dots in her present state.

"Are you sure you are not him?" she managed to wheeze.

"I'm sure I'm not who you seek," the old man said enigmatically.

"Could you tell us where to find him then?" asked Thomas. "We have a gift for him from Devana."

"Give it to me," the old man said greedily. "I'll pass it on."

"No," said Cassie. "We have to give it to him personally and tell him that Devana wants to end their quarrel."

"I've heard that before," said the old man bitterly. He began to quiver before their eyes. "*Give it to me now!*" he shouted in a towering rage and grabbed at the bottle.

But Thomas held firm to it.

A sudden storm erupted overhead and hailstones dashed down from the sky. The old man disappeared. The children ran to shelter under a nearby stand of trees but branches broke off and crashed to the ground. The whole forest quaked in the violent storm as if an invisible fight was taking place between the sky and the earth. Boughs crashed to the ground, branches were blown off and the very earth itself trembled.

"That old man *was* him," said Cassie. "He was just playing around with us. We'd better do as he says."

Cassie ran out into the hailstorm and placed the gold and silver bottle on a tree trunk.

"Here is your gift from Devana, Leshii," she shouted above the crashing noise of thunder and lightning.

Instantly the storm ceased and the old man once more materialised before her, smiling broadly.

"So who is it you really seek?" he wheedled. "Can I do you a favour?"

"No," said Thomas resolutely, remembering Devana's advice about the price being your soul. "We are trying to escape the Baba Yaga," he went on quickly. He'd dealt with tricksters from the Otherworld before and they nearly always lied.

"In which case you must journey north," the old man said slyly, pointing through the trees to the open clearing beyond. "You have to cross the meadow and skirt the mountain, then continue to the forest's edge. That will bring you to the open steppes. Keep going until the moon is high in the sky and you can avoid her by going through a golden field of corn where huge red poppies grow."

Thomas bowed slightly and, grabbing his sisters by the hands, ran across the meadow and into the forest. Then they slowed down, breathless, and trudged through the forest, skirting the mountain until they came to where the trees thinned at the forest's edge. Behind them was the snowy cap of Magic Mountain. Ahead of them lay miles and miles of fields of golden corn and wheatfields that gleamed before them like a golden sea.

"Let's look for the field with the giant poppies," he said. "My guess is Leshii will betray us to the Baba Yaga out of spite. He means to trick us by sending us into her lair in the field of poppies. But what he doesn't realise is that we want to be captured."

"When he said he gave a spell to a mortal who has to sacrifice a baby, do you think he could mean Vladimir?" pondered Cassie.

"It must be him," said Thomas. "But remember Leshii is a trickster. We can't believe anything he says."

After another couple of miles, they reached a field swaying with huge stalks of golden corn and dotted with giant red poppies, their dusty heads bobbing lightly in the breeze.

Cassie gazed at the golden field flecked with red. She felt her stomach lurch. They were about to enter the lair of the Baba Yaga and face trials unknown. But it would bring them closer to rescuing the babies. She pictured the innocent open faces of the twins, Lorcan's big smile and the pretty face of the tiny Tatiana framed by her lick of dark hair. Was anybody caring for them? Did anyone know that Mattie like to be tickled under his chin and Matilda on her tummy? Or that Lorcan could hurl himself into the air and land on his bottom? Would anybody hold Tatiana tight and soothe her to sleep? The thought of any harm coming to them was too distressing and strengthened her resolve. Gathering all their courage, the Chingles entered the corn-field.

CHAPTER 10

A s the moon rose, the Chingles tried to settle in the field of corn to sleep. The cornfield was a thicket of stalks with the swaying ears of corn stretching far above, growing in their light green husks with silken tassels. Here and there were giant poppies with spiky serrated leaves and stems of bluish green. The giant scarlet poppy heads seemed too heavy for their delicate stems. Even though the long fibrous leaves on the corn stalks were ticklish, the giant poppies exuded a powerful aroma that made the children feel languorous and listless. The dusty pollen made Cassie sneeze.

Their limbs felt heavy as they curled up together. As they drifted into sleep, a wind caressed the field. Then it gathered force, cleaving through the corn like a giant broom. A current of air nudged them in their nest. At first it was almost pleasant, like a gentle kiss. But as it gathered force it began to feel like being caught in the crosswinds of a gale.

"It's the Baba Yaga!" squealed Cassie.

"What do we do?" cried Thomas.

"Nothing," said Cassie, her fear mounting. "We have to let her capture us."

Nancy gripped her stomach. "She's up there!" She pointed towards the sky as the moon peeped from behind a bank of clouds.

Terrified they watched as a spirit flew across the star-seared sky. The giant form of a bony old woman with a huge nose, flying in a kind of basin, loomed over them. Behind her she swept the field with a giant brush, beating it with large angry strokes.

The corn was bent flat to the will of the wind. Above, the sky darkened as deepest night fell and stars winked out in the sky. As the brush approached nearer, the children were battered and tumbled forward. But then it withdrew and they were left, breathless and covered in chaff, fifty metres from where they'd slept.

The Baba Yaga flew straight at them and a terrible laughter pierced their eardrums. They heard the swish of beaten corn, the steady beat of her brushstrokes. The basin passed over their heads. The Chingles tied their kerchiefs around their faces and locked their arms tight.

"Good luck!" shouted Thomas as the giant brush advanced towards them.

They were swept up in an instant and brushed out of the cornfield by the rough giant bristles. The force of the brushing pushed them all apart. They were roughly shoved among ears of corn, the scarlet petals of poppies, chaff and dust raked up by the Baba Yaga's giant brush. It was as if they were so much fluff in a tumble-drier. Their stomachs flipped as they were rolled across the earth. A stink worse than a thousand pigsties filled their nostrils. All of their senses cried out to resist but they knew they must succumb to her terrible force if they were ever to see the babies again. All night they were tossed and brushed hither and thither and their bodies were black and blue with bruises. They were swept against rocks, tree trunks and prickly bushes. But they never got left behind in the cloud of dust and debris that threatened to choke them.

In the whitening light of dawn, they abruptly came to a stop. Behind them, the field of corn was as it should be, gently rolling in a light wind. They had come to land in an area of harvested stalks, all scratchy and rough. The air was heavy and oppressive and filled with smoke.

Dimly through the murk, they made out shapes even though their eyes streamed and smarted from so much dust. Ahead of them, the landscape was pitted and scarred. There were no proper trees but acres of blackened stumps as if all vegetation had been struck by lightning. A horribly oozy black river flowed sluggishly past the twisted trees. Even the blades of grass were burnt black. Any flowers that remained looked scorched and burned.

Through the burnt forest they made out a quaking shape. It looked like a house with a high fence before it. But they felt dizzy, as the house appeared to be revolving.

"This must be her house," quaked Thomas, suddenly afraid of the ordeal that lay ahead of them. He thought about Ivo and how damaged and fragile he seemed. He had survived his encounter with the Baba Yaga but he had paid a price. Suddenly, Thomas wished he was back home in his bed in Inish Álainn with the security of Connle and Áine and the distracted presence of Jarlath. Or back home with his father and mother living their uneventful life in East Croydon. Even the dreary drudgery of school was preferable to this. The wind howled and the acrid air caught in his throat. There was also a low hum like a growl that buzzed in their ears.

Cassie peered at the building. It seemed to tilt and sway. It was no bigger than a cottage but was tall as if it was perched on something. In fact, it looked rather nice despite its bleak setting, like the gingerbread cottage that tempted Hansel and Gretel in the fairytale. Then she saw the skinny outlines of the chicken's legs. She made out the pimply flesh. It was indeed moving on giant chicken's legs. Somehow the cottage didn't seem so nice after all.

The house was surrounded by a high fence topped with lights that on closer examination was a ring of fire. They approached carefully, their legs like lead, wrapping their cloaks around them. The fence also heaved and moved. As they got closer flames licked out from the fence. They jumped back.

"The fence throws flames when someone approaches," said Thomas. "That's why the landscape is so blackened and scorched."

They tiptoed round, looking for a way in, tying their kerchiefs over their mouths and noses to stop from gagging. There was no gate or entrance that they could make out.

In the grey light of early dawn they got a better look at their surroundings and saw that Jarek the polewik had been right about the raw materials from which the fence was made.

It was constructed out of skeletons! They inched closer. They saw the heads of the skeletons revolve, and then tongues of flames came out of their bony mouths. A smell of rotting flesh hung in the air.

"I'm going to be sick," said Cassie, gripping her stomach.

A voice growled out, so Cassie blew on Ogma's ring.

"What stupid children dare to face us?" said a hard, cruel voice. They realised it was coming from one of the skeletons. "We will bleach your bones before you go too far!" The skeleton blew a flame from its mouth that scorched the ground inches from where they crouched.

"There's no way in," whispered Thomas. "I'm too sore and tired to attempt a salmon leap."

"They would just shoot the flames upwards at us," said Cassie.

"Oh, come in, little children," cried another scratchy voice. "Our mistress likes a tender bone to chew on."

The voice was so screechy they had to cover their ears. They felt frozen to the spot, unsure how to proceed.

"Maybe if we could persuade the other children to come back with us we might be able to storm the citadel," said

Thomas. But he knew this was a bad idea. For a start, there was no way Ivo would let the children leave the camp. The wild children, for all their cunning, had no magical skills. It would be putting them in danger.

"We need water to stop them burning us," said Nancy.

"If only it was that simple," said Cassie. "If only a fire engine would turn up and help douse the flames by attaching a hose to that dirty river!"

Nancy wasn't deterred. Her sister was always pooh-poohing her ideas but sometimes she was right, even if she was little.

"From the sky," said Nancy. "If it rained hard enough, the flames would go out."

Cassie just sighed but Thomas looked thoughtful.

"She's right, you know," said Thomas. "Leshii made it rain so hard in the forest we could barely stand and tree boughs came crashing down."

"It's too dangerous to get involved with Leshii again. The price of asking a favour of him is your soul," Cassie said.

Nancy felt something stir in her pocket. She put her hand in and felt the little wooden doll Ivo had given her. She took it out and held it in both hands, looking at its painted smiling face framed by black spiral-shaped curls peeping out from under its red headscarf. She liked its cheerful yellow cloak and its orange flower. It was only a small object but it felt solid and reassuring.

She balanced it on the palm of her hand. "What should I do, Vasalisa?" she asked it earnestly.

The little doll spoke in a high, musical voice.

Startled, Cassie blew on Ogma's ring. "Ask her again, Nancy," she said.

"What should I do, Vasalisa?" repeated Nancy.

"Little ones must pick Perun's flower," said the doll.

"Then it will rain at your appointed hour."

"So where can we find it?" asked Thomas.

"Not far, little one, not far,

You seek the fiery bloom shaped like a star."

"Which way?" asked Thomas.

But the doll said nothing.

Nancy put it back in her pocket. Then she felt the doll nudge her. "She's telling me the way!" she cried. "She's guiding me!"

Vasalisa led them away from the house of the Baba Yaga towards a stand of blasted trees by the black oozing river, nudging Nancy in the right direction. The trees looked diseased with black spotted foliage and gnarled branches like twisted limbs. Scarlet toadstools with orange spots grew from the slimy, rotting forest floor. Lightning had split many trees and decaying branches lay on the ground.

"I don't like the feel of this place," said Thomas with a shiver. "I bet the Eretsuns are about." Just as he spoke, he thought he saw a bony arm shoot down from an overhead tree and almost grab him from the side. But it was only a low-lying branch stirred by the wind.

Bizarrely it was almost dusk, though it was hard to tell

in this ruined landscape. Perhaps it existed in a perpetual gloom or a whole day had been swallowed. As the light extinguished in the sky, the trees took on more ominous and frightening shapes.

Nancy took out the little doll.

"Tonight at midnight the Osmunda fern will flower.

It's golden red in colour and has magical powers.

It can summon rain or sun for the space of one day,

But the demons will want it for their own evil play."

"So how do we get it?" interrupted Thomas.

"You must do what I say

To harvest the plant without delay."

A heavy hailstorm broke from the sky, strafing them with hailstones the size of golf balls. They held their cloaks tightly about them but had to take shelter under the rotten trees. The vegetation was sparse overhead and they ended up soaking wet and bruised from the vicious hail. Beneath them the ground was muddy and made a kissing sound and retained the shape of their feet when they pulled them up. They felt miserable, wet and cold not to mention scratched and sore. Their stomachs felt hollow and they realised they were very, very hungry.

"You must gather birch strong and stern

And make a circle around the fern," said the doll.

"Speak to no spirit, no matter what they say.

Now you must wait. Don't speak or sway."

"How are we going to find birch twigs and branches in this horrible place?" wailed Cassie through chattering teeth.

Her hair was sopping wet and rivulets of water ran down her face.

The doll moved in Nancy's pocket and she signalled to them to follow her. They walked several paces in the deepening gloom. There was barely any visibility. But at the edge of a tiny clearing, miraculously they found a bundle of silvery birch twigs and branches. And nearby in the centre of the clearing, poking its head through the rotting leaves of the forest floor, they saw the pale green frond of a fern, like a small clenched fist.

Quickly, they made a circle of birch twigs around the fern as instructed by the doll.

They stood inside the circle of birch branches and twigs surrounding the unfurling Osmunda fern in the blasted forest, battered by wind and rain. As night fell, it was truly hard to stand stock still for such a long time and not speak to each other. Cassie wanted nothing more than to chat to her brother and sister. Thomas thought he'd die if he didn't sit down. Nancy longed to curl up in the branches of a tree and fall asleep. But they held their ground and stood solid as statues. As time wore on, Cassie felt more and more sceptical about the tasks that were being set for them. Nothing made sense. The Baba Yaga was supposed to kidnap lost children but even though she had swept them in her path, she hadn't captured them. Nor could they get past her fiery fence of skulls. Maybe it was because of Leshii, she thought. He's warned the Baba Yaga and she doesn't want us near the babies.

As the half-moon rose and the night thickened, the ravaged limbs of the trees made frightening silhouettes. The moon rose over the clearing. Close to midnight the frenzy started. Pearly moonlight filled the sky with soft light and at first it seemed the forest swayed and danced. Then they heard a wrenching, heaving sound as if trees were being uprooted. There was the warm, earthy smell of freshly disturbed soil. Thomas blinked and realised the trees were pulling themselves up by their roots and moving about. The children were used to the kindly trees of the Sacred Grove but these damaged and diseased trees were hostile and frightening. They bore down on them in a sinister manner, scraping their necks with their boughs, but they didn't cross the circle.

As time wore on, a thick fog filled the forest. It was cold and clammy.

And then creepy, disturbing shapes began to emerge out of the fog and push up against the circle of birch. But the branches seemed to have formed a protective barrier.

Angry, distorted shadowy figures with fangs and claws pushed in. Moonbeams illuminated the clearing and the threatening shapes became more solid. It felt like hundreds were pressing in on them. Demons, thought Cassie. Her blood ran cold. The menacing shapes began to caper and shout, tempting them.

"Cassie!" a hideous voice called out.

"Thomas!" leered another.

"Nancy!" screamed a third.

But the children said nothing, warned by the little doll not to speak to the spirits.

Thomas suddenly buckled at his knees but managed to stop himself falling.

Cassie sensed he was rattled. But she couldn't see what he was seeing. She looked at Nancy who shrugged. She couldn't make out what it was either. They are going to tempt us all in turn, Cassie thought.

Thomas was transfixed by a horrible two-headed monster that rose before him – one head that of a huge fox and the other a bear slavering at the mouth. They began to shout and bawl. Thomas stared urgently at the pocket where Cassie kept Ogma's ring and she realised he wanted her to blow on it. She managed to do it without moving about too much.

"Thirsty are we, little man?" the fox head leered, holding out a drink.

"Worried about your little brother and sister?" said the bear head. "I can give you what you want if you give the flower to me when you pluck it."

To Thomas's amazement, in the next instant the bear/fox creature held a twin in each giant paw. The babies both whimpered softly. Then Mattie woke up and looked at him with his big brown eyes, beseeching him to come to the rescue. Thomas immediately sprang towards the creature but Nancy grabbed his arm. She shook her head vigorously in warning. Thomas hesitated. It must be a trick, like the doll said. He halted at the barrier. The two-headed demon moved closer and slavered in his face.

"Last chance," growled the bear head while the fox barked loudly.

Thomas stood stock still, paralysed, every fibre in his being fighting his natural instinct to snatch the twins.

The fox head let out a terrifying whoop and bent down and bit off Matilda's head. Then the bear head took Mattie in his slavering jaws and swallowed him in one gulp. Thomas wanted to scream in agony. He had failed. He was about to jump out but both Cassie and Nancy restrained him.

"It's a trick," Cassie mouthed.

Thomas shook and wept silently. It was almost too much to deal with.

"Cassie!" a dark voice hissed. "Want to play?"

Cassie watched in terror as a reptilian demon with fangs and horns tossed a small bundle in the air to another demon with a green body covered in scales. It too held a large bundle that it tossed in the air. The bundle screamed out as it was thrown too high. It was Lorcan. In a ray of moonlight she saw the other baby was little Tatiana. The tiny baby screamed as she was flung in the air and caught roughly in the beast's slobbering jaws.

Cassie closed her eyes tightly. It's an illusion, she told herself inwardly. These are not the real children. She heard the screech of the babies so cruelly tossed.

"Mama!" she heard Lorcan cry out.

Despite herself she opened her eyes. The demons were laughing hideously as they threw the babies to each other,

215

pretending to drop them and catching them roughly. Cassie willed time to move on and their ordeal to come to an end. She glanced down. The fern was getting bigger, increasing frond by frond.

Nancy put her hand in her pocket and gripped the little doll.

Just then a nymph, as tall, thin and stately as a stalk of waving corn, approached the edge of the circle. Her white cloak billowed around her. In her arms, she awkwardly jostled four babies.

"Won't you come and help me mind the babies," she crooned to Nancy. "I am so busy with them all!"

The little doll stirred vigorously in Nancy's pocket.

No, Nancy thought. I have to trust the doll.

"Please help!" the spirit woman pleaded as she wavered. "My arms are so heavy I am going to drop one."

Nancy clenched her fists and screwed her eyes shut.

"Quick," pleaded the spirit. "I'm going to drop them, now!"

Nancy's eyes shot open when she heard babies screaming in fear. She took a step closer to the edge of the circle.

The little doll positively jumped up and down in her pocket. Cassie saw Nancy's stricken face and held out her hand. Her little sister gripped it tightly.

For what felt like hours, the demons and the moving malevolent trees pranced about, laughing viciously. It felt like their ordeal was never going to end. Just as they were about to give up hope, a golden light sprang from the fern. They saw the radiance was coming from the fern head, gently unfurling to reveal a golden-russet spiked flower like an exotic star. It was beautiful and glowed with new life and beauty.

Immediately Nancy sprang forward and seized it. It throbbed with a red-gold light. Instantly the woods grew silent, the fog dispersed and the horrible shapes of the demons disappeared.

"*To Perun, you must offer the flower,*" said the doll to Nancy, "*But keep one petal for another hour.*"

Nancy plucked a red-gold petal from the bloom and put it in her pocket. Above, a large being appeared in the sky. It was a god with a silver head and a golden beard.

"I am Perun," he said. "I grant you one wish of rain and thunder."

"Please rain on the Baba Yaga's fence," begged Nancy. "But not until we reach it." She held the glowing flower, minus one petal, up to the god.

Perun nodded his great head. Immediately the flower exploded into sparks and flew into the air. The little doll nudged Nancy and they ran from the forest, the god hovering overhead.

Once more they confronted the fiery skulls on the Baba Yaga's fence but this time, as the flames licked out, Perun in the sky above howled back, unleashing thunderbolts and lightning and a crashing rainstorm. The lightning struck the fence. It was like a fireworks display. For a moment the fence burned and whizzed like a Ferris wheel at a fun fair, dazzling colours rising into the sky. The skulls and bones fizzed and crackled.

"Welcome to your doom!" shrieked one on the left, flames licking from its rictus grin.

"Death waits for you!" screeched a cracked skull on the right, through stumps of teeth.

Then the rain crashed down on the fence. Shards of bone exploded through the air as if cleaved by an axe. In minutes the fence was dashed to smithereens, leaving just fragments of bones here and there. The house was no longer moving around on its chicken legs.

"The doll was right," Nancy said happily and led her brother and sister up to the front door.

It was a forbidding sight. The keyhole was a mouth filled with sharp teeth. The knocker was a blackened skeletal hand. The keyhole snarled as they approached but to their surprise the door sprung open.

They ventured inside, gagging with every step, their way illuminated with candles glowing in blackened skulls. There was a powerful, sickening smell of boiled cabbage and an intensified reek of pigsties. The floor felt tacky and greasy underfoot. Every surface was covered with a layer of grime so thick it was impossible to work out what kind of furniture was in the house.

They walked through a corridor towards the back of the

cottage where a boiling, bubbling noise compelled their attention.

They pushed open the door. They could hardly see for the steam that poured out at them. They glimpsed several large blackened pots boiling away on hissing fires. Once more the same grease and grime covered everything. The foul stench of rotting vegetables filled the air. Their breath became ragged in their throats. Horrible blowflies gathered on discarded bones and rotting meat at their feet. Maggots squirmed from cows' and pigs' heads. Cassie thought she would faint in the steam and stench.

Then the steam cleared a little and they saw her. Tending the pots with a giant ladle was the huge and hideous old woman who had flown in the basin, quite the ugliest they'd ever seen. Her face was a mass of wrinkles and warts. Her nose was long and hooked and so sharp it seemed to be made of iron. Her tangled grey hair hung down her back. She clutched the ladle in her gnarled hands and licked her black lips when she saw the children. Cassie blew on Ogma's ring.

"Fresh meat, my pretties, who's first for my pot?" she slavered. A slick of saliva hung from her slack jaw. "I am very hungry," she belched. Her greedy eyes popped in her head and a bony hand shot out, grabbing Nancy by the neck. The children screamed as she dangled Nancy over the pot.

"No, please!" pleaded Cassie. "Please don't harm her!"

Nancy clutched the little doll in her pocket. As the

Baba Yaga lowered her towards the heaving, churning pot the little doll moved and inspired her. Even though she was almost choking in the steam, she managed to speak.

"Please let us help you!" said Nancy. "We will do whatever you want!"

Abruptly the Baba Yaga flung Nancy to the floor and seized Thomas around the waist. She held him in front of a fireplace where they could see a roasting spit and a roaring fire.

"A bit skinny but more tasty if roasted," she said, licking her blackened lips. To Thomas's horror, she sniffed him hungrily. Aghast, she dropped him to the floor. "You smell of nicey-nicey ways, kind and caring," she spat. "I cannot abide that in my house."

Whipping out her other hand, she snatched Cassie by the leg and dangled her so close to a boiling pot that the bottom of Cassie's hair dipped inside and was coated with a gluey, slimy green liquid that singed the bottom of it. Cassie's stomach heaved.

"Please let her go!" Nancy said. "We will do whatever you want!"

The Baba Yaga dropped Cassie, as if she was the one who had burnt her. The horrible hag-witch shuddered.

"There is something about you children I don't like," she said. "Too goody-goody. I will release you if you stay and work for me for two days and nights. If you carry out my wishes, I will grant you one wish and let you go."

The children nodded their heads vigorously.

The Baba Yaga leered at them. "Ha, ha," she said going out the door. "Clean my house by daybreak. Lickety-split!" She laughed hideously and was gone.

The slam of the door echoed through the small building.

In the glowing light of the burning fires in the kitchen, the children looked at each other in despair.

"Where do we even start?" said Cassie, desperately trying to get up from the filthy floor but feeling she was being sucked down. The floor was very uneven and spongy underfoot. She peered down realising she'd disturbed something. She felt something slither up her leg. It was impossible to see the real floor as it was covered in a layer of writhing insects. She jumped up and down in repugnance and tried to push away the horrible slimy things that were burrowing into her flesh. She lifted her hand and maggots clung to it. She thrashed around, causing Thomas and Nancy to do likewise.

"I'm going to be sick," shuddered Cassie, who hated anything crawly and slimy coming near her. She jumped up on a half-rotten stool.

"Try not to think about them," said Thomas through gritted teeth. "Look on the bright side – we have a licence to search the house for any trace of the babies."

Cassie calmed down. "We'll never get it all done by dawn," she said. And I hope we don't make a grim discovery, she thought, but said nothing. Gritting her teeth she jumped down from the stool, careful to land light on her feet, and began to search the kitchen with Thomas and Nancy. She peered into bubbling pots and poked through the horrible floor with a ladle made out of arm-bones and a skeletal fist with the fingers torn off. Thomas armed himself with a stirring stick that was a long shin bone and rooted around the tables that heaved with rotting heads and maggoty meat but to his relief they all seemed to be of animal origin. Nancy peered into crevices and corners and saw all kinds of wriggling beasties and slithering creatures. But there was no sign of any babies and to their great relief no evidence of baby skeletal remains. They waded through the churning floor and looked behind a tattered curtain to what they supposed was the Baba Yaga's bedroom. This consisted of a bed of rotting wood covered in rags so tattered they resembled a swarm of flies. Cassie touched the bed and a dense cloud of nasty bluebottles rose up! The bed was covered in crawling and flapping insects and wriggling black larvae. But there was still no evidence of the babies. They bolted as quickly as they could from the room.

Now all they had to do was tackle the worst cleaning job ever devised.

"I hate evil monsters and witches," sighed Thomas. "But cleaning and housework comes a close second." He looked at the ceiling that was mired in some icky, rotting substance and back at the floor where millions of insects crawled and burrowed into a layer of something like compost or manure.

Cassie scratched around the kitchen and found some filthy rags in a corner. Thomas came across a bucket of water, but it was the black, oozing substance from the river they'd passed and was more like oil than water. Everything they touched was covered in about fifty layers of slime and grime.

"It's hopeless," said Thomas, coughing in the steamy fug of the dirtiest, most unhygienic kitchen the world had ever seen.

"I don't know where to begin," said Cassie.

"Oh, I hate to think of poor little Mattie and Tilda, Lorcan and tiny Tatiana being in this hovel!" cried Thomas in despair.

They realised that every surface moved and quivered with squirming, buzzing insects. That was the low growling sound they'd heard from outside.

Nancy felt the little doll stir in her pocket, so she took her out.

"What do you think we should do, Vasalisa?" asked Nancy, her eyes streaming from the steam and rotting smell.

The doll brightly jumped from Nancy's hand.

"*Let me help you clean the rot,*" she smiled.

"*Soon we'll have it all spit spot.*"

She skipped over the cleaning rags that they held. Thomas's was transformed into a sweeping brush, Cassie's into a feather duster and Nancy's into a sparkling cloth.

"*The tools will only do your bidding*
   If every child is very willing," the little doll said brightly.

Thomas suddenly laughed and so did Cassie.

"This is like some stupid TV commercial to get you to buy cleaning products," she sniggered.

223

"Worried about your kitchen? Scared the Baba Yaga might eat you?" piped up Thomas, imitating the voiceovers of adverts. "Try Little Doll's magic cleaning product for a miracle clean!"

Both Cassie and Nancy joined in, miming to his voiceover as if they were housewives from the 1950s.

Heartened, the children set to work. Miraculously, Thomas found that his sweeping brush did indeed sweep all before it. Cassie opened the windows and began to dust the filthy surfaces. To her amazement, the swarms of insects rose in a black cloud and buzzed out the windows. Nancy followed in Cassie's wake and wiped everything that she had dusted. To her surprise, tables and chairs emerged gleaming and shiny.

Thomas burned all the accumulated rubbish in the grate.

As the night reached its darkest hour, the only grimy things left in the house were the children, who had become blackened and dirty through their efforts. They slumped on the floor and stared blankly ahead, beyond exhaustion, too tired to talk or sleep.

The Chingles felt a sneaking pride as they heard the Baba Yaga's thunderous footsteps return at dawn, even though they were disappointed not to have found one single clue to the babies' whereabouts.

She barged into the house, breathing her sulphurous breath and carrying a steaming bag of bones. Her nose twitched as she entered the kitchen. She looked around as the early morning sun illuminated the sparkling kitchen.

"What is that horrid smell?" she gasped, flailing round the room, running her hands over the sparkling surfaces and recoiling as if burned. "It's fresh air," she said with horror and banged shut the windows.

She tore open the newly cleaned curtain to her bedroom and stopped as if struck by lightning.

"Why is there no buzzing sound to help me go asleep?" she cried angrily. "My bed is white: its brightness hurts my eyes." She staggered out of the room, horrified at the cleanliness and order in her household. She gazed down at the floor with distaste, gnawing on one of her bones, the origins of which the children had no wish to speculate on.

Her face crumpled in disappointment as her feet stamped about the immaculate floor. She threw herself on the ground and banged it in a passionate temper tantrum, spitting and seething like a wild animal.

Then she jumped to her feet. "You have succeeded!" she shouted in a fury.

Then she bent down towards them and brought her horrible warty nose close to their faces, spittle flying from her mouth and overpowering them with the noxious fumes of her breath.

The children staggered back, overcome and exhausted from their night's exertions. They felt giddy and fragile from lack of food and sleep.

"Ah," breathed the Baba Yaga with a cunning and wicked gleam, "but you didn't know I have an upstairs!"

"But it's just a cottage," protested Thomas. "You don't

have an upstairs." The Baba Yaga fixed him with an evil glint in her eye. "I do now," she said, laughing hideously.

Cassie inwardly groaned as she led them to a corner of the room. Thomas's legs buckled under him as the Baba Yaga pushed open a door they hadn't noticed before. All at once, an avalanche of dust cannoned down a stairway and enveloped them, dirtying again the newly cleaned kitchen. The children, wracked with coughs, wiped the dust from their eyes and watched in dismay as all their work was undone in one fell swoop.

"I am going to sleep now," called the Baba Yaga, laughing. "When I awake, all must be clean and ready. And no going upstairs before you clean up the kitchen, mind. I like things done in their proper order. And I will wake up immediately if you disobey me!" She laughed so hard she coughed and spluttered herself.

As soon as she was gone off behind her curtain, Nancy fetched out the little doll.

"It's no use," said Cassie. "The more we do, the more work she will create."

"Look, we don't even know if we can trust her," said Thomas, clenching his fist in frustration. "I just want to find the babies! Should I risk sneaking upstairs to search? I think I will."

"Noooo!" said Cassie. "You heard what she said! We have to play by her rules, so we have to clean the downstairs first and then we can check. Ivo told us we have to obey her."

"And we have to listen to the doll," Nancy said.

"You're right," said Thomas, "but I must say cleaning is the last thing I expected to have to do as a superhero!"

"Surely you don't think girls like it any better?" scolded Cassie. "What matters is for a hero to do his best no matter what the task is!"

"I guess you're right," said a chastened Thomas. "I'm not going to let her get the better of me."

"Let's ask Vasalisa," Nancy said.

"*If Baba Yaga gives us trouble*

Then our efforts we redouble," said Vasalisa the doll brightly.

She jumped on the brush, the duster and the cleaning cloth and they magically split into two. The children were now armed with a cleaning implement in each hand. The doll jumped on each of their shoulders for added measure and each child was filled with a renewed surge of energy. Even their hunger was banished. They launched themselves into a cleaning frenzy, barely pausing for breath.

But even with two sweeping brushes, Thomas found it harder. A deep sucking sound rose from the floor as the brushes were wrestled from his grasp. Horrified, Thomas saw that a mass of seething giant worms and maggots were crawling all over the brushes. The whole floor was a carpet of writhing, oozing insects a metre deep. The Baba Yaga had done something to make it worse.

Taking a deep breath, Thomas plunged his hands in. He had to force himself to reach down through the sickening slurping, writhing mass to grasp the brushes. Within seconds he himself was covered in a wave of maggots. They crawled into his nostrils, into his mouth. He thought he was going to pass out but managed to scream "Help!"

His sisters ran to his aid. Nancy used her cleaning cloths to beat the insects off him while Cassie brushed him with her dusters and helped him to his feet. Cassie tried to summon in a large intake of air through gritted teeth to perform the Breath Feat and blow away the insects but the air was too thick with buzzing insects for her to manage. Together, they jumped around the kitchen, trying to stamp out the writhing mass with their feet and beating every surface. But each strike caused another wave of horrible flying beasties to take to the air. They felt they were going to drown in the avalanche of nasty creepy-crawlies.

Then the little doll jumped from Nancy's pocket and began to spin, creating a vortex that repelled the insects and maggots. The children saw what she was doing. Thomas tried to open the windows that the Baba Yaga had closed but the pressure of the buzzing flies was too great. He borrowed one of Nancy's cloths, wrapped it around his arm and, summoning all his strength, smashed the glass with his elbow.

The little doll spun around and slowly a line of insects rose and was sucked out the hole in the window. Then Cassie, Thomas and Nancy copied her example and spun on their heels. The vortexes created a counter current, repelling the insects, maggots, blue bottles and worms and with gathering speed they were sucked out the window. Then the force of the insect storm became so great it blew out the glass in the other windows. As the insects were expelled, they made a noise like a low scream. The air was thick and black and the children spun for what seemed like hours. But finally the air grew clear and the buzzing, screeching noise stopped.

The children stopped spinning and sat down on the clean floor in a daze.

"Now all we have to do is fix the windows," Thomas said wryly.

But Nancy and the little doll had already thought of that. As Nancy flicked her cloths, the little doll blew from her little painted mouth and, magically, the glass was restored.

They all looked around, amazed to see that the kitchen was returned to its clean state.

But with dismay they realised it was almost evening and they still hadn't gone near the upstairs. Gathering their courage, they tackled the staircase.

All seemed ominous and quiet. Nancy faltered on the narrow stairway of high uneven stones, her not-yet-five-year-old legs struggling to climb up. Cassie glanced back at her sister and held out her hand to help her up, which her little sister gratefully accepted. Cassie realised with a jolt just how young Nancy was. They were always forgetting that because of her extraordinary courage and abilities. Gazing at her little sister's sweet face made Cassie think of those other dear little things, Mattie and Matilda. How helpless babies were! And Lorcan and Tatiana – she pictured them smiling and gurgling in their cradles. Lorcan was big for his age and boisterous but he was still a baby and his abundant energy would get him into trouble. Not everyone might have the patience to deal with him, particularly not an evil warlord like Vladimir. He was happy to torture people over a few trifling debts. What chance did a baby have? And poor little Tatiana. She was only a few months old. How would she survive without her mother's milk? A tear came to Cassie's eye at the very thought of it.

As if reading her mind, Nancy gripped her hand tightly before letting it go and taking the doll from her pocket for a moment. "We are going to find them," she said earnestly.

Cassie wiped the tear away. "Of course we are!" she exclaimed brightly, with more certainty than she felt.

Thomas had reached the door at the top of the stairway. He tried pushing it but it felt like someone or something was leaning against it on the other side.

"Come on, give us a hand!" he called to his sisters.

They all put their shoulders to the door and opened it a crack.

Thomas peered in but could see nothing except a wall of blackness. Then the blackness began to crumble and tumble through the door. They were looking into a wall of dust.

The trickle of dust soon became a landslide that tore the door from its hinges. They clung to the stairwell, managing to lodge their toes and hands in cracks in the stonework. But the torrent of dirt made them choke and splutter. They managed to hold on and soon the stream of dust came to an end. In despair they realised the kitchen was now full of dust again. "The kitchen!" groaned Thomas. "The Baba Yaga said we had to clean it first."

"Technically, we have obeyed her by doing it already," spluttered Cassie. "And we've got to search upstairs for the babies before the Baba Yaga wakes up and we can't do it at all!"

"Right. Let's do the upstairs now and deal with the kitchen later."

The air was still thick with dust and they could hardly see their way through it. They could barely breathe. Gradually the air cleared a little and they were hugely disheartened to see a corridor with several rooms off it. The rooms were cramped, filled with yet more dust and the accumulated filth of centuries. They conducted a quick search but there was no sign of any babies whatsoever or traces that they were ever there.

Cassie sneezed uncontrollably until the little doll jumped from Nancy's pocket and touched her nose.

"It's horrible," Nancy said. They felt they were going to suffocate in the dust and set about the task with heavy hearts.

"*Spit spot, spit spot!*" said the doll.

"*We will soon clean out the lot.*"

A bucket of clean water and a scrubbing brush appeared

out of nowhere. Even though his legs felt heavy with tiredness as if filled with a sack of nails, Thomas got down on his hands and knees and started scrubbing. Nancy went around the room and with a cloth in each hand set to scouring walls and furniture. She worked fast, aided by the little doll in her pocket.

Armed with her two dusters, Cassie went into the next room. She climbed up some horrible knobbly furniture to reach the ceiling where giant cobwebs, heavy with dust and dirt, hung like hammocks from the ceiling. She ran her dusters across them but they were as strong as if woven from steel. After several attempts to dislodge them, she dropped the dusters and jumped onto a web, determined to dislodge it with her body weight. But as she dangled above the floor, the dust in the room started to form into a mass, taking on a ghoulish shape. It was some kind of fiend made of dust.

An angry sawing sound rose from the shape that spun like a dervish. It came towards her and soon she was gazing into its angry eyes. It lurched from side to side and threatened to engulf her. She tried to let go but the cobweb held her in its gluey, sticky grasp. Fighting back her disgust, she forced herself to perform the Breath Feat; it was her only chance to repel the dust devil. She swallowed mouthfuls of dead fly, moths' wings and other unknown pieces of debris and dirt. Trying not to gag, she summoned her strength and blew it all out again in a stream in her hot breath.

The dust devil sizzled and subsided on contact but then

came back, twice the size. Cassie continued to blow, despite almost blacking out with the effort. She writhed and wriggled to escape the cobweb and struck out against the dust devil with her foot. But it split in two and become two dust devils.

The hissing, snarling noise alerted Nancy and Thomas, who ran into the room. Thomas immediately jumped up and bashed the cobwebs with his brush and Cassie was released from their sticky grasp. Her body weight dislodged a giant cobweb that fell onto the dust devil like a blanket, trapping it beneath. Nancy took the doll from her pocket and it sprang from her hand and hopped around the web, releasing points of light. This shrivelled the web and the dust devils down to a manageable size that Nancy flicked away with her cloth.

"All done!" said Nancy brightly.

"If we could find out the secrets of these cleaning materials, we'd make a fortune," said Thomas. "Think of all those dumb adverts on TV. We'd clean up!"

It wasn't a particularly good pun but for some reason it made Cassie and Nancy laugh very hard. Their laughter was infectious and soon they were all in hysterics. Even the little doll laughed until tears were squeezed from her painted wooden eyes.

When they finally stopped laughing, they felt renewed and ploughed on through the many rooms.

After what seemed like days, they finally came to the end of the corridor where to their horror they realised there was a small door hidden under the dirt. They dragged open the door and saw that there was a rickety staircase leading up to the attic under the eaves of the roof.

Conscious of the time, Cassie suggested that Nancy, Thomas and the doll tackle the attic on their own while she went back downstairs to clean the kitchen.

"All the dirt that cascaded down the stairs when we opened the door is still waiting for us," she groaned.

But the little doll shook in Nancy's pocket and Nancy told Thomas to join Cassie, that the little doll wanted her to go to the attic alone. They reluctantly consented and with a pang left their little sister to face whatever was in the room all by herself.

Nancy pushed the door open carefully and tiptoed into the room. The first thing that hit her was the stench of rotting vegetables. The room must have been some sort of storeroom. All around it, split and torn sacks spilled their rancid contents to the floor: mouldy grain, flour crawling with beetles, sticky sugar, damp salt. The whole place was a mess and reeked with a nauseating stench. Nancy tied her kerchief around her mouth.

Nancy moved closer to one of the sacks, unsure what to do. She thought the Baba Yaga probably liked her food half-rotten, so she decided to refill the sacks. But as she approached the first sack's mouth she fell back with a shudder. For the sack was moving!

It heaved and breathed as if it was a living thing. There was something horrible about it that made Nancy's stomach lurch and her throat constrict. But she was used to facing horrors, so she took a deep breath and gave the sack a shove with her foot. It fell over and spilled its contents to the floor, including hundreds of writhing, screeching rats!

They scurried frantically around and their high-pitched squealing alerted all the other rats in the room to a human presence. Soon there were thousands, squealing and tumbling over each other.

"Wait!" squeaked Nancy in a range on the edge of ultrasound, inaudible to a human. "I mean you no harm!"

But this only caused further disarray. The rats ran in every direction, their whiskers twitching and brushing.

"*Get her!*" she heard one scream.

Suddenly a horde of rats formed themselves into a writhing mass and prepared to throw themselves at Nancy. She saw with terror they meant to overpower her. She glimpsed a thousand little mouths snarling at her and little beady eyes fixing her with murderous intent. She froze, unable to run for it as she was surrounded. Frantically, she grabbed the little doll from her pocket and held it above her head.

In an instant the rats ran up her legs and body, piercing her clothing and clinging to her with their sharp little claws, their high-pitched squeals numbing her. She felt a thousand nips as sharp little teeth pierced her skin, and her flesh was lacerated with a million tiny lashes from their thrashing tails. They reached her neck in a flash and were about to bite into it when the doll let out a high-pitched scream, barely audible to a human. But the rats heard it.

As if suddenly electrocuted, they fell away from Nancy's body and ran headlong towards the door. The room was filled with their panic. Seeing an alcove, Nancy jumped into it and watched as a million rats made a run for it, driven mad by the scream of the doll.

Down the corridor they tumbled, a stream of rats, heading for the stairs.

In the kitchen, Cassie and Thomas stood overwhelmed by the filthy mess caused by the avalanche of dust from upstairs. But then they heard the stampede above their heads. The noise grew into a loud rumble combined with a cacophony of high-pitched squeals that nearly made their ears bleed. Then they heard a rush of sound on the stairs.

"Quick!" shouted Thomas, pointing to a mantelpiece near the ceiling just above the fireplace. They held hands and salmon-leaped together, clearing the ground just before the first wave of rats launched themselves at the newly restored windows.

The combined force of so many small bodies pushed the glass out. Cassie and Thomas watched in amazement as a river of rats ran in a torrent through the kitchen, driven outside by some unseen, powerful source.

Nancy must be doing something to cause this, Thomas thought. But both of them worried for her safety. They felt bad about leaving her to deal with the final room on her own, even though the doll had insisted.

"The doll must have known that Nancy would be better at this task alone," said Thomas, voicing both their thoughts.

The house quaked and shuddered and Cassie and Thomas realised it was jumping around on its chicken legs. It tipped to one side, dislodging the rats even quicker. Cassie and Thomas just about hung on to the mantelpiece.

Then as suddenly as the tumult had begun, it stopped. The kitchen was cleared and there wasn't a rat to be seen.

Cassie and Thomas surveyed the damage. But the avalanche of rats had also cleared away the layers of dust and dirt and, apart from the broken windows, the kitchen was spick and span once more. Miraculously the pots were all sparkling clean and continued to bubble on the fires.

Seconds after, Nancy appeared, weak but smiling, through the few remaining motes of dust that were caught in the beam of the sun streaming through the broken window. Her clothes were ragged and she was covered in tiny little bites and grazes all over her body. But she was alive.

Cassie ran towards her little sister and threw her arms around her. "You're safe!" she exclaimed.

"Don't say you doubted Nancy!" Thomas joshed as the little doll leapt from her pocket and repaired the windows.

"Now I must heal Nancy's bites," sang the doll.

"With my magic points of light."

She jumped around Nancy, beaming a point of light onto her many bites and grazes. Soon Nancy's cuts were healed.

"I'm glad we're all together here now," said Cassie. "I don't like it when we are split up."

237

"So why are you going to split us up by going to Tír na nÓg?" Thomas said.

Cassie looked away. Thomas let it drop. He didn't know why he had brought that thorny subject up at that particular point.

But the sound of snoring like an oncoming train, which had been rumbling behind the curtain, suddenly stopped. They heard groaning, creaking sounds as the Baba Yaga rose from her bed.

"Finished your work?" the Baba Yaga growled, leering at them as she ambled into the kitchen. She sniffed the air and regarded the clean kitchen with distaste. Then she went up the stairs to check their work. She returned to the kitchen with a strange expression on her face.

"You got rid of the rats," she growled. They couldn't tell if she was happy or sad.

"We have once more done your bidding," said Cassie. "Now it's your turn to honour your side of the bargain."

The Baba Yaga shrugged her crooked shoulders and let out a low grumble.

"I have no choice but to aid the pure of heart," she said, disappointed.

"Don't try and trick us," warned Thomas.

The Baba Yaga turned on him and stuck her bony nose in his face.

"Vile boy!" she screeched. "I am not a trickster!"

"Well, give us the four babies you have!" Thomas demanded, leaning back out of her foul breath.

The Baba Yaga raised herself to her full height. "I cannot give you what I haven't got!" she shouted at him.

Thomas looked at his sisters with dismay. For some reason she sounded totally convincing.

"But I don't understand," he shouted, losing his fear. "We were told Vladimir had the babies kidnapped and they were being held by you!"

"They were for a day not so many moons ago," she mused, scratching her hairy chin. "Tasty morsels they were too!"

The children gasped in horror. It was too late. This vile old witch had already eaten the babies! Thomas grabbed a huge frying pan. Cassie took hold of a large spoon. They were about to lunge at the Baba Yaga when the little doll let out a screech, stopping them all in their tracks. Cassie and Thomas dropped their weapons.

The Baba Yaga spoke again.

"But this was just a temporary hiding place. Vladimir has taken them away. Maybe he was afraid I would eat them."

"Are they still alive?" asked Cassie as she got a grip on herself, her brain clouded with images of the babies' faces.

The Baba Yaga shrugged and growled. "They were when I last saw them. I do not know what Vladimir might have done since."

"You must tell us where they are!" said Thomas. "You promised."

The Baba Yaga laughed. "Why should I?"

The little doll piped up from Nancy's pocket: "You are bound to aid the pure of heart."

The Baba Yaga growled and sighed and led them towards another small door in the house they'd failed to notice before. She opened it and they saw it led down to a basement deep in the bowels of the earth. They realised the house was no longer revolving on its chicken legs but had settled down on the earth.

"You can't expect us to clean underground cellars as well," complained Thomas.

The Baba Yaga laughed, a hideous wheezing sound that was more frightening than her roar. "Underground," she said, pointing with her bony finger. "Vladimir has taken them to a fortress underground. They are probably dead already. And you will be too. The fortress is guarded by an army of the Undead."

Before the children could do or say another thing, the Baba Yaga roughly nudged them down the stairs with her bony fingers. Just before she slammed the door shut, Thomas stuck his foot in it.

"You must give us a light," he demanded.

Laughing, the Baba Yaga thrust a stick at him with a lighted flame in a skull at its top.

Cassie shuddered, already feeling claustrophobic.

Then the door slammed behind them and they were on their own.

CHAPTER 11

Thomas held the hideous skull lantern of the Baba Yaga aloft, the flame darting from behind its grinning mouth like a fiery tongue. As far as light spilled, they saw steps descending into the deepest pit of the earth. They walked down the stone steps with heavy hearts.

"I'd really hoped we'd found the babies," said Cassie despondently, her voice echoing in the gloom. "I don't think my nerves can bear it any more. I'm so worried about them – they are so little and defenceless."

"Lorcan's not little. He's nearly as big as I am," said Nancy. "But he's much littler than a vampire man."

"At least we think they're still alive," said Thomas, trying to lift his sisters' mood. "Look, let's just concentrate on finding them."

They trudged down the stairs but Cassie's worried thoughts kept eating away at her.

"I wonder if Vladimir has worked out which baby is

Tatiana. I hope he's not conducting gruesome experiments," she said out of the blue, unable to keep quiet about what was on her mind. "Maybe he thinks he can somehow, I don't know, extract supernatural power from her. The obvious thing would be to drink her blood . . ." She shuddered and Thomas turned on her.

"Look, this kind of conversation isn't helpful!" he said, alarmed.

Cassie heard the panic in his voice and shut up.

After hours of walking, their legs were too heavy and they couldn't continue any further. The stone steps seemed to go on forever. The air was dry and oppressive, making breathing difficult. It was eerie the way the deep earth absorbed all sounds and there was no echo of their footfall on the stone steps. After a while they settled down on the cold steps exhausted and fell asleep.

They awoke, startled, to feel hard rain beating down on them. Cassie opened her eyes. It wasn't rain but lumps of soil and stones and they hurt! Like her brother and sister, she tried to shield herself by curling into a ball. Large stones pinged off their skin, denting their flesh. Their instinct was to run or shout out "stop" but they were in strange territory and needed to assess who or what they were up against. It could be Eretsuns!

Finally the stones stopped raining down on them. Thomas saw the stones glinting like glass in the beam of the skull lantern and thought it was some trick of the light. He picked up a handful.

"These aren't stones," he exclaimed in wonder. "They're glass beads!" He held out his hand for his sisters to marvel at the assortment of green, red and glassy stones glistening on his palm.

Cassie looked closely at the stones. She was used to admiring her Nan Nelson's jewellery and often was allowed to play with it. She lifted up a clear glass bead that had a lustrous sheen and bit it. Then she held it up to the light and watched as it flashed fluorescent blue and phosphorescent yellow. It was almost as if there was a fire in the stone.

"That could be a real gemstone," she said in astonishment. "Maybe even an uncut diamond." She picked up another stone about the size of a pebble. It was blood red and shot through with fine lines like silk. "This might be a ruby," she said.

Nancy handed her a luminous green stone.

Cassie examined its radiant green surface. "I think this is an emerald," she marvelled. She compared the stones to the beads on Willa's necklace and they seemed to have similar qualities.

"I remember learning in science that you cannot scratch precious metals with a steel point. It's one of the tests for real gems," she said.

Thomas took off his steel watch and using the corner of the clasp tried to scratch the stones. It didn't leave the tiniest mark on the transparent, green, blue or ruby red stones.

"I would bet these are real diamonds, rubies, sapphires and emeralds," marvelled Cassie.

"Let's gather them all up. We could make a fortune," said Thomas greedily.

But Cassie restrained him. "We are in fairy realms," she said. "They could be enchanted or not real at all. Remember what happened when the leprechauns gave us fairy gold and silver coins on Inish Álainn?"

Thomas dropped the stones. He remembered only too well how they became lumps of coal and ordinary stone.

"Stones of the elements," mused Cassie. "Have these something to do with Vlad's spell?"

Just then they noticed a few pinpricks of light at the bottom of the tunnel and heard the sound of scurrying. Nancy shuddered, worried that she might encounter rats again. But there was a calm feeling in her stomach. They descended the steps cautiously and realised they were nearly at the bottom. They found themselves in a tunnel but a mound of earth that looked like part of the collapsed roof blocked their path.

There was enough space for them to squeeze past the pile of red earth.

"Please be careful! We could be in some disused mineshaft and the tunnel could collapse again on our heads," said Thomas.

They inched forward and felt the smooth surface of the tunnel to their backs. At the end of the tunnel the ground under their feet became stone. Thomas shone the lamp and realised they were now on a walkway carved out of rock that extended over a vast underground cavern. They advanced cautiously, realising they were indeed in some kind of disused mineshaft. Metal ladders extended up and down the cavern's walls. All around it were burrowed-out holes, and piles of stone and earth littered the floor. Strange metal towers that looked like winches stood at intervals and there were chutes and large metal containers like grain silos.

Ahead of them the walkway branched into a network of more tunnels burrowed into the earth. More metal ladders extended from the walkway to the cavern floor. There was no sign of the pinpricks of light. The skull of the Baba Yaga made vast looming shadows in the huge space.

They crept along the walkway, their senses on high alert.

Nancy felt a fluttering in her stomach. "I think there's somebody about," she whispered and pointed a little way ahead to where a ladder joined the walkway.

They heard a scurrying, scraping sound and a clinking like glass bottles. They fell back aghast as a head poked up from the ladder. But it was grinning and seemed friendly.

It was a fat little man with flat features and a sort of soft fur covering his head. He pulled himself up onto the walkway. He looked like a human mole. He carried a lamp of a luminous mineral that seemed to shine with its own light. He began to speak so Cassie blew on Ogma's ring.

"We've found them! The Amber People! The prophecy came true!" exclaimed the man. He waddled towards them and jumped up and down in excitement.

He was followed by another, this one looking like a

woman. They were a bit taller than Nancy and wore extraordinary gemstone-studded clothes shot through with sparkling mica, silver weave and gold threads. They wore many belts of precious stones, which explained the clinking sound. They danced around the skull light, held by Thomas, as if possessed. They were both ecstatic and hugging each other and almost oblivious to the children. Cassie caught a glint from their faces and realised their eyes and teeth were made of precious stones, the man's bright emerald and the woman's ruby.

Finally, they stopped, breathless.

"So you are who exactly?" asked Thomas.

"Dodek and Morecha," said the little fat man. "Oh happy day! Now we will be sung about in stories."

The children were bewildered but said nothing.

The man gestured to them to follow him down the ladder that he'd ascended. Nancy nodded, so there seemed no reason not to trust him.

"Let's try and find out as much as possible before giving anything away," whispered Thomas. "They seem to be expecting us."

"Wouldn't it be easier to just tell the truth?" said Cassie.

"Let's see if we can trust them first," said Thomas. "They think we've been sent in fulfilment of a prophecy and are more likely to help us if they believe we are these Amber People. Then when they know us a bit better they won't be so disappointed that we're not who they think we are. We might even *be* these Amber People!"

"Funny how people keep thinking we've been sent in fulfilment of a prophecy," sighed Cassie. But she did as Thomas asked. He seemed to have a knack with magical and strange folk and after her dismal efforts with Ivo she didn't want to put her foot in it again.

At the bottom of the cavern, Dodek and Morecha led them to a cave.

It was their lair – a hollowed-out crystal cave with a low bed fashioned out of red rubies, chairs of rose quartz and a table of gold and silver inlaid with precious metals. The children gasped. It was like a king's room in a magical kingdom but pride of place seemed to be given to a dried leaf and a piece of bark in a cabinet studded with gemstones.

"You are admiring our treasures," said Morecha gesturing with pride at the mud and dried leaves. "Very rare in our world."

"You have beautiful furniture," said Cassie.

"Oh, these old things!" replied Morecha. "I'm so bored with precious metal. I hear humans have whole houses made out of wood!"

"So, Dodek, how exactly would you like to be sung about?" asked Thomas.

Dodek sang his answer with great confidence. "They will sing that all the Karzeleks had given up hope, enslaved by the Blood Man Vladimir. But Dodek and Morecha waited a thousand years for the return of the Amber People with the gift of light from the Baba Yaga!"

"You've been waiting for us for a thousand years?" asked Thomas in amazement.

"Well, that's a slight exaggeration. It might be a thousand days," admitted Dodek. "But it's a very long time. Down here it's hard to measure time."

"And the Amber People, that's us?" asked Thomas.

Dodek looked at him, puzzled, as if Thomas was a half-wit. "The prophecy was that the Amber People would return with the light of the Baba Yaga in our time of need and here you are. It is a well-known legend among the Karzeleks."

"I've forgotten so much while we've been away, and dealing with the Baba Yaga has affected my mind," said Thomas, trying to look a bit confused. "I've gone so silly, I've nearly forgotten who the Karzeleks are!"

Morecha smiled kindly at him, betraying ruby teeth. "Why, we are all Karzeleks – the miners of the stones of the earth. How could you have forgotten that!"

"Oh, I remember it now that you've reminded me," said Thomas, crossing his eyes for effect. "And us Amber People, are we also Karzeleks?"

"Of course!" said Dodek,

"What stones do we mine?" asked Thomas.

Morecha looked at him with exasperation.

"Oh, he's such a tease!" said Cassie heartily, sensing Morecha was losing patience. "Best just to humour him when he gets like this," she said in a big stage-whisper.

"I hope *you* haven't forgotten," Morecha said, her eyes glinting at Cassie.

"Of course not," said Cassie. She risked a guess. "Amber People mine amber, of course!" To her relief, Morecha nodded.

"Humans find it on the sea floor in places like the Baltic," Cassie continued slowly to Thomas. She nodded at Morecha, seeking confirmation.

"That's right," said Morecha slowly. "The Amber Tribe live beneath one of the Earth's seas that you call Baltic and they mine it from the other direction to the earth dwellers. But the Amber People are closer to the earth than the rest of us and have amber-coloured eyes."

Thomas, who was running through his whole repertoire of idiotic expressions, looked quickly away. While Nancy had brown eyes and Cassie hazel, a mixture of green and brown, his were most definitely blue.

"And we have been enslaved by Vladimir, that wicked man," said Cassie.

"We are treated most cruelly," continued Morecha. "Vladimir forces us to give him all our precious stones. He kidnapped our leaders and all our power stones. As you know, us Karzeleks live a very long time. But our leaders are ailing and all our power stones are fading."

"Oh, that's terrible," said Cassie sympathetically. "Vladimir must have tricked you? Oh, I mean us." Then worried she was once more betraying their ignorance, she added, "We have been out of touch – you'd better fill us in."

"But of course he tricked us," sighed Morecha wearily, eyeing them with suspicion. "Isn't that why you went to get the fire from the Baba Yaga?" Cassie winked at her and prodded Thomas who was giving a very realistic display of idiocy. "Just humour him," Cassie whispered with a pleading expression.

Morecha sighed and nodded.

"Our dealings with humans are always difficult. We should have known better," said Dodek patiently. "You remember we used to give stones to the humans for healing properties but when they started to exploit us and we found out they were using them for decoration and fighting over them, we retreated farther into the earth."

"Humans can be very vain and frivolous," said Cassie disapprovingly, making sure Willa's sparkling necklace was concealed under her jumper.

"But the humans had things that helped us prolong our lives like nectar for our skin and sands to polish our stones," continued Dodek, "and when Vladimir said he would help us get them we were glad once more to have a friend above ground. He was the first human to find us in a long time."

"We were happy to help him build his city underground," said Morecha. "But little by little the relationship changed."

"At first, he was our ally," said Dodek. "He brought us the things we needed from the Upper World. But then he began to demand more and more gemstones. We had to work night and day to mine them. Then he captured some of our leaders and power stones that resonate with life and before we knew it we were his slaves."

"Then we discovered he had been collecting all the precious stones of power," said Dodek. "He believes he can use them somehow to unlock great power. I don't know how yet but we feel things through the resonance of stones. We pick up signals."

Thomas felt a cold prickle up his spine. Stones of the elements. Vladimir must have enslaved the Karzeleks so he could capture their stones of power for his evil spell.

"But now that the Amber People have come with the Baba Yaga fire we can rise up against him," said Morecha enthusiastically. She looked closely at the children. "You are strange-looking Amber People," she said. She looked at Nancy. "You look more like humans than Ambers. They too have stone eyes. Although the colour is right, you have squishy soft eyes."

She took up her finger and was about to jab it into Nancy's eye, when Thomas stayed her hand. Her skin underneath the soft fur had a peculiar texture, like polished marble.

"We have been much changed in our dealings with the Baba Yaga," he said diplomatically. "My eyes have even turned blue!"

Dodek patted him sympathetically. "Come, we must hurry! We can use the light to set the tar pits on fire and encourage our people to rise up."

Thomas looked at Nancy and Cassie. "We cannot just give you the light," he said.

Dodek and Morecha looked crushed. The light in their stone eyes darkened and clouded.

"We have a mission," Thomas explained. "We have to rescue four prisoners."

"It's not a good idea to rise up when Vladimir is also keeping your leaders prisoner and holds your power stones," said Cassie. "How do you know he won't just kill your leaders at the first sign of trouble?"

Dodek looked at Morecha with something that resembled alarm. Their stone eyes registered every emotion like a television screen. They clouded over when they were confused, shone brightly when they were happy and went dark when sad. They were easier to read than humans. The Karzeleks were clearly a trusting people. No wonder they felt humans were treacherous.

"The Amber boy with the wonky eyes is right," said Morecha. "Foolish Dodek has spent all his time composing his songs and not thinking up a proper plan."

Dodek looked down at his feet, ashamed. He looked like he was trying to think of something to say. He clearly wasn't very bright. "Ah, but the Amber People can deal with Vladimir!"

"I can see it must have been very easy for Vladimir to enslave this lot. They are so naïve," muttered Cassie.

"Have you heard tell of four human babies who are being held prisoner?" asked Thomas. "We must rescue them before we do anything else."

Dodek and Morecha exchanged puzzled looks.

"Why would you be asked to rescue the human babies?" said Dodek.

Cassie flashed Thomas a look and mouthed "tell them the truth". But Thomas shot her a warning glance.

"We got the light in exchange for promising to find the babies." Well, he thought, it was nearly true.

"We believe he has the babies because he needs them to make a spell to give himself supreme power," said Cassie gravely. "One of them is not of human mother. The spell also requires he has the stones of the elements. Could these be your stones of power? You said he has captured them all now."

Dodek and Morecha let out a gasp.

"This would make sense," said Dodek. "Vladimir has the Alatyr Stone, which is the Amber Stone of your tribe, the source of all rivers. He has the ruby like the earth's sun that is Morecha's tribe, the emerald of my own people like the grass, the sapphire blue like the soft evening sky, the diamond like the light of the world. He has captured our leaders. He even has the bloodstone – much prized by humans as symbolising the warm red stuff that runs inside them. All our stones correspond to elements in the human world. It is said that anyone who can join the power of elements above and below the earth will rule the world."

"Vladimir needs a baby born of a supernatural being to complete the spell," explained Cassie. "That is why he has kidnapped the babies. He took four of them because he didn't know which one was of divine origin. We learned this when we were above ground."

"He has locked the stones for safe keeping in the city of New Selene, which is underground," said Morecha. "Maybe he also has the babies there."

"New Selene, you say. Can you take us there?" Thomas asked, remembering the city of vampires mentioned by Tadgh back in the library in Inish Álainn.

The two Karzeleks nodded, their bright gem eyes glinting in the flare from the Baba Yaga's light.

"If you promise to give us the sacred light later," said Dodek.

The children nodded their agreement.

"Is New Selene in the same location as the old one," said Cassie, remembering Tadgh said it was somewhere near Belgrade in Serbia.

But the Karzeleks shrugged.

"That was, I think, in a different place," said Dodek.

They set off across the cavern floor towards one of the tunnels at the opposite end. The children were glad to have guides because the earth was so pitted with holes and entries, it looked like a Swiss cheese. They had no chance of navigating down here.

They ploughed through a series of tunnels and soon they entered a vast cavernous hall, with a vaulting roof of crystal. The light underground seemed to come from gems so translucent they were almost invisible. It was beautiful yet sombre.

All around the hall, groups of Karzeleks toiled and worked. The Chingles could almost touch the unhappiness of the small stone people.

Everywhere was the glint of gemstones, the gleam of metal tools and the flurry of movement. Thomas squinted and the whole scene shifted in pinpricks of light like a kaleidoscope.

Dodek approached a group of workers who were loading a large metal cart. The largest, a small fat man with a bushy beard, downed his tools. Up close the children saw that the workers were loading emeralds. It was hard to work out how old they were, or even if they were male or female. The small fat man with large emerald gems for eyes seemed to be some sort of foreman. He squinted at Dodek and Morecha.

"Is it really you two?" he asked.

Dodek couldn't suppress a triumphant smile. "We have the fire of the Baba Yaga, brought by the Amber People as told in legend," he said.

"I am Rarok of the same tribe as Dodek," the small fat man with the bushy beard introduced himself to the children. "Greetings, Amber People."

A hush went through the crowd and one by one they downed tools. In a minute, the children and their stone friends were surrounded.

"We can now rise up against our bloodsucking oppressor with the help of the Amber Fire," said Morecha. "We need an alliance of all the stone tribes because if we are united it is easier to defeat him."

Rarok scratched his head. "But how can that be? Vladimir has all our leaders and our sacred stones in his care. At least on sacred days we can touch our stones. We risk losing everything."

"We were so stupid to help him build that city,"

explained Morecha to the Chingles. "Vladimir convinced us that we needed a fortress to protect our stones. He tricked us."

"But Vladimir has other plans for your stones," warned Thomas. "We know he has found a place of magnetic resonance where there is a fault line near the remains of a magical being who once stalked the earth. And he has kidnapped babies, also for the spell. I'm not sure exactly what he might plan to do with your stones but you can bet it will be nasty."

The Stone People uttered gasps of alarm.

Cassie glanced at Thomas. "We should tell them who we really are," she whispered. He nodded his head.

"We ought to tell you the truth," Cassie said. "We aren't Amber People. We are human."

A low grumble went through the crowd. Dodek and Morecha gasped.

"So that's why you knew so little," said Morecha with a reproachful look at Thomas. "You tricked us!"

"Sorry, we let you believe we were Amber People because we weren't sure you would help us if you knew we were humans," he mumbled.

Morecha wagged her finger at him but sort of smiled, so he hoped she wasn't too mad.

"Ah, that explains your squishy eyes!" said Dodek. "Now you see why we don't trust humans. They never tell the truth."

"Told you," Cassie whispered to Thomas.

"Yes, but admit it, Morecha and Dodek. If you knew we were human from the beginning, you wouldn't have trusted us, would you?" said Thomas.

"You are correct. Especially after Vladimir," said Morecha.

"So you see, we had no choice," said Thomas.

Morecha and Dodek looked rather confused.

"Let them speak," said Rarok. "We may not like or trust humans but these have the Baba Yaga's fire and must be pure of heart."

"We come from the place where Vladimir may find the magnetic resonance he seeks for the spell, an island far away," said Thomas. "We are trying to rescue the four babies he has kidnapped."

There was another hushed silence. The stone people began to mutter and talk among themselves.

"But we are your friends and also want to defeat Vladimir," Thomas said. There was a tense silence. Finally Dodek spoke.

"I count it an honour to have squishy-eyed friends," he said. "Maybe you are not to blame that we thought you were Amber People. The prophecy maybe said the brown-eyed ones would bring the fire but we think of Amber as the brown stone. By the way, we will have to fashion stone eyes for you, in case Vladimir and his followers detect you."

Thomas told them about the havoc Vladimir was wreaking on the earth, about the wild children and the kidnapped babies.

The Stone People stayed quiet as they digested the

information. But then like a wave, they began to be emboldened.

"Let us defeat the oppressor!" shouted one.

"We must storm the citadel!" cried another.

Soon they were shouting and cheering and throwing their shovels in the air. The chamber resonated with the clang of metal on stone.

Rarok looked at his people. He stopped scratching his head and stood up straight.

"We will join your alliance," he said solemnly.

"There is one condition," said Cassie. "We cannot kill any of the Eretsuns. They are people whose souls have been snatched by Vladimir and we've made a promise not to kill them."

"We are glad to hear it," said Rarok. "We do not believe in killing. We will find other ways to restrain them."

A great cheer arose that echoed all around the vast chamber.

As it died down Rarok turned to Dodek and said, "Now what do we do?" Dodek looked with puzzlement at Morecha and the children.

But Thomas had been thinking.

"Don't worry," he said. "I have a plan!"

Cassie shot him a worried look. "I would like to consult with my brother and sister if I may," said Cassie to the Stone People.

Rarok nodded his assent and the Chingles withdrew behind a group of metal carts.

"And what exactly is your plan, Thomas?" Cassie asked, arms folded.

"Oh, you of little faith," he said breezily. "First we are smuggled into the fortress. The Karzelek tribes each send a party of soldiers to gather outside the vampire city. Then we rescue the babies. Next we imprison Vladimir. On our signal, the Karzeleks rise up and defeat the vampires. We get out of here and bring the babies home. Ta da!" he finished proudly.

"As simple as that," said Cassie sceptically. "First of all, it may not be so easy to capture Vladimir. Second of all, we don't know that the Karzeleks will succeed. Third of all, we promised Ivo that we wouldn't kill the Eretsuns and would help him find a way to bring back their parents. Fourth of all –"

"Technicalities!" Thomas intervened. "You always have to be so negative, Cassie."

"But your plan has so many flaws," she continued, like some junior lawyer. "And it's complicated by the fact we've offered help to so many different groups. The Karzeleks and the wild children both want different things."

"No. We all want to defeat Vladimir," said Thomas.

"Thomas is good at making plans," said Nancy loyally.

Thomas shot her an appreciative look.

"But Ivo and the wild children want us to save the Eretsuns. I just don't know how we're going to defeat Vladimir without harming them," worried Cassie.

"But we need to try. The Eretsuns are not dead. They are

259

the living vampires created when a sorcerer possesses the soul and revives the body of one on the brink of death. Somehow, Vladimir has mastered this black art. There has got to be an antidote. We know from our experience with Caitlín of the Crooked Teeth that the souls and life force don't go away – they have to be put somewhere. We can do it."

"We can help them," said Nancy, feeling her stomach ping. The closeness of so many gemstones was sending pulses of electro-magnetic energy through her, renewing the strength of the Star Splinter traces that remained in her tummy.

"Yes and Sennan, who is like the best ever druid, has disappeared into Donn's Kingdom of the Dead in search of a solution. If he hasn't solved the mystery I don't know if we can!" Cassie pointed out.

"Well, maybe when you become immortal you can sort it all out," Thomas retorted.

"Well, maybe I will," said Cassie and they stopped talking to each other.

There was a long silence when all they could hear was the grinding of wheels, the clinking of the gemstones and the muffled voices of the Stone People.

"Well, can you think of a better plan?" asked Thomas.

Cassie said nothing at first and then had to admit that she couldn't.

"At least if we get inside the fortress, we have a fighting chance of getting the babies. We'll figure out the rest later," said Thomas reassuringly.

"I believe you," said Nancy quietly. "My Star Splinter has a good feeling."

The Chingles returned to the Stone People and explained their plan.

"We need you to smuggle us inside the fortress," said Thomas.

"We can hide you in a consignment of jewels that we have to bring to the fortress," said Rarok. "It will not be comfortable because you are squishy people."

"We must also give them gemstone glasses to disguise their eyes," said Dodek. "The Eretsuns will recognise them otherwise."

"What about their smell?" said Morecha. "The Eretsuns will pick up their scent."

"We can try sewing carefully selected jewels into their clothing," said Rarok. "Their crystalline structure may protect the energy field of the children. And the gems will give off a vibrational frequency that might disrupt the Eretsuns' sense of smell."

"Clever idea," said Morecha.

"We told you before that gemstones can have healing properties," Dodek explained to the children. "No one understands the subtle magic of stones better than Rarok."

"But it may not be foolproof," warned Rarok. "The effect might be intermittent or disrupted by the stones used to build the fortress."

"Still, it's better than nothing," said Morecha.

The Stone People set about making their preparations

in workshops and forges in a series of caves. Rarok gave instructions to one group about the best gems for disguising the children's human scent.

The Karzeleks were obviously clever metal-and-stone workers. They had the most beautiful tools: emerald hammers, diamond knives with gold handles. Their practical instruments were more finely wrought and intricate than the jewellery of royalty. Immediately they set to work adapting sacks used for carrying the jewels.

Rarok introduced them to a skinny Karzelek with bright blue sapphire eyes.

"This is Plono our friend from the Sapphire Tribe," he said. "She was the principal architect of the city fortress at New Selene."

Her eyes flickered with a look of both pride and shame. They watched with interest when she led them to a replica of the city. It was a model carved in forbidding-looking black marble.

"It is a square city built in a huge cavern under the earth's crust surrounded by a moat of lava with a fortress at its core," Plono explained, her sapphire eyes sparkling.

The main part of the city consisted of many intersecting squares with lots of ugly freestanding black buildings like miniature mausoleums. In the centre of the city loomed a huge round fortress that rose all the way up to the earth's surface.

"The fortress is actually built into the root of a vast table-topped mountain that falls away to steep cliffs. The fortress tower rises up through the mountain and has an opening on the earth's surface on the flat top. There is a deep trough between it and the next mountain." She pointed out the glass top of the fortress tower.

"Do you know exactly where the tower leads to in the Carpathian Mountains on earth?" asked Cassie.

Plono shook her head.

"Is it near a human city?" Cassie asked.

"No, it is very isolated," said Plono.

Cassie tried to remember Tadgh's map but her memory of the geography of the Carpathian Mountains was hazy. She vowed to pay more attention in her geography lessons in future – that's if she ever went back.

"The fortress is the hub of the vampire city and is built on three levels," continued Plono. "You cannot see the top levels of the fortress from the city as the second level is built into the heart of the mountain. And the third level rises as a tower up through the mountain to the earth's surface."

She slid off the front panel to show them the floor plans and pointed out the various features as she continued.

"You enter the fortress in the main city built in the cavern. This first level is used as a customs depot. Once you are inside, you pass through customs, then into a hall."

She pointed to a grille in the hallway.

"This is the entrance to a straight staircase leading to the next level. This level is a network of tunnels leading to corridors with rooms off them built into the mountain."

This part of the fortress looked intricate and complicated with a labyrinth of tunnels.

"The third level is the fortress tower leading up to the outside world. It contains the inner chamber. The roof is a skylight that opens out to the earth's surface, as I told you," she said, demonstrating the opening. "There is a helicopter pad nearby. Both the opening and the helicopter pad are cleverly camouflaged so they could never be spotted from the air. The tower is the most secure part of the fortress, at least from underground entrances, and my guess is any special prisoners would be kept here. Vladimir demanded many security features there, like spring-loaded nets and cages hidden in the walls. There are also concealed rooms built around the chamber."

"So where exactly is the entrance to the inner chamber?" asked Thomas.

"There is a long spiral staircase between the second and third levels. It leads to a trapdoor that opens out onto an annexe on the third level. This contains the entrance to the inner chamber." Plono pointed out the location of the staircase.

Its entrance was surrounded by a maze of tunnels. It wasn't going to be easy to find their way around. The children peered intently at the model, trying to memorise the layout.

"What are all these rooms off the tunnels for?" asked Thomas.

"I don't know," said Plono. "They may be used for

storage or for something else. I think it is where they keep and hatch the Eretsuns."

Cassie shuddered. "Do Eretsuns guard the city?"

"Yes. There are many of them there," confirmed Plono.

"But how will we ever find our way? It's a maze," exclaimed Thomas.

"We Karzeleks always know the way," Plono shrugged. Presumably the Karzeleks' resonance with stone and magnetic energy gave them an inbuilt sense of direction.

"It's a shame you can't come with us," said Thomas.

But Plono shuddered. "I could never bear to go there again."

Cassie felt uneasy. They would surely get lost.

"Maybe my Star Splinter will help," Nancy said brightly.

Maybe, thought Cassie, but she was doubtful.

Thomas felt disoriented looking at the fortress. It didn't exactly follow the logic of human buildings and there was something forbidding and hostile about it. Presumably that was Vladimir's intention.

"The city is certainly of ingenious design," he said.

Plono nodded her head with a mixture of pride and regret. "I am a clever architect but I wish I'd never agreed to make this city for that evil man," she said sadly. "I have vowed never to set foot in it again."

Thomas noticed a series of narrower tunnels on the second level that interlinked with the main tunnels. "What are those?" he asked.

"It is best to avoid them," said Plono. "They use them as

sewers and for waste. Though they can be shortcuts. They are too small for the Eretsuns to use. Even children like you would have to crawl on their bellies in them."

"What about any locked doors or gates we may encounter?" asked Cassie.

Plono smiled. "As you will see, there are some of a cunning Karzelek design. But in theory also quite simple. For each one you just have to locate a knob. Then you whistle softly by the spot. The Eretsuns and Vladimir don't know this. They have keys. I began to distrust them and built in one or two little secrets in case we might need them. But I had to work quickly and disguise what I was doing so some of them might be faulty."

"Do you know which ones mightn't work?" asked Thomas.

"Most of those on level one and two are okay, I think," she said. "But on level three I had problems creating an emergency exit under Vladimir's nose beside the inner chamber. I have secretly designed the air vent beside it to convert into an exit but the mechanism was installed in a hurry and it was a tricky design. It should work with a very low whistle."

She ushered them to another area in Rarok's cave. The Chingles watched as the Karzeleks prepared a cart, large enough to take six sacks. It was fashioned out of metal with four great wheels and seemed to work on an ingenious spring-loaded mechanism that required no power to run it. The Karzeleks clearly had their own highly sophisticated technology that didn't rely on power sources.

Morecha arrived carrying three pairs of crystal eye-glasses that were almost invisible to the casual observer. The children tried them on. Slight flaws and cracks in the quartz crystal fractured their view like a kaleidoscope when they looked into a light source. They tried on their jewelled clothing, as heavy as a suit of armour. Cassie and Thomas felt like a King and Queen. Willa's necklace throbbed and glowed around Cassie's neck. It had become more lustrous since they'd come into the domain of the Karzeleks. Nancy was delighted with her clothing that shone and glistened with amethysts, diamonds, rubies, sapphires and crystals. It made the traces of Star Splinter in her stomach fizz even more.

Rarok gave them a marble box to hide the skull head of the Baba Yaga.

Then he and a group of his followers led them to the cart and the sacks where they would be hidden and smuggled into the city. These were spun from wires like chain mail and were surprisingly supple.

"It's amazing you've managed to convert these sacks so quickly!" said Cassie with admiration.

Rarok beamed with pride. "Our metalworkers are gifted and fast," he said.

Thomas dreaded being covered with a load of gemstones. But the Stone People were clearly ingenious metalworkers. When each child got into the sack, it was secured with a false lid that operated with another crafty spring mechanism. Dodek showed them a tiny knob for locking and unlocking it from the inside. This one worked by touch. Once they were all safely inside the sacks and had secured the false lid over their heads, the top of the sack was filled with a layer of jewels. Precious stones lined the sides of the sack but the Karzeleks had taken care to choose smooth, polished stones. They felt cool to the touch. There was even a little spy hole in the side of each sack. It may not have been the most luxurious hideaway in the world but it was definitely the most expensive.

As they said goodbye and set off, a great cheer resonated through the crystal hall. It sounded like the tinkle of a million glasses.

～

The journey to Vladimir's underground fortress took days, as each time they came to a new mine, the miners of each gemstone tribe had to be won over to the cause. They came first to a cave where miners tunnelled out a blue-green semi-precious gem called turquoise. It didn't take long for Dodek and Morecha to persuade the Turquoise People to join the alliance. They agreed to send a troop of armed miners to wait outside the vampire city and to join the battle when word was sent. The Chingles and their Stone Tribe helpers journeyed on. Such was the wave of resentment against Vladimir they had no trouble engaging everyone in their mission. The Quartz Crystal people, the Diamonds, the Sapphires, the Garnets, the Purple Amethysts Tribe all followed in succession.

As they neared the fortress, the children felt a mounting fear and excitement all mingled together. Inside their sacks, hidden among other sacks of precious gemstones, they had little idea of where they were. Being deep in the earth's crust was disorienting. It was hard to see much through their spy-holes. They had a vague sense of tunnels and machinery, like being in the underground in London or Paris. But their solidarity with the Karzeleks gave them courage and hope.

As they reached a cavern that sounded busy and lively, Thomas risked peeking through his spy-hole. He discovered they were nearly at their destination. The noise was deafening as thousands of Karzeleks made their way through a maze of tunnels and walkways below, with carts of every conceivable shape and size. The tinkling sound of gemstones rubbing off each other in their sacks was amplified as they came into a wide and open space.

CHAPTER 12

A s they were at a height, Thomas had a good view as they approached the city. His eyes nearly popped out of his head with amazement.

Before his astonished eyes rose the Underground City of New Selene. Nothing in Plono's model had prepared Thomas for the grandiosity and size of it. It was carved out of black volcanic rock and was surrounded by a moat of molten lava. The entrance was a huge black marble gate. Each gate-head was mounted with a lion biting the head off a tiger. He saw with a shudder another statue with the snarling head of a bear and the open jaws of a fox, just like the demon that had terrorised him when they picked Osmunda's flower. Everything was elongated and massive, as if the city was home to a tribe of giants. Beyond the gates, the vast round bulk of the fortress extended beyond the roof of the cavern up to the earth's surface. The vast scale of the

Vampire King's citadel dwarfed the Karzeleks, who looked like little mice scurrying through the streets.

Their cart joined a long line waiting for admittance to the city. Fearful of being detected, Thomas shrank back into his sack but not before he caught his first real close-up of an Eretsun that was pacing among the carts.

The creature's appearance was deeply unsettling. It looked like an experiment that had gone wrong. It was covered in coarse brown hair like a werewolf but protruding from its top jaw were fanged teeth like a vampire. The limbs seemed longer than a human's and although it stood upright, it was shambling and awkward. It gave off a negative vibration of desperation and savagery. But what really caught his attention were the dead, soulless yellow eyes. There was also an overpowering rotting smell, like bad meat. One was bad enough but an army of them would be unthinkable! He had to suppress the urge to throw up when he shrank back down in his sack.

As the cart trundled towards the entrance of the city across a marble bridge suspended over the lava, a distant bell tolled. They seemed to be stuck in a long line on the bridge. After what seemed like ages, their cart moved forward again. Then they heard a clanking, sawing sound and the distant bells tolled again. Eretsuns roared roughly at each other. The gates were opening. They were in the city. Cassie, Thomas and Nancy in their separate sacks could hardly breathe as their fear mounted. Soon they would have to face the Eretsuns and the Vampire King! Yet soon also they would rescue the babies. All their focus was on the trials ahead.

Through her spy-hole, Cassie caught a glimpse of the centre of the city. They were looking down a long street lined with mausoleums in front of a huge circular building in black marble. It had to be the fortress entrance – the customs depot on the ground floor, or level one as Plono called it. It seemed to mix various styles but was very imposing. There were several alcoves bearing terrible gods and devils from various mythologies. One looked like an Inca mask, eyeless and bloodthirsty. Another was some sort of snake god of Ancient Egypt. Yet another had devil's horns and a forked tongue. Their faces were hideous and frightening.

The fortress loomed up at the intersection of several streets. Cassie tried to recall Plono's replica. There should be four main streets each lined with tombs and smaller buildings. The cart trundled by pitch-black tombs and mausoleums illuminated with a sickly yellow light. Large, ugly imposing statues lined the streets. Birds perched on the top of the buildings. But on closer inspection these crows, buzzards and vultures were made of stone. The whole place felt dead and soulless and filled her with a gnawing sense of dread. It was more like a graveyard, a kingdom of the dead. No place for little children, she shuddered, goosebumps pimpling her arm. No place for anybody.

But they had arrived at the customs depot at the entrance to the main fortress. Cassie remembered it from the model. She heard raucous laughter and snarling and froze when a hand was thrust into the sack. She heard a clumsy hand rummage through the gems in the false compartment millimetres above her nose. Luckily the hand stopped short before it hit the metal of the false lid.

They heard a snarl and the ring of metal as an Eretsun beat the sacks with something.

Cassie's heart rattled in her chest so loudly she feared it would betray her. The Eretsun was clearly not satisfied with the sacks. She held her breath. A sword was thrust at the sack but just clanged against the gemstone lining. She willed herself to stay as still as stone.

Thomas gripped his fists tight, forcing himself not to move a muscle. Every fibre in his being wanted to leap out of the sack and fight. He was so pent up with anger at Vladimir, he no longer felt any fear. This inactivity was agonising. But he forced himself to be patient. Pick your battles, he remembered Scáthach, their wise teacher, telling them. Know when to hold back and know when to fight. He gripped the marble box tightly. The tip of a lance bit against the gemstone lining of the sack. He held his breath, not daring to move.

Deep in her sack Nancy felt her stomach fluttering. The traces of the Star Splinter gave her an extra intuition, like a sixth sense, and she knew something was about to go badly wrong. She tensed and readied herself for action.

The Eretsun guard was still not satisfied. Cassie heard him sniff the air loudly and fear curdled in the pit of her stomach. She hoped Nancy and Thomas were all right.

They heard him tip over one of the other sacks and each

of the Chingles had to stop from crying out in relief when they heard the steady cascade of gems hit the ground.

Then Cassie felt a rough hand pull at her sack. They were going to empty out her sack!

She fingered Willa's necklace around her neck. She had no choice but to shape-shift and willed herself to change. As the gemstones were emptied onto the ground, with blood-tingling effort she managed to turn herself into a black beetle and scurried away before the vampire noticed. But what if he realised the sack was mostly empty and discovered the false compartment? But before the Eretsun could register the phoney sack, another full sack of jewels tipped off the cart spilling its contents on the ground. She saw with her beetle eyes that Dodek and Morecha had pushed it off.

The Eretsun grunted and thumped Morecha who fell to her knees pleading forgiveness.

She heard the disgruntled vampire mutter incoherently at Dodek and Morecha as he shuffled off. But he seemed to be satisfied.

The children and the Karzeleks were alone with the sacks. They were in a place that felt like the interior of a mausoleum except, instead of coffins, it was lined with vast metal boxes and weighing scales.

Dodek and Morecha replaced the jewels in the sack.

"One of the children has gone missing," Nancy heard Morecha whisper anxiously to Dodek. "I think it is Cassie."

Nancy knew she would have to act soon.

Cassie, who was scuttling back towards the cart, was just about to change back when a group of Eretsuns burst through the door. They walked clumsily and one of them nearly trod on Cassie. Just in time she scuttled away from the large hairy foot but, panicked, she ran in the opposite direction from the cart. In her fear, she lost her bearings. Oh no! She saw through her large beetle eyes that the Eretsuns were walking towards her and the one who had nearly trodden on her spitefully lifted his ugly foot to stamp her out. She noticed a frieze up the wall along one side of the building. She scurried up the smooth surface of the marble and joined the frieze. It featured a praying mantis, a black widow spider, a mosquito and a deadly viper. It really was quite repulsive and ugly. She clung on as the group of Eretsuns shambled past. Suddenly one sniffed the air, grunted and scowled around. Had he picked up her scent? They stopped at the frieze, grunted and swore and became agitated. She didn't dare move in case they squashed her. She stayed still, hoping she blended into the frieze. One of the Eretsuns climbed up on another's shoulders and struck out blindly at the frieze. But some other insect seemed to sting him and he fell back. With a few blood-curdling cries, the Eretsuns passed on.

Cassie breathed a sigh of relief in her beetle state. But her escape was short-lived. Just as she was summoning the energy to change back, she saw through her beetle eyes the praying mantis approach towards her. Then the deadly viper's head slithered in her direction. She tried to inch away but they were faster. In her panic she couldn't marshal the concentration to change. Seconds passed like minutes. She saw the evil yellow eye of the black marble viper, the clutching claws of the praying mantis.

Then all was blackness. All was lost.

Am I dead? she thought. She was in a void. But then she felt a comforting familiar presence. No, I am safe, she thought. She felt herself being carried a little way.

"Just as well they didn't bother searching Thomas's sack," said Nancy as she let Cassie down gently by the cart. "He has the Baba Yaga's fire." Nancy was the only one of them who had mastered the art of talking once she'd changed shape. She had transformed herself into a magnificent black stone crow, like the ones that populated the top of the buildings, along with buzzards and vultures. She was so convincing she looked almost made of stone. Just in time she had scooped Cassie, in her beetle state, up in her beak.

That's a relief, thought Cassie. Judging by the behaviour of those Eretsuns, they were going to need the Baba Yaga's fire.

They transformed back into themselves behind a pile of gemstones. Dodek gestured to them that the coast was clear. They could see why. A little way off, the first Eretsun guard who had examined the sacks had come back and was absorbed in feasting on a raw sheep's carcass. Blood ran down his face and he grunted and ground his jaws with satisfaction. Cassie turned away in disgust and, without delay, climbed back into her sack.

They heard the Eretsun grunt at their group. He must have been ushering them on, as the next thing they heard two huge marble doors grind open and next time they peeped out they found themselves inside the large black marbled hall. The proportions were once again huge. They felt dwarfed and little. It was grand and imposing yet also repulsive and dead.

"You can come out now," said Dodek. "We have to wait here for five minutes for the Eretsun escort to arrive to pass us through. They are getting sloppy."

The children got out of their sacks, glad to have survived so far. Dodek was right. Security seemed somewhat lax. Vladimir obviously felt so confident of his invulnerability and his control of the Karzeleks that he barely saw the need to defend his gleaming, repulsive black city.

"Remember Plono's model," said Morecha. "We are on level one. Level two has the network of tunnels where the Eretsuns might be kept. There is a long spiral staircase leading up to the inner chamber of level three. On the second level, try to make your way to the centre to find the staircase. Good luck. We will wait for your signal to rise up." She pointed to a metal grille just inside the main doors. Beyond it stone stairs led up to the tunnels.

They heard a shuffle along the corridor, the shambling gait and grunts of the Eretsun. Without hesitation, the Chingles slipped through the vast grille and hurried up the stairs.

They climbed the staircase several hundred metres,

terrified that they would meet an Eretsun at any moment, and eventually reached a wide tunnel. Smaller corridors led off in every direction. Then they reached an intersection with another tunnel. But they soon lost their bearings. They had no idea which direction to turn. It really was a warren of tunnels.

Thomas's watch had a built-in compass but the needle whizzed about uselessly.

Cassie fingered her bloodstone necklace for inspiration. Nancy patted her stomach, seeing if she could pick up any resonance that might give away the location of the babies. Then both of them pointed left and exchanged glances in agreement.

So they turned left.

On the left-hand side of the tunnel they passed a steel door with an eye-level grille in it, like a prison door. Nancy felt a spasm in her stomach and insisted they check it out.

Cassie stood on tiptoe and peered through into a narrow room. There was empty space in front but dimly, about halfway across, she made out solid metal bars cutting the room in two.

They heard a groan.

"What was that?" said Thomas anxiously.

Cassie squinted and to her astonishment made out spectral shapes jerkily moving behind the bars. Then she saw a hand grip the bars.

"There are some people in there!" she gasped. "I don't think it's Eretsuns. It's some kind of prison cell!"

They heard a thin voice call out in desperation.

"We'll have to go in," said Thomas.

The door was strong but he noticed the locking mechanism was similar to the ones Plono had told them about. He whistled gently. It worked! The door flew open and they padded in, tensed, not sure what they would find. There was barely any light but, on the other side of the metal bars, they saw men and women packed into a cell. They looked half dead, their skin grey, their eyes sunken in their heads, their clothes in tatters. They lay on the floor, many too weak even to groan, their eyes staring into space. The children nearly wept with pity. There was no sign of any locking mechanism to release the prisoners but many of them looked too weak to move or were in chains so it would have been futile to open their cell.

"Who are you?" Thomas asked a man who was struggling to stand by holding onto the bars. He had a long, thin beard and deep-brown sunken eyes.

Cassie blew on Ogma's ring.

"My name is Doctor Gregor. We are Vladimir's prisoners," he said.

"We are the Chingles," said Thomas. He wanted to explain their mission but the man was desperate and wanted to talk about his plight.

"Please, I don't know if you can help. We are near death. Vladimir takes us and turns us into Eretsuns. If we die before he has time to do this, he feeds our poor old bones to them. The Eretsun guard hinted yesterday that

Vladimir intends to kill us all without waiting for the brink of death."

"But that's like cannibalism!" said a horrified Thomas. "Vladimir is really evil." And he must be in a hurry to move on to the next stage of his plans, he thought.

"Can you help us?" asked Doctor Gregor.

"Of course we'll try to help," said Cassie.

"Tell us what you know about Vladimir and his plans," said Thomas.

"I was a doctor in a large hospital on the edge of the Carpathian Mountains –" The man's breath rasped in his chest and he had to stop for a moment. But after closing his eyes for a few seconds, he bravely continued. "Vladimir came and offered grants to build a new wing. But then people started disappearing. Others turned up with weird puncture-marks in their neck. I began to have suspicions that something strange was happening. To my eternal stupidity, I turned to our local politician to air my worries. He was in the pay of Vladimir. Vladimir immediately had me imprisoned. And I now await my fate."

"Do they have little babies here?" asked Nancy. She gently stroked the doctor's hand. Even though he wasn't an old man, his face was deeply lined as if he had suffered great pain.

He smiled faintly at Nancy's kindness. "Is this why you have come?"

The children nodded.

"They have them on level three, in the inner chamber," he said, "where the fortress tower rises up through the mountain and has an opening on the earth's surface. I understand that is how Vladimir enters and leaves the fortress from his nearby helicopter pad."

"Are they still alive?" asked Thomas, half-fearful of the answer.

The doctor rallied a little and smiled. "Very much so!"

Thomas, Cassie and Nancy sighed in relief.

"But only because Vladimir has some grizzly plan for them," continued Doctor Gregor. The children blenched. "But it does not all go Vladimir's way. He is encountering difficulties." There was a note of hope in his voice that gave the children heart.

"What do you mean?" asked Thomas.

But just then a sudden stirring alerted the Chingles to one of the men lying in chains on the floor. He didn't look as thin and wasted as the other prisoners but there was something familiar about him. Especially the twitching moustache.

Cassie couldn't believe her eyes. "Finbar Flash!" she exclaimed. "What's he doing here?"

Finbar Flash just stared into space. He was in some kind of shock, as if he'd seen the worst thing ever!

"He has been struck dumb," said the doctor. "He has suffered a severe trauma."

"He must have followed us here," exclaimed Thomas. He felt very sorry for him all of a sudden. Whatever it was that had happened to Finbar Flash was something he wouldn't have wished on him.

"You said the babies are in the inner chamber," said Cassie. "We've come to rescue them and I promise when we get them, we'll set you free."

"But I must tell you – there is a strange phenomenon with the babies," said the doctor.

"Are they all right?" asked Thomas anxiously.

The doctor smiled. "I can assure you they are in perfectly good health. Too good for Vladimir's liking. They were installed in their cots on a special elevator-platform under the exit to the earth's surface. Vladimir uses the platform as a lift to transport stuff to and from the helicopter. But then, through some strange means, the babies erected a force field – some kind of protective shield. Nobody can go within a yard of them. Nothing gets in and out of the barrier. A most strange phenomenon. That evil sorcerer Raznik who is helping Vladimir with his dark plans asked me there to check if it was something medical but I could not help them."

The children gasped in relief.

"It must be Granny Clíona's blessing!" exclaimed Cassie. "She's our ancestor and a witch and she gave them her blessing using a spell. It had something about them having a protective shield when they needed it."

"A spell?" said the doctor. "Perhaps. Or it may be that they have erected a barrier of protection through some kind of telepathy. I have never encountered this before. How they are feeding and being changed is a mystery. But it is causing Vladimir problems. They are supposed to be cared for by two nurses. There is something odd about the nurses that I cannot put my finger on. They are not Eretsuns but neither are they human."

"Perhaps they are spirits," wondered Thomas. "We had information that the babies were kidnapped by two old spirit women called Doma and Poula. It might be them."

"I do believe I heard those names," said Doctor Gregor.

"Where can we find them?" Cassie asked urgently.

"I was blindfolded but I memorised the route," the doctor said. He paused, trying to get his breath, as he was so weak.

The children desperately wished they had some food to give him.

He then explained that they had to go right, onto the next tunnel, and turn left again. There they would find the spiral staircase that led to the trapdoor opening out onto the inner chamber in the tower.

"I wish we could do something to help you," said Thomas.

The doctor smiled and said, "If you rescue the babies that would be enough. I hate to think of such young little things falling into Vladimir's hands."

"The fire," said Nancy suddenly. "We could give them some fire."

Thomas looked at his little sister with gratitude. He indicated to the doctor to pass him a taper and he opened the marble box.

"This will at least protect you from the Eretsuns temporarily," he said.

But frustratingly the taper wouldn't light.

"Will we encounter any Eretsuns on our way to where the babies are kept?" Thomas asked.

"The Eretsuns howl when they smell human blood. I did not hear any roar as I passed by on my route," said the doctor.

"Then you need the Baba Yaga's fire more than we do for the time being," said Thomas, handing over the box.

The doctor's eyes flashed with gratitude.

"But we promised it to the Karzeleks!" said Cassie.

"These people need it urgently," said Thomas. "Besides, I don't want Finbar Flash's death on my conscience. You will give it back to us, Doctor?"

He nodded in agreement.

"You are good children," he said. "Thank you for the gift of fire. Now we have a chance of evading our fate. But you have given me one thing even more precious: hope. I wish you luck."

The children left the cells and headed towards the staircase to the inner chamber.

They moved as quickly as they could, turning right onto the next tunnel, then left again. Ahead, they could see the spiral staircase that would take them to the next level. But to their surprise they heard a low rumbling sound coming from a corridor on the left just before the staircase.

"But I thought there were no Eretsuns," said Cassie, dismayed. "I wish we had the fire."

"They must be newly hatched," said Thomas. "They can

smell us. The protective effect of the jewels in our clothing must be wearing off. We'll have to risk it."

They flew past the corridor, their hearts pounding, but there was no pursuit.

Then they mounted the spiral staircase to the trapdoor leading into the inner chamber. They climbed hundreds of corkscrew steps and felt themselves ascending gradually towards the earth's surface. Finally, they reached the trapdoor. It was also secured with several Karzelek locking mechanisms. Thomas whistled softly at the various knobs, hoping the sound wouldn't betray their presence. The trapdoor sprang open and they crawled through. Once through the trapdoor they were in a quite large square annexe. On one side, there was a tall door with a grille high at the very top. They heard the low murmur of voices. Thomas knelt on Cassie's shoulders so they could get the lie of the land. His heart was pounding, half-dreading what he might see.

The first thing he saw was the four babies dozing in four wooden cots painted white, laid out like the shape of a cross on top of a circular wooden platform. Two worried-looking nurses fretted about at the side of the room. His heart leapt for a moment with joy. He gazed down at his sisters and gave them the thumbs up.

"They're still alive!" he whispered.

But the sight of the little faces made him feel more keenly how defenceless they were.

One of the women had an abundance of wild springy black hair and wore an old-fashioned peasant skirt and an apron. The other looked rather similar except her head was covered in a scarf tied back behind her ears. The room was most extraordinary. A large black mobile hung from the ceiling. The figures on it were stuffed blackbirds, ravens, crows and vultures. Blackened teddy bears that looked fire-damaged lined the room. Some were deformed with ears, legs and arms missing. Mutilated dolls with torn clothing lay in heaps on the floor. It looked like a playroom designed by somebody with a sick mind. The women began to chatter so Cassie blew on Ogma's ring.

"We must hurry with the feed before the babies wake up, Doma," said the dark one.

"I am going as fast as I can, Poula," grumbled Doma, the one in the headscarf. "Don't rush me because I might make a mistake."

"Raznik wants to try one final spell," said Poula. "We must feed them before he comes as they get very cranky when he is about. And so does he."

"It's not as if they ever drink our milk," complained Doma.

"But it reminds the big one to fill their bottles," said Poula.

Thomas was puzzled by their words. How on earth were the babies surviving if they didn't drink the milk prepared by the nurses? And who was "the big one"?

On cue, the four babies woke up and started to wail. As far as Thomas could see, they were all right if a little pale and grumpy looking. Certainly their lungs were working.

"Mama!" roared Lorcan, who seemed even bigger than they remembered him, perhaps the size of a three-year-old child.

"Yes, my precious," cooed Doma. "Mummikins has made your bottle. You see, I am your real mummy."

Lorcan let out a big wail and screamed, "Naaah!"

These women really seemed to think the children were their own. Doma tiptoed over to the platform as if trying not to step on a bomb. She stopped short, careful not to hit into something. Thomas supposed it was the invisible protective shield. Then she carefully laid the two bottles down on the ground. Poula did the same.

As soon as the bottles were down and the women stood back, Lorcan jumped out of his cot and gathered up four empty bottles that were thrown on the floor inside the invisible barrier. He tapped each of them on the side and immediately they all filled with milk. He downed his in one and threw it back on the floor. Then, tossing the twins their bottles, he fed Tatiana, who gurgled and snuggled in his arms.

Thomas felt his heart melting and understood what the women had been talking about. Somehow, magically, Lorcan was filling the babies' bottles with milk. He wondered if the same magic was cleaning their dirty nappies! He wrinkled his nose: there was no smell that he could detect.

As soon as the twins had finished they tossed their bottles out of their cots. They crashed off the barrier and rolled around inside their invisible prison. Lorcan put

Tatiana back in her cot and climbed back into his own. Then he let off the loudest burp in the world.

"Good babykins!" cooed Poula. "Perhaps Mummikins can have a little cuddle today?" She approached the platform, holding out her arms with a demented look on her face. But as soon as she came to the edge of it, she walked smack into the invisible barrier. She went flying across the room and was hurled into the wall. The babies all looked at her with interest.

Across the room a concealed door sprung open and a tall, gaunt man in a black cloak with a magenta lining strode into the room. He looked arrogant and cruel. He carried a large steaming phial in his right hand.

This had to be Raznik.

"Stay back," said Raznik. "I will now throw this new potion at the barrier. Let's hope this one works. Vladimir is losing patience."

Thomas tensed as Doma threw herself on the floor and grabbed Raznik's legs. "Please, our children don't like it when you do that! It makes them fretful."

Raznik kicked her away as if she was a dog. "Shut up, you stupid woman! They are not your babies. We need to find out which one is Willa's child before we can complete Vladimir's experiment. You have no idea how angry he is about this. If you had done your job properly in the first place and got the right one, we wouldn't be having this problem!"

"That was the fault of that stupid vampire Natalya," whimpered Doma.

"And those silly, selfish mermaid creatures! We asked

them which baby was not of human mother born but they said they were bound by the God of the Sea not to tell or they would be turned into codfish!"

The Merrows must have thought they were talking about Lorcan, thought Thomas, and they were bound not to speak of Áine.

"They told us some of the things Vladimir wanted to know but the stubborn creatures wouldn't give up the amulet either!" snivelled Poula.

"Shut up, you useless idiots! I'm sick to death of listening to your feeble excuses! Out of my way!"

"But they are our babies!" wailed Doma, picking herself up from the floor. "You mustn't harm them!"

"Forget the babies and fear for yourselves! Vladimir blames you for this stupid invisible barrier around the babies. He's itching to do away with you."

Thomas was thinking furiously. The doctor had referred to the platform as an "elevator-platform". There must be a way to raise and lower it from the inner chamber to the earth's surface above. He scanned the room. There was a console on the wall with metal buttons. Maybe they used some ingenious Karzelek system to raise and lower the platform.

Thomas lowered himself from Cassie's shoulders. "We'll have to make our move right now," he whispered. "You take Lorcan, Cassie. I'll grab the twins and Nancy can manage Tatiana. And whatever we do we mustn't reveal which baby is Willa's."

"But what if we can't penetrate the barrier?" asked Cassie.

"At least we can stop Raznik throwing that potion at them. They might die! Come on! We have no time to lose!"

Cassie's heart flipped. It wasn't looking good.

The door had the same Karzelek locking mechanism. Thomas gently whistled and the locks softly sprang back.

"Just do as you're told!" Raznik was saying. "I am going to throw this acid mixture at the babies to make this barrier shrivel. It is infused with alchemical herbs, devil's root, witch's tooth, the venom of an adder and moss from a three-thousand-year-old grave. One or two of the babies might die in the process but the supernatural one will survive."

The three Chingles charged through the door and burst into the room.

"Stop what you are doing!" Cassie shouted.

Raznik and the two nurses froze.

Pandemonium ensued. The four babies immediately began to clamour and Lorcan, Mattie and Matilda tried to crawl to the Chingles but couldn't escape their own force field. Raznik threw the potion up in the air and it cascaded down on Poula, who shrivelled into ashes and rose as a spirit shape. The women really were some kind of fairy creatures, Thomas realised in that split second. Cassie performed a rope trick and tied Raznik in knots, managing to gag him with a loop of rope at the same time. Nancy didn't have to do much to defeat Doma. The sad creature just ran off and whimpered by the wall.

Thomas scanned the roof and saw a series of metal boxes in line with the raised platform of the children's cots. He headed over to the metal panel and pressed a button. Immediately the ceiling opened, revealing a skylight. Light flooded the room and for a second the children closed their eyes and bathed their faces. It had been so long since they'd seen the light. Thomas opened his eyes and blinked, adjusting to the sudden light. He pressed another button but nothing happened. He tried another and whistled this time. Yes! the wooden circular platform was elevated on a metal plate that rose slowly out of the floor. Under the metal plate were rods of thin steel. He whistled again and the platform rose a little further. He scanned the room again and noticed a steel ladder ascending to the skylight.

"We can transport all four of them together on the elevator-platform," he said urgently. "That's how they got them in. And we can escape through the skylight by the ladder."

"How are we going to get them home?" asked Cassie.

"We'll figure something out, once we get them out safely," said Thomas.

The four babies cried and gurgled. The twins shouted, "Cass Tom-Tom Na-na!" which was their name for their brother and sisters. Lorcan screamed and shouted, "Wah wah!" Tatiana seemed to have fallen asleep again.

Thomas and Cassie both began to whistle.

But the platform didn't move. It was about half a metre off the ground. Tentatively Thomas approached it, mindful not to crash into the babies' invisible shield. He crouched down to take a closer look.

"There seems to be a kink in one of the rods. Perhaps if we whistle close to it, it will iron itself out," he said. "I can't think of anything else to do!"

His sisters joined him near the damaged rod of the platform and began to whistle.

They were so intent on their task that they didn't notice a figure slip into the room and press a button on a console on the wall.

Within seconds an intricately rigged steel cage flew up from the floor, trapping all three Chingles. Too late they remembered Plono's warning about cunningly contrived security devices.

"We're trapped!" Thomas exclaimed in amazement. "You, Doma – whatever your name is – let us out!"

"I'm afraid that isn't possible," said a quiet voice with no trace of a foreign accent that sent shivers up their spines. "So here are the Chingles. We meet at last."

The three Chingles turned round to be confronted by a small man dressed impeccably in English tailoring like a banker. But there was something cold and bloodless about him that chilled them to the marrow. He had a pathetic attempt of a blond moustache on his upper lip. His hair was so light and transparent, they could see his scalp. His eyes were so pale they were almost no colour. A slight, sneering smile played about his lips.

The Chingles were in no doubt about who he was.

"Let us out of here immediately," said Thomas hotly. "You have kidnapped these babies illegally and are breaking the law."

Vladimir reached his gloved hand through the bars of the cage and summoned Thomas over to him with a gentle gesture. He leaned in as if he wanted to whisper something in Thomas's ear.

Thomas's instinct was to shrink back but Vladimir was gently insistent. But as soon as Thomas came near him, he pulled off his black glove and smacked him hard across the face. Thomas shrank back in surprise. Vladimir coolly replaced his glove.

Cassie immediately lashed out at Vladimir through the bars of the cage like a wildcat and all the babies started to wail. Vladimir merely laughed, grabbed Cassie around the neck and held her at arm's length, his gloved hand tightening around her throat. He put his other hand through and stroked her hair.

"Quite a temper we have, my lovely," he said in his soft, sinister voice.

Cassie tried to shrink back, gasping for breath. There was something completely repulsive about this man that frightened her more than Caitlín or Balor or any other monster they'd ever encountered.

Vladimir released her and casually turned his back on them.

Panicking, Cassie grabbed the necklace around her neck and summoning all her energy tried to change into something small so she could scuttle out of the cage. But her brain was clouded and she couldn't concentrate.

"Shape-shift," she whispered to her brother and sister.

Nancy and Thomas tried to focus their energy into a point, but they too found their powers shattered by the grip of panic and fear.

"So here are the famous Chingles, who have beaten the Baleful One with the Evil Eye and the Cat Woman with the Bad Breath!" said Vladimir, turning round to confront them.

"It was Balor of the Evil Eye and Caitlín of the Crooked Teeth," said Cassie quietly.

"And we defeated them in battles, shape-shifting and using our warrior skills!" said Thomas, trying to sound brave.

"I'm not sure I believe you were capable of such things. Where did you have these great battles?" Vladimir asked, sounding as if he didn't care about the answer. He pulled off his glove and picked at his beautifully manicured nails.

His hands were small, Cassie noticed, and didn't look like they ever did any work.

"Mind your own business," said Thomas. "Why should we tell you?"

"Please yourself, little boy," said Vladimir. "I have other informants. I know, for instance, that a certain amulet was never recovered from the scene of Balor's demise – on the fault line in Inish Álainn – would that be correct?"

Cassie and Thomas said nothing, struck with the same

thought. Those wretched Merrows! In their spite and silliness they had blabbed to Doma and Poula – and doomed the world to a terrible fate.

"Oh, cat got your tongues now?" he said in his slimy voice. "But the look on your faces tells me all I need to know."

"What's it to you?" said Cassie stubbornly.

But Vladimir said nothing. The silence was unnerving.

"He wants the amulet!" Doma suddenly shrieked. "The Merrows have it – they wouldn't give it up! But he'll get it anyway! He'll harness the power that lies from a tower to a fault line where a giant was killed! The Merrows told us all those things exist on the island! This will happen when there is a blood-red moon caused by the earth's shadow. He needs the blood of a supernatural baby. I've figured it out! He will kill my babies!"

She sprang up like a wildcat and launched herself at Vladimir. He punched her hard in the face and then, picking up Raznik's phial, poured the remains of the potion over her. She immediately shrivelled and her clothes fell to the floor, while a white spirit shape rose in the air and disappeared in a puff of smoke. The children shrank back, shocked.

Vladimir turned to them and smiled.

"So the foolish old woman thinks she can see into my mind!" he laughed. "She is a spirit – a type that is so desperate for a baby they rob other people's. Foolish spirits! Bringing back four babies and failing to identify the one I need! Then blaming Natalya and those mermaids! The truth is, they didn't really *want* to find out which one was Willa's baby. They got greedy and took the opportunity to take them all! Then they got the stupid idea that the babies belonged to them. I kept them around because they were useful. But they have become a liability."

"And what they told you was nonsense!" cried Cassie. "All lies! That amulet is worthless!"

"It's pointless going to Inish Álainn!" cried Thomas. "There's no fault line there! And the tower is just an ordinary dwelling place with no magical properties!"

"Nice try," said Vladimir, moving towards the cage.

Thomas shrank back.

Vladimir looked him coldly in the eye and smiled mysteriously. "Well, I suppose there's no harm in telling you, since you will be dead in a few hours. And knowing how my plans will destroy everything you hold dear will make your last thoughts before death more bitter. The discovery of Inish Álainn with its tower and fault line and the amulet was just the breakthrough I was looking for, as I was lucky enough to, shall we say, extract a prophecy a little while ago."

"*A baby not of human mother born . . . a tower of power,*" Cassie said.

Vladimir stared at her and smiled. "Ah, the little Chingles have been finding out my secrets. Big deal, even stupid Doma figured it out." He felt inside his jacket and took out a small battered parchment.

The children were silent.

"Paid a high price I did for this, from Leshii, the Forest God," Vladimir boasted, fondling the parchment. "It's written on human skin in my own blood."

Thomas felt a wave of repugnance and shrank back. "But you lost your soul," he mumbled.

"What do I need a soul for when I will soon have ultimate power?" Vladimir snapped.

He unfurled the parchment and began to read.

"The sacrifice of a baby not of human mother born,
At a fault line where a giant sleeps,
By an island with a tower of power.
From above, a space stone of the soul splitter,
From below, the gems of all elements.
When the earth's shadow darkens the blood moon,
All power will be yours, Vampire King of All Worlds."

"It won't work," said Cassie in a small voice.

Vladimir suddenly began to rave and shout. "This is my destiny, my fate! I am the chosen one and nobody will get in my way! Already I have more power than anyone could have dreamed of. Soon I will be the Vampire King! I have the spell!" He shook the parchment at them in his little fist and was almost spitting with fury.

The children shrank back.

"But where was I?" he resumed. "Let me outline it for you in detail. As you can see, everything is in place. I have a baby not of human mother born. Balor's remains lie on a fault line directly in line with a tower that can channel magnetic resonance. The Merrows have the amulet –"

"The Merrows are very wilful and stubborn. They won't give you the amulet," said Cassie through clenched teeth.

"Everyone has a price," Vladimir said coldly. "Even you, my sanctimonious little Chingles!" He threw them a look of such pure hatred they recoiled.

Cassie blenched. She knew the Merrows couldn't be relied upon.

"And with the amulet, I can capture the magical rays of the lunar eclipse. The amulet will then become the instrument to animate the gemstones that I have rescued from the Karzeleks. They correspond to all the elements of life on Earth and I will be their master." His mean little colourless eyes glistened with pleasure.

Cassie felt she would be sick. Thomas slumped in the cage, drained. He felt powerless against this man. Nancy was crying softly, holding her stomach. Vladimir's presence was causing her physical pain. Thomas quietly took her hand and held it.

"Ah, Inish Álainn is perfect! Not only does it possess all the ingredients for my spell but I can also tap into Balor and Caitlín's power at the time of the eclipse. To think I cursed Willa for escaping, when all the while in her stupidity she was leading me to greater power! And what luck that Natalya tracked them down and had the wits to recognise that Inish Álainn was the location I was looking for! But it was not just 'luck' – it was destiny! It *proves* that it is my destiny to succeed! Soon all the secrets of the occult world will be revealed to me. I will be the Vampire King. But I won't bore you with my plans for world domination. Alas, you won't be here to enjoy my new world order."

"Take me instead of the babies. I have magic powers," pleaded Thomas.

Vladimir merely looked at him and snorted. "You are not even good enough to be fed to the Eretsuns!" he laughed.

"But you have too many babies," said Cassie. "That may wreck your spell!"

Vladimir stopped laughing. "So . . . are you going to tell me which one is Willa's baby?"

The Chingles said nothing.

"Maybe I should tell you exactly what I plan to do with the babies," Vladimir said. "You see, the supernatural baby who is half-human and half-divine is the catalyst. It is necessary for the spell to work because it combines the real world and the divinity of the Otherworld. I will fuse the baby, or in this case *babies*, into the amulet, so all power will be mine."

"When you say 'fuse' what do you mean?" asked Thomas in a small voice. "Will the babies die?"

"I'd be amazed if they survived," laughed Vladimir. "The spell calls for a sacrifice or weren't you listening? Their essence will be reduced. Naturally they'll die."

The children looked at each other in horror. Of course they knew all along that Vladimir intended to destroy the babies. But to hear it stated so starkly made their blood run cold.

"So are you going to tell me which one is Willa's baby? It seems so wasteful to kill them all," goaded Vladimir.

"Could it be the large one? He seems to have special powers." He pointed at Lorcan, who immediately went into a rage and smashed his rattle against the invisible barrier with tremendous force. "Or maybe the twins? That would be nice, twice the power," he gloated.

Thomas felt he would burst. All he had to do was say the twins were his brother and sister, say their names and they might be spared. Cassie threw him a warning sidelong glance. He struggled but realised it was a trap. There was no way Vladimir would let any of them escape alive. On the other hand, he couldn't touch the babies as things stood. No one here knew how to undo the protective shield.

Only Granny Clíona, Cassie suddenly thought. But she was missing back on Inish Álainn.

"And what about the little one?" Vladimir wheedled in his cold voice. "She, I must confess, is my least favourite. The most sickly and uninteresting. But perhaps it is her. She is so new. No great loss really. She's hardly been alive." He laughed his high-pitched phoney laugh and they wished he would choke.

But still the Chingles said nothing.

"Ah, never mind! Since no one will tell me which one is Willa's, I will kill all four babies. There is a risk that the human ones will pollute the spell but that is the risk I have to take." He regarded them coldly.

The children looked at him in horror.

"One last chance. If you care to reveal to me which one is Willa's, you could save three of the babies and save me a lot of trouble. And, of course, if any of you know how to undo the force field, I might consider a deal."

Thomas tried to think straight. He would do anything to save the babies and he loved the twins above all but this was a hideous bargain.

Nancy felt the little doll stir in her pocket for the first time since leaving the Baba Yaga's domain. "Don't tell," she whispered.

But Thomas looked like he was about to speak.

"Don't trust him, Thomas!" Cassie shouted. "Why would he spare the babies when he plans to kill us all! It's a trick!"

Vladimir laughed. "So much cynicism in one so young." He put his hand through the bars again as if to touch Cassie's face, but she shrank back, petrified. "You might be pretty but you are also very tiresome," he snapped.

Thomas tried to stop the tears in his eyes but he was weeping uncontrollably. Dimly he felt ashamed of himself but also powerless.

"We won't let you win!" said Cassie.

Vladimir laughed. "Brave talk. Even if through some miracle you do escape and follow me back to Inish Álainn, it will just make it all the more interesting for me. I like a bit of sport."

"We are more of a threat than you think," said Thomas in a croaky voice. "We are here, aren't we? We have breached your citadel."

"Crying like a baby!" sneered Vladimir. "Tell me, how do you think you got into my fortress? *Because I let you.* I have been tracking your every move since the Baba Yaga let you go. I told her to. You see, I harboured a dim hope you might be able to break the force field. Otherwise I would have let her eat you."

"But what if the spell has got it wrong?" Thomas cried desperately. "Maybe it would work without actually killing the babies?"

Vladimir laughed thinly. "You really are pathetic. Of course the baby has to be sacrificed. That is the way of the gods. As for the protective barrier around the babies, that is a temporary hindrance. I will find a way around it even if I have to blow them all up."

Thomas slumped down, utterly defeated.

Vladimir untied the sorcerer Raznik, who was spitting with fury by this time, and bid him raise the babies up through the skylight where a helicopter hovered overhead. Raznik went to the metal panel and pressed a hidden button. This time the platform rose without any problems. The Chingles stared as it rose on the metal rods and the babies were elevated towards the helicopter.

The Chingles watched in anguish. They heard the babies' wails and heartbreaking sobs. Cassie, Thomas and Nancy crouched together in terror, feeling weak and little.

"Just so you know what will happen to you," said Vladimir. "In five minutes the newly hatched Eretsuns will be released. They will be driven wild by the smell of human blood. They will hunt you down and then they will tear you limb from limb. And if you manage to stay intact you will become vampires yourselves."

"But . . ." said Cassie, and stopped. She had stupidly been about to boast that the Chingles were not alone, that the Karzeleks planned to rise against Vladimir. "If you leave the Eretsuns here, you will be useless without your army of vampires."

Vladimir laughed coldly. "You are thinking of the Karzeleks. Soon, you will discover your little friends are powerless. As for my troops, you don't think I was dependent on those peasants! I have my own elite troops for special missions. I have been, shall we say, experimenting with different types of vampires. I have raised the most evil from the dead. Heartless and highly trained. Well, nice to meet you." He paused. "You know what the greatest pleasure is?" he sneered. "All the time you thought you were saving your precious island and behaving like superheroes, you were unwittingly bringing me closer to my goal! And deceitful Willa, in trying to escape, merely helped me. Hah!"

And with that he walked up a ladder on the side of the wall that led to the skylight, followed by Raznik. Pulling the ladder up after them, they climbed on board the helicopter.

CHAPTER 13

"Now what do we do?" asked Cassie, pulling at the bars of the cage in despair. They all felt badly shaken by their encounter with Vladimir.

"I hope we made the right decision not to reveal who Tatiana was," fretted Thomas.

"The doll told us we shouldn't tell," said Nancy.

"There was no point in giving him that information anyway, as the babies are all bound together," said Cassie. "They must have triggered the protective shield when they encountered Vladimir."

"That's right!" said Thomas, rallying a little. "Granny Clíona's blessing was that they be protected from harm when they needed it most."

"The only one who can break that protective shield is Granny Clíona," said Cassie. "But where is she? We've got to find a way to get back to Inish Álainn and thwart his plans."

"Vladimir doesn't know we have the Baba Yaga's fire,"

said Thomas. "He thinks we only survived because of his orders. But the Baba Yaga is bound to reward the pure of heart. We've got to get back to Doctor Gregor and retrieve the flame before the Eretsuns get us, and then we have to get to Inish Álainn."

"What about the Eretsuns and our promise to Ivo?" asked Cassie.

"Let's deal with one thing at a time," said Thomas. "What do you think, Nancy?"

"We will find a way," she said with a confidence not shared by her brother and sister. But the doll didn't stir again in her pocket.

"They took the ladder up with them," said Cassie. "We'll have to find another way out."

They gazed up at the sky through the skylight. They saw another fleet of helicopters take off. Some of them were winching huge gemstones.

"Look, they're transporting the Karzeleks' stones of power," said Cassie. "They must be heading to Inish Álainn."

"Let's see if we can shape-shift and get out of here," said Thomas. "We have to rescue the prisoners and get back to Inish Álainn."

As he spoke, the skylight leading to the earth's surface closed over. The panel with the control buttons flew off the wall and shattered into pieces.

"Vladimir must have generated some time-delay explosive to wreck that control panel," said Thomas. "We won't be able to escape through the skylight now."

"At least he's gone. None of us could shape-change when Vladimir was here," said Cassie. "I've never felt so weak and powerless. He must have been releasing some counter-magic."

"Maybe it was the vapours from Raznik's potion. Let us all hold Willa's necklace and see if we can summon our strength," said Thomas. "We should become something small to get out through the bars."

Cassie removed the necklace from around her neck and each of them held it with one hand. They felt a very weak pulsation through the jewels.

"*With all the powers that are strange*," intoned Thomas. "*Change, Chingles, change!*"

With the help of Willa's necklace and the combined force of their effort, they managed to shape-change into mice to escape through the cage bars. Each of their hearts pitter-pattered in their mouse bodies and they trembled as they eased through the bars, their tails flicking against the cold steel. But feeling weak, once they were through, they changed back into themselves almost immediately. Thomas felt a foreboding and worried their powers had been damaged.

They went back through the trapdoor into the annexe. No sooner were they through it than heavy metal doors sealed the entrance. They searched but could find no Karzelek locks. It looked like any escape through the inner chamber was now barred.

"We might be able to get out through the air vent.

Plono said it converts into an escape exit," said Cassie. But they couldn't find it.

But they would have to deal with that later. First they had to descend the spiral staircase and re-enter the system of underground tunnels below the third level of the fortress.

But as they neared the end of the staircase, they were met with a wall of sound. It was the baying of hundreds of newly hatched Eretsuns and it turned their blood to ice.

They staggered towards the corridor where the prisoners were kept. But in their panic, they lost their sense of direction. Each of the tunnels looked the same. Feeling dizzy, Cassie tried Willa's necklace but there was no response. Nancy felt no guidance from the Star Splinter trace in her stomach. Frantic, they ran up and down tunnels.

"I can't feel anything with this noise," Nancy shouted.

"I'm completely disoriented," screamed Cassie in despair. "I've lost my bearings. Everywhere seems the same down here."

They turned down a wide corridor but as they did so they knew they'd made a terrible mistake. The snarling, screeching howls hit them like a wave. This corridor was large and lined with cells, the walls glistening with their own light. They had mistakenly entered the Eretsuns' wing.

Desperately they tried to turn back, but a metal grille flew down, trapping them. They tried to open it by whistling near the knobs but it remained shut. Maybe it was faulty. The only way out of the long corridor was to pass the long line of the Eretsuns' cells and exit the other end.

"Let's run!" shouted Thomas.

But just then at the far end of the corridor over a hundred metres away, a cell door flew open and a shambling creature shot out, half-human, half-wolf with large fangs. They saw the snarling open mouth of the Eretsun and his outstretched claws as he advanced towards them, baying for their blood. But he was only the first of about twenty behind him as cell doors flew open, all pushing and snarling, baring their horrible teeth like baying hounds and extending their clawed, hairy hands. The children were facing into an onslaught of Eretsuns. The creatures moved slowly at first, not yet steady on their feet, but with awful pounding force.

Then the Chingles heard another noise. Nancy, who was nearest to the entrance that had just been blocked by the grille, turned round. She saw snarling heads and ripping claws trying to reach them through the bars.

"They're behind us as well," she cried, fear cracking her voice. But at least the beasts couldn't break through the grille.

"Shape-shift!" shouted Thomas.

They concentrated every muscle, every sinew and fibre and willed themselves to change. Thomas tensed until beads of sweat broke on his brow. Cassie shivered and couldn't focus.

They looked at each other in despair.

"It's no use," said Thomas. "I used up all my energy escaping from the cage."

"Where's Nancy?" asked Cassie, scanning their surroundings. She looked down into the eyes of a little mouse.

"I'm here," squeaked Nancy's little voice.

"Run for help!" Cassie shouted desperately. "Get the Baba Yaga's fire. We'll try to hold them off."

Nancy in her mouse shape scurried through the grille. The Eretsuns screamed as she ran through their hairy feet and tried to stamp on her. Others scraped at the ground with their outstretched claws. Thomas and Cassie could only pray that she'd made it.

Thomas and Cassie stood side by side.

"We'll just have to fight them with our bare hands," said Thomas resolutely, his voice calm, even though his insides felt like jelly. "Good luck, sister," he said bravely.

The Eretsuns, now gathering speed, advanced towards them like a pack of hyenas sizing up when to move in for the kill. They began to howl even louder. With every step the stench of death increased, almost overpowering Cassie and Thomas.

Cassie felt frozen and quickly embraced her brother. As she did, she felt the Karzelek stones sewn into their clothing bash against each other.

The Eretsuns were about to move in. They were snarling like starving beasts, their jaws wide open and slavering.

An idea came to Cassie.

"The gemstones!" she said suddenly, ripping a few jewels from her clothing.

Thomas understood and tore several large rubies and emeralds from his jacket. With an Eretsun within spitting distance, he took aim and hurled a large ruby.

It hit the Eretsun right between the eyes with the force of a bullet. The Eretsun cried out, as much in surprise as at being hit. But the impact had temporarily stunned it and it crumpled to the floor, pulling down another couple in its wake.

Cassie also took aim. An Eretsun with large frightening jaws wide open bore down on her, arms extended, claws at the ready. In seconds it would be at her throat, feasting on her blood. She threw a handful of jewels with all her might and her projectiles flew into the Eretsun's jaw. The creature choked and gurgled. Its eyes rolled in its head. Black bile rose from its throat and it fell to the ground. In its frustration, it clawed at the walls that shone with their own light. It seemed to be going mad and fell to the floor rolling and twisting.

But the next wave of Eretsuns merely stepped over the bodies of their companions. Once again, Thomas and Cassie took aim. This time Thomas landed a big emerald in an Eretsun's eye, thrown so hard it rammed there. The creature tore at the jewel and pulled out its own eye. Cassie hit one hard on the nose with such force the creature was knocked to the ground.

But no matter how hard the children fought, the Eretsuns kept coming like a swarm of locusts and Thomas and Cassie were running out of jewels. But at least now the Eretsuns had to clamber over the bodies of their wounded companions. The tunnel reverberated with howling and screaming. Behind the children, the Eretsuns behind the grille shook and tore at it, impatient for the kill.

Soon, Cassie and Thomas were down to their last jewel each. Facing them were more and more Eretsuns, each more savage and bloodthirsty than the one before.

"Never give in," said Cassie.

"We are the Chingles!" roared Thomas. He gave a Shout of Battle so loud it temporarily stopped the advancing Eretsuns in their tracks. Cassie joined in.

But it only bought them a few seconds. Soon the Eretsuns had adjusted and bayed even louder themselves.

Both children had thrown their last jewel.

"Come and get me," taunted Cassie bravely. "I'll fight you with my bare hands!"

"I'll tear you limb from limb," shouted Thomas.

They knew they were doomed but were going down fighting.

The Eretsuns howled and bayed. But Thomas noticed a different quality in their roaring. The sound of fear.

He realised the Eretsuns were still moving towards them but now it was as if they were fleeing something. They seemed to be stunned into some sort of fright. Those further away fell to the ground as if struck by some mysterious hand. And then he saw why. Above their heads a skull floated with a burning light. Tongues of flame flickered from its grinning jaw. It was sending the Eretsuns into a frenzy. It was the Baba Yaga's fire.

Fear rippled through the Eretsuns. Those who were injured writhed and brayed on the floor.

The skull advanced. Those whom it came near

collapsed, foaming at the mouth like rabid dogs, black bile spilling from their jaws and dribbling from their terrible fangs. The sight of the skull aloft, the burning flames, was enough to have stopped them in their tracks.

Soon Thomas saw little Nancy's curly hair. She walked purposefully, shining the flaming skull at the Eretsuns. She had entered the corridor at the other end.

"Make them go back into their cells, Nancy!" shouted Thomas. "We can lock them in again!"

Little Nancy walked proudly towards the cowering Eretsuns. Amidst the confusion and danger, it was something to see, thought Thomas. A little girl holding a skull aloft, beating back a pack of newly hatched vampires. The Eretsuns cowered and shivered as Nancy loomed nearer. While she shone the skull at each of them in turn, Thomas, waving his hands at them and shouting, ushered them back into the cells. Frantically Cassie ran around securing the doors. The air was filled with low moans and whimpers. It was hard to believe that only minutes before the Eretsuns were a braying pack of monsters intent on tearing them limb from limb. The ones trapped behind the grille that had blocked the entrance to the corridor were cowering on the ground, whimpering at the sight of the fiery skull.

Thomas ran back to the grille and whistled and twiddled with buttons. This time it worked. The grille shot up. With the Baba Yaga's fire it was an easy job to herd the Eretsuns back into the cells.

"We've got to hunt down and lock up any other Eretsuns on the loose and release the prisoners," said Thomas.

"Let's release the prisoners first," said Cassie. "We are safe now we have the Baba Yaga's fire."

"And the prisoners are defenceless," Thomas added ominously.

Nancy led them back down to the prisoners' cells. This time they ran purposefully and proudly, safe in the knowledge that most of their enemy was locked up or cowering in fear. As they approached the prisoners' quarters, there was a tentative cheer, a slight rustle of interest, but many of the prisoners were so weak they barely registered their return.

Doctor Gregor was thrilled to see them: his lined face lit up with a smile. Cassie re-examined the cell bars looking for the locking device. Then she spotted each bar had a separate button. She whistled and pressed the knobs and each bar retracted into the ground. At first many of the prisoners just stared, unsure what to do.

Finbar Flash cowered in a corner, his eyes open but unseeing. Nancy had to take him by the hand to lead him out of the cell. He held on to her hand as if he was the child and she the adult.

"We are here to rescue you," said Cassie. "You will be safe from the Eretsuns, thanks to the Baba Yaga's fire."

Many of the prisoners were too weak to walk.

"We need the help of the Karzeleks to get these prisoners above ground," said Thomas. "Even though the

313

inner chamber entrance and the skylight have closed over, they might be able to tunnel a way to the earth's surface or help us find Plono's dodgy air vent."

"But even if we send Nancy to fetch them, they won't get past the Eretsun guards without the light of the Baba Yaga," argued Cassie. "And we need that light to protect the prisoners from any stray Eretsuns who may be roaming the tunnels. We'll have to go together and get as close to the surface as we can."

So they set out, heading back towards the spiral staircase that led to the upper level and the earth's surface. Some of the prisoners were so weak they could only crawl on their bellies. It was a pitiful sight. As they reached the end of the tunnel, many of the prisoners were too weak to go on.

"It's no use, they'll never climb that endless spiral staircase onto level three," said Thomas. "You stay here and I'll make my way back to the city to bring a party of Karzeleks to carry them."

Cassie nodded in agreement. It was risky but they were never going to make it otherwise. And Finbar Flash was holding so tightly to Nancy's hand, there was no way she could leave him for now.

"Take the Baba Yaga's light," said Cassie. At her words, many of the prisoners quaked in fear.

But Thomas shook his head.

"There are more of you. Your combined scent may draw any rogue Eretsuns still on the prowl. Besides, I think I might use the network of smaller tunnels Plono showed us and it would be difficult to manage with the light. The Eretsuns are less likely to use those tunnels and they are shortcuts."

Thomas set out. He needed to get back to the entrance of the fortress in the heart of the city. The main tunnels were built of the light shining stone that Dodek and Morecha called sunstone and were tall enough for an adult to walk down. He located the other passageways that linked the main walkways. They were dark and low and he would have to crawl through on his belly. He hoisted himself up and crawled into a dark interior. It was airless and smelled sour and the walls were slimy. It was obviously a sewer. Thomas tied his kerchief around his mouth, tried not to think about it and slithered forward on his belly. With great effort he inched along. But soon he came to an opening onto a long, badly lit corridor. He spotted another small opening at one end and dashed towards it. All his senses were on red alert for any twitch, any atmospheric change that might betray the presence of an Eretsun. He barely noticed the horrible black gunge that clung to his clothes, matted his hair. He tried to keep his bearings. He needed to keep going to get to the lower level of the fortress where the Karzeleks were waiting.

The next sewer was easier as it had grooves in the rock that gave him hand- and footholds to climb along and avoid the gloop below. He breathed heavily, concentrating on making it to the other end. To help himself, he began to count each move forward. Thirty, forty, fifty. When he reached ninety-four, he noticed a faint light at the end. He wondered if he could make it in one hundred steps, a nice neat number. He quickened his pace and tried to take longer stretches. One hundred, he mumbled under his breath as he reached the end. He almost wanted to cheer. But instead he quickly surveyed the corridor as he lowered himself down. His heart leapt when he saw, about forty paces to the left, the beginning of the staircase. He rushed forward, almost at his goal.

But as he was ten paces from the staircase, he crashed to the floor.

He lay sprawled for a second, stunned by the fall, wondering how he could have slipped. Then his hairs stood on end as he felt a presence loom over him. He turned over and to his horror found himself looking straight into the jaws of an Eretsun. It must have been downstairs in the customs depot or on the loose somewhere. It was so close he saw the yellow eyes, the red irises, the back of its open throat. In two seconds he was going to be bitten.

He grabbed the Eretsun's ankles, reared up and head-butted the creature. Then he slithered underneath the creature's legs, thankful for the horrible gunge from the tunnels. He sprang to his feet. His best bet was to make a run for it. The creature snarled and lunged at him. But Thomas was quick. The Eretsun screamed and launched itself towards him. But he was lumbering and clumsy. Thomas sensed he could beat him.

Just as Thomas reached the staircase leading to the

customs depot on ground level one, the Eretsun made one last desperate effort and dived for him. He grabbed Thomas around the neck, his fingernails digging in, threatening to break the flesh. Thomas kicked and screamed but the Eretsun held him firmly in his grasp. In a matter of seconds he would sink his teeth into Thomas's neck. And that was that: Thomas would become an Eretsun in the sway of Vladimir.

"Please," Thomas gasped, "spare me, in the name of whatever little bit of humanity you might have left!"

Their eyes locked. Thomas looked into the dead yellowish eyes with the red pupils. For a brief second, he thought he saw something flicker there, a tiny shard of the person this monster might have been. Then he noticed a wooden cross around the creature's neck.

Suddenly, he remembered the wooden cross Ivo had mentioned around his father's neck and found himself saying: "I am a friend of Ivo."

Taken off guard, the Eretsun dropped his head and growled but then he suddenly lunged towards Thomas. Blindly, Thomas lashed out but the Eretsun dodged and Thomas flailed about, grabbing hold of the cross around the Eretsun's throat. The Eretsun reared back and the cross came free in Thomas's hand. Winded, the Eretsun momentarily collapsed and let go of Thomas's neck. Thomas struggled free. The Eretsun shrank back, examining his own hand – almost, Thomas thought, as if horrified that he was capable of inflicting pain. Thomas seized his moment and dashed towards the stairs. The Eretsun lunged and attacked again. He managed to scrape Thomas on the leg but it was a half-hearted effort.

Thomas felt a slight burning sensation where the Eretsun had scythed his leg. The Eretsun howled and screamed and then limped off as if it were wounded.

Quickly, Thomas examined his leg. His trousers were torn and blood-beads had formed where he had a deep graze. He felt a slight tingling and numbness but he tested his foot and was still able to walk. He carried on, with each step feeling a growing sense of relief that he'd escaped. But then he worried that the Eretsun had drawn his blood. Will that make me a vampire, he wondered.

At the bottom of the staircase he was relieved to see Dodek and Morecha waiting for him in the custom hall.

"By the Blessed Stone of Alatyr," exclaimed Dodek, "he's alive!"

"Something extraordinary is happening," said Morecha. "All the Eretsuns seem to have gone into a frenzy. We have been able to stun them and round many of them up. And we've been able to rescue our leaders but the stones have disappeared. Hard to believe Vladimir is so careless."

"More like arrogant. We encountered him in the inner chamber and he revealed he now has the means to create other more hideous vampires and raise them from the dead," said Thomas. "As we thought, he believes he can animate your gemstones to create extraordinary power to take over all the worlds. We believe he's taken the stones to Inish Álainn."

Dodek and Morecha gasped.

"And the babies?" Dodek asked. But he could already see in Thomas's face that their mission had failed.

"Vladimir and Raznik have taken them to Inish Álainn," said Thomas. "They have fled the city. We have captured the newly hatched Eretsuns but there must be many more on the loose. And we have rescued many prisoners. We need your help to lead them up to the earth's surface. The exits at the top of the fortress are sealed off so it looks like we'll have to dig our way out if we can't find the air vent."

The Karzeleks who had gathered in the hall jostled forward, eager to help. A group was deputised to locate tools for digging and another sent to track down any Eretsuns still on the loose. The rest would accompany Thomas, Dodek and Morecha back to the freed prisoners.

On the route back there was no sign of the stray Eretsun, to Thomas's relief. When they reached the prisoners at the bottom of the spiral staircase that led to the third level, the Karzeleks used their cloaks as makeshift stretchers.

Soon they were back in the annexe outside the inner chamber, which they turned into a field hospital for the prisoners. But no one could get the metal doors that had closed over the trapdoor to budge. There was no hidden Karzelek mechanism to be found and no sign of the air vent.

Cassie drew Thomas and Nancy aside.

"The prisoners are so weak. If the Karzeleks manage to get us out of here, who will help us with them? They need care, water, food and medicine soon or they will not survive. The Karzeleks can't live for long on the earth's surface."

"And what are we to do about the captured Eretsuns?" asked Thomas.

"I've been thinking. The only ones who can help us are the wild children and Ivo," said Cassie. "But Ivo will not leave the forest."

"If he knows we've have found the imprisoned Eretsuns, he will," said Thomas. "I think I met his father." He showed them the cross.

"I can still shape-shift," said Nancy. "I will get him."

"Ivo can help – it's our only chance," said Thomas.

"I will tunnel as a mouse, I will run as a deer and fly as an eagle," said Nancy resolutely.

Thomas handed his little sister the wooden cross. "It might convince him his father is here."

"But how will I get out of here?" said Nancy. "I don't know if I can find my way through that big black city."

Just then Morecha approached. "We have found the air vent built alongside the chamber – look left! It's faulty but we can widen it and get out that way."

It was a narrow air vent, too small for even Nancy to fit through unless she shape-shifted.

Suddenly Cassie's brain was whirring. "Plono mentioned that a low whistle converts it into an escape exit!"

"Ah, clever Plono!" said Morecha. She whistled gently but nothing happened.

"But she didn't say how low . . ." said Cassie despondently.

"So it's just a matter of figuring out how low to whistle to widen the mechanism," said Morecha.

"Cool!" said Thomas. "But let's not waste time. Nancy can change into a mouse again, scurry up the vent and go for help. In the meantime, Dodek and Morecha can try to work out how to convert the vent into an exit. Hopefully we can get the prisoners to the surface where the wild children will take them into their care. Ivo knows about healing and the Karzeleks can guard the vampires until we figure out what to do. Perfect!"

Cassie sighed. "You always make things sound so easy!"

They kissed their little sister goodbye before she shape-shifted back into a mouse, thinking how very brave she was to carry out this mission alone. But if anyone can carry it off, it's Nancy, thought Thomas as the tip of her tail disappeared through the vent.

"Good luck, Nancy!" he called and then he winced. His leg was stinging. He showed it to Cassie.

"I don't like the look of that," she said, her forehead creased with worry lines.

But Thomas brushed it off. "He didn't bite me, that's the main thing," he said cheerfully, though he had his fears. "And I got the wooden cross. It might just convince Ivo to help us. We'll be back on Inish Álainn soon and Áine can take care of my wounds."

"Áine is trapped in a force field along with Willa and Connle, remember," said Cassie. She insisted Doctor Gregor examine his leg.

"You are safe," said Doctor Gregor reassured him. "He barely scratched the surface. They have to drink your blood to change you. Though it might leave a nasty scar."

Thomas exhaled in relief.

Cassie felt dreadfully anxious. Vladimir was probably at Inish Álainn already. She tried not to think what he might be getting up to. "The sooner we can get out of this hellhole the better," she said. But her thoughts continued to hover around the babies. At least their force field seemed to give them some measure of protection.

❧

Meanwhile Nancy had reached the earth's surface. She discovered she was in a shallow crater in a mountain-top plateau surrounded on all sides by a sheer cliff face of black rock. It was completely inaccessible – a barren wasteland covered with volcanic ash. Not a blade of grass grew; there were no trees or any life at all. The terrain at the bottom of the high plateau was punctured with rocks and the soil was blistered and cracked. On one side the nearest mountain was in the foothills of the Carpathian Mountains but between it and the plateau there was a huge chasm like a kind of dried-out lake surrounded by steep jagged rocks on both sides. She gazed around and saw the outline of the Magic Mountain in the distance. Her Star Splinter told her she wasn't so far from the camp of the wild children. She rose to the air as an eagle and took wing.

❧

In the middle of the camp, Ivo was amazed to see a bird of prey swoop towards him and land on a rock opposite. It was an eagle.

But in the blink of an eye it became a little girl, Nancy. He smiled to see her.

"We have found some of your people," she said. "You must come."

Ivo's face darkened and he hesitated.

"You must help," pleaded Nancy, grabbing his hand and placing the wooden cross in it. He minutely examined it, turning it over and over. He looked at Nancy with a mixture of awe and shock. "How did you get this?" he asked, his voice choked with emotion. "This was my father's."

"Thomas got it – it was on an Eretsun," said Nancy.

Ivo swallowed hard. "Then he is alive!"

"Only you can rescue him," Nancy urged. "Please come."

Ivo hesitated but this time he had no choice.

Out of the trees, from behind rocks, in the middle of carrying pitchers of water and chopping firewood, the wild children ran to Nancy.

"Please, Ivo, let us go!" they clamoured.

Ivo stood silent for one minute.

"You are our only hope," said Nancy. "The prisoners need help and so do we."

Ivo fingered the cross, its rough wood given a patina by much handling. He looked into the pinched faces of the children, which for the first time bore the light of hope. He mutely nodded his head in accord. The children cheered.

He gestured them to be quiet.

"We have much to prepare. Be quick."

Like a well-oiled machine, the children immediately sprang into action. Nancy handed back Vasalisa and Ivo placed her in her special box. Then he packed a huge sack of medicinal herbs while the children gathered up as much food as they could carry. Soon they were ready.

Meanwhile, back at Vladimir's fortress, Cassie and Thomas found it tough waiting to see if Nancy would successfully reach Ivo and the tribe. They tried to do what they could to make the prisoners comfortable. Cassie even attempted to comfort Finbar Flash, who had got horribly upset when Nancy had to leave, but he just stared at her mutely and rocked back and forth.

Dodek and Morecha were also frustrated. They had located a lot of knobs and buttons cunningly concealed on the inside of the vent but they couldn't work out how to operate them to convert it into an escape tunnel. They hoped there wasn't a serious fault in the mechanism. So they sent a messenger to Plono, who'd vowed not to return to the city herself.

The journey was a long one. All day and night they struggled to carry their loads through the forest along a route that had taken Nancy just a few hours in her animal

324

state. But the children were so excited about seeing their parents they ploughed on, not even wanting to stop for food.

Ivo let Nancy lead the way, marvelling at this small child who had so many powers.

But when they got to the chasm between them and the plateau where the entrance to the underground city was, all their hope drained away. They looked down a sheer rockfall. The jagged walls on either side were too steep and treacherous to climb. Ivo could barely look and felt dizzy and disoriented.

"You can wait here," said Nancy. "I'll go get help."

"It's hopeless," said Ivo. "Even if you can reach the others, you'll never get the prisoners across to here."

"The Karzeleks can help," said Nancy brightly.

"Impossible," said Ivo. "From what you've told me they cannot survive for long in the outdoors. Besides, they do not like humans as a rule."

"They like us," said Nancy. "We helped free them from Vladimir."

"It feels so cruel to know my father may be in there and I can do nothing to help him!"

He slumped down and buried his head in his hands. He sounded like he was choking in an effort not to cry. But soon all the other children were weeping.

"It's horrible for us to come so far and lose all hope," said one little girl with huge wracking sobs.

"We are just little," said another. "The world is big."

Nancy gazed at them sympathetically. "I am a Chingle and we always find a way," she said resolutely and with that she took wing and rose in the air as an eagle.

Back at Vladimir's mountain, she found her original exit point, the air vent, and shape-shifted into a mouse again. Soon she was scurrying her way back down into the fortress. A distant bell tolled.

It didn't take her long to reach the annexe. The first people she met were Dodek and Morecha, who were still puzzling how to turn the air vent into a tunnel. She changed back into herself and explained about the tribe of wild children across the chasm on the earth's surface.

They told her how they had failed to discover the secret of converting the air vent and how they had sent a messenger to Plono.

"It is true that we are not able to survive for long above ground," Dodek said. "But we must get the prisoners to the surface. The air is getting thinner as the air circulation system is beginning to break down and they will all suffocate to death if they do not go above ground."

"We do not need so much air as humans," said Morecha. "But even we are feeling uncomfortable."

Nancy already had begun to cough and wheeze. Her head felt slightly dizzy.

Cassie and Thomas, who had been over at the far side of the annexe attending to the prisoners, realised their little sister had returned and were overjoyed to see her.

Nancy explained how Ivo and the children were stuck

on the other side of the chasm. Cassie felt mixed emotions. On the one hand, she surprised herself by feeling somewhat glad at the thought of seeing Ivo. On the other, she was exasperated by his lack of spirit, his changing moods.

Dodek sighed and looked worryingly at the narrow air vent above.

"We're going to have to move soon but it will take forever to convert all of this into a tunnel if we have to do it by hand," he sighed. "And there's no sign of the messenger from Plono."

Morecha was peering at the sides of the air vent above her again, still racking her brains. She showed Nancy the cleverly concealed knobs and buttons.

"These knobs and buttons are there for a reason," she said to the little girl. "There must be some kind of way to open these locks with a combination of pressing and whistling but we've tried a thousand times and nothing happens!"

"We've even tried bangs and whistles!" said Dodek. "And the lowest whistles you ever heard!"

"Let me try," said Nancy.

"It's no good, Nancy," said Cassie impatiently. "We've all tried. Plono said some of these mechanisms might be faulty because she had to do them quickly in secret."

"Then maybe what is needed is a faulty whistle," said Nancy stubbornly.

"That's silly, Nancy!" said Cassie. All these difficulties were getting her down.

"No, it's not!" Nancy insisted. "Like sometimes when you try to whistle and it comes out like a blow instead."

Morecha looked at her with interest, her eyes glittering.

"Let the little one try," she said.

Thomas lifted Nancy up.

Nancy took a deep breath and blew on the knob as if it were a birthday-cake candle.

"See?" said Cassie.

But just then there was a click.

They all stared at the vent but nothing happened.

But Morecha was staring at Nancy in great excitement. "It's working!"

With that, she blew rapidly on all the knobs and buttons in succession.

To their astonishment the shiny metal walls concertinaed out and became a tunnel wide enough for a person to pass through. There was even a stepladder.

"Clever Morecha!" exclaimed Dodek.

"More like clever Plono!" said Morecha.

"And how about clever Nancy?" said Thomas.

"Brilliant!" said Cassie. "Thomas, you organise the prisoners to start making their way up with Dodek and Morecha's help! Nancy and I will go up to the surface and see if I can think of a way to get the wild children across."

Soon, Cassie and Nancy reached the earth's surface.

Cassie gratefully burst through into the air, and breathed in deep gulps. She lay on her back for a moment and let the air caress her. She felt that fresh air and sunlight was better than all the gold and jewels in the world. But then she stood up and looked across the dangerous precipice of the chasm. Great spikes of rock rose out of the chasm floor like a giant dragon's teeth. The rocky walls joining the plateau to the mountain were two jagged blades of granite. It was sheer, vertigo-inducing rock. She could suddenly sympathise with Ivo's despair. But they needed to do whatever was necessary to get back to Inish Álainn to rescue the babies.

If only it was a lake, she thought, they could sail it. And then her eyes lit up.

"Nancy, do you still have that petal from Perun's flower?"

Nancy scratched about in her pocket and found the petal.

"It's worth a try," said Cassie.

She stood on the mountainside and summoned Perun. Above, the clouds swirled and spiralled, forming into banks. The children trembled as a large shape loomed in the sky. It was the faint image of Perun. His golden beard looked like sunbeams captured in the cloud at sunset. His dark hair was like the shadow of the moon.

"Can you send us water?" she begged.

"I have already granted that wish," he said in a stern voice.

"But please!" Cassie begged. "It's our only hope."

"I do not need to grant your wish," he thundered. "You have only a slight claim on me."

"But all the children are crying!" pleaded Nancy. "They

have no mummies and daddies. You must help them. I still have a petal. Vasalisa the doll told me to keep it."

"Where we come from, the tears of children have magical properties," said Cassie. "Once we released a ghost from a bottle – our very own ancestor. Tears can heal and renew. Doesn't the sight of so many children crying move your hard heart?"

The spirit of Perun with his golden moustache looked over at the children, his expression unchanging and seemingly unmoved. The wind blew and the cloud hovered over the other side the chasm. It descended on the children and then was gone.

"Much use that was!" fumed Cassie. "These gods and goddesses are all so capricious. They only stick to the rules when it suits them."

But Nancy tugged her arm. "I can hear a funny noise," she said.

Cassie strained to hear. Her little sister had exceptionally good hearing. Then Nancy pointed over in the direction of the tribe of wild children across the chasm. A stream had begun to trickle down the sheer mountainside.

"It's coming from them," said Nancy. "It's from their crying!"

Cassie screwed up her eyes. To her amazement, the tears of the children were so copious they were running in rivulets down their faces and mingling and pooling below them. The pools began to form into a single flowing stream.

The tears of children have magical qualities, she

repeated to herself. That's what Connle had told her once and with their tears they had released the ghost of Granny Clíona from her bottle. And she felt her own eyes wet, with relief and sadness and happiness all mixed in together.

The water began to cascade down the side of the mountain and rose steadily.

Even Ivo felt himself break down and for the first time he expressed his grief for the loss of his father. He remembered again the pain of his torture, his own horror at not being able to do anything. He cried for all the little children in his care and how useless he felt as a replacement for their fathers and mothers. He cried for missing his grandmother and her soft hands and gentle laugh. Such a lot of tears.

And what of the other children of the Lost Tribe? Ivo's cousin Conchy remembered his mother's long fiery hair, like a sheet of beaten copper, as red as his own, and how she would brush it absently behind her ear when she bent down to kiss him. Basher, for all his outer toughness, felt his heart melt when he thought of his mother's floury hands after she'd been kneading bread, how she would tease him and chase him around the kitchen table claiming to be the Flour Monster and they'd collapse with laughter. It had been a long time since he'd laughed. It made him sob to think of it. Kicker remembered his parents dancing on their wedding anniversary, just the night before they were captured, and couldn't bear to think of their bright shining eyes now dimmed.

All the children thought of their parents, their smiles,

and felt keenly how much they missed them. They remembered all the nights they felt alone and cried themselves to sleep. The little ones shivered and sobbed as they felt again the gnawing pangs of hunger, the cold breeze in the branches as they hid. They cried for the long nights hiding in trees and damp hollows as the Eretsuns went on the prowl. They cried for their friends who did not make it, who were in the wrong place at the wrong time and were kidnapped and killed. They remembered the smiling faces of their mothers and the warm hugs of their fathers and sobbed for the loss of their stolen childhoods.

And then they thought of all the children all over the world who were robbed of their childhoods. The children bleeding and wounded and dying, caught up in war zones in conflicts of adults' making. The children whose parents beat and abused them and showed them no love. Children maimed and killed because of careless adults and selfish people who drive too fast or leave guns lying around. And for the children whose time is short because of illness or accidents. They cried a million tears for a thousand sorrows.

And as they cried the rivulets fed a stream and the stream became a cascade. The water dived to the bottom and pooled, first just wet soil, then a puddle. But increasingly a lake. And as the lake rose, something happened to the children. The boulder of sorrow broke in their hearts. They noticed the water rising. And soon the tears turned to ones of joy.

"It's a lake!" exclaimed Cassie. "A lake of tears!"

The children stood on the brink of the opposite cliff. The sight of so much water made them pause. Such a lot of sorrow in their hearts to fill a lake with tears. But Ivo felt something else stir. For the first time since his father had disappeared he allowed himself to believe there might be something else in the world apart from sorrow. He might be able to live, not just endure.

Cassie's heart was beating fast. They could now leave the evil city of New Selene and hunt down Vladimir. She filled her lungs with air and roared across the divide.

"Make up boats!"

The water was now level across the top of the cliffs. On the opposite bank the children began to form their carrying poles into makeshift rafts. Ivo rushed about securing the flimsy crafts with twine and belts, cloaks, anything he could lay his hands on.

A fair wind began to blow and the children set off on their flimsy crafts. The vessels scythed through the water as if they were the most sophisticated boats ever devised. Soon they were all across.

"You came," said Cassie as Ivo disembarked.

They smiled at each other, eyes shining, and exchanged an awkward clumsy hug. Cassie reddened and she felt oddly embarrassed.

"You fulfilled your promise," said Ivo. "I wasn't sure you would."

"We still have to get them to safety and I haven't figured out yet how to save the Eretsuns," said Cassie.

She led them to the place where all the prisoners had been taken up to safety through the widened air vent. The children held their breaths and felt nervous, yet excited.

"The prisoners are very weak," she said. "You must be gentle with them." Ivo nodded his head.

The wild children streamed onto the plateau and as each one did so, they gasped in surprise.

The prisoners barely stirred. But soon cries of joy followed by tears were heard as some children found their parents. Others ran frantically from person to person, desperately seeking out the face of a loved one.

Cassie almost cried at the sadness in Ivo's eyes. She went to him and pressed his hand in a gesture of friendship.

"Your father will be among the Eretsuns imprisoned below," she said kindly. "We have to leave them locked in the cells until we find an antidote. You must talk to Thomas."

Ivo and Cassie found Thomas resting. His leg stung and he was weak. Quickly Ivo dressed his wounds. Thomas told him about the encounter with the Eretsun who he thought was Ivo's father.

"I must go," said Ivo, heading towards the air vent.

"No," said Cassie. "It is too dangerous."

But Ivo was already heading down the ladder leading back into the fortress. Without hesitation, Cassie followed him.

"Please, Cassie, don't try to stop me – this is just something I have to do," said Ivo, his eyes pleading with her.

"You will need the fire of the Baba Yaga," said Cassie. "It is with the Karzeleks. They will only give it to me."

Ivo nodded his head, accepting her help.

When they reached the annexe on the third level, Dodek and Morecha, who with the other Karzeleks had rounded up all the stray Eretsuns, were just about to head back to the underground cavern. They held the flaming skull of the Baba Yaga. Cassie explained that Ivo was seeking his father whom Thomas had encountered. Dodek and Morecha agreed to accompany them.

They headed for the second level of the fortress and retraced Thomas's steps to the top of the staircase where he'd encountered the Eretsun with the wooden cross. As they passed by corridors with cells in them, any Eretsuns locked up howled in frenzy.

At the staircase connecting to the first floor, they saw blood on the floor but there was no sign of any creature.

"I seem to remember locking up an injured Eretsun around here," said Dodek, "but I don't know where exactly. It could be him."

"Maybe," said Cassie hopefully. "Thomas said he limped as if he were wounded. But if he is still loose, he will flee from the Baba Yaga's fire. Dodek and Morecha, we will have to go ahead and you will have to follow behind us and be ready to intervene with the fire if there is any trouble."

Cassie and Ivo proceeded alone. About twenty paces from the staircase, Cassie noticed some drops of black bile.

"It is Eretsun blood," said Ivo.

There were more drops leading to a storeroom on the right-hand side of the tunnel. Ivo looked in the top eye-level grille.

"I think there's an Eretsun in there," he said. "I want to see him alone." Cassie nodded her assent but motioned Dodek and Morecha to come nearer with the fire of the Baba Yaga.

"That's the injured one we rounded up," said Morecha.

"You can go in alone but I will stay at the door with the fire nearby," said Cassie. She whistled into the knob on the unlocking mechanism to open the door.

As Ivo was about to go in, she touched his arm.

"He will be much changed," she said.

Ivo nodded gravely and proceeded in.

Cassie watched keenly from the door as Ivo approached the creature rolled in a ball in the corner of the room. He was gnawing on his own hand. His eyes stared blankly ahead. She couldn't begin to imagine how Ivo felt to see his father like this, a wretched mutant.

Ivo stopped in the centre of the room and fell to a crouch.

"Father, I know it is you," he said gently.

The creature growled and stirred and lurched forward but when he saw Ivo, he shrank back again. He howled and held his own arms and legs as if trying to restrain himself from moving.

The creature was very weak and thin, Ivo saw.

"Father, if you can hear me, we are doing everything we

can to fight Vladimir. This girl here," he gestured to Cassie, "is helping us. The boy you struck is her brother. He is all right. Please don't give up hope. We will restore you soon."

But his father just continued to howl and whimper in the corner. Ivo backed off, unsure what to do. Eventually Cassie entered the cell, with Dodek and Morecha standing watch on the door, and put her hand on Ivo's shoulder. Without a word, Ivo let her take him by the hand out of the cell.

They secured the door.

"We must get him food," said Ivo, breathing hard. Cassie saw that he was making great efforts to control himself. "I am sorry you have to see him like this. He is a proud man."

Cassie smiled gently. "You have much to be proud of. He retained enough of his humanity to draw back from attacking Thomas. And he seemed to know you."

Ivo visibly pulled himself together. "We must do everything now to defeat Vladimir and find a cure to convert the Eretsuns back into human beings." There was a new note of resoluteness in his voice.

A thought struck Cassie. "Dodek, Morecha, you once said your gemstones had healing properties. Do you know of any antidote to restore an Eretsun?"

Dodek's emerald eyes clouded over. "The stones have great power. But the only person who will know how to undo the spell is he who made it."

"Vladimir," said Ivo through clenched teeth.

"And he is in Inish Álainn," said Cassie.

"In which case you must hunt him down," said Ivo.

They agreed that, with the help of the Karzeleks, the wild children would tend the needs of the Eretsuns until the Chingles found a cure. If they ever found a cure, Cassie thought ruefully.

Cassie and Ivo made their way to the surface. Back at the makeshift camp on the plateau, Ivo gathered his followers and told them of the plan. Then he joined the Chingles. They were tending to Finbar Flash, who was still staring blankly ahead.

"This prisoner has lapsed into a catatonic state from shock," Thomas explained. "He followed us here and was unprepared for what he found. Can you help him?"

Gently, Ivo anointed Finbar with some herbs while Nancy held his hand. After a while, even though he was still weak, he seemed more relaxed and the desperate expression fled from his eyes.

"You have got to get back to Inish Álainn," said Ivo to the Chingles.

"Our best chance is to hook up with Jarlath and Sasha on the submarine," said Thomas.

"As I flew over on my way back to Ivo's camp, I saw no sign of the sea," said Nancy.

"Then we need to get to civilisation to try and get a call through to our friend Dick Headley," said Cassie.

"We have lost so much time," said Thomas.

Then suddenly Finbar Flash stirred. He raised his hand

and weakly patted his jacket. His voice was barely audible and Nancy bent down to listen to him.

"He says he has his phone," she said. "We can use it to get help. He said something else but I couldn't understand. Something about Dick Headley."

Cassie's eyes widened in surprise. Concealed in his pockets and hidden in a false lining were the components of Finbar Flash's mobile phone.

Cassie smiled as she pumped the code into the phone. But just as she was about to hit the send button to dial Dick Headley, Finbar got into a flurry. Nancy leaned in to hear him.

"No, no, don't ring Dick Headley. That's what he's saying!" she cried. "He says the governments are gargling internal airs and Dick Headley has been rested. He said call the submarine!" She said the words slowly because they were rather big words for a child not yet five.

"I think she means Dick has been arrested and the governments are guarding international air space," said Thomas.

"Let's hope no one has detected the submarine," said Cassie. And to her surprise Finbar Flash shook his head vigorously.

Nancy listened again. "He said no one has detected the submarine. It has vanished into thin air."

"We told Jarlath and Sasha to make their way to the sea nearest the Carpathian Mountains. Do you think they might be here?" asked Cassie.

"Is it possible they might have somehow evaded the dragnet of security?"

"It's worth a shot," said Thomas.

"Manannán must have covered them with his cloak of invisibility," said Cassie.

Finbar Flash groaned.

"He says he's very sorry he got us into trouble," said Nancy.

"He nearly got himself killed!" said Cassie. "We'll have to take him back with us."

Doctor Gregor told them that he was too weak to move but Finbar clung so desperately to Nancy that they had no choice. They decided it was for the best to take him.

"The signal for this phone might be picked up," said Thomas. "Nancy can shape-shift when we get to the sea and get the submarine to come pick us up. If Sasha and Jarlath are still under Manannan's spell they won't think anything of it."

"Are we far from the coast?" Thomas asked Doctor Gregor.

"At least three hundred miles to the Baltic Sea, I think," said Doctor Gregor.

"We can do it," said Cassie. "We'll have to shape-shift into eagles and fly. I think Perun's visit has helped give me back my strength. We can carry Finbar in a cloak."

"I can find the submarine with Willa's necklace and the Star Splinter," said Nancy, resolutely rubbing her stomach.

Without hesitation Ivo produced his sky-blue cloak from his medical bag. "Use this to carry Finbar," he said.

As they made their preparations, Ivo took a moment to speak to Cassie on her own. She felt slightly nervous and hoped he wasn't going to start an argument. He took her hand and looked into her eyes. His large green eyes were luminous with intensity.

"Thank you," was all he said. But with those two words he said much more.

A new understanding passed between them. Despite the adversity ahead, despite the desperateness of their situation, Cassie felt something sing in her heart.

The Chingles said goodbye to the Karzeleks, the prisoners and the wild children. The clock was ticking and they'd lost so much time.

But at least Ivo doesn't hate me, thought Cassie as she readied herself to shape-shift.

They transformed into magnificent eagles, snatched up the cloak containing Finbar and soared into the sky.

CHAPTER 14

*I*nish Álainn looked different underwater. The island came up on the monitor of the submarine as a sloped landmass stretching to the depths of the ocean. Unsurprisingly Sasha and Jarlath knew very little about what was going on, except that they were under suspicion for killing their wives and children. To Thomas and Cassie's relief, they asked no questions and were clearly still under the binding spell put on them by Manannán Mac Lir.

"As I said, I think Manannán put his cloak of invisibility around the submarine," said Cassie. "It's the only explanation for how they could have evaded the most sophisticated military in the world. And thank heavens Manannán put a spell on them to co-operate with us."

"I don't know," said Thomas. "These submarines can be very good at evading surveillance. I wonder if Vladimir and Raznik have been able to get on to the island, if the fairies of the Midnight Court are still operating their force field."

342

"But Raznik is not necessarily supernatural, is he? It's only a rumour about him being a vampire," Cassie said. "And Vladimir is still human even though he styles himself the Vampire King and plans on taking over this and the Otherworld. He could just walk straight in."

But they soon understood that evil Vladimir and his sidekick had no need to go to the island. There was a lot of activity around Poolbeg Rock, which was outside the fairies' force field. It was here they'd set up their headquarters.

Even though they didn't think they could be seen, the submarine kept its distance while they tried to gather information. Luckily the sub was fitted with the latest in high technology and they could survey the territory.

The children gathered around the monitor. First objects appeared as blurs of green light on the blue screen. But then Thomas pressed a button and the cameras homed in closer. The objects still had a greenish tinge but the children could make out what they were.

They didn't like what they saw. Missiles surrounded Balor's wreck. They could also make out a distinct crack in the sea floor.

"Look, there's the fault line. It must have been widening since Balor's demise," pointed out Thomas in dismay. "Vladimir really does have the elements he needs for his spell right here in Inish Álainn."

Between the missiles were cages filled with huge glowing gem stones – diamond, amber, ruby, emerald, sapphire. But the Alatyr stone – the huge amber stone the Karzeleks had told them about, occupied pride of place. It throbbed with a soft amber light and within it they could see traces of fossils, dinosaur footprints, delicate plants like filigree, tiny flowers. It was like an underground sun and extended to just below the waterline. But there were also underwater missiles and defences, black and forbidding. Poolbeg Rock was booby-trapped. It was too horrible to think what Vladimir might be planning. Perhaps he was going to destroy the beautiful stones and ravage the island so he could unleash his horrors. Perhaps he was going to blow the babies up!

Crabs and lobsters and countless shoals of fish swam between the missiles and the precious Stones of Power. A cluster of magnificent jewelled anemones had even grown on one large black weapon. Cassie thought she caught the flick of a large tail. Then she glimpsed long, pale, flowing reeds and realised it was blonde hair. The Merrows, she thought.

Just then they came into view. And around the neck of Mara, Cassie spotted the amulet. It throbbed and glowed red, the wondrous remnant of a meteor that had fallen to earth in North America where their friend Grey Wolf had found it.

Cassie and Thomas watched as the Merrows circled lazily, even deliberately, around the missiles as if they were keeping guard.

"Vladimir seems to be setting everything up for some giant activation," said Cassie. "Mara still has the amulet but, from the way the Merrows are behaving, I would say they are obviously in on the plot. How stupid it was of me to lose that amulet to them of all people!"

"Don't blame yourself," Thomas said. "At least now we know what we are up against. Let's just hope we can rescue the babies before Vladimir does whatever it is he's planning. At least it seems he can't penetrate their protective shield without Granny Clíona."

The children decided it was safer for Sasha and Jarlath to stay away from the island so they landed in a specially designed dinghy while the men stayed in the submarine out at sea.

The Chingles had only got onto the sand when the Boogan ran to greet them. His seaweed body quivered and shook.

"Oh, you have returned!" he exclaimed. "I have been keeping lookout since you left. You cannot believe the things that are going on here on this island!"

"Please fill us in," said Cassie.

"Well, that Vladimir fellow has come and set up his headquarters at Poolbeg Rock. There's a deep underground cave that tunnels under the water there and we think that's where he has the babies. You remember that dwarf Polewik? He saw them arrive. He cannot get onto the island because of the fairy's force field but luckily I was out there on the rock. The magical barrier doesn't seem to affect me. I don't know why. Maybe because I am a creature of the sea as well as the land. I was out with the dolphins at the time they put up their force field, so maybe that was it."

"It's a very faulty spell," said Thomas.

"Luckily, nobody pays me any attention because I can look like just a great floating mass of seaweed," said the Boogan. "Polewik is still there, poor lad, because he looks like a hummock of grass and they just walk all over him. I know how he feels."

"So Vladimir is waiting for the lunar eclipse," said Cassie. "He told us his plans when he captured us in the inner chamber of the Vampire City. This island is the perfect place for his spell to become Vampire King of All Worlds."

"How does it work?" asked the Boogan.

They told him how Vladimir had cruelly outlined the precise workings of the spell, glorying in the irony that the Chingles' victories over Balor and Caitlín had worked in his favour.

"So it looks like he has all the steps in place," the Boogan said. "But you got away from him, that's something."

"But we failed to rescue the little ones. And the worst part is that he plans to sacrifice them," said Cassie. "It's too horrible to contemplate! What are we to do?"

"Are Áine, Willa and Connle still in suspended animation?" asked Thomas.

"Afraid so," sighed the Boogan. "Yerra, it's a divil of a force field!"

"And what about the Merrows?" asked Cassie. "They're helping Vladimir, aren't they?"

"Those stupid women are so intent on spiting Áine, they don't know what they're doing," he replied.

"Vladimir says everybody has their price," said Cassie.

"Why doesn't Manannán intervene?" asked Thomas. "Surely he doesn't want to unleash a power like Vladimir's? After all, he's helped us by protecting Sasha and Jarlath and creating a cloak of invisibility around the submarine."

"He says that's as much as he's prepared to do. He's still sore with Áine and I'm afraid he doesn't really understand the black hearts of humans," sighed the Boogan, shaking his great seaweed head and sprinkling them with seawater. "He says it's up to yourselves to sort it all out. That's the way of the gods, I'm afraid. But I think it also means he must have faith in you."

"We are on our own," said Cassie. "All the deities who would help us have been disabled by the fairies' force field."

"There's one other thing," said the Boogan. "Vladimir has rounded up all the islanders and is keeping them prisoner. Some makeshift prison on a warship."

The blood drained from Cassie's face. She exchanged stricken glances with her brother and sister.

"Everyone?" she cried. "Tadgh, Róisín, the twins, Mrs Moriarty? That can only mean one thing. He plans to turn the islanders into Eretsuns!"

They thought about the poor prisoners in the underground fortress of New Selene and how they were starved to near death. How gaunt and weak they were. And they realised how fond they had grown of all the islanders. Of Tadgh their dear librarian friend who always helped them out with knowledge. Mr Mulally the publican and his warm hugs and smiles. Stephen Guilfoyle the hardworking farmer who always gave them lifts and free vegetables. Mrs Moriarty who put her heart into her knitting. Even Mrs Prendergast the sour old teashop owner – beyond her crustiness, she was still a person. Podge the ferry captain and his brother Patch the pilot . . . It was too terrible! A tear slid down Cassie's cheek but she hastily brushed it away.

They made their way back to the house. The island seemed eerie and deserted. There were no lights on. When they got to Fairy Fort House it was still lonely and forlorn. There was decaying half-eaten food on the table, proof of the haste of their departure.

But one thing really cheered them up. Nancy came running in from the garden, her face alight, in her hand a familiar silver bottle.

"Granny Clíona!" cried Cassie.

"It was hidden in the grass near the path!" said Nancy. "I found it when I kicked it with my foot!"

They were overjoyed to find Granny Clíona still inside, safe and sound. Obviously the silver covering had made her immune to the fairies' magic.

However, they kept the stopper half-closed while they explained to her what the fairies had done and the fate of Connle, Willa and Áine.

"Aye, pet, keep the stopper on, will ye?" she cried. "In case I get sucked into the fairies' evil net!"

"How did the bottle end up there on the grass?"

wondered Cassie. "It couldn't have *jumped* out of your jeans pocket as we walked up to the house, Thomas!"

"Unless Lorcan threw it from the window later?" said Thomas.

"He couldn't have – he was sleeping deeply that whole evening," said Cassie.

"You know," said Thomas slowly, "I must have got it wrong when I thought I had put it in my pocket. That enchanted sleep we had after the picnic must have confused me. Lorcan must have grabbed it at the picnic before we put him back in his buggy and he was kidnapped. Then it could have fallen from the buggy as we pushed it up the garden path."

"Anyway, it doesn't matter!" said Nancy. "We have Granny Clíona back again and I found her!"

Thomas spoke into the half-stoppered bottle. "What are we to do, Granny?" he sighed. "Vladimir has occupied Poolbeg Rock. He plans to fuse the babies with the polluted amulet during the eclipse so he can raise a diabolical army of vampires with his new power. The babies will die. The Merrows are in league with him. He is protected by an elite troop of Eretsuns. We know he has influence and can call on the protection of the international navy. We daren't move against him because he still has control of the babies."

"I think you will have to fight cunning with cunning," mused Granny Clíona. "Your only chance is to spring a surprise."

The Chingles felt emboldened and energised by Granny Clíona's presence. They felt the dim stirring of a tiny hope.

Maybe Vladimir didn't hold all the cards. Maybe they could do something to challenge him.

"The babies are locked in some invisible protective shield. Do you think it is your spell?" asked Thomas. "Can you get them out of it? I mean if somehow we were able to reach them."

They heard a chuckle from the bottle. "Could be, could be! In which case you must take me with you."

"Let's go right away," said Thomas, reaching for the bottle.

"Hold your horses!" shouted Granny Clíona. "That's only half a plan. We need to get the fairies to release their net so we can draw on the powers of the other deities."

"But perhaps the net is also keeping the Eretsuns out," said Cassie.

"The fairies' spell is faulty," said Granny Clíona. "It's only a matter of time before our enemies breach it anyway, especially if Vladimir is going to give himself more supernatural dark powers. It's not long to the eclipse."

They hesitated, realising the truth.

"This is war," Cassie said. "Remember what Scáthach told us before? Battles are not only won by the powerful. We have the weapon of the weak: that our opponent underestimates us."

"We must get the fairies to dismantle the magical barrier so we can have a united front of supernatural power," said Thomas.

"Then we somehow have to foil Vladimir's plan," said Cassie.

"Maybe we can negotiate with him," said Thomas. "Now that we have Granny Clíona, we have the means to undo the babies' protective shield. We know he's desperate to do that."

"But that's no use unless we can get all the babies away from his clutches," said Cassie.

"Yes but it gets us in the right place, close to the babies. I am the only one who can release their invisible barrier," came Granny Clíona's voice from the bottle. "If we approach him saying that I promise to undo the spell, we might have a chance to rescue the babies."

"But how can we do that?" asked Cassie. "Rescue the babies from right under Vladimir's nose, I mean."

They all lapsed into thought.

"We trick them like they did us," said Nancy suddenly.

"What do you mean?" asked Thomas.

"The sticks," she said. "In the cradle."

"You mean we kidnap the babies and replace them with changelings?" said Cassie. "We'd never get away with it. Besides, we don't have changelings."

"Hang on," said Thomas. "If Granny Clíona is allowed to break the force field around the babies, logically Vladimir is going to want to know the identity of the supernatural baby. We can only get him to agree to giving Granny Clíona a shot at breaking their invisible barrier if we reveal Tatiana's identity. Even if we save the others we might have to sacrifice her!"

"Not if we've replaced her with a changeling and the real Tatiana is safe with us," said Cassie.

"But what if it isn't Granny Clíona's spell that has caused the force field?" said Thomas.

"Then we are sunk," said Cassie. "But what else could it be?"

"It's worth a try," mused Thomas. "It has two advantages: it saves the babies and foils Vladimir's spell with one stroke. Can you think of a better plan?"

Cassie shook her head. It was a long shot but she really didn't have a better idea.

"Courage, my pet," said Granny Clíona from deep inside her bottle. "We overcame Balor and you saw off Caitlín. Vladimir doesn't know what he's up against!"

Cassie smiled faintly. "Let's get to work!"

CHAPTER 15

As the children approached the fairies' court, in exile in the Sacred Grove in the castle grounds, they were surrounded by a posse of hostile fairies keeping sentry. They instructed the Chingles to go away in no uncertain terms.

The Pooka sidled over as the children stormed off, disgruntled.

"You lot just never learn how to talk to them little creatures, do you?" he said scornfully. "Did you never hear all that flowery nonsense Connle gives them when he's trying to get round them? They lap it up."

"I wish Connle was here," sighed Thomas.

"So do I," said the Pooka.

They looked at him sideways. The Pooka wasn't known for his attachment to anyone.

The horse coughed, embarrassed. "You know what I mean, I miss teasing him."

But Cassie and Thomas smiled.

"So maybe we should bring them a present? But what do you give to fairies?" pondered Cassie.

"Get them back their Fairy Field," winked the Pooka. And with that he was gone.

"That means trying to persuade that miserable old beggar, Viracocha, to go shift," sighed Cassie.

"He's got no power now – why don't we just boot him out or frighten him with our lances?" said Thomas.

"Because if we do by some miracle succeed in getting the fairies to remove the magic net, he'll get all his powers back and destroy us to nothing, stupid!" said Cassie.

So they set off for the Fairy Field. But as soon as they approached it, they realised it was waterlogged.

"Poor Verruca!" said Nancy. "He's been crying and crying."

"It's Viracocha, Nancy," laughed Thomas. "A verruca is a wart on your foot!"

They saw a sodden lump of clothing in the middle of the field. They called out to him. But he didn't stir.

"Please, Viracocha, we need you!" pleaded Cassie.

"Go away," he gulped between big wracking sobs. "I no like humans. They always let me down." He curled up in a ball, hugging his knees.

As he shifted about, Thomas noticed some small brightly coloured creatures in a small enclosure fashioned out of mud by his side. There was a glorious tiny butterfly with shimmering gold wings, a multicoloured lizard as small as a baby's finger, a tiny spotted jaguar and a brilliantly coloured macaw, the size of a thumbnail. It looked like a miniature zoo, except the creatures moved as if real!

"What's that?" marvelled Thomas, bending down for a closer look.

Viracocha sighed. "I miss the animals from my home, so I make some – how you say – copies. I tired of humans."

"Are they real?" asked Cassie, reaching her hand in to stroke the minute jaguar, then recoiling as the little creature snarled and bared his jaws.

"No. They just, how you say, replica. They not last long. Tomorrow they become mud. I do not have the magic or the desire any more to make real things," he said dejectedly.

"But they're so lifelike," enthused Thomas.

The little golden butterfly flew up and alighted on his finger. It was no bigger than his fingernail. Thomas held it up to his eye. He admired its tiny quivering antenna, its delicately scaled golden wings with black eyespots. Then the tiny winged creature flew off and alighted on Viracocha's nose. The god brushed it roughly aside and the little creature crumbled away to dust.

"Ah," said Cassie, "that's a pity! It was so sweet!"

"But it was just clay," shrugged Viracocha. "Tomorrow they all mud and I make some more."

He picked up a piece of dirt between his thumb and forefinger, rolled it about and flicked it up towards the sky. In a flurry it became another tiny golden butterfly. The children exclaimed, amazed.

"You really are quite clever," said Cassie appreciatively.

"I bet you could make anything you wanted," said Thomas thoughtfully.

"Please leave me alone," sighed Viracocha, burying his head in his hands. "I no longer speak with humans. Always let me down."

"But we are only little children," said Nancy. "Give us a chance."

"What do you want?" he said gruffly, raising his mournful face to glance at them briefly.

"We just want you to leave the field for a while so we can get you back your powers," said Thomas. "The fairies are awfully attached to it and, well, you must be uncomfortable there, what with all the water and everything."

"I am very dump, how you say?" he moaned. "Very old, and dumpy and watered."

Cassie suddenly had a brilliant idea. "We know a nice place where you could sleep in a crystal bed," she wheedled. "It's a house that belongs to the former Sun Goddess and it's cosy and warm."

Thomas and Nancy's faces lit up. Surely he would say yes to that!

Nothing happened for ages but just as they had given up hope, the bundle of damp clothes stirred. Viracocha rose up mournfully. He scooped up his little menagerie and put them in a pocket inside his poncho.

"The sun, I miss the sun. Your sun here is very weak. Water comes from sky too many times. Clouds are always crying – you no need me here to make water. Sun Goddess must be very lazy." He shook his mournful head in disapproval.

"If you must know, she is married to our uncle and her sister is looking after the sun as well as the moon!" thundered Cassie. "And if you didn't spend all your time crying and feeling sorry for yourself, you might be able to get yourself back to your home. They obviously need you more there. Though fat lot of use you are to anyone, lying in a soggy heap!"

Viracocha was taken aback by her reprimand and for a moment bristled. But then he looked up at the sky as a soft rain began to fall. The gentle misty rain caressed his already damp face.

"Perhaps you speak the truth," he admitted. "My people need me and I must try get back to them."

Then, to their great surprise, he quit the field sharply, leaving big puddles as he walked away.

Soon they had him installed in Áine's house where he soon fell into a deep sleep on Áine's crystal bed.

"That was easily done," said Thomas as they bailed out the field in preparation for the return of the fairies. "For once, Cassie, your sharp tongue has come in handy."

"He was getting on my nerves, just feeling sorry for himself," Cassie replied. "Well, let's hope the fairies will fulfil their side of the bargain."

"And I think we might have found a way to manufacture some changelings," said Thomas with a smile.

"Yes!" said Nancy.

Cassie stared at Thomas, puzzled. "Viracocha's skill with clay!" she suddenly realised. "If we can get him to play ball!"

"We just have to ask him nicely," Nancy said. "Or Cassie can shout at him."

"But maybe he can only make miniature replicas," said Cassie doubtfully.

"Well, he's a creator god," said Thomas. "He should be able to make full-size ones if he wishes."

"That remains to be seen," sighed Cassie.

As soon as they'd managed to clear Viracocha's tears from the field with a bucket and a wheelbarrow, to their surprise a shower of petals descended from the sky. There was a flurry of wings and high-pitched laughter as the fairies descended back to their field, carrying rush matting.

King Finbhearra and Queen Úna, their eyes shining, ran to thank the children.

"You are twice welcome, oh fly-abouty lovely little thingies," said Thomas, trying to talk in the flowery manner he knew they liked – but not quite succeeding.

The king and queen looked at him blankly as if he was talking double Dutch but then smiled anyway.

The king bowed low. "And we are now forever in your debt."

"In which case you can repay it by removing the magical barrier," said Cassie, cutting to the chase.

The king and queen shuffled their feet and looked down, embarrassed at this.

"We would like to help," said the queen. "But, alas, our fairy followers don't agree."

"Well, you'll just have to make them," said Cassie, growing impatient.

"But they cannot be bidden like that," said the king evasively. "Besides we want to feast and sing our return to our home."

"If you don't help, we'll get that beggar Viracocha back," warned Thomas. "Don't forget, your force field is keeping people in as well as out. They can't leave even if they want to. And Viracocha definitely wants to go home."

The king looked shifty.

"It's something else, isn't it?" said Cassie.

"The truth is we don't know how to reverse the spell and remove the force field," admitted Queen Úna, her cheeks red with embarrassment. "The spell went up in something of a rush and a mishmash."

"Well, you'll just have to work on it," said a furious Cassie and, grabbing Thomas and Nancy, she stormed out of the field.

Granny Clíona was equally perplexed by the fairies' inability to reverse the spell.

"Ach, but let's continue with our alliance-building with other deities," she said brightly from her bottle. "Something will occur to me."

And something did occur to her when they told her about Viracocha's skill with clay and their notion that maybe he could manufacture changelings.

"Have I ever told you about my talent for the little things?" she asked them from her bottle.

They looked at each other, puzzled.

"I'm good at spells that reduce things in size. It's not a very useful talent, more a party piece. But if I can make the real babies very small – temporarily, mind you – it might help us smuggle them out."

"You mean if you made them tiny we could put them in our pockets?" asked Thomas. "Why don't you miniaturise all our enemies and I could squash them underfoot?"

"Och, I'm not that clever. I've only ever been able to do it with objects. But I think I could manage wee babies!"

"I like it!" said Cassie. "It's worth a shot."

"You never told us before you were able to do these kinds of spells," said Thomas.

"Och, when you've been stuck in a bottle for two hundred years you forget all kinds of things. It's only just come back to me!" said Granny Clíona. "Now let's crack on with seeing our visitors."

They salmon-leaped to Glimmering Lake and discovered the Eight Chinese Immortals were hidden behind a cloud, too weak to move about. They could barely talk.

The philosopher Han just managed to say, "Ah, the very clever not very old persons of busy habits," before falling into a faint.

"Oh dear," said Cassie. "We'll have to remove the force field soon. It's destroying their strength."

The Eight Immortals just sighed and moaned, collapsed on their cloud.

"Now just nod your heads for yes," said Thomas. "If we get rid of the force field will you help us fight Vladimir?"

As one they nodded their heads. The children smiled. Well, at least that was something. Though in their weakened state the Eight Immortals couldn't fight a mosquito, never mind an evil, power-crazed man and an army of the Undead.

"There's still the wee dilemma that the fairies don't know how to reverse their spell," said Granny Clíona from her bottle. "We need to find an antidote."

They heard Han the Philosopher croak something. Nancy crept nearer. She listened intently to him as the others debated among themselves about what to do next.

Nancy tugged Cassie's sleeve.

"What now?" said Cassie impatiently.

"They might have to do what they hate most. That's what Han says," said Nancy.

They heard a shriek from the bottle.

"That's it! I remember once we had a similar problem in my time! In fact it was when they tried to ban me from the island! The antidote required they do what they hate!" exclaimed Granny Clíona. "Let's away to them wee folk and knock their wee heeds together!"

So they salmon-leaped back to the Fairy Field.

They landed right in the middle of a fairy feast to the annoyance of the assembled company.

"Shoo!" shouted Dris the Blackberry Fairy thunderously. "We are thinking of banning outsiders from our field!"

"Just answer one question and we'll go," pressed Cassie.

"Very well," said King Finbheara.

"What do you all hate most?"

With one voice the answer came.

"HARD WORK!" the fairies shouted.

"We like only to play and feast and dance," agreed King Finbhearra.

"We use spells for everything – like preparing delicious food and dressing ourselves in beautiful garments," said Queen Úna.

Thomas suppressed a smirk of amusement. "Well, work is what you have to do to lift the force field."

There was a murmur of disapproval and annoyance that turned into a crescendo of carping and complaining.

"How do you know?" demanded Dris, his purple little face scrunched up in annoyance.

"Granny Clíona remembers a similar incident from her time," said Thomas.

"Don't you remember trying to get rid of me in the same way?" piped Granny Clíona from her bottle. "And yer spelling was just as rubbish then as it is now!"

King Finbhearra looked shamefaced and many of the other fairies hung their heads. They broke into fevered discussion and debate, ignoring the Chingles and Granny Clíona.

Finally Queen Úna bid the piper sound a shrill note. The sound was so insistent, it caused them all to be quiet.

"We are all agreed the force field isn't working," she exclaimed, standing on her little tiptoes.

There was a grudging sort of agreement.

"It is sapping all our energy and making us too tired for feasting and fun," added King Finbhearra.

The weary fairies nodded their heads.

"It's boring having to maintain it," admitted Cam, the idle Fairy of the Buttercups. "But what is hard work? It is so long since we have done any."

Thomas smiled with a wicked gleam and glanced over at Cassie. "I'm remembering the Baba Yaga. I'm thinking dust and grime and sweeping and polishing," he said. "Follow me."

He led a troop of fairies up to Fairy Fort House.

"Now all you have to do is clean our house. It's a bit dirty and neglected since we've been away but I'm sure you'll have it spick and span in no time."

The fairies groaned but began to half-heartedly clean the house.

At first Dris and another group tried to do a magic spell but Cassie insisted they did it the hard way – manual labour.

Never before had the children seen such a group of work-shy lazybones. The fairies were absolutely useless. It took four of them an hour to roll one crumb out from under the table and then they spent the next hour arguing about where to put it. Queen Úna cried, actually cried, when she was asked to scrape out a congealed porridge bowl. Then she fell into a dead faint. King Finbhearra fell asleep after five minutes trying to polish a fork. It was hopeless. They really didn't know how to do any work. The only light relief was

Granny Clíona's merry chuckles from her bottle as Thomas, Cassie and Nancy gave her a blow-by-blow account of the fairies' miserable efforts to clean the kitchen.

"Dris nearly drowned in the sink," reported Nancy after she fished him out by his little neck.

"Cam has fallen into the butter dish because she was so busy trying to lick it," Cassie told her.

"The flying fairies have all developed sneezing fits from the cobwebs on the ceiling," tittered Thomas.

Thomas decided to check out the force field and went outside.

Queen Úna saw her chance and said she'd better accompany him, as she'd know better than him if the antidote were taking effect. He took to the air as an eagle with Queen Úna on his back.

"It's having no effect at all," Thomas told them all on their return, downhearted.

Some of the younger fairies started to wail.

"There's something not right then. It worked in my day," said Granny Clíona. "It should have had even a little effect."

"Perhaps it's not the thing they hate most now," said Cassie thoughtfully.

She went into a huddle with Granny Clíona and Thomas.

"Can we think of something they hate more than hard work?" said Cassie.

"Ach, the fairies hate so many things it's hard to know where to start," sighed Granny Clíona.

"They hate all the new gods," Nancy piped up.

Thomas looked at her as if she was a genius and gave her a hug.

"Of course!" he exclaimed. "That's the perfect antidote. They put the force field up to repel outside deities. To bring it down they have to do the exact opposite!"

"They have to welcome them to their feast!" laughed Cassie. "Oh, wait until we tell them. This I can't wait to see!"

Within half an hour the Fairy Field was adorned with beautiful flowers woven into a carpet. Garlands of blooms hung from the hawthorn trees. A table was laid out with the most beautiful fairy food on silver and gold plates. Drinks were served in goblets inlaid with diamonds.

Queen Úna and King Finbhearra looked impressive in their woven clothes. Queen Una's hair was decorated with beautiful blossoms. The members of the fairy court were dressed in their finest costumes.

The court had never looked so magical and beautiful – but the fairies had never looked more miserable in their lives. They looked almost as dejected as Viracocha.

The children watched from a haystack as the fairies welcomed those they hated most into their heartland – the magical creatures and gods and goddesses from outside. Despite feeling tense about whether the antidote would work or not, tears of laughter ran down Thomas and Cassie's cheeks as they watched Dris bow low to Viracocha and nearly faint at the smell of the old Beggar God. Queen Úna and King Finbhearra looked like they were sucking lemons as they extended a hand to each of the Eight Chinese Immortals. The funniest was when Almudj, the Aboriginal Crocodile, back to his normal size, devoured the entire contents of the table, goblets, plates and all, and the fairies had to just smile nicely and refill the table with a magic spell, only for him to do it again.

"I feel sorry for the outsiders having to put up with such a frosty reception," whispered Cassie.

Thomas was intently watching Queen Úna who was looking up at the sky with a concerned expression.

"It's not working yet," said Thomas. "I'm getting worried that we'll never lift this force field. We'll have to face Vladimir alone."

But then the fairy music started and a magical thing happened. The foreign gods began to revive a little. Han the Philosopher Musician took up his flute and joined in the play. Immortal Woman played on an instrument that looked like a kind of lute. Then Viracocha revealed some panpipes hidden under his moth-eaten poncho.

The children listened transfixed in the hayrick. The music, at first slow and tentative, swelled as the different instruments weaved around each other. The sound was truly magical and heavenly, like birds singing, wind rustling over the ocean, a baby's laughter. Compelled by its beauty, the children were drawn to the Midnight Court. And joining hands, all the fairies and other Chinese Immortals, even Almudj the Crocodile, began to dance.

The music increased in tempo and the dancers whirled around in a frenzy, passing by each other in a blur. And as the musicians drew to a climax, something seemed to burst. They could all feel it though it was invisible to the eye. This time Queen Úna looked up to the heavens with shining eyes and gave a happy smile to Thomas.

"I think it's working!" he gasped, breathless from the dance.

"I think you might be right," said a familiar voice.

"Connle!" Cassie exclaimed.

To the Chingles' great delight, Connle strode into the court followed by Áine and Willa.

"We're back from our little holiday," he said, wagging his finger at the fairies.

"But the babies, are they alive?" asked Áine, barely able to say the words.

"They are still alive, but held prisoner by Vladimir," said Cassie.

"My poor Tatiana!" cried Willa.

Cassie told them about Poolbeg Rock and Vladimir's plan to carry out his spell at the time of the eclipse that was nearly upon them. They listened carefully, horror growing on their faces.

"But if the protective shield is in place surely whatever he does he won't be able to kill the babies?" said Cassie.

"We don't know how strong the protective shield is," said Áine. "It's too risky. It might be penetrated by powerful explosives."

"And Raznik is constantly experimenting with ways to breach it," said Thomas. "He might find a way."

"It's true," said Cassie. "Vladimir seems confident that he's found a way to sacrifice all four babies. He is, after all, going ahead with his plans, despite the problem of the protective shield."

"Well, we have a plan too!" Thomas declared.

Cassie looked at him doubtfully. They really only had half a plan and she somehow felt bad about giving Áine and Willa false hope. On the other hand, sometimes what she thought of as Thomas's half-baked notions proved surprisingly effective.

They left the fairies and the foreign gods deep in surprisingly friendly conversation and returned to Fairy Fort House, where Granny Clíona came out of her bottle and they discussed possibilities.

"Our goal is to rescue the babies *and* foil Vladimir's spell," said Thomas. "We think we've found a way to achieve both goals at the same time." Áine, Willa and Connle listened intently.

"Vladimir's spell depends on the workings of lots of elements in the right order," said Cassie. "Our plan is that if we wreck a key element we can undermine it."

"We are thinking that we could rescue the babies by substituting changelings for them," said Thomas. "Then Vlad's spell won't work because we've ruined a vital part."

Áine and Willa gasped at the daring of the plan.

"But how will you get near him to do that?" Áine asked.

"Vladimir's weak link is that he's not sure of the identity of the divine baby," said Thomas. "He has to sacrifice all of them but there is a risk the human ones will contaminate his spell. He's more worried about this than he lets on. We go to him with Granny Clíona and reveal to him that it was her blessing that caused the force field around the babies. Then we say she can break it."

"But can you do it at the right moment, Granny Clíona?" asked Áine. "Even a clever witch like you can't always dictate the timing or the precise workings of her spells."

"Och, that's true," she agreed. "Look what happened with the babies' protective shield. It seems the babies themselves chose the moment to activate it."

"We have to believe you can," said Thomas soberly. "Everything depends on that."

"That's just one of the risks," said Cassie. "There are others. For instance, will he allow us to get close enough to them to swap them for changelings?"

"But the biggest problem is that we're sure he will only agree to co-operate if we reveal which baby is Willa's," said Thomas.

Willa gulped and looked anguished but said nothing.

"We also have to make the switch, somehow distract him, substitute the changelings for the babies and escape," said Thomas.

"But we need to know that Willa agrees to us revealing which baby is Tatiana," said Cassie. "If we manage the switch she'll be safe. But something could go wrong and she's the most at risk."

There was a tense silence. Finally Willa spoke.

"Your plan is maybe good, I think," she said. "You have to tell Vladimir who is Tatiana. But you already rescue her and leave behind this changeling?"

"Yes," confirmed Thomas. "We will rescue her and leave her replica behind."

"Then I agree," said Willa. "After all it is my fault everyone is in danger."

"So how are you going to make the swap?" asked Áine.

"Granny Clíona has a very elegant solution," said Thomas.

"I make the real babies very wee, so we can smuggle them out," said Granny Clíona.

Willa looked at her in puzzlement.

"She means she can reduce the babies in size and then hide them so we can sneak them out," explained Connle.

"Och, that's what I said!" cried Granny Clíona.

"And you can do this?" asked Willa, her eyes wide with wonder.

"I've always been a dab hand at making things tiny," said Granny Clíona with a note of pride. To demonstrate, she blew on a cup on the table and reduced it to the size of a fingernail. Willa placed it on the palm of her hand, amazed.

"If the real babies are very tiny we can put them in our pockets," said Nancy.

"Or better still, in Granny Clíona's bottle," said Connle.

"This is a brilliant idea," said Áine. "Granny Clíona, do you think you can make them tiny even if the force field can't be broken, all four together? Then we could wait until they are back on the island to break their force field."

"Och, I can but try!" said Granny Clíona.

"And you can make them full size again?" asked Willa.

"Of course, my dear!" Granny Clíona blew on the tiny cup, now on the table, and in the twinkling of an eye it was restored to its proper size.

"And how exactly are you going to make the substitution of changelings under Vladimir's nose?" asked Áine.

"I will have to trick Vladimir into putting out all the lights, so we can switch the babies with the fakes," said Granny Clíona.

"No better woman!" winked Connle appreciatively.

"We will need some very convincing changelings," said Áine.

"We know the very person, or I should say god, who can help," said Thomas. "Viracocha makes brilliant tiny replicas of animals. We just have to persuade him to make babies."

"I'm sure the Chingles can talk him round," said Áine.

"Cassie terrified him into leaving the Fairy Field," said Thomas. "I'm confident we can rely on her."

"What if, despite all our efforts, Vladimir succeeds in making his spell work?" asked Áine in a small voice.

"We will fight him in battle," said Thomas. "We have to

371

drive him and his vampire troops away whether or not his spell works. Now we also have the help of Viracocha, the Eight Chinese Immortals and Almudj the Rainbow Snake."

"The other gods may not have their full powers yet," said Áine. "Even if they regain some of their strength, their powers here will be weaker than in their own place. It is by no means certain we can beat him."

"There's another complication," said Cassie. "We can fight the Eretsuns but we've made a promise to their children not to kill any of them, as they are all the unwilling victims of Vladimir."

"But, Cassie, don't forget these Eretsuns are not the parents of the wild children," said Thomas. "Vladimir said he had created a new elite group of vampires risen from the dead. I think we will be facing ghouls."

"That's even more worrying," said Cassie.

Áine looked intently at the children. "You have bravely fought Balor and Caitlín. You have used your gifts wisely and well but this may be your most difficult battle yet. You are up against an evil human who does not understand the powers he is unleashing. He has hostages and you may not be able to kill his fighters."

The Chingles looked at her gloomily.

"Doesn't sound like we stand much of a chance," said Cassie.

"But you have come up with a clever plan," said Áine. "You can use cunning and skill to outwit him. Even an enemy with superior magic and weapons can be defeated if you use your minds. But what of these Eretsuns? How did you defeat them without killing before?"

"We pinged stones at them. Well, precious stones, diamonds and stuff," said Thomas.

"Maybe it will work again," said Áine.

"We don't exactly have lots of jewels lying around, apart from Willa's necklace and that won't last long," sighed Cassie.

"I gladly give it," Willa said

"Yes but Vladimir has, under the sea!" cried Thomas. "If we can get hold of one of his gemstones and break it up, we'd have weapons. I'm sure the Karzeleks wouldn't mind."

"It's a thought," agreed Cassie.

"And the tainted amulet? Does Vladimir have it or does Mara still hold it?" asked Áine.

"Last we saw, Mara was wearing it but the Merrows are out there around Vladimir's missiles at Poolbeg Rock and we're sure they are in collusion with him," said Thomas. "Anyway there's no chance she'd give it to us. Or to you either, Áine."

"Especially not to me. It is their jealousy of me that has caused so much trouble," said Áine.

"They'd only give it to you in exchange for Jarlath," said Cassie. Áine went pale. "Not that I'm suggesting that. Good grief! I'd never let them get their hands on dear Uncle Jarlath. And I'm not even sure that would work now that they are under Vladimir's sway."

"If Vladimir plans to fuse the amulet and the precious

stones underwater, perhaps we should also have underwater support," suggested Cassie.

"We could call on Rónán and Tethra – they've helped us before," said Thomas. Rónán and Tethra were dolphins, brother and sister of Lugh the God of Light.

"And don't forget we have Jarlath and Sasha in the submarine. They are invisible for the time being," said Cassie.

Áine and Willa exchanged a look.

"We'd rather they didn't get involved," said Áine. "We really don't want them to know about our being of the Otherworld."

"I'm not so sure they haven't guessed," said Cassie.

"Even if they have, we can ask the gods to make them forget," said Willa. "These are very delicate things between a man and a woman. It is better that they think we are of humankind."

"They may think we have bewitched them if they discover we are from the Otherworld," explained Áine. "Besides, I run the risk of total annihilation by the Tuatha Dé Danann if I reveal my divine origins."

Áine and Willa exchanged a sisterly hug.

Thomas threw them a worried look. "Áine, Willa knows your secret. Is this not dangerous for you?"

"Willa is also of the Otherworld. I did not tell her, she guessed. She knew without being told. It is different. The gods cannot punish me for that. The most important thing is that Jarlath never finds out."

Thomas shrugged. He thought it might be rather great to know your partner was a magical being but grown-ups often saw things differently to children. It was strange that Jarlath had never guessed. But he was a scientist and mathematician and disinclined to believe in the airy-fairy, even when it was right under his nose.

But there was one thought playing on all their minds, the unspoken understanding between all of them. Even if, and it was a big if, they managed to stop Vladimir seizing total power, there was a strong possibility that the Chingles, their allies and the babies wouldn't live to tell the tale.

CHAPTER 16

"I t feels a bit like being an army general," Thomas whispered to Cassie as they got ready to brief the motley crew of international magical beings gathered together to take on the might of Vladimir. They had all met in Áine's cottage in the north-west of the island. As the most magical house on the island, it seemed to offer some protection and was far enough away from Poolbeg Rock not to arouse suspicion.

The Chingles stood on the doorstep, anxiously looking at the sky. It was pitch black and the bright, plump full moon was high in the north of the sky. Thomas noticed its left-hand portion was already in the earth's shadow. There wasn't much time. They had maybe an hour and a half before the total eclipse.

"How exactly are we going to get the babies away from Vladimir on Poolbeg Rock once we make the switch?" asked Cassie.

"Luck, cunning, superior magical ability and better fighting skills," said Thomas.

"And me," said Nancy. Thomas hugged his little sister.

"You mean you haven't a clue," said Cassie.

"How can I? I don't know what we'll be facing," shrugged Thomas. "We will have to rely on our instinct and ingenuity honed over many battles."

"Perhaps at the right moment we can shape-shift and create a diversion to allow Connle to escape with the babies," said Cassie. "I bet we'll have to go into Vladimir's presence unarmed. We'll be surrounded by Eretsuns. We're in much the weaker position."

"As I've told you before, the one thing we've got more of is our minds," smiled Thomas.

Cassie turned her eyes up to heaven. Her brother was irrepressible.

"I'll know," said Nancy. "The Star Splinter will give me a clue. I'll nod at you when the time is right."

"Just as well we don't have to rely on Thomas's mind all the time," laughed Cassie. She knew it was a perilous mission, even suicidal, but at least they were in it together. "I have a terrible feeling we're doomed and this is just one last brave, heroic mission so we can go down fighting."

Nancy slipped her hand into Cassie's. "Don't give up," she said softly. "We can do it."

Cassie smiled weakly at her little sister and ruffled her curls but she wasn't convinced.

They went back inside to organise their allies.

"Now, as we have explained," Thomas began, "the plan is that Cassie, Nancy, Connle and I go to Poolbeg Rock and beg safe passage to see Vladimir. We will take Granny Clíona, who will use her magic to rescue the babies. We will have to go unarmed but with the substitute babies concealed about our persons."

"We have the help of a very talented god to make the substitutes," said Cassie, nodding at Viracocha who humbly bowed his head.

"They will be leetle figures and will grow at the right time," he said. "But I need a lock of hair for each from a member of family."

Áine produced a scissors and cut one of her own blonde locks. She also cut hair from Willa, and from Cassie and Nancy, who both had dark hair like the twins.

"But these replicas will be powerless and will stop the spell?" asked Willa.

Viracocha shrugged. "Always before they are not so good. Maybe last one day before come dust. They no way help Vladimir in his spell, is you no worry, my amigo."

"Okay – Granny Clíona reduces the real babies in size and we switch them with the changelings," said Thomas confidently. "We get out of there. Vladimir's spell falls apart and we chase him and his horrible vampires out of Inish Álainn."

Everyone knew the plan was risky but they were buoyed by his spirit.

"I have one good piece of news," said Áine. "Finnen will be joining you. She contacted me to say so."

Viracocha perked up. He was curious to meet the Irish moon goddess who was also looking after the sun.

"In the meantime, Almudj will go with Rónán and Tethra the dolphins who are standing by. They will try to take a chunk out of each of the sacred stones," said Thomas. "Almudj will crush them in his teeth and we can use them to defeat the Eretsuns."

The crocodile creature clicked and roared.

"He is happy to help but hopes his teeth are still sharp enough for biting stones," translated Nancy.

"So do we," agreed Cassie. "The Eight Immortals will come to help us get off Poolbeg Rock. We will hand them the babies and try to capture Vladimir. We will also try to rescue the islanders who are held on his warship."

"The fairies will operate as a back-up force. They can be messengers and will stand by with weapons in case we need them," said Thomas. He pointed to a replica of the island and Poolbeg Rock laid out on Áine's crystal table. "As we speak, the Boogan is relaying a message through the Merrows, offering that we meet Vladimir." Thomas did indeed sound like a young army general. "If all goes to plan, we shall be setting off for Poolbeg Rock shortly."

"This mission is fraught with danger," said Cassie. "We do not know that we will succeed in undermining the spell. We do not know that we will be able to defeat the Eretsuns or prevent the fusing. But we will all certainly try."

All the various fairies and Magical Beings cheered and shouted out good luck in their own tongues. For a brief moment they felt brave. Just as everyone was about to leave,

Finnen arrived. The Eight Chinese Immortals immediately fell prostrate to the floor. She looked more radiant than ever, her gown of sun and moon symbols whirling with light of every hue.

Finnen bowed back to the Chinese Immortals and also bowed low to Viracocha. "Lord Viracocha, I hail you as a creator god!"

Cassie and Thomas looked at each other in amazement. They were surprised to see Finnen showing such reverence to the miserable old beggar, even if he had recently gone up in their estimation.

Then Viracocha did something extraordinary. He smiled.

Quickly, they filled Finnen in on the plans. She digested all that they told her and looked thoughtful.

"I am sure Viracocha will make wonderful replicas," Finnen said.

Viracocha reached into his poncho and took out his miniature menagerie of animals. Everyone marvelled to see the tiny creatures held in the palm of his grimy hand. Then he folded his palm over and was left with a handful of clay. He took the four locks of hair, mixed each with a pinch of clay and fashioned tiny balls. He spat on each in turn and then began to hum softly, falling into a trance, rolling them in his hands. He let out a wild shout and suddenly became tall and imposing, a crown of sunbeams shining from his head. The children had to shield their eyes from his brilliance. Tears rained from his eyes and he cried onto the four balls of clay. For a moment the balls glowed and pulsated. Then Viracocha breathed on them and closed over his hand. He shut his eyes and intoned something in a strange tongue and once more became a beggar again. He handed the four balls to Thomas.

"They will turn into the babies when you need them," he said. "Just mumble 'Viracocha' under your breath."

The children regarded the little clay balls in awe.

"Let's hope your magic isn't too powerful and they don't turn into real babies," joked Cassie.

"I'm sure Viracocha knows what he is doing," said Finnen. "But I must warn you – the power of an eclipse is very special. You never know what can happen!"

The air felt like a cold slap in the face as the Chingles and Connle set off for Poolbeg Rock in a currach, a traditional boat with a wooden frame covered in animal hides. The little craft was tossed in the hostile sea as they tried to row through the churning waters around the rock. The shadow that was now over halfway across the moon was beginning to faintly light up, like a piece of iron heated in a forge that was just beginning to glow. It was a beautiful but eerie sight. The sky seemed darker than usual and the clusters of stars brighter. There wasn't long to go before a total eclipse.

No one spoke as they pulled the oars through the water. Nancy cradled the silver bottle containing Granny Clíona. Thomas made sure the four balls of clay that would become replicas of the babies were safe in his pocket. As soon as they got closer to the island, they heard the peal of a distant bell and the howling of a horde of Eretsuns who had caught the scent of fresh human blood drifting over the waves.

"Let's hope the Boogan has negotiated our safe passage," shouted Thomas through chattering teeth.

As they got closer they saw that the island was guarded by snarling, screaming vampires. At first they thought they were going to be attacked but then they saw that the demons had collars around their necks and were padlocked to the rocks on large steel chains. But it wasn't just Eretsuns. There were ferocious-looking creatures with animals' heads, talons and snarling jaws. One looked like Labartu, the Babylonian vampire. She had a hairy body, a lioness's head with donkey's teeth and ears, long fingers and fingernails and the feet of a bird with sharp talons. She was holding vicious snakes. Another had the body of a snake, ten heads, each with terrifying fangs, and leathery wings like a giant bat.

Vladimir is already raising other vampire spirits, Thomas thought grimly. His power is growing.

As they drew up to the island, they saw that Raznik the sorcerer was waiting for them, amidst the howling creatures they had summoned from the underworld. Thomas made ready to throw the rope over but Raznik held up his hand.

"We will take only the witch," said Raznik. "You others must remain in the boat."

"No way," said Cassie. "It's all of us or you don't get Granny Clíona." She signalled to the others to row away again.

Just as they were moving away, Raznik called them back. "Disembark and we will search you!" he roared.

On land, four blank-eyed Eretsun guards dressed all in black leather searched the children. They wore muzzles and eye-visors. Beneath their masks Thomas caught a glimpse of hairy faces and long fanged teeth. These must be the elite Eretsuns Vladimir had raised from the spirit world and had been training. They were armed with machine guns and rapiers and had a savage power. But they gave off an inhuman chill and the stench of death. Thomas felt very disinclined to fight them.

When the search was finished the guards grunted and the Chingles were led to a dark cave, guarded by more elite Eretsuns. These were equipped with even more frightening equipment: what looked like miniature ground-to-air missiles and semi-automatic machine guns.

Before entering the cave Thomas took one more anxious look at the moon. Its tip was like a pale yellow sliver in contrast to the three-quarters in shadow that glowed with the intensity of the embers of a dying fire. It looked a bit like a Japanese lantern. The start of the total eclipse was maybe less than ten minutes away!

Raznik waved them into the cave, which felt cold and dank. A large light hung from the cave's ceiling. There was a strong smell of brackish seawater and rotting seaweed. At the back of the cave was a trapdoor.

A guard opened the trapdoor. On the other side were several flights of stone stairs descending under the sea. They corkscrewed down the stairs for what seemed like miles, nobody talking.

Eventually they came to another trapdoor, where Raznik pressed a combination-lock number to release it.

"You are wise to co-operate with Vladimir," said Raznik in precise English. "He was planning to blow all the babies up in a controlled explosion before the eclipse, reckoning that the supernatural one would survive. At least this way you get to save three of your precious babes. Personally I would have been happy to see the back of them."

The children shuddered. They'd made their offer just in time.

The door slid open and they were in an underwater globe-shaped glass room fronting directly above the site of Balor's wreck. They hadn't seen this globe in the submarine survey. It was lit with powerful arc lamps. Outside around the wreck the great precious stones glinted and shone, many-hued and phosphorescent under water. The remains of Balor's yacht were in the centre like the ribs of a rotted whale. Along the sea floor the fault line was clearly visible like a long sinuous crack in the earth.

It was like being in a goldfish bowl. Thomas looked down through the glass floor and thought he saw the flick of a Merrow's tail. Then he saw a sight that truly horrified him. Large sharks with vampire-like fangs swam among the stones above the wrecked boat. A tail flicked by and a shark turned and attacked the glass. They saw the beast's huge maw of a mouth and flinched, even though the glass was a buffer. These were the horrible beasts that Almudj and the dolphins, Rónán and Tethra, would have to face.

The babies were sleeping in their cots on their platform, which was right up against the glass. On closer inspection the glass was fitted with detonators. Vladimir was seated on a high platform made of pearl, just beside the babies' cots. Above the cots a glass tube that finished in a round bulb hung down from the ceiling. There was a hole in the bulb, large enough to insert a baby. This contraption was clearly where Vladimir meant to place the baby sacrifice.

On the other side of the glass room there was a clock and a television monitor linked to a camera showing the night sky. The moon was now glowing bright red with only its outer rim still to pass through the earth's shadow. It was countdown to the full eclipse.

"Instruct the witch to break the spell. You may then take the three human babies. You will leave Willa's baby here. You will have five minutes to get to the outer chamber," Vladimir said in his cool, unemotional voice. There seemed no room for discussion.

Connle held up the silver bottle and tapped its neck. The ghostly form of Granny Clíona oozed out of the bottle. A slight tremor passed through Vladimir's jaw as she fixed him with a stern eye and rose to her full height.

"I'll not break the spell until you guarantee safe passage for the babies you do not want," she said firmly.

Vladimir sneered down at her. "Shut up, you tiresome old woman!" he said. "You are in no position to negotiate.

Every second you waste in discussion leaves less time for your escape."

Granny Clíona said nothing and passed through him, which made him shudder. But he soon regained his composure. Then mumbling an incantation under her breath, she circled around the babies' invisible barrier.

Sure that nobody was watching, Thomas emptied the tiny clay figures into his hand and passed one each to Cassie, Nancy and Connle.

Granny Clíona continued to move around the outside of the invisible barrier, preparing her spell to miniaturise the babies. Everyone held their breath.

Cassie glanced anxiously at the video monitor. Nearly all the moon pulsed red except for a faint shadow at the top. The total eclipse was almost upon them.

As if on cue, the three Merrows, Mara, Sionna and Fand, swam around the outside of the glass globe. Each of them wore an expression of triumph that was so extreme it seemed slightly mad. Mara wore the amulet around her neck. She stared directly at Cassie through the glass and threw back her head in laughter. Cassie saw something disconcerting. Mara had large vampire-like fangs. Vladimir had them in his power. Fand and Sionna also laughed revealing their fangs. Somehow he had turned them into vampire Merrows. Such powers allied with their cold hearts could only mean trouble. Cassie felt her guts go cold. She had never liked the Merrows but they had always seemed to her more foolish than evil. But now Vladimir had turned them. He corrupted everything he came in contact with.

Mara removed the amulet and, swimming above the globe, placed it in a special cavity in the roof of the glass. It fell into a chamber that was part of the tube suspended from the ceiling.

Vladimir looked at Granny Clíona with contempt. "Well, you useless old woman? Admit you can do nothing!"

"I was merely preparing my antidote," Granny Clíona pronounced. "You need to put the lights out."

Cassie glanced anxiously at Connle, hoping Vladimir would fall for their ruse. He blinked quickly.

"I don't trust you, stupid old ghost. Why do you need the lights out? You have wasted enough of my time," said Vladimir icily.

"It is the only way I can break the binding spell locking the babies in the invisible protective shield," said Granny Clíona.

"You mean to trick me," said Vladimir.

"You risk ruining your spell, contaminating it with human babies," said Granny Clíona calmly.

"Do as she says and we will reveal what you want to know," said Cassie, her voice quivering. "The identity of the divine baby."

Vladimir smiled. "So you are prepared to betray Willa's baby." He laughed coldly. "It will be worth it to see the proud Chingles behave just like everybody else. Your betrayal is very dear to me."

"The child you want is the youngest baby, Tatiana," said Thomas in a low voice.

"Very well, old hag!" said Vladimir. He gave the signal and all went dark except for the television screen showing the moon glowing red.

In the flickering light of the phosphorescent jewels in the ocean, Granny Clíona whirled around the babies' platform, creating a vortex.

Connle gave a high-pitched whistle and in one move the children and he tossed the clay replicas towards Granny Clíona's spinning form. Under their breaths the children mumbled "Viracocha".

There was a great empty sound as if all the energy had been sucked out of the room. There was a brief tremor in the glass globe.

"Raznik, restore the lights!" Vladimir shouted.

Four babies lay sleeping on the floor in their blankets. The platform and cots had disappeared. Granny Clíona had also vanished but it looked like her spell had worked. Connle held the silver bottle.

But there was something odd about the replicas, Cassie realised. Lorcan's had raven-black hair instead of his blonde mane, Tatiana had a mass of curly brown hair instead of her raven-black hair and the twins, Mattie and Tilda had long blonde hair. Somehow Viracocha had mixed up the hair samples and given them to the wrong babies. Cassie held her breath. But neither Vladimir nor Raznik seemed to notice.

Raznik swept forward and scooped up Tatiana and placed her in Vladimir's arms.

Vladimir's eyes shone greedily. He whipped out a dagger with a gleaming pointed blade. The children gasped.

The replicas looked convincingly real. The Tatiana replica began to cry. Cassie felt the panic in her heart. Vladimir nodded at the two commander Eretsuns, who roughly picked up the twins and Lorcan.

"These are surplus to requirement," sneered Vladimir. He turned to the Eretsuns. "You can deal with them all after I've made my transformation. I want them to watch."

"But you risk contaminating your spell with human blood by our presence!" shouted Cassie.

"Ah, but you will all be alive, at least until after the spell has worked," sneered Vladimir. "I only need to sacrifice the baby not of human mother born. The only risk was in sacrificing all four and you have saved me that trouble."

"You've betrayed us! You liar!" shouted Thomas, trying to grab the twins. Even though he knew they were replicas, they were all too convincing and he suddenly felt very protective towards them.

"I will let you go soon enough," said Vladimir.

Cassie held her breath and glanced at Thomas. They both looked at Nancy but she shook her head, telling them not to move. They looked over at the snarling Eretsuns. There was no way they could defeat the Eretsuns without weapons. There was no point in trying to shape-shift because the heavily armed Eretsuns would kill them while they made the change. When Vladimir realised the spell had gone wrong, they probably would have to fight their way out anyway or create a diversion to let Connle escape. And Vladimir would be more vulnerable then.

Maybe in the confusion of the spell going wrong they could seize their moment to escape. Cassie and Thomas were both thinking the same thing and exchanged a look of agreement. Now was not the right time to make a break. They had no choice. They didn't trust Vladimir but they would have to stay.

Everyone waited for Vladimir's next move. He was now glued to the television screen, absorbed in waiting for the right moment during the eclipse. Raznik was preoccupied with dealing with Tatiana. He placed the Tatiana replica in the opening of the glass bulb that was directly beneath the amulet. She screamed, her little face pushed up against the glass.

Vladimir glanced up at the clock and screen. Cassie followed his gaze. Vladimir watched the television monitor counting down the seconds for the exact moment of the total eclipse that would release a surge of power. The whole of the moon's surface now glowed a fiery blood red. It looked smaller and more three-dimensional than usual, like an illuminated ball suspended in space.

Vladimir brandished his dagger towards the baby in the glass bulb. Everything went black. The sound of a baby's screams rent the air. There was a tremor in the earth. Cassie prayed with every fibre in her being that they had succeeded in fooling Vladimir. That the baby's scream was not the sound of Tatiana being sacrificed. That soon he would discover that he had no special powers and they could escape.

The blood-red moon appeared again on the television screen. The eclipse was at its height.

With a shout of triumph, Vladimir proclaimed, "I am the Vampire King of All Worlds!"

Cassie held her breath. But then the lights came back on. The moon still throbbed red on the monitor. There was no sign of the baby or the dagger but the amulet now lay in the bulb of the tube and glowed with a blood-red light.

Vladimir smiled in triumph and, to Cassie's shock, he now had the long incisor teeth of a vampire. He grabbed the amulet from the tube and put it around his neck.

Cassie looked in horror at Thomas, her heart flipping backwards. She knew from his white face that he felt equally at a loss. They looked to Nancy but she seemed to have gone into shock. Their plan was in tatters and now seemed a totally stupid idea.

Somehow, the spell had worked, even with a replica of Tatiana – if it was a replica. It was a disaster. They had totally miscalculated and had allowed the monster to seize absolute power. Vladimir truly now was the Vampire King.

CHAPTER 17

Vladimir snarled and screamed with success. But he was so absorbed in his transformation, he forgot about their presence. There was a weird lull with everyone transfixed by Vladimir's continuing metamorphosis. He twitched and convulsed as he became more animal-like. Eventually he noticed them and with a dismissive wave signalled to the Eretsuns to take them away and dispose of them.

The replica Tatiana had disappeared into the amulet that now throbbed with supernatural power. Outside the glass pod the power stones glowed and fizzled with supernatural light.

Thomas's mind went numb. He was unsure what to do. Somehow they would have to get away from Vladimir and the Eretsuns and gather their magical troops to face their enemy in a battle they were doomed to lose. Nancy gave them no signal. Maybe her Star Splinter had been adversely affected by the lunar eclipse. But he too felt curiously powerless. He had no way of knowing if the babies had been saved. He feared something had gone wrong with the switch. Once again, the children felt feeble in the presence of Vladimir.

Then suddenly the Eretsuns pushed the Chingles and Connle out the door into the tunnel to be disposed of. As they climbed the stairs, the elite Eretsuns became more wild and unsettled. They tore off their visors and masks. Their jaws dripped with saliva, their tongues hung out and they licked the replica Mattie, Lorcan and Matilda, sizing them up for the kill. Thomas felt sick to the stomach and had to keep reminding himself that they weren't his real brother and sister and cousin, merely very convincing clay replicas. It helped that they all had the wrong coloured hair. But apart from that they were all too human. It filled his heart with fear to see the Eretsuns' savagery at such close quarters. They were waiting to attack, relishing every moment. Thomas realised the Eretsuns planned to savour their kill when they got out of the tunnel. There was no point in trying to fight them here. The Chingles had no weapons and they felt like sitting ducks.

The entrance back into the cave was only a minute away. The closer they were to the opening of the cave the more chance they had of allowing Connle to escape from the Eretsuns. They could shape-shift and attack the creatures and create a diversion. But the Chingles felt curiously weak. Nancy felt no messages from the Star Slinter in her stomach. It made her want to cry. Maybe the power of the eclipse had damaged their powers. The Eretsuns began to howl loudly. In a moment, the door would be opened and Cassie dearly hoped the Chinese Immortals would be there to help Connle ashore. But just then Nancy felt a twinge

"Cassie, Thomas," she shouted. "Watch out for Connle. Something's going to happen!"

But just as they reached the door a huge explosion rocked the tunnel and blew them all from their feet. A large boulder dropped towards Connle but Cassie and Thomas pushed him out of the way. Huge chunks of rocks broke off and fell into their path. One giant boulder trapped two Eretsun guards and immediately they disintegrated away to dust. Seawater began to flow in through a hole behind them in the roof of the tunnel. Cassie and Thomas flanked Connle, who held the silver bottle, keeping him steady on his feet as they waded through the filling tunnel. The replicas of the twins and Lorcan that had fallen from the Eretsuns' claws began to disintegrate in the water. Thomas was appalled but also felt a curious sense of relief. They are not real, he told himself – the true babies are safe in Granny Clíona's bottle held by Connle. That meant even Tatiana must be safe. He hoped with all his heart this was true.

"We'll never reach the cave," cried Cassie.

"Help me!" cried Nancy. Her leg was trapped under a lump of rock. Thomas waded back to her and pushed it off. Her leg was badly bruised but otherwise she was uninjured. The seawater continued to flow in. They were up to their waists now. Cassie and Thomas kept Connle upright as he held the bottle above the water. They were going to have to exit through the breach in the tunnel.

"We'll have to swim for it," cried Thomas. "Connle, try to make it to the shore! Get all our allies to gather. We will have to face Vladimir in battle. There is some time, as he is still transforming, but we should stay down here and try and take him on." He felt some of his power returning and saw his sisters felt the same.

"Maybe we can try to stop the amulet transforming the gemstones," said Cassie.

"But first let's get Connle to the surface. Hopefully the Eight Chinese Immortals can rescue him and take him to safety on the island."

They pushed themselves upwards from the blasted tunnel towards the water's surface. They held on to Connle, who was badly winded but still clutching the silver bottle containing Granny Clíona and, they hoped, the real babies now reduced to tiny versions of themselves. But it was agonising. The water gushed and swirled, knocking them against rocks and debris from the tunnel explosion. Anxiously Cassie, Thomas and Nancy turned into salmon, nudging Connle towards the surface. With supreme effort they broke through the skin of the sea. Thomas saw a cloud hovering above the waterline. It was the Eight Chinese Immortals coming to help Connle. In seconds he was subsumed in the cloud.

The Chingles as salmon dived back under the waves towards the site of Vladimir's transformation at the fault line.

The water emanated a greenish glow. Large chunks of rock and glass floated treacherously. The Chingles stuck close to the sea bottom, their silvery scales glinting in the greenish light. They surged forward, cleaving a path to Vladimir's globe off Poolbeg Rock. As they swirled around Balor's wreck, they noticed many of the gemstones had been damaged in the explosion. But there was no sign of the defences or the glass globe. They must have been damaged in the explosion. But what had happened to Vladimir? Had he been blown up too? The whole area pulsed with a strong magnetic power. Cassie flicked her silver belly through the water and thought she saw the tail of Almudj, the dreamtime crocodile, swim among the gemstones.

Their fish natures sensed the danger before they reached it. Below the water, they spied the dark bulk of the wrecked hull of the yacht where Balor's remains lay. Other menacing shapes circled round.

The Chingles hid behind a rock. A dark, large creature dived down towards them through a snapping wave. They saw its fin and the white underside of its body. It was a killer great white shark about seven metres long, the size of a small truck. Its great blunt nose surged through the water and as it came closer, it bared its teeth with huge front incisors. It was a vampire shark! Another one of Vladimir's deadly experiments in mutant species.

The last thing they needed to be now was salmon or human beings. They were at a loss to know how to take their deadly enemy on. If they turned into white sharks, any contact with his sharp teeth could infect them with his vampire blood. They felt the eddy through the water as his huge body moved ever closer.

And then they saw a stream of precious stones fly towards their deadly enemy. Thomas looked around. Almudj the crocodile was launching precious stones from his jaws towards the killer vampire shark as if emptying barrels from a shotgun.

The precious stones surged forward, one hitting the shark in the eye. This only enraged him and he pushed ever forward. Thomas watched the cascade of stones sink through the water like spent bullets. Quickly he turned into an octopus.

He propelled forward in the water and with his eight arms garnered as many stones as he could. Then targeting the vampire shark's mouth, he began to hurl stones at him. Quickly, Cassie and Nancy followed his lead.

The shark thrashed about in the water, unaccustomed to such a barrage. The three Chingles as octopuses circled about him, all the while launching stones at him, confusing him.

Bull's-eye! thought Thomas as he flung three stones together that lodged in the shark's throat.

At the same moment, one of Cassie's stones blinded the shark in his other eye. The sharp flipped and thrashed. Blood came out of his mouth and he sank to the ocean floor.

They felt exhausted but kept going. Above them in the water they saw the dark outline of the steel keel of a boat. That's the warship, thought Cassie, where the islanders are interned. We ought to try to rescue them. They drew closer in to the craft. Almudj cruised beside them in the water. Then they saw dark shapes circling the boat. Thomas spied three vampire fish peel off from their watch and surge towards them in the water. The crocodile flicked his tail and barked underwater. Nancy understood.

She concentrated and hurled herself upwards through the surface. As she broke through the skin of the sea, she became a white-tailed sea eagle with broad wings and a wedge-shaped tail. She let out a high-pitched call and dived back towards the waves. Cassie and Thomas looked up and saw her coasting on a current of air. They felt the lash of the movements as the three killer vampire sharks drew nearer.

Just in time, Cassie and Thomas changed too, leaving the crocodile to deal with the killer vampire fish alone. He rose on his tail in the waves and gnashed his spiked jaws, taunting and luring them towards combat. The sharks took the bait, not realising their real quarry were now sea eagles.

The warship rocked in the bitter sea, tossed on treacherous currents. It looked forbidding and impenetrable. Howling Eretsuns roamed the deck, baring their teeth and roaring at the sky.

The three eagles flew over the vessel, surveying its defences. It seemed unbreachable. They couldn't even see an entry point to below deck where the prisoners must be.

Then a siren sounded and a fresh group of Eretsuns issued from a trapdoor concealed in the bulwark. At the back of the ship, a lifeboat was suspended over the side. The sea eagles landed in it and changed back into the Chingles.

"We're going to have to reach that trapdoor," whispered Thomas. "We'll have to fight them with our bare hands."

His sisters nodded.

"If we lure them to one part of the ship, we can push them overboard," hissed Cassie.

They moved stealthily up the ladder leading up to the upper deck. But just as Cassie popped her head level with the deck, a hairy claw lashed out. She pulled back just in time and, prodding her brother and sister, they fell back into the lifeboat.

Four snarling heads hung down over the side, screaming and bellowing. Then one Eretsun realised there was a ladder and started to descend.

Desperate, Cassie cast about and finding a lifebuoy hurled it at the beast, who merely shrugged it off.

"We'll have to jump back into the water," cried Thomas. But then he felt something hard pinging against his face. He looked out to sea. Almudj was sending a jet of jewels in their direction.

Quickly Cassie and Nancy grabbed the tarpaulin and made it into a makeshift receptacle to catch the precious stones. Thomas grabbed them as they came and took aim at the Eretsun's mouth.

His first shot was the most satisfying bull's-eye he'd ever hit. It lodged right in the Eretsun's throat, who gurgled and fell down the ladder into the boat. Its body disintegrated on impact. The second one he stunned with a shot to the forehead. The third one took him by surprise, leaping straight onto the lifeboat and catching Thomas by the neck, as he turned round to take aim. Once more he came eyeball to eyeball with an Eretsun. But Thomas didn't flinch. He had a diamond in his mouth and spat it full force down the Eretsun's throat. The fourth slipped on the ladder and stunned himself on the lifeboat.

The Chingles distributed the jewels among themselves and Cassie carried the rest in the makeshift tarpaulin sack. Nancy found some pieces of rope and two sticks and fashioned a sling. They shimmied up the ladder and stealthily crept towards the trapdoor.

The children had the element of surprise. Nancy took out her sling and pelted several Eretsuns on deck, who fell to their knees. They noticed several of the Eretsuns had blood running from their mouths as if they'd been in for the kill and had slaked their ravenous thirst for blood. Each of the children felt sickened and fearful about the fate of the islanders but they couldn't waste time. Soon, they had lowered the trapdoor and found themselves inside the cavernous interior of the warship.

The metal door clanged behind them and echoed through the vast metal belly of the vessel. There was little sign of human habitation, no smells, noises, nothing to betray the whereabouts of the islanders. Along both sides of the hold were large bolted doors without windows or obvious locks.

Cassie inspected them. "They look pretty watertight to me. Even if we became tiny microbes we'd never get through them," she said ruefully.

Towards the back of the ship they heard a clattering screech. They moved quickly through the eerie blue light of ship's interior. Their footsteps clattered in the echoing gloom. The boat lurched and Cassie felt a sickening twist in her stomach. The airless, windowless emptiness was getting to her.

"That screech. It's a small creature. They are trying to say something to us," said Nancy. She began to run towards the back of the ship.

Thomas immediately followed her. Cassie, trying to suppress her nausea, followed more slowly.

Thomas and Nancy got there before her.

"Oh no!" Thomas cried, looking distraught.

Nancy began to utter a series of high-pitched noises.

"What is it?" Cassie breathlessly asked.

But all Thomas could do was point.

This hold had a glass front and the interior was lit by an eerie light. The bottom was strewn with a weird array of objects: knitting needles, a bodhrán, a wooden spoon with cake mix still on it. There were shoes and bits of ripped clothing lying around and the walls were covered in blood.

Cassie began to recognise the objects. Mrs Moriarty's knitting needles, Donnacha's bodhrán, the wooden spoon decorated with Celtic symbols belonging to Róisín the post mistress that she said added a magical ingredient to her scrumptious cakes. Slowly the realisation kicked in. Something awful had happened to the islanders.

"He has – Vladimir and the Eretsun – the – oh no! They've killed them," she managed to stutter.

But Nancy shook her head and pointed to the top right-hand corner of the hold. Crushed into its side were a group of tiny bats hanging upside down.

Nancy began to communicate with them in a series of squeaks and squeals at a high frequency.

"It's the islanders," she explained to her brother and sister.

"Vladimir must have changed them into bats," Thomas said.

"What's happened?" Cassie asked desperately.

Nancy continued to talk to them.

"They were attacked by the Eretsuns," Nancy translated. "But they didn't become Eretsuns. They turned into vampire bats. They say they won't bite."

"Why did they turn into bats?" asked Thomas.

Nancy listened to a flurry of squeaks.

"Róisín says they have a bit of magical protection because they live on Inish Álainn," she translated. "The bats won't harm humans. They drink animal blood."

"So even though they had to turn into some kind of vampire, they managed to make it the most innocent kind there is," said Thomas.

"Oh, our poor friends!" wailed Cassie. "It's all our fault. We lured Vladimir here."

A tiny wizened bat screeched and flapped its wings.

"It's Róisín – she says we are not to blame," said Nancy.

"But how can we help them?" asked Cassie.

"They said they won't come out. They don't even want to drink animal blood," said Nancy.

Cassie slumped to the floor and put her head in her hands. Tears spilled out of her eyes.

"So this will be the future for the human race if Vladimir has his way. All people will be turned into beasts. Nobody will be able to trust another person for fear of contamination. I'd rather be dead than live in Vladimir's world. Just as well I won't have to. I'm glad I'm going to Tír na nÓg!"

"But we can't turn our back on people," said Thomas. "We've got to find Vladimir, make sure we defeat him. I won't rest until we do. And we've got to figure out how to rescue the people of Inish Álainn and the Eretsuns of the Carpathian Mountains."

Oblivious to the others, Nancy continued her conversation with the bats.

"Do you know what has happened to Vladimir?" Nancy asked.

"*North, south, east and west. He's everywhere, he'll never rest,*" said a furry little bat that was Mrs Moriarty.

"He is the power of three," said a skinny bat that used to be Donnacha. "He's married the phantoms in his blood."

"Can you explain? What's a fant tum?" asked Nancy in bat language.

"He's found a way to access the power of Balor and

Patricia Murphy

Caitlín," said the Róisín bat. "That's what the Eretsuns said. And then something horrible about him killing a baby."

"But at least we tricked him out of the blood sacrifice," said Cassie. "We shrunk the babies and put them in Granny Clíona's bottle. Or I hope we did."

"The spell giving Vladimir power still worked. I don't know how," said Thomas. "Ask them where Vladimir is."

Nancy solemnly nodded her head. "They don't know but they say the Eretsuns said he now has the power of three. He made the spell work and has the power of horrible old Balor and Caitlín as well."

"Imposs–" Thomas began but he didn't get to finish his sentence as the children felt the boat lurch and, before they knew it, they were sliding down the narrow stretch of corridor. The boat had tipped on its side!

"Aah!" screamed the children as they tumbled together.

"Turn into seabirds," shouted Thomas. "We may be able to ride the storm."

The children were shaken and upended like peas in a drum. Their legs and arms crashed against the cold metal of the warship. They tried curling into balls but they were bounced around so much they feared they would be bashed to death. But each of them concentrated, knowing their life depended on it. They willed their bodies to change shape, their form to change to their need. And then it happened. Their bodies contracted as if they were shrinking, their noses became beaks, their eyes moved to the sides of their heads. Their bodies were covered in feathers and their arms became

404

wings. They were razorbills – black and white seabirds used to being buffeted and riding out storms.

The warship was standing on its side and seawater gushed into the corridor. The Chingles dived into the dark, turbulent water to get away from danger, pushing their small feathered bodies hard against the current. Down, down they dived, passing several startled fish. Soon they reached the lowest point of their nosedive and skimmed back up through the waves.

As they reached the air, several things seemed to happen at once. The boat was lifted up clean off the sea, water sluicing down its side. It was as if a giant hand had plucked it out of the waves. Thomas's bird sense picked up a great mass ahead of them. He rose in the air and his sisters followed him.

The ship had indeed been picked out of the sea by a giant hand as if it was some child's toy in a play pool. Thomas could barely digest what he was seeing. The hand was huge, with talons instead of fingers and long black nails, filed to a point. He'd seen that hand before. Surely it couldn't be Caitlín? Surely Vladimir hadn't raised her from the dead?

Cassie looked down and saw a giant foot planted in the waves. It was misshapen, with thirteen toes and ugly nails like bone. She knew that foot. She spiralled up following the ship, dreading what she might see: Balor back from the dead.

Nancy rose higher in the air, straight as an arrow. A hot gust of fire blew towards her. She dodged it by dropping lower and then rising fast again. She saw fangs and the long jaw of a werewolf but she could have sworn the cold, fishy eyes belonged to Vladimir. And around its neck was a red-gold amulet! It must have expanded magically to fit his bulging neck.

"*Cawwh!*" Thomas and Cassie screamed.

The three seabirds alighted on a rock and turned back into the Chingles. They crouched, horrified, in the gathering storm.

"Caitlín is back!" shouted Cassie.

"No, it's Balor – I saw his foot," screamed Thomas, teeth chattering in the gathering storm.

"Vladimir has become a giant Eretsun!" Nancy cried. "And he has the magic amulet around his neck!"

And then they felt a hot breath reach towards them. The earth shook. The metal ship was tossed from a vast hand and crashed back into the ocean.

"The head is coming from the clouds," shouted Cassie pointing upwards. "You'll see, it's Caitlín – I saw her hand!"

"No, it's definitely Vladimir," said Nancy through chattering teeth. "I saw it with my own eyes."

"And I know it's Balor," averred Thomas. "But we can't all be right."

But as the head bent towards them, they realised they all were. Of all the horrible, sickening sights they'd ever seen, this was the most gruesome.

"It's all of them!" shouted Cassie. "The power of three! The islanders were right!"

For rearing up in front of them was a three-headed beast, with Caitlín's long Corra neck on the right and on the left Balor's huge, ugly misshapen head with the Evil Eye covered. And in the middle was Vladimir, his face transformed into a werewolf's with sharp vampire teeth issuing from his slavering foam-and-blood-flecked mouth. The creature attacked with a taloned hand like Caitlin's and stomped forward on one ugly misshapen leg, the exact same as Balor's. They saw springing from its back the hideous wings of the Corra, slick like oil, covered in matted black feathers. Somehow Caitlín and Balor had merged with Vladimir's body, creating a monster more hideous than each of them individually.

"This is an abomination! How can we ever fight this?" shouted Cassie.

A taloned hand shot out, just short of where they watched. Then the other hand, with six misshapen fingers like Balor's scooped through the water and tossed foam in their direction. The creature seemed to be playing with them.

Then the mysterious words of Devana came into Thomas's head.

"The three of us must make the three-headed beast choke on the bloodstone! Remember what Devana said. I didn't understand it at the time but I think she gave us a message. We must use the bloodstone to defeat the beast!"

"Why don't I just throw it down his mouth?" said Cassie.

"There's a risk he might spit it out," said Thomas.

"Then I'll fly in with it," said Cassie bravely.

"I'm not letting you go alone. I'm coming to make sure you can escape. Besides, Devana said it had to be the three of us. Maybe it won't work if the three of us aren't present."

"I'm coming," said Nancy.

Cassie held the bloodstone in her fist and Thomas and Nancy clasped her hand in theirs.

"All for one and one for all," said Thomas. "We've always been stronger together." His sisters smiled brightly at him. "Follow me. Each one of us must enter a different mouth!"

He changed back into a razorbill and flew towards the mouth of Balor. Cassie headed for Caitlín's disgusting mouth, the jewel in her beak, and Nancy braved the slavering jaws and fangs of Vladimir.

This was the last thing the three-headed monster expected. Each little bird flew deep into the stinking mouths of their enemies all joined at the one neck. But the three mouths of the horrid creature obviously sensed they'd swallowed their prey because the three-headed beast began to bellow and the children were swept down the throat by a gush of bile-green saliva.

Luckily, as razorbills they navigated the rush of bile as if it was seawater. Down the throat they went and rested on Vladimir's tonsils. Briefly they changed back so they could talk to one another.

Vladimir's throat constricted and the Chingles felt themselves tossed around on his pulsating tonsils. Black foam from the backwash of his swallowed saliva flecked their clothing and left little pinpricks of rotted fabric.

"We can't stay here," shouted Thomas, grabbing his sister. "Cassie, throw the bloodstone and change into insects again!"

Quickly, Cassie hurled the bloodstone down the monster's throat.

It began to have immediate effect, as Vladimir gagged and his tonsils swelled under their feet. He gnashed his vast teeth. They felt a horny hand come to his throat and then three fat fingers were pushed into his mouth.

"It's Balor's hand!" shouted Cassie. "Quick, change, Chingles, change!"

It was difficult to focus with the gagging and retching going on in Vladimir's throat but finally they managed it and each became a yellow-and-black-striped wasp.

Cassie and Nancy flew free of his mouth but, just as Thomas was about to go through, Vladimir gnashed his giant pointed teeth. Thomas narrowly missed being crushed but, as he launched back into flight, he found his way blocked by the tightly clenched teeth. There was nothing else for it. He stung Vladimir on his engorged tongue.

Vladimir roared and began to spew some horrid green bile. Thomas just managed to get out from behind his teeth but he had to fly with all his might to escape the spume of bile issuing from Vladimir's stomach.

Exhausted, Thomas flew high in the air and was glad when a current of air caught him and carried him in to land.

He sat nervously with his sisters on the cliffs of the island overlooking Poolbeg Rock, surveying the rampaging giant that loomed over the island. The vampire head of Vladimir lolled on its chest, stunned, green bile foaming from its mouth. The heads of Caitlín and Balor convulsed and roared, jerking around uncontrollably. Balor's horny hand tried to rip the eye-patch away to reveal his baleful Evil Eye that could kill at one glance. But the giant was unco-ordinated. Caitlín's talons struck out, trying to uproot the island from the ground. The children shivered.

"We could get the fairies to fetch our weapons and leap back on the giant. You severed Caitlín's head last time," said Thomas.

"Vladimir isn't dead yet," said Cassie. "Only stunned. We have to finish him off."

"No!" a voice came from behind. The Chingles turned round. It was Willa. She had climbed up to the top of the cliff with Áine and Connle.

The children were overjoyed to see them.

"You've survived!" said Cassie to Connle. "And the babies?"

"They are safe but now they are tiny. Granny Clíona succeeded in miniaturising them all too well," said Connle. "She won't attempt to dismantle their protective force field until she has them the proper size."

The children exhaled a huge sigh of relief.

"Granny Clíona is minding them for now," said Connle. "But we felt you needed our help more."

"We need to keep Vladimir alive so we can find out the antidote for rescuing the Eretsuns," Áine said.

"I just don't see how we can defeat this three-headed monster without killing it," said Thomas.

"There may be a way. But you will need the help of all your magical friends to achieve it," said Áine.

The monster lurched forward, its arms flailing towards the land. But Poolbeg Rock got in the way. So the beast, using both its hands, tore it from the earth and dashed it against the cliffs. Everyone screamed and shrank back. But Áine let out a high, lilting burst of song that soared over the island.

It had the effect of summoning all the magical creatures who were currently living on the island. Soon they were joined by the Eight Chinese Immortals, Finnen, Viracocha, Almudj the Aborigne God, who swam in underwater, and a multitude of fairies of the Midnight Court. Even the Pooka turned up.

"Finnen and Viracocha will head your army as you try to defeat the giant," said Áine. "Vladimir's power is awesome but we must do what we can."

Finnen and the Inca god stepped forward. He was utterly transformed. They realised he no longer looked like a beggar but had a crown of sun rays around his head and the tall erect bearing of a god.

"Viracocha, you look very different," said Cassie.

"My power is returning slowly but not enough to defeat this Vladimir," he said. "But my replicas they work only too well. It better than I think. I feel guilty. I feel bad the spell work and Vladimir becomes a monster."

"At least we saved the babies. It definitely wasn't a child, was it, some kind of clone of Tatiana?" asked Cassie in a hushed voice.

"No, my leetle one. It was clay replica. But because her mother a goddess and I use her hair, it gave the copy some mysterious power," explained Viracocha.

"She had my hair!" said Nancy.

"You also have special powers, my leetle one," said Viracocha ruffling her curls.

Cassie felt relieved. It had been horrible to hear the screams of even a replica baby.

But Thomas looked at him thoughtfully. "Viracocha, you are a sun god and Finnen is a moon goddess who is now also looking after the sun. If Vladimir's power can be created by an eclipse could it also be undone by an eclipse?"

"Perhaps," said Finnen. "But a solar eclipse is not due for a while."

"Couldn't you create one by magic?" Thomas asked.

Finnen and Viracocha looked at each other and a look of complicity flashed between them.

"We do not like to alter the path of the heavens but Vladimir is a threat to all worlds," said Finnen.

Viracocha looked up into the skies. The light was dim but night had passed. "This time the moon should block the light of the sun."

"We can create a solar eclipse," said Finnen. "We will alter the sun and moon path very briefly. We will do what we can."

Out at sea the monstrous three-headed shape of Vladimir belched and heaved, beginning to revive. This made up Finnen and Viracocha's minds.

The magical army watched as the Swan Maiden from Inish Álainn and the creator god of the Incas ascended into the skies.

The clouds began to clear and the sun appeared bright and glowing in the east. Immediately the sky was filled by an eerie light as the moon began to block out the light from the sun.

"It's working!" exclaimed Thomas.

"We don't have much time," said Áine. "You need to form three concentric circles around the heads, two spinning clockwise, the one in the middle counter-clockwise. Then after sixty seconds you need to summon all your power into a shaft of light."

The sun was half covered by the moon and became a semicircle of gold. "Chingles, each of you needs to be in a different circle," Áine instructed. "Cassie, you go underwater as a salmon with Almudj the crocodile, Tethra and Rónán – Nancy, go in the middle around the creature's belly and, Thomas, you must circle his head. Both of you assume the shape of eagles."

So all of the magical creatures did as they were asked. The Eight Chinese Immortals flew with Thomas around the three heads of the beast. Nancy was joined by the fairies of the Midnight Court who formed a circle around the creature's heart. The beast was so large, it was just as well that thousands of fairy creatures had turned up. No one had ever seen so many in one place before.

Willa was about to join the circle around Vladimir's head but Áine stopped her.

"No. Tatiana and Lorcan need their mothers," she told her friend quietly. Reluctantly Willa agreed. Áine smiled at her. But they watched anxiously as the magical army pitted its strength against the belching, heaving monster with the three hideous heads of Vladimir, Caitlín and Balor. The beast was merely temporarily stunned and pulsated awesome power. It was in the balance who would win.

Everyone began to spin as the moon moved towards the sun. A surreal twilight descended as the moon crept over the face of the sun. Within minutes the sun sliver was almost covered by the dark moon. Below, Cassie in the shape of a salmon swam in a furious circle with Rónán, Tethra and Almudj. The beast jumped up and down trying to stamp them with its foot but they were deft, expertly cleaving through the waves. Soon they formed a band of light whirling through the water.

It was hard for Nancy and the fairies to evade the flailing arms of the beast that tried to tear at them but they moved so fast they formed a band of light.

Thomas and the Eight Chinese Immortals had the hardest job. The heads of Balor and Caitlín continuously spewed green bile and black spit in their direction and howled. They just about managed to circle its neck but there was a worrying gap.

But soon the black disc of the moon replaced the sun's bright rays. A beautiful gossamer halo of light surrounded the dark moon in a rosy hue. It was the corona, the outer layer of the sun's atmosphere circling the black moon in a ring of glowing red gold.

"Away!" shouted Áine as a bolt of blue light issued from the eclipse and hit the spinning bands of light.

Underwater, Cassie saw that their band of light had become independent of them and radiated a deep emerald. Together with Almudj, Rónán and Tethra, she swam away. They watched as the band of green light constricted and tightened around the creature's leg.

Above the water, the creature's arms hung limply by its side as the shining band of ruby-red light created by Nancy, and the thousand fairies thickened and burnished. It too was struck by the sapphire-blue light from the eclipse and the fairies, and brave nancy were able to withdraw as it became a separate band and tightened around the creature, causing it to gasp and moan.

But the Corra head of Caitlín and the writhing head of Balor continued to spit and roar. There was a worrying break in the circle of diamond-white light. The power of Thomas, and his friends the Eight Chinese Immortals wasn't enough.

As the blue light from the eclipse moved up the giant's body, the middle vampire head of Vladimir began to stir!

Frantically Thomas in his eagle shape beat his wings and tried to close the gap. But the three heads began to blow, knocking the Chinese Immortals from the air. They managed to stop themselves mid-fall and regain their place but it was becoming increasingly difficult to maintain the shape of a circle.

The blue beam from the eclipse moved up the giant's body but it struck the head of Vladimir through the gap in the circle.

"Hah!" roared Vladimir's vampire head, revived. "You have miscalculated. You have only succeeded in channelling the sun's power through the moon to give me back my strength." He let out a blood-curdling screech.

Seeing what was happening, the others in the circle tried to help bridge the gap. Nancy and the flying fairies joined her brother's circle and Cassie rose from the water transforming from a salmon into an eagle. They regrouped. But the heads spat and foamed, forcing them to spread ever wider. The band of diamond light became an intermittent chain of sparks.

There was still a worrying break. The creature began to spit chunks of rock and breathed fire from its mouth. Several fairies had to retreat, injured. Two of the Chinese Immortals plummeted into the water. They were losing the battle with the three-headed monster.

The sky began to lighten again. The eclipse was nearly over. Áine didn't hesitate. No prohibition of the gods was going to let her sacrifice the safety of the world when she could make a difference. She flew upwards towards the circle to fill the gap.

But she was too late. Willa had got there before her.

"Go back, Áine! It is my fate to face Vladimir!" Willa roared.

Reluctantly, Áine retreated to the cliff.

"So we face each other at last," roared Vladimir as Willa joined the spinning circle.

In the dying embers of the eclipse, the creature roared and thrashed. With Willa's involvement, the band of light began to intensify. This time there was no gap. The band shone with diamond brightness, a brilliant ring of light, blinding the three heads. The blue bolt once more came from the sky and connected with the ring. It began to constrict, strangling the single neck of the three-headed beast. The magical creatures and the Chingles flew to the cliff top.

The band split into two and wrapped itself around the jaws of the Corra and Balor, leaving the head of Vladimir untouched. The head of Balor spun around three hundred and sixty degrees. Then it exploded in a vile mess of blackened bone. The other band severed the Corra's head and it fell into the sea and sank to the ocean floor. The amulet around Vladimir's neck that had magically grown to fit his monstrous size was blown to smithereens.

Only Vladimir's vampire head remained. He foamed at the mouth and his eyes rolled in his head.

"Please, spare me!" he roared.

Willa rose in the sky and flew in front of his eyeball.

"And why should we do that, you wretched creature?" she demanded.

She gestured towards the blue beam that joined together

417

and once more encircled Vladimir's neck. It tightened and Vladimir fought for his breath.

"The Eretsuns!" he gasped.

"Tell us how we can save them and your miserable life will be spared," spat Willa.

"The Alatyr stone," he breathed. "It holds their souls. It must be dissolved in a bath of tears."

"Of course! The Karzeleks said it was the stone closest to humans," said Cassie to Thomas and Nancy as they watched from the cliff top. "It doesn't just hold fossils."

But something was happening to Vladimir. Steam began to rise out of his ears, nostrils, mouth. His teeth gnashed in his jaw. His giant body convulsed and he began to shrivel. He crashed into the sea and writhed in the waves until he regained his normal size. Thomas swiftly changed into an eagle and, swooping from the sky, picked him up in his beak.

They brought Vladimir back to the Fairy Field. He looked pathetic. He was covered in carbuncles as if all his evil was trying to escape. On one side of his neck was a blackened stump where the head of Balor had been and on the other a deep red gash where the neck of Caitlín had been severed. His teeth were blackened and one of his arms had withered. He seemed to have become blind in one eye.

Willa approached him.

Vladimir fell to his knees and put his head in his hands.

"No, don't touch me," he begged. "Please don't come near me again." He fell to the ground and rolled himself into a ball.

"Pathetic human!" said Willa contemptuously. "Get him out of my sight!"

Very willingly four fairies approached him and began to weave a filigree web about him, as light as a cobweb but as solid as metal chains.

"We need to decide his fate," said Áine. "He has violated the contact between this world and the Otherworld. Not just our domain but other realms as well."

Thunder and lightning flashed across the sky. The children looked up awestruck as clouds formed into beings. First they saw the Celtic gods, with Manannán the God of the Sea riding a white horse of foam. Then the Dagda the Good God, and another cloud looked like Ogma. Three cloud-shaped crows flitted across the rosy sky and turned into the Morrigan and her Sisters, the three terrifying Goddesses of Battle. And then they merged into the shape of Devana, the Goddess of Hunting in the Carpathian Mountains. The shining path of a rainbow vaulted across the sky and Heimdall, the Norse god who guarded it, appeared. The three Norns, the sisters of fate of the Norse gods, emanated from the clouds. And they were joined by the brilliant shining form of Lugh. Spirit forms in the shape of gods thronged the sky. Viracocha appeared in the sky and was merged with Perun from Slavic mythology.

"It's as if all the gods are telling us they are similar," said Cassie, awestruck at the swirling heavens that throbbed with gold and silver light.

"Yes, they are all aspects of the same forces and elements," agreed Thomas. "Like the sun and moon, thunder and light."

"You have learned well in your travels to the Otherworld," said Áine. "Each place and people bring forth their own gods. But we all have much in common. The fairies here failed to realise that you cannot have false barriers between us. Look how powerful we were when we joined forces against evil."

"It's the same with humans," said Cassie.

Just then, Connle arrived breathless.

"Granny Clíona can't break the force field or get them to become normal size," he wheezed.

"This is a major problem," said Cassie. "We can't leave them like that."

"Perhaps we should ask the gods for help," suggested Thomas. "But how can it be?"

"It must be that the babies have somehow created the spell themselves," said Áine. "Granny Clíona's blessing may have triggered the protective shield. But all of the babies have a magical connection. They must have reinforced it with their own powers. There is no other explanation."

Suddenly the sky lit up with the prismatic colours of a rainbow; then all the heavenly shapes merged together and became the shape of Cernunnos the Hunter and God of Shape-shifters, holding a snake in one hand and an apple in the other. Around his head was a crown of thorns and ivy.

"Chingles," he spoke, "once more we meet." He gave them an enigmatic smile. "I have come to tell you the gods are pleased with you."

Cassie, Thomas and Nancy stepped forward.

"Thank you, but how do we break the spell that binds the babies?" asked Cassie urgently.

"Do you know its cause?" asked the god in the sky.

"We think the babies have created it themselves," said Thomas. "Granny Clíona cannot break its hold."

"Then only the babies themselves can reverse it," said the god. "But you can help them by reminding them how to be babies."

"What do you mean?" asked Thomas.

But Cernunnos just continued to smile his mysterious smile.

"What about Vladimir?" asked Cassie. "What shall we do with him?"

"He has violated the contracts between the heavens and the earth. You have proved worthy heroes. It is the gods' decision that the Chingles can decide his fate," said the shape of Cernunnos.

"That's a tough responsibility," said Thomas.

"Great power brings great responsibility," said Cernunnos. "But you have proved worthy, Chingles. That is why the gods have offered you immortality."

"We don't have to tell you now, do we?" Thomas asked, alarmed. "I thought we had until the end of the summer to decide whether to accept!"

"Yes, you do have until the end of the summer," Cernunnos said, "when I will return to learn your decision."

"No need as far as I'm concerned," said Thomas. "I'm not going."

"Nor me," said Nancy empathically.

Cernunnos nodded.

Cassie gulped, she was still unsure of her decision, but Cernunnos was speaking again.

"You do not have to tell me your choice yet. Summon me when you decide. But there is someone else here who must return."

"I know," said Willa stepping forward, trying not to cry. "I break the laws of the heavens by taking mortal shape without permission. But using my magical powers while mortal to join the fight against Vladimir, it seal my fate. But I ask for mercy. Whatever about me, it is wrong to punish Sasha and my child. Is there any way I can keep in touch with them?" Willa fell to the ground weeping.

Perun and Devana appeared in the sky as Cernunnos faded.

"Please," interjected Thomas bravely, "she only violated her human shape to save both this world and the Otherworld from Vladimir. If she hadn't acted we wouldn't be having this conversation."

Devana and Perun hovered in all their majesty. Then Perun spoke.

"For three months in the summer time of the year, Willa can live with Sasha and Tatiana in the Carpathian Mountains. But the rest of the time, she must spend in the Enchanted Forest as a spirit."

"I thank you with all my heart!" cried Willa.

"Farewell, mortals," said Perun.

"Hang on!" cried Cassie. "Just exactly how do we break the babies' force field? Your decrees mean nothing unless we can do that. Tatiana won't be going anywhere!"

But Perun and Devana had already disappeared.

Weeping tears of joy, Willa embraced Thomas in her gratitude for his help.

"I don't know how he does it but he always seems to get around the gods," marvelled Cassie.

"But I can't get their help in releasing the babies from their force field," he replied downhearted.

"We are the Chingles!" said Nancy. "We always find a way."

CHAPTER 18

The Chingles sat in the kitchen with Áine and Willa, waiting for Connle to return with Granny Clíona's silver bottle that contained their ancestor and the babies. Everyone felt tense, knowing Willa had to return to her Otherworld and they still hadn't returned the babies to their real size or managed to get them to break their mysterious protective shield. They sat in uneasy silence.

"It is okay. I understand that I must return," Willa said finally.

"How about you?" said Áine to Cassie. "Have you thought any more about your decision?"

Cassie felt faint with the agony of trying to make up her mind.

"What would you do?" she said desperately to Willa.

"I would happily change places with you," Willa said quietly. "Humans can change and grow."

"But we die," said Cassie. "And grow old and life is hard."

"Life is sweeter, knowing that you will lose it. Eternity is a long time," said Willa.

"Áine, what do you think?" asked Cassie.

"I know the privileges of both and it is lonely being a goddess. You know I take human form every time I can," she smiled.

"If we go we will live forever and have many adventures and powers," said Cassie. "We'll never have to go to school or grow old. We will be better than human."

"You'll never see me again, or the twins, or Mummy and Daddy, or Inish Álainn," said Nancy, surprisingly angrily for her. "I'll hate you forever if you go." She ran at her sister and meant to thump her but instead flung her arms about her with a big kiss. Thomas joined them in a hug.

"Please!" begged Nancy.

"After all we've been through?" said Thomas, with a lump in his throat. "I want to see the twins after all this."

"But it's true, isn't it, Áine, that you lose your powers when you become a grown-up? And I'm the oldest so it will happen to me first!"

Áine nodded.

Cassie felt torn. She hated school; she hated East Croydon. She was nearly a teenager and would be the first of them to grow up. It was okay for Nancy. She had years to go.

She was relieved when Connle walked briskly into the room carrying Granny Clíona's silver bottle. "We have to try to figure out what to do with the babies." He smiled kindly at them all, as he took the stopper from the bottle and out whooshed Granny Clíona.

Then Áine shook the bottle into her hand and a little platform that fitted snugly into her palm popped out. Four miniature babies lay on it, sound asleep. All their hearts melted and Willa tried desperately not to cry, aching to hug her daughter.

Áine held them aloft.

"Och, I've got tae crack this spell," boomed Granny Clíona. She turned to the children. "I think if I can break the force field, then I'll be able to get them big again. I'm at my wits' end. Have ye any ideas?"

Cassie shook her head.

"I feel it is my fault," sighed Granny Clíona. "I'm more rusty than I thought."

"The more I think about it, the more I'm sure it's not in your power to undo the spell," said Áine.

"Yes. Cernunnos said something about the babies maybe having special powers themselves," said Thomas. "Oh, and then he said maybe we can help them by reminding them how to be babies. I don't know what he was on about. I like riddles but honestly sometimes I wish you Otherworldly folk could just talk straight for a change."

Áine looked thoughtful. Granny Clíona scratched her ghostly head. She looked at Áine.

426

"The force field is of the baby's own devising," said Áine. "Your blessing may have triggered it but the interpretation is their own work."

"Aye. My spell was that the bairns always have strength when they need it most to protect themselves from harm and that they be surrounded by a protective shield of love."

"It's hard to believe because they are so young. None of them can even talk but they have generated a protective shield," said Áine. "*They* did it to protect themselves from harm and have more power than they know. It makes sense. Tatiana and Lorcan are of half-divine origin. It is likely they have some special powers. And Mattie and Matilda – well, they are related to the Chingles and look what you can do!"

"That's kind of cool," said Thomas.

"Och, but they don't have the sense to unlock their spell. We'll have to find a way," said Granny Clíona. "I used to be good at antidotes. All those wasted years trapped in my bottle have dulled my talents."

"But why did Cernunnos say we must remind them how to be babies?" asked Thomas. "The answer is there if we could understand it!"

"Maybe babies know things and then forget them," said Nancy.

Granny Clíona spun round.

"That's it!" she exclaimed. "They've frozen themselves in time and have forgotten how to grow. We'll have to remind them that they have to move forward."

427

"And just how are we supposed to do that?" said Cassie sceptically.

"Och, by showing them something we all had to learn!" said Granny Clíona mysteriously. "Get everyone with human blood to gather now in the Sacred Grove."

"There are only us and the Eight Chinese Immortals. They all started as humans," said Cassie.

"That's not enough," said Granny Clíona.

"What about the islanders? They are still all bats. And Jarlath and Sasha?" asked Thomas.

"Well, turn them back to islanders. Didn't Vladimir reveal how to change vampires back? The more the merrier, except perhaps for Vladimir," said Granny Clíona. "Áine will devise a draught so that any human who shouldn't know about it forgets it all afterwards."

"We have to make a decision about Vladimir. The fairies will get bored guarding him," said Cassie. "I vote that he turns himself in to the authorities and stands trial."

"That's a great idea," said Thomas.

"Well, I know a journalist who could do with the scoop of his life! Vladimir has committed enough human sins without even bothering to delve into the Otherworld stuff."

Half an hour later, equipped with a healing and forgetting draft from Áine, Cassie, Thomas and Nancy flew as eagles to the submarine, carrying Vladimir in their three beaks. As Thomas and Nancy hovered above, Cassie shapeshifted into a salmon and dived down to the submarine then, changing back into herself, knocked on the porthole to an astonished Jarlath.

First they administered Finbar Flash the forgetting and healing draft, so his memory was wiped clean of his adventures in Vladimir's underground city. Fortified, Finbar Flash listened awestruck as Vladimir confessed to running the mafia, kidnap, arson, bank robberies, fraud and enough crimes to send him to prison for a thousand years. Within minutes of his telephoning Interpol and the world's press, a division of the international navy sped towards the submarine to arrest Vladimir.

"I spent a long time hating your guts, Chingles," Finbar Flash said to them contritely. "But I've got to hand it to you. You really are the most remarkable children!"

Thomas smiled at Cassie. Just as well he didn't know about their magical powers!

Jarlath and Sasha, in a daze from Áine's draught, headed in towards the shore in the dinghy landing craft with Nancy. They didn't even blink when a collection of sorry-looking bats landed on the craft. And they merely nodded hello when a bizarre-looking crocodile threw a chunk of amber and a scallop shell as big as a basin into their boats.

"So the remedy for restoring those turned into vampires –" said Thomas

"Or vampire bats," Nancy piped up.

"Is to place the Alatyr stone in a bath of tears," said Cassie.

"Think about Willa leaving," said Thomas.

And soon the Chingles had cried enough to fill the scallop shell. They placed the stone in it and in turn each of the bedraggled bats took a bath.

If Jarlath and Sasha were surprised to see bats change into their friends from the island, they showed no signs of it. Cassie and Thomas gave Mrs Moriarty, Róisín, Muiris, Donnacha, Stephen Guilfoyle, Mrs Prendergast and the others a drink of Áine's draught of healing and forgetting. If they thought it was odd to be crowded onto a dinghy with Sasha, Jarlath and the whole island, none of them showed it.

There was a gentle onshore breeze and the waves merrily swirled and sloshed around the dinghy. Seabirds hovered on the wing in a sky of puffy, scudding clouds. It was as if they were on some special day trip. The boat danced over the lively waves. Cassie watched fish slither underwater and the brilliant sun tinged the waves with silver.

It will be hard to leave all this, she thought. She looked across at the golden sands of Boogan Beach sparkling in the summer sun, the glittering emerald of the fields beyond and the gentle rolling mountains. If Inish Álainn was so beautiful, how much more stunning would Tír na nÓg be?

Yet what would she do with herself all alone in Tír na nÓg, she thought as the dinghy thudded forward on the water. All of their adventures were only enjoyable because they were together, united as the Chingles.

I will live forever, she reminded herself. I will be like a goddess. I would love to be immortal. But not as much as I love to see my family, the thought snuck into her mind. Cassie debated fiercely in her head; every fibre in her being was shaken by her fear of taking the irreversible step. An image of the twins came into her head. Then her mother's smiling face and her father's kind eyes. She glanced over at Nancy, who gave her a happy smile. She remembered the time when they found Nancy with the fairies after they thought Balor had eaten her.

As if reading her thoughts, Thomas uncharacteristically gave her a brief hug as they sat in the boat. She thought how Thomas had saved her life when they fought against Caitlín. She remembered the three of them meeting the Sean Gaels and the wedding of Jarlath and Áine.

She remembered Ivo and his bright-green eyes. How he disapproved of humans who craved immortality and how they had reached a new understanding when she helped him find his father. She'd never see him again if she went to Tír na nÓg. So many thoughts swirled around her brain. But the priority for now was to get the babies to change back. She was glad there was so much going on and she didn't have to remain with her thoughts gnawing at her brain.

Before they knew it they were back on dry land.

❧

Soon there was a sizable crowd gathering in the Sacred Grove. Áine walked among them scattering daisies, violets, the spray of flowers called babies' breath and rose petals.

"What's going to happen now is something special," said Granny Clíona with relish. "We're all going to become babies once more to help these wee ones realise growing is the best way to heal all ills." The Chingles looked at her perplexed but soon were lulled by Áine's mantra.

"Be all you new,
Like morning dew,
To babyhood may you return
And show the way the spell to spurn."

The sky became a hazy blue. The air was filled with a crackling electricity. And then an extraordinary thing happened. Each person began to go backwards in time. The older islanders like Róisín passed from old age to middle age, then the prime of life, teenage years, young children and then smiling babies. Jarlath sped backwards through spotty adolescent, gangly boy, chubby toddler and became a jumping little baby that couldn't sit still. Sasha became a dark-eyed little baby who sang in baby language. Sour old Mrs Prendergast went from middle age to her youth without really changing, then briefly she was an astonishingly pretty girl before becoming a chubby, smiling baby. I wonder what happened to make her so miserable today, Cassie briefly wondered before finding herself shrinking into a seven-year-old, then a three-year-old and finally a bonny baby not yet able to walk. Even Nancy, not long out of babyhood herself, went backwards and was soon a gorgeously cute infant with a mass of dark curly hair. They glanced over and there was Thomas, with his smudge of blond hair, trying to crawl and laughing as he sprawled on his stomach. Baby Cassie laughed to see she was near an extraordinarily hairy baby with a quiff of red hair and dark eyes. It was Connle looking just like the little foundling that Granny Clíona had rescued.

The Sacred Grove was filled with baby laughter and gurgles. Briefly the wise old trees sparked into their human shapes and smiled at the assembled baby parliament surrounding the platform of the four tiny babies joined in their invisible force field.

Cassie, Thomas and Nancy felt shot through with the intensity of the feeling in the Sacred Grove. For together, the babies who'd gone back in time sent out a force to Lorcan, Tatiana, Mattie and Tilda that could only be described as love. The feeling rose through their laughter and gurgles and soon the four trapped babies began to laugh too.

And then they began to grow back to their normal sizes.

That was it, Cassie realised in her baby state – the four kidnapped children had forgotten to laugh!

It's not just the tears of children that have magical properties, thought Thomas, so does the laughter.

There was a high, thin tinkling sound as if an invisible plane of glass had been shattered. Suddenly the babies began to clamour and call for their mothers.

In a split second, everyone returned to their normal selves.

Cassie, Thomas and Nancy dashed to the twins. This time there was no invisible barrier keeping them apart and they grabbed them and hugged them close. Áine and Willa rushed forward and scooped up their babies, hugging them as if they would never let them go. Thomas, Cassie and Nancy managed to hold the twins between the three of them and jumped and shouted for joy.

If the islanders were surprised to find themselves at some kind of gathering, they didn't show it. Connle, now again over five hundred years old, rushed around administering the draught of healing and forgetting. Within minutes they had all journeyed on their way, back to their daily lives. Clearly Áine's draught of forgetting was very effective.

Willa embraced her husband and some understanding beyond words passed between them. She held Tatiana and hugged her close. Then she explained to Sasha that she had to return to her homeland and could only see him for three months a year. Sasha seemed to understand.

"When you are not with me, you will be like wife of my soul." Sasha smiled through his tears and embraced his wife and baby. "Don't cry – we see you very soon. Three months with you worth twelve with anybody else. And I inspired now to write most beautiful songs."

Willa kissed her baby and husband.

The Chingles saw that Willa was about to leave and she beckoned them over to say goodbye.

"I will return now with the Alatyr stone to help cure the Eretsuns. Thank you, Chingles – your deeds will live forever in song and story."

"Your necklace," said Cassie, removing it from her neck.

But Willa stopped her. "Please, you keep it to remember me," she said.

"I can't, it's too valuable," said Cassie.

"Okay, keep it until some day maybe Tatiana needs it," laughed Willa. Hers eyes shone and she looked beautiful. The children realised it was the first time they'd seen her laugh.

Willa bowed at Thomas. "Thanks to you, the gods showed me mercy."

"Say hello to the wild children for us," said Thomas.

"And Ivo," said Cassie. "The boy who is their sort of leader. Tell him he might be right about being human."

"Perhaps one day you can tell him yourself," said Willa.

Cassie realised she might rather like to do that. Thomas shot her a questioning look but didn't say anything. And with that Willa was gone.

Then, in turn, the Eight Chinese Immortals and Almudj came to say goodbye.

"So long, clever younger persons of Chingling," said Immortal Woman. "You have given us courage to face our own fight."

"But you must promise come visit us," said Han.

"If you ever need a spare Chingle," grinned Thomas.

435

"And bring the beauteous Swan Maiden, Fillen," said Iron Crutch Li.

The Eight Immortals bowed low, then ascended in their cloud to the sky.

Almudj clicked them a goodbye, translated by Nancy. He too invited them to visit him in Dreamtime.

Lastly, Viracocha came to speak to them. "Maybe people aren't so bad after all. But now I help Goddess Finnen clear up the mess of three-headed monster. Make sure no come back. Then I go back to my own people."

Later that evening, the children sang to the twins as they got them dressed for bed.

"Have you thought any more about Tír na nÓg?" Thomas asked Cassie as they put the twins into their pyjamas.

"Of nothing but!" groaned Cassie.

"Well?" asked Thomas in trepidation.

"You are simply not allowed leave us!" said Nancy.

Mattie suddenly lunged forward and grabbed a handful of Cassie's hair. Matilda grabbed her arm.

"See, they won't let you go either," said Nancy.

Thomas and Cassie laughed. She cuffed Thomas playfully on the shoulder.

"Who else will be here to keep you in check?" she said, mock stern. "I don't think I'll be summoning Cernunnos."

Thomas laughed and the twins picked up his humour and gurgled loudly. Nancy kissed Cassie on the cheek.

Cassie felt a warm glow inside her. She was lucky to have brothers and sisters who loved her and were worth fighting for.

They laid the twins in their cots and tip-toed from the room.

"I wonder how it's going with the wild children and the Eretsuns," Thomas said as they went down the stairs.

"So do I," said Cassie. "But hopefully they are all restored to their normal lives now. I wish we could go visit them. But we can't usually visit real places in dreams without magical help. We've never been able to use these powers just to visit someone."

"I wish we could go," said Thomas, all keyed up from the day's excitement. "I can't sleep now."

"What happened to the Merrows?" Nancy suddenly asked.

"That's a very good question," said Thomas. "I'd very much like to know about their fate!"

"Well," said Cassie, "let's find out!"

When they were sure the babies were fast asleep, the Chingles crept out of the house. They rode on their bicycles towards Poolbeg Rock, which was now lopsidedly jutting out of the sea since Vladimir's three-headed monster had plucked it out of his way.

They took to the air as seagulls and were amazed to see three very wrinkly old hags sitting by a rock pool. One had straggly grey hair like weeds and was as fat and bloated as a porpoise. Another had sparse blonde wisps on a nearly bald head, a large drooping moustache and looked very like a walrus. The third had a few sad curls under her red cap, which was perched at a sorry angle over her very lined brow. Her face looked distinctly fishy with bulging eyes and a loose-lipped mouth that kept opening and closing. Her skin was so wrinkly she resembled an alligator. Then they noticed the fishes' tails in the water. Thomas sniggered. The Chingles landed on Poolbeg Rock and resumed their normal shapes.

"Hello, venerable ancient old Merrows," Thomas said brightly. "We are looking for three young Merrows. They have a tendency to be cheeky."

The fat old Merrow that looked like a porpoise turned on him. "Sod off, you little whippersnapper! It's thanks to you that we've ended up like this." Her teeth were blackened stumps and her little eyes almost disappeared in her blubbery face.

"Why, you look like Fand, except maybe two hundred years older. Are you perhaps related?" baited Thomas.

Before she could reply, the blonde mermaid caught sight of her walrus face in the moon's reflection on the rock pool.

"Don't say anything," she wailed, tearing at her sparse blonde hair. "We *are* them Merrows. That grey oul wan is Fand. I am or was Mara. Oh my bee-oot-iful hair!

Manannán has punished us for helping Vladimir. How were we to know he was so evil!"

"That must be very hard on you. Will you stay like this forever?" asked Cassie.

"Manannán said if we do good deeds for a year he might reconsider," shrieked Sionna, her battered red cap falling over her fishy face.

"That's going to be even harder for you," Thomas said, trying to sound sympathetic but hardly able to suppress his giggles.

"And we'll never be able to get sailors to stay with us now we look like old walruses, or at least Mara does," sniped Fand, shaking her blubbery head, obviously not liking being described as an "oul wan".

A thought struck Cassie. "Have you claimed Raznik, Vladimir's sidekick?" she asked. "We haven't seen him. He must have drowned in the explosion out under the sea near Poolbeg Rock."

"Oh, him!" sniffed Mara. "He was a weirdo. We turned our noses up at him. So this big, ugly, horrible fish called the Black Widow trapped and suckered him and he'll stay attached to her forever, dwindling to one hundredth of his size."

Cassie and Thomas exchanged glances. It sounded like a fitting end for the evil sorcerer henchman of Vladimir.

"So have you done any good deeds yet?" asked Thomas.

The Merrows looked startled at the very thought. Eventually the fish-faced Sionna spoke.

"Go on, ask them!" she urged her companions.

"Ah, it would kill me!" moaned Mara.

"Do you want to stay this way for ever?" complained Fand.

"Can we . . . do you a good deed?" asked Mara, barely able to say the words.

"What was that?" asked Thomas. "I didn't quite hear you."

"She said, you little toe-rag, can we do you a good deed or sod off annoying us!" roared Sionna, her red cap slouching over her fishy eye.

"Well, actually, perhaps you can," said Cassie smiling. "Can you fetch Manannán?"

"Oh, thanks for nothing," moaned Fand. "The last personage ever in the whole wide world we'd like to see."

"That's why it's the perfect punishment," winked Thomas, all innocence. The Merrows scowled mightily at him before diving into the sea.

Ten minutes later Manannán Mac Lir rose out of the sea enveloped in a soft sea mist. He was a towering figure seated in a carriage pulled by seahorses. His eyes were the aquamarine of oceans, his hair the curling spume of a mighty wave. The Chingles stood awestruck as much by the fact that the Merrows had actually done as they were asked as by the presence of the God of the Sea.

"Manannán, we have a request to make. We have the power to travel in dreams to the Otherworld and to other locations with magical help. But we do not have the power to visit another part of the world in real time without magical aid," said Cassie.

"These are the rules of your powers. Why are you telling me?" boomed Manannán impatiently.

"You helped cover the submarine in the cloak of invisibility, didn't you?" said Thomas. "Would you permit us to travel over the ocean to visit the Carpathian Mountains to see how our friends fare?"

"Ah, go on," they heard Fand the Merrow say. "What's the point of asking us to arrange good deeds if you won't play ball?"

"Don't be all mean and curmudgeonly," Mara cried.

Manannán grimaced. "I will carry you across the oceans in my cloak of invisibility and you may shape-shift to visit them for a short time. But you can only look."

In what seemed like seconds later, three ravens flew over an encampment deep in the Carpathian Mountains. The area teemed with parents and their children on what looked like a day trip. They were dressed in normal clothes and it was hard to recognise the neat, clean children as their friends in the wild tribe. It was even more difficult to associate the calm, responsible adults with the savage Eretsuns.

They watched as a red-haired boy, Conchy, showed a flame-haired woman with dancing eyes where he slept in his circular tree house like a swift's nest.

"My son!" she said as she hugged him.

Conchy looked up to see three ravens alight on the tree house and his eyes filled with happiness.

The Chingles took wing and rested on a bush. Nearby, Basher, the stocky boy with dark hair, shared a picnic with two people who looked like his parents. The woman, who was plump and jolly, handed him a plate heaving with food and Basher laughed to see it.

Down by the river, a boy with straw-blond hair played ball with his sister and father and mother. He looked up as he saw three ravens fly by and land on the branches of a broad-limbed beech tree. "Thank you!" he mouthed to the birds, then seemed baffled that he'd greeted ravens.

The three ravens circled the camp. Everywhere they saw scenes of contentment, parents happy to be with their children, children basking in the warm love of their mothers and fathers.

Finally the ravens alighted in the branches of an old tree. At the foot of the tree, a man with sandy hair greying around the temples sat with his back to its gnarled bark, his eyes closed, savouring the last of the summer sun. Around his neck he wore a wooden cross, polished by much handling. Nestled in the branches of the tree was a tall blond boy with luminous green eyes. He was writing a letter.

One of the ravens flew up and perched on his shoulder. The boy didn't stir.

"*Dear Cassie,*" the letter began. "*Our parents think we children have been in separate refugee camps and it is better they believe this. Only we ever need know the truth. I want to tell you . . .*"

The raven flew back to her brother and sister. It was time to go back to Inish Álainn.

Cassie could wait to read what Ivo was writing to her. In the real world where she knew now she belonged – at least until their next adventure on Inish Álainn – she still had a long time to grow up. The three ravens took wing and flew off into the sky.

THE END

Pronunciation Guide to "Chingleworld"

The list (using the English spelling system) is to help you pronounce some of the Irish and Slavic words and names in the book. Remember it is a rough guide only!

I have borrowed freely from mythology and folklore and made many familiar legendary figures take part in my story – so I hope they don't mind.

On Inish Álainn

Inish Álainn (*In/ish awl/ing*)	–	"Beautiful Island" – somewhere off the west coast of Ireland
Bo Men (*Boe men*)	–	ghostly creatures of the bog who tickle people to death

Boogan (*Boo/gan*)	– seaweed creature
Cam (*Cam*)	– fairy of the buttercups
Cernunnos (*Ker/nuh/nohs*)	– God of Shape-shifters
Clíona (*Clee/on/ah*)	– sixteenth-century witch in a bottle and ancestor of the Chingles
Connle (*Con/leh*)	– a gruagach (see below) and caretaker of Fairy Fort House
Dris (*Driss*)	– fairy of the blackberries
Muiris (*Mwir/ish*)	– the island postmaster
Róisín (*Roe/sheen*)	– post mistress and wife of Muiris
Rónán (*Roe/nawn*)	– seal brother of Lugh
Rua O'Rogan (*Roo/ah Oh Rogue/an*)	– mischievous fairy a "Fear Dearg" *see below*
Sean Gaels (*Shan Gales*)	– "Old Irish" – name given to a select group of warriors which includes Sennan, Lugh and Scáthach for the purposes of this story!

Sennan *(seh/nan)* — druid and member of the Sean Gaels

Tadgh *(Tie-ig)* — the island librarian

Tethtra *(Teh/trah)* — seal sister of Lugh

Irish Mythology and Folklore

Áine *(Awn/yeh)* — a sun goddess

Balor of the Evil Eye *(Bal/ur)* — evil one-eyed Formorian Giant

Caitlín of the Crooked Teeth *(Cat/leen)* — wife of Balor and sorceress

Clurachaun *(Cloor/ach/awn)* — spiteful kind of leprechaun

Fear Dearg (Far dar/ug) — literally the "Red Man", fairy dressed in red

Finbhearra *(Finn/vara)* — King of the Fairies and husband of Uná

Finnen *(Finn/en)* — a moon goddess, sister of Áine

Gruagach *(Gruuh/uh/guhk)* — "The Hairy One" – fairy creature with shaggy long hair

Lugh (*Luu*)	–	God of Light
Manannán Mac Lir (*Mon/an/awn Mac Lir*)	–	God of the Sea, father of Áine
Merrow ("*murúch*" or "*muruach*")	–	English form of Irish word for mermaid
Ogma (*Oe/mah*)	–	God of Eloquence and Letters
Scáthach (*Skaw/huhk*)	–	"The Shadowy One" – legendary woman warrior and teacher
Tuatha Dé Danann (*Tuu/ah day dan/an*)	–	the collective name for Irish gods and goddesses, literally the people of the Goddess Danu
Úna (*Uuh/nah*)	–	Queen of the Fairies

Slavic Mythology

Slavic deities and folklore spirits often have a number of names and pronunciations since each Slavic nation and language has their own local version. Below are the most widespread pronunciations.

The Baba Yaga   –   witch who flies through
(*Bah/bah Yah/gah*)   the air in a pestle
                           and mortar

Devana (*Deh /van/ah*) –   hunter goddess, a Slavic
                           version of the Roman Diana

Dodola (*Doh /doh/lah*) –   Goddess of Clouds
                           and Rain

Eretsun (*Eh /reht /soon*) – Living vampire whose
                           soul has been possessed
                           by a sorcerer on the
                           point of death

Karzeleks (*Kar/zeh/lek*) – underground miners who
                           guard gems and precious
                           metals

Leshii (*Lesh /ee*)   –   Forest Lord who often
                           appears dressed as a
                           peasant

Perun (*Peh/roon*)	– God of Thunder and Lightning
Polewik (*Poh/leh/veek*)	– field spirit
Vasilisa (*Vas/il/ees/ah*)	– magical painted doll
Vila (*Vee/lah*)	– wood nymph with beautiful voice

Norse

(In Norse the stress is usually on the first syllable)

Bifröst (*Bee/frost*)	– "Shining Path" – the sacred rainbow
Heimdall (*Hame/dahl*)	– Guardian of Bifröst, the sacred rainbow
Hel (*Hell*)	– Queen of the Dead, daughter of Loki
The Norns (*Nornz*)	– the Fates, the Three Sisters of Past, Present and Future

Other

Almudj *(Al/mudge)*   – Australian Aboriginal
                             creator god with a
                             kangaroo head, crocodile
                             tail and snake's body. Also
                             known as Rainbow Snake

Eight Immortals   – Chinese deities who were
                             once human and who have
                             each attained immortality
                             and special powers

The ones featured in the story are:

Han *(Harn)*   – the flute-playing philosopher

Immortal Woman   – whose symbol is a lotus
                             blossom

Iron Crutch Li *(Lee)*   – ugly old man who walks with
                             the aid of a crutch and
                             carries a gourd bottle

Penglai Shan   – mountainous island in the
(Pung/Lie Sharn)   mysterious East, home
                             of the Eight Immortals

Viracocha   – Inca creator god from South
Veer/ah/coach/ah   America, the God of Sun and
                             Storms who disguises himself
                             as a beggar

ACKNOWLEDGEMENTS

Thanks as usual to sterling editor Gaye Shortland for her valiant re-chingling. To publisher Paula Campbell for her faith and vision and David Prendergast for guiding the book through production. Also to Lynda, Niamh and Kieran at Poolbeg for their hard work and dedication. I am grateful to Jim Stanton for his brilliant cover design across the whole series. The continued enthusiasm and support of sales agent Conor Hackett is much appreciated. Much thanks to my agent Stephanie Thwaites at Curtis Brown for her support and wise words.

Thanks also to my first reader, Elsa, for her sharp eyes and to Aoife, Michelle, Cynthia, Orla, Ivan, Louis and Molly for their encouragement. Also to my family and friends for their continued cheerleading.

For background on Slavic mythology and folklore I am indebted to *Forests of the Vampire* by Charles Phillips and

Michael Kerrigan. For inspiration, to *The Dictionary of Imaginary Places* by Alberto Manguel and Gianni Guadalupi. And for reference, to the *Oxford Dictionary of World Mythology* by Arthur Cotterell.

453

Also published by poolbeg.com

THE CHINGLES GO WEST

PATRICIA MURPHY

ON HOLIDAY IN THE WEST OF IRELAND ON REMOTE INISH ÁLAINN, THE CHINGLES – CASSIE, THOMAS AND NANCY – JOIN THE SUN GODDESS ÁINE IN HER DANGEROUS QUEST TO FIND HER SISTER FINNEN THE SWAN MAIDEN WHO IS "HIDDEN AMONG THE STARS".

Their search for the Swan Maiden takes them into perilous other worlds in Europe and America and even the glamorous world of Hollywood movies. But their special powers seem useless against the wicked sorceress, Caitlín of the Crooked Teeth, who has vowed vengeance on the Chingles for their defeat of her husband, Balor of the Evil Eye.

Will they manage to crack the mysterious Ogham code and master Celtic battle craft to find Finnen and defeat their most deadly enemy yet?

ISBN 978-1-84223-218-7

THE CHINGLES FROM THE EAST

PATRICIA MURPHY

Legend has it that the giant Balor of the Evil Eye will return bent on revenge to destroy the remote island of InishÁlainn in his search for a magical stone. The only ones who can stop him are the mysterious 'Chingles from the East'. But what does this have to do with Cassie, Thomas and Nancy who are spending their summer holiday on the island with their Uncle Jarlath?

Before they are even off the ferry, the children are plunged into an adventure where they encounter mischievous and dangerous creatures from Irish myth, learn of the mysterious powers of shapeshifting and meet the magical trees of the Sacred Grove.

If that wasn't enough they also have to contend with Sir Dignum Drax, the nasty tycoon who wants to cover the island in concrete. What is his link to the evil giant Balor and can the children master their new-found magical skills in time to take on Balor and his awesome powers?

WINNER OF POOLBEG'S
'WRITE A CHILDREN'S BESTSELLER'
COMPETITION

ISBN 978-1-84223-216-3